"Bending the Arc by Don Thomps[...]n [...] race and gender relations in the United States from a very personal perspective, and, without sermonizing, shows how it disrupts not just family ties, but societal cohesion. Thompson does a masterful job of weaving the historical and social background of neo-Nazi and other extremist movements into the story without disrupting the flow or halting the action. A thoroughly entertaining read that will also make you think, this is recommended reading for every political and community leader in the country. As the title implies, even when things appear hopeless, there is still hope. As Dr. Martin Luther King, Jr. said, 'The arc of the universe is long, but bends toward justice," but as the protagonist discovers, it only bends when people take a stand against intolerance. I absolutely could not put this down. Kudos to Don Thompson for a five-star book." Charles Ray, Awesome Indies Book Awards.

BENDING THE ARC

Don Thompson

AIA PUBLISHING

Bending the Arc
Don Thompson
Copyright © 2020
Published by AIA Publishing, Australia
ABN: 32736122056
http://www.aiapublishing.com

All characters in this publication are fictitious and any resemblance to real persons, living or dead, is purely coincidental.

All rights reserved. No part of this publication may be reproduced, stored in a retrieval system or transmitted in any form or by any means electronic, mechanical, audio, visual or otherwise, without prior permission of the copyright owner. Nor can it be circulated in any form of binding or cover other than that in which it is published and without similar conditions including this condition being imposed on the subsequent purchaser.

Paperback ISBN: 978-1-922329-06-6
Cover design by K. Rose Kreative

In loving memory of my parents,
Frank and Janice Thompson

"The arc of the moral universe is long, but bends toward justice."
Theodore Parker, as paraphrased by
Dr. Martin Luther King Jr.

*"If we extend unlimited tolerance even to those who are intolerant,
if we are not prepared to defend a tolerant society against the
onslaught of the intolerant, then the tolerant will be destroyed,
and tolerance with them."*
Karl Popper

1999

L uke Mason squinted at the old cabin through his dusty windshield. Once a lively retreat for fishing friends, work-week escapees and an eclectic family, it was now much too quiet. He stepped out of his truck after the three-hour drive from Seattle, trudged across the weed-infested grounds and up to the faded porch. The soul once ensconced in the place seemed to have leaked out through the cracks and dissipated in the air among the young firs and cedars blocking the former lake view. He pulled on the stubborn door. It took three tries with foot braced against doorframe, but eventually the warped wood yielded, and cool darkness spilled onto his face. The sooty remains of long-dead fires seasoned the air.

As if to let the darkness seep out into the summer sunshine, Luke left the door open and turned back to walk the perimeter before venturing in. A Northern Flicker pecked out its staccato refrain and Luke looked up, trying to locate it, hoping it wasn't practicing its skills on the cabin's siding. But the only evidence was the soft swoosh of wings as the bird made its exit somewhere overhead to the left. The silence in its wake was so profound that Luke hesitated to break it, even with soft footfalls in the cedar-padded earth.

Once a place of laughter and recreation, this was now merely a location on the map at the end of an unnamed dirt road in the North Cascades. The windows were dark and dirty, the cedar siding grayed, the door to the old shed missing. Luke had hoped to be engaged by the past, maybe even comforted by it, but instead he found it strangely absent. Instead of triggers for reflection, he found lifeless objects of only present significance:

a rusted hinge on the ground near the shed, an abandoned bird's nest in the dense branches of a drooping old hemlock, the cold thin crescent of an aging moon barely visible in the late morning sky.

Luke let his gaze fall from the moon and settle on his old kayak stowed under an open edge of the cabin. He expected it to evoke something, some real memory: the sound of a paddle in water, the sight of an eagle soaring over the lake, a picnic on the island, something. But no, the vessel was just inert wood and fiberglass abandoned in the dim crawl space. A bowline secured one end of an old nylon line to the boat while the other end lay untethered and frayed in the dark soil under the building. *I probably tied that very knot*, he thought. But trying to force an actual memory of the event, straining to feel his fingers form a loop in the rope, he failed and looked away.

Yet another memory did come. A second kayak, his brother's boat, once lay in the dark space beside his. As unwelcome as this memory may have been, it was no stranger to Luke, nor was it a surprise. He shook his head at the paradox of self-deception and walked again, around the shaded back of the cabin, through a sea of ferns on the far side, and down the overgrown trail toward the dock. The truth was that memories of the absent kayak and its missing owner were always with him in one form or another, towed along just below the surface like fated fish on a stringer.

Luke picked his way down the slope through a blackberry tangle and stepped onto the dock. It was in surprisingly good condition given years of neglect. A little moss grew here and there, but Luke felt no movement as he walked out to the end. *Solid, just as we over-built it those many years ago.* A rainbow trout rose, and sunlight flashed off the ripples as a newly hatched bug became breakfast. Luke lifted his eyes from the fish swirl and scanned the more distant water. The glassy surface revealed fish activity everywhere. *Stoneflies. That's what they're after this morning.*

Luke turned to retrieve his fly rod from the truck but a painful catch in his lower back stopped him mid-step. His doctor had long ago attributed this to stress; and the cabin, originally serving as an antidote, had now become another source. Luke knew that he and Jen would soon need to either sell the property or invest heavily in its maintenance. The rest of life, with all its opportunities, demands and expenses, like the blackberries along the trail, had simply taken over. Thinking about selling, Luke felt his connection to the cabin being slowly ripped out by the roots. Maybe Jen felt it, too, but he doubted that the intensity was similar. Jen was the pragmatic one. Luke became unreasonably attached to things, or so he'd been told.

This isn't just a thing, he argued to the silence. *It's an enabler of experience, a catalyst for relationships. It is — or was — a place where memories are made and held.* But when he tried once again to appreciate the beauty of the lake and the promise of hooked fish, he felt foreign, like a trespasser on his own land.

He searched the distant shoreline for any sign of new construction. Thankfully, he found none; just the same three cabins he'd grown accustomed to seeing over the years. Two of them, Johnson's and Bullock's, were built after his, and Luke remembered feeling a sense of encroachment when the structures first began to take shape on the cove a half mile down-lake. He knew at the time that this was selfish and that his hopes of a perpetually undisturbed view and a kind of default ownership of the cove itself were unreasonable. And yet, the emotions held sway. Of course, the cabins did get built, and as they gracefully aged into the landscape over the years, Luke slowly began to see them less as invaders and more as natural elements in the environment.

And now, there they are, more permanent in this place than I am, Luke reflected. He tried to take comfort in the fact that he wouldn't need to worry about lakeside development and property maintenance if they sold the cabin. He tried to see this as a new kind of freedom, as Jen had gently suggested several times. He tried, but it wasn't working.

Instead, Luke's thoughts fell back to a time when he couldn't have conceived of this odd form of freedom. In 1981, he and Finn had dreamt of building a cabin on the forty acres their parents had acquired years earlier with the same plan in mind. That original plan had never materialized because of their father's stroke and their mother's subsequent decline; but, after their parents' passing, Luke felt that he and his brother had inherited the dream along with the property.

Finn was the older brother by two years, but they were both still in their twenties in 1981 and too young to understand – or perhaps to admit – that hauling tons of lumber, brick and cement up the steep washed-out dirt road from Rockport in a rented trailer would be a nearly impossible task. So Finn and Luke hired the cheapest architect they could find, and simply began. It took them nearly a month of frequent half-days away from their real jobs just to get the materials up the mountain. Then the first winter set in. Their young Seattle minds hadn't really thought that one through. They covered everything with heavy blue tarps and waited impatiently down at sea level.

Spring doesn't fully arrive in the North Cascades until early June, but even so, the brothers made several optimistic but abortive starts in April of '82. By the end of May they had managed to hire a backhoe – something their budget didn't account for – and had the foundation dug and poured. The framing went quickly, and the roof was in place before the first snow in October. It took them two more summers to add plumbing, set up a permanent generator, build the fireplace and finish off the three-bedroom interior.

Finn was the finish carpenter. Luke had creative skills in other areas, but he was the first to admit that fine woodwork was not his specialty. He could build things that would last but Finn could make them worth lasting. Somewhere in the not-so-deep recesses of their young minds, the brothers had hoped to make the place aesthetically acceptable not only to themselves and their fishing buddies but also to women. So they imagined that Finn's fine carpentry skills and another thousand dollars in furniture and decor would do the trick. The brothers had no specific women in mind at the time, but the general concept was motivation enough.

As it turned out, a nicely finished cabin and wishful thinking weren't sufficient. The only visitors for the first two years were male colleagues and friends from sea level, but that was fine. In those early days, they all enjoyed fishing and beer drinking, and the visitors helped them sink the pilings for their new dock. It wasn't until the next year, in August of 1984, that their luck shifted, and the real story of their lives began.

1984

Even though the United States and the Soviet Union were still conducting regular nuclear weapons tests in 1984, it didn't turn out to be a particularly Orwellian year. Ronald Reagan returned to the White House for a second term in a landslide victory against Walter Mondale, Carl Lewis won four Olympic gold medals, Archbishop Desmond Tutu won the Nobel Peace Prize, and telescreens were nowhere to be seen.

Finn was becoming quite the Reagan fan, much to Luke's chagrin. It wasn't as though Luke gave much thought to politics; it was just that President Reagan struck him as one-dimensional and astonishingly immune to facts. Even the staunch conservatives John Wayne and William F. Buckley Jr. had torn into Reagan about his opposition to the Panama Canal treaty back in 1978. Luke just couldn't get his head around Finn's budding infatuation with this man.

Maybe his consternation had more to do with his chosen profession than it did with politics. Luke had just started teaching creative writing to undergraduates at the University of Washington and couldn't imagine Ronald Reagan as a believable character in anything but a hard-core comic book, and even that seemed a stretch. His own students wrote more nuanced characters and most of them were in class only to check off an elective.

On the other hand, Luke had a great deal of respect for his brother, and Finn was far from alone in his admiration for the president, so Luke had to consider the possibility that his own blinders might fit just a bit too snugly. He resolved to loosen them up and move on.

Finn made that easy in those early days. In addition to the brothers' shared genetics, they had some common, if rather shallow, goals: finish the cabin, meet some interesting women, catch a lot of fish. The former and the latter came naturally and served to strengthen their fraternal bond. The other, not so much. Or, perhaps Luke would say it was more complex. Much more complex.

In September of that year, Luke, Finn, Jennifer Lassiter and Amy Carpenter jammed into Finn's Jeep and headed north out of Seattle. Finn and Jennifer had been dating for a few months and Jennifer's friend, Amy, had apparently been convinced that this fit, five foot ten Luke with wavy light brown hair was at least harmless and perhaps even mildly interesting. The group was headed to the cabin for a day or two of fishing.

Slim Jennifer, her shiny brown hair pulled back in a ponytail, sat up front with Finn, and Luke found himself crowded into the small back seat with pretty, blond Amy. He felt awkward when turning toward her to talk because there was really no public space between them. So he stared straight ahead, only glancing sideways from time to time as the conversation seemed to require it.

"So, tell me again where this place is?" asked Amy. "You said something about Rockport before?"

"Right, It's not too far from there. And Rockport's about forty miles northeast of Burlington. It'll probably take us another, oh, couple of hours, to get there," Luke replied, glancing at his watch. "After that we've got a stretch of four-wheeling up a rocky Forest Service road and then a private dirt track to the cabin."

"Is it dangerous – I mean driving up that last part?" asked Amy with a little frown.

"The four-wheeling? No, I wouldn't say dangerous. Just a bit rough. It's really more like a trail than a road, but the Jeep will handle it just fine."

"Oh, okay. I've never done anything like that before and I was just, you know, sort of wondering."

"No, it'll be fun, don't worry," said Luke, turning slightly toward his date. "Finn's got lots of experience. All you have to do is hang on and enjoy the ride."

Amy nodded as she searched her purse.

"Want a mint?" she asked.

Luke wondered about the implications of Amy's offer but quickly decided that it held little, if any, significance.

"Sure," he said. "Thanks."

Luke stared out the side window, sucked on the mint and pretended to be interested in the freeway scenery. They were passing through a section of wetlands just north of Everett and there were, in fact, things to be seen and enjoyed. But in less than a minute Luke felt the back-seat silence descend like a dark cloud and began to feel responsible for changing the weather.

"So, you work with Jennifer, right?" he asked.

"Well, yes and no. We work for the same company. I'm in space planning and she writes software. We're growing like crazy, so I stay pretty busy with all the moves and re-orgs. Jen and I met during one of the big moves."

Up in the front seats, Finn and Jennifer were chatting away, but Luke caught only bits and pieces of the conversation over the noise from the Jeep's off-road tires. Jennifer's ponytail whipped back and forth as she looked between the window and her tall, dark-haired boyfriend who kept his eyes on the road.

"How many people now?" Finn was asking something about the growth of the company that Jennifer had recently joined as an entry-level software developer.

"Around six hundred. Something like that."

"Joining the big boys…. That thing with Apple…"

"Uh huh… Bill decided to… kind of risky…"

"All that land in Redmond… really going to…?" Finn was getting serious about his job in commercial real estate and he was interested in anything that had to do with local development. Luke could see his focus sharpen.

"Definitely... couple of years. ... a complete campus."

Finn took a freeway exit and the road noise dropped.

"But let's not talk about work," said Jennifer as she put a hand on Finn's shoulder. "Let's talk about the day ahead. I can't wait to get back out on the lake again. Do you guys ever get tired of it?" she asked, glancing back at Luke. "Does that gorgeous view start to seem ordinary after a while?"

Her smile told Luke that she knew the answer, but he wanted to respond anyway.

"Not yet, and I hope it never does," he said. "Everything's different up there. The air's a little thinner; the sunlight's a little brighter. It affects me in new ways each time, I think."

Jennifer turned around as far as she could without loosening her seat belt. "How do you mean that, Lucius?"

Luke detested his given name and was never able to get a straight answer from his parents as to why they inflicted it upon him while favoring his brother with such a friendly and uncomplicated moniker. The nickname was okay, but when he had to explain its derivation it always lost a great deal of value right off the top. Still, he heard nothing negative in Jennifer's pronunciation. In fact, she imparted an unusual liquid quality to its sound which Luke found himself liking. But still...

"Please, call me Luke. Well, for me there's a kind of weird dichotomy going on. On the one hand, arriving at the lake is like coming home. Everything in the cabin is just as we left it the last time. There's a sort of calming familiarity to it. It grounds me, like home. You know what I mean?"

Jennifer nodded. "Yes, I think so. What about the other hand?"

"I guess it's the changes," said Luke. The whole environment changes from visit to visit, even hour to hour. There's always something different about the lake and the woods around it. Maybe a tree has fallen into the water. Or eagles have made a nest in one of the big firs. Or maybe it's just something as simple as a gust of wind that ripples a stretch of water and changes its reflection of the sky."

9

"But how does it affect *you*? That's what you said, right?"

"Right. That odd combination of stability and change – I think it puts me very much in the moment. I just seem to settle down and pay more attention to the 'right now.' And the moment is always a little different each time, so it keeps me interested. I don't know, sounds like a load of BS when I actually try to describe it."

"It doesn't to me. Not at all." Jennifer turned back around and stared straight ahead.

"Anybody for coffee?" asked Finn as he pulled into a parking lot.

The foursome walked into one of the new Starbucks coffeehouses which had just begun to spread across the Pacific Northwest, ordered drinks and looked around. The tables were small and the place so crowded that they had to split up. Luke brought two tall mochas back to the first table and placed one in front of Amy, who was again fishing around in her purse. She thanked him quietly and then looked back down at the table.

"Hey, what's wrong?" Luke asked.

I'm sorry, Luke. This is stupid." She slowly shook her head as if trying to find the next words. "Really stupid."

"No, no, it's okay. What is it?"

"It's just that… I don't… I don't know. Talking to you feels weird. It seems like you don't really want to be here with me. And that's okay, I guess. I mean, why should you? We don't even know each other."

Amy looked up and Luke saw some genuine beauty behind her pretty, sad face.

"Don't you hate blind dates?" he said. "Two people thrown together and expected to act like a couple?"

Amy nodded.

"So, maybe we can just get that out in the open and move on. Have some fun today. Get to know each other a little." Luke reached across the small table and patted her hand.

A smile and another nod. "I'd like that."

Back on the road, the conversation turned to the cabin, the mountains, and fishing. Amy said she'd been fly fishing once before and had always wanted to try again. Jennifer had never fished, even though she loved being on the water, and said she wasn't sure how she felt about it. Luke got the impression that her reluctance might have something to do with cleaning the fish, so he tried to reassure her that they usually just released them.

"So why bother catching fish in the first place?" Jennifer asked.

Luke shrugged. "I think there's something primal about it. Something about choosing a fly, casting it into the water where you think a trout might be lurking, then seeing the fish rise to the fly and take it. Bam! It feels like, I don't know, being part of the whole predator/prey thing – right down at the level of the fish."

Luke immediately felt embarrassed. *The level of the fish? Really?*

But Jennifer was nodding as she turned back to look at the road ahead.

The Cove

The Jeep pulled up to the cabin in early afternoon, and the cedar air held the fragile warmth of autumn as Luke walked down to the edge of the clearing. Several yellow and orange deciduous trees burst through the otherwise dark evergreen background along the lake, and a light breeze rippled the surface. He scanned for signs of fish. *Hard to tell right now.* He noticed an uptick in his heart rate and attributed some to altitude and some to anticipation. *It's good to be here. Good to be back.* An otter was swimming toward the far shore, leaving a V-shaped wake behind, quickly erased by the wind — an ephemeral history with Luke as its only reader.

"Hey, brother! A little help?" Finn's voice pulled Luke from his reverie and back to the task of unloading the jeep and setting up the cabin. He turned to see Amy and Finn toting backpacks and food. "Grab the fishing gear, okay?"

"Got it!" Luke said, jogging back up the slope.

Luke moved fly rods, vests, waders and a fly-tying kit into the third bedroom which would be his for the weekend, then headed for the kitchen. Jennifer was there, already busy cleaning and organizing. Luke walked in to see if he could help.

"No, I'm good," she said with a bright smile. "But I think Finn wants to get the kayaks down to the dock. Maybe he could use a hand. Amy's making beds."

"Oh, sure, definitely."

The kayaks were doubles so it took two people to move each one down the winding trail through small trees and blackberry thickets to the lake. Finn and Luke slid them into the water, tied them off to dock cleats and stood for a moment, taking in the long view down the lake. The wind had dropped, almost to a calm, and Luke noticed a few dark clouds in the distance. A fish swirl appeared not more than ten feet off the dock.

"Thunderstorm tonight?" he mused.

"Maybe. Smells like it. Probably be much cooler after that," said Finn.

"I'll bring in some firewood," Luke said, turning to make his way back up the trail.

The brothers had built a small lean-to against the shed to shield their stash of wood from the frequent rains. Luke grabbed a large armful from the pile and hauled it back to the cabin, adjusting the load so he could see the stairs up to the door. He nudged the half-open door with a foot, spilled the wood onto the hearth, and went back for a second load.

When he returned, Amy was there arranging the dumped firewood into a neat pile.

"Thanks," Luke said. "So, what do you think of the place?"

"It is *so* beautiful here, Luke. I didn't know quite what to expect but you guys really have something special. Did you say that you and Finn built this cabin yourselves?"

"We did over ninety percent of the work. Had some help on the foundation, but after that, yep, pretty much."

"Well, I love it. Thanks again for letting me be part of this," said Amy with a shy smile.

"Of course! So glad you're here," said Luke, trying to straddle the line between politeness and encouragement. "Wait 'til you get out on the lake. I think you're gonna have a great time."

Amy nodded. "Speaking of that, any plans for the rest of the day?"

"I was thinking of taking the kayaks out for a short trip. You know, just to help everyone get their bearings. Maybe tomorrow we'll paddle all the way out to the island and do a little fishing. Sound okay to you?"

"Are you kidding? That sounds amazing."

"Alright, let's go talk to the others." Luke took Amy's hand to help her up from the hearth.

After a quick discussion, everyone agreed, and they all headed down to the dock. Luke helped Amy into the forward seat of one kayak as Finn assisted Jennifer in the other. Luke untied the line for Finn's kayak, secured it to the boat's small foredeck and gave them a little push away from the dock.

"Uh, Luke?" Finn said as Luke made his way back to his own boat.

"Yep?"

"Paddles?"

"Shit – sorry! I don't know what I was thinking." Red-faced, Luke loaded all four paddles into his boat, handing three to Amy, and paddled over to his drifting brother and laughing girlfriend.

Amy handed off two paddles and they followed Finn and Jennifer out onto the smooth gray water.

"Let's head over toward the cove!" Finn shouted from his position twenty or thirty yards in front. "Better keep an eye on the weather!"

"Sure!" Luke yelled back, thinking more about the graying skies than any particular destination.

The first distant peal of thunder came about fifteen minutes later. Luke increased his stroke rate and told Amy to do the same. "Let's catch up to them and talk about this. I think we should head back."

Amy needed no convincing and it took them less than a minute to intercept the others, who had slowed their pace and were looking back. Amy was silent and Luke could tell by her wide eyes that she was frightened.

"Okay," said Finn. "We've got a choice. We're well over halfway to the cove. We can either keep going and hunker down on shore there or we can turn around and paddle like hell back to the dock. Whatever we do, we need to get off the water."

A bolt of lightning lit the sky, hitting the shore a few miles down-lake. The thunder roared soon after.

"I vote for the dock. We'll be safer in the cabin," Luke said, nodding back toward the shore. "Better than being exposed out in the woods."

"I don't know," said Finn, glancing the other way. "We make it to the cove quicker. Jennifer, Amy?"

"Let's take the quick route," said Amy, her eyes still wide. Jennifer was silent.

Finn and Luke nodded at each other and set a furious pace toward the cove as the third lightning strike hit somewhere behind them near the cabin. This time the thunder was almost immediate, and Luke could feel adrenaline coursing through his body in response. Heavy drops of rain began tentatively and then became a torrent.

"Go! Go!" he shouted.

Less than ten minutes and as many strikes later, the soaked and tired group reached the shore within the cove and hauled the kayaks out of the water. They ran into the woods.

"Down there!" Luke pointed ahead to the left where a small ravine divided the terrain. "Get down low, away from these tall trees!"

He charged ahead, only looking behind after spotting an overhung rock ridge. *Perfect.* Finn and Jennifer were right behind him.

"Where's Amy?!" Luke yelled, scanning back along our trampled path through the ravine. *Damnit!* "Amy! Amy!"

The rain was so heavy that the tree cover was no longer serving as an umbrella. Water poured through the canopy as it became saturated. Lightning hit a nearby tree and turned the surroundings into a hideous high-contrast monochrome scene, and that is when Luke spotted Amy, high above the ravine, standing a few yards away from a tall tree with her head down and shoulders hunched. *Why didn't I take her hand? Why did I leave her alone?* He turned back and ran toward her.

The next bolt of lightning was so close that the deafening explosion of thunder and the searing light were simultaneous. Luke tripped and went down.

What is that light? Why is it still there? Luke's addled mind was unable to distinguish between the former lightning and a flaming tree above the ravine. Another flash and explosion. He stumbled to his feet and ran toward his last vision of Amy.

Reaching the edge of the ravine, he rushed past the smoldering remains of the doomed tree, now steaming as rain threatened the fire's demise. *Where is she?* Luke jumped a moss-covered log, and nearly landed on Amy's prostrate form. Her face was turned to the side and Luke gently shifted her. Her lips were blue and her face ashen in the dim forest light but there were no signs of burns on her body or clothing that Luke could see. He remembered hearing of situations where enough current can flow through the ground near a lightning-struck tree to cause cardiac arrest in someone standing nearby. *Still, better than a direct hit. What do I do? I need to remember!*

Luke felt for a carotid pulse along the side of Amy's neck. Nothing. Tried the other side. Nothing. He grabbed a wrist. Nothing there either. Straining to remember bits of a long-ago CPR class which he regarded then as a singular waste of his valuable time as an eighteen-year-old immortal, Luke recalled the correct cadence: the old Bee Gees song, Staying Alive. *Use that beat. Oh, oh, oh, oh, stayin' alive, stayin' alive.* Luke tore open Amy's shirt, found what he imagined to be the right spot on her chest just about the center of her bra, and began compressions. He stopped to give her breaths. They went in. He'd forgotten to check her airway but it seemed okay. He went back to chest compressions. *Come on, Amy, come on! Please!*

Finn and Jennifer caught up and were standing over the other two. Finn knelt down to hold Amy's head. More breaths. Amy jerked and coughed hard. Luke flew back in revulsion before he realized what this meant. She threw her head back, gasped for breath, retched and coughed several more times. Luke found himself shaking as he turned her to the side and tried to clear the vomit from her mouth. She was breathing again. *Breathing again.* Jennifer bent down and did her best to cover Amy with the ripped shirt. Luke turned to the side, cold sweat running down his face, and fainted.

When he awoke, Luke saw relieved faces looking down at him. "Where's Amy?" he asked.

"She's fine. She's right over there." Jennifer pointed to a boulder a few yards away. Amy was sitting up against it and looking much more alive. The rain had stopped and the storm seemed to be moving away.

"Thank God," Luke breathed, struggling to his feet.

"Well, actually, thank *you*," said Jennifer. "You saved her life."

"I don't know…" Luke straightened up and brushed wet cedar fronds from his clothes.

"*I* do," said Amy, from her seat against the rock. "I wouldn't be here right now without you. I'll never be able to thank you enough."

Luke walked over and sat down next to Amy. "I'm so glad you're okay. That was just too close. But if I hadn't been here, Jennifer or Finn would've done just the same."

"But you *were* here. It *was* you. Thank you." Amy laid her head on Luke's shoulder and he could feel her softly breathing. He put an arm around her and pulled her closer.

The Hemlock

The storm blew through quickly and the air turned cold behind it. Amy was up, walking around, and everyone wanted to get her back to the cabin as soon as possible. The paddle to the opposite shore was choppy but otherwise uneventful, and no one spoke as they pushed ahead. The occasional sound of thunder was now muted and distant.

Once back at the dock, Jennifer helped Amy up to the cabin while Finn and Luke hauled the kayaks onto the dock and turned them over.

"How's she doing?" Luke asked Jennifer as he stepped into the cabin minutes later.

"She's okay. Tired. I think she's resting now."

"Good. That's good."

Luke went to Amy's room and gently knocked on the door. "Come in."

"Hey, you. How're you feeling?" Luke sat down at the foot of her bed and patted a covered leg. "Kind of a tough way to get introduced to the lake, huh?"

"I'm okay. I little sore, I guess. But good, I'm good." Amy smiled and sat up with a wince.

"I'm glad. Can I get you something to eat or drink? Maybe some tea?"

"No thanks. Jen brought me some earlier." Amy nodded toward a mug on her nightstand. "Can you stay here with me for just a little while?"

"Sure. Let me grab a chair from outside." Luke got up from the bed.

"Wait. Please don't go. Can you just lie here beside me for a while?"

"Of course."

Amy moved over a few inches and Luke stretched out on the bed next to her. Their arms were touching, and he thought it best to hold her hand, to comfort her. Within a half hour, her slow rhythmic breathing told him she was asleep.

Slowly, Luke slid off the bed and made his way toward the door. Hearing Amy turn over, he froze in mid-stride. When he was certain she was sleeping again, Luke opened the door, stepped outside, and silently pulled the door closed behind him. He heard and smelled the comfort of a crackling fire in the living room and moved toward it, being careful to avoid the one floorboard he knew would creak.

Jennifer was there, sitting on the hearth, tending the fire.

She looked up as Luke approached, the glow from the fireplace reflecting in her brown eyes. "How is she?" she asked.

"Sleeping. She seems fine. Just tired," Luke replied, sitting cross-legged on the floor in front of the fire. "Where's Finn?"

"Oh, he went down the mountain to pick up a few things we forgot to bring. And a bottle of wine to go with dinner tonight."

"Sounds good. How're you doing after all the excitement today?" Luke asked.

"I'm fine, really."

"Yeah?"

"Yeah."

Jennifer laid another small log on the fire and stirred the embers below it. Flames licked up and around the new wood, igniting it as they watched in silence. The ticks and snaps of the fire filled the minutes comfortably.

"Actually..." Luke heard Jennifer's voice through the haze of near-sleep and felt his eyelids rise. "Actually, I thought I was fine until I started to build the fire. But then I found my hands shaking while I tried to arrange the wood in the fireplace. They wouldn't stop. Until now."

"Of course," Luke began, looking up at Jennifer as she turned toward him. "You almost lost a friend today. How could you *not* react like that?"

"I felt so weak, and I hate feeling that way. I wanted to be of more help to Amy, like you were. All I could do was bring her some tea."

"That was probably all she needed right then. You were there for her."

"Maybe."

"Not maybe. You were there. You were exactly strong enough."

Jennifer nodded and gazed back into the fire. The two sat again in easy silence.

Later, a crunch of gravel outside the cabin intruded as the jeep drove up. Luke rose and opened the door for Finn while he took off his boots and came in with a bag of groceries. The sun was setting, and its orange glow spilled into the room, joining the firelight.

"Hey you guys; how're you doing? How's the patient?" Finn held the bag in one arm and gave Jennifer a quick squeeze with the other.

Luke realized at that moment, with a little flush of shame, that he hadn't checked on Amy since he left her room. "Oh, she's good. I was just going in to check on her again."

"While you're there, see if she's up for a glass of wine, okay?" asked Finn.

"Sure."

Luke found Amy sitting up in bed, leafing through a magazine. A bit of color was back in her face and she looked better.

"Hi. Looks like you're about ready to rejoin the world."

"Yes, I think I just needed a little sleep. I'll be out in a few minutes, okay?"

"Sure. Hey, Finn got some wine; feel like a glass?"

"That'd be great. Thanks."

A few minutes later, Amy emerged with brushed hair, new jeans and a maroon-colored sweater. Her hazel eyes smiled as she entered the living room.

"Wow. What happened to the patient and who are you?" said Finn. "You look great."

"I feel a whole lot better, thanks." Amy sat down next to Luke on the rug in front of the fire and tucked her legs sideways under her.

"Here, have a glass of the house red," offered Finn. He handed Amy her wine.

"Well, here's to Amy," said Luke, raising his glass. "And to the tree that took the hit for her!"

"To Amy…and the tree!" toasted the group.

"You know, if that tree hadn't been standing there next to you up on the ridge, the whole trip would've been ruined," said Finn with a half-smile. "Would've really pissed me off!"

"What kind of tree was that, anyway?" asked Luke amid the awkward laughter that followed.

"Why does it matter?" said Finn.

"I don't know. Just wondered."

"I think it was a hemlock," said Jennifer.

"Okay," said Luke. "So, if a hemlock seed hadn't germinated under that particular patch of soil fifty years ago, and if it hadn't managed to avoid being eaten as a sapling, and if it hadn't gotten enough sunlight and water over the next few decades to grow tall enough to take the lightning hit, Amy might not be here drinking that glass of wine right now. And her daughter wouldn't be born and grow up to be President later on down the line."

"A woman president?" interjected Finn. "You really are a story-teller, aren't you, Luke?"

"Come on, Finn, really? You're not serious," said Jennifer.

"Dead serious. Hey, I have a ton of respect for women, but I just don't think…"

"Think what?" said Jennifer.

21

"I don't know. I guess I just don't feel like most women could handle the range of responsibilities, the pressures, you know…"

"No, actually, I *don't* know," said Jennifer. "Those two things you just mentioned both happen to be major strengths many women have today, and there're lots more that apply here, believe me. So, if you want to come up with some other objections, let's talk about those, too."

"Look, you're just making my point, letting your emotions get in the way."

"Finn, that's not emotion; that's rational argument," rejoined Jennifer. "Maybe you're not familiar with the concept."

"Look, this isn't the time or place for this kind of thing," said Finn, tossing back the last of his wine.

Amy and Luke had been trading nervous glances during this exchange, and Luke began to feel responsible for the conflict.

"I'm sorry I brought this up," he said. "I didn't mean to cause this mess, even though I have to say Jennifer has some good points here."

"Well, 'this mess,' as you call it, is important, at least to me," said Jennifer, with a dark glance Luke's way.

"Me too," said Amy, looking down.

"…and, I don't know what a better time or place would be," Jennifer added. "But okay, let's put this aside for now. But just for now."

Learning to Fish

L uke awoke the next morning to smells of bacon, coffee, and a wood fire. The room was cold, and a glance outside the window reinforced his desire to stay under the blankets indefinitely. The ground was white with frost and the little section of lake visible from his room was like a sheet of gray glass. The occasional crackle of the fire lulled him back into sweet sleep more than once. Ultimately though, persistent thoughts of bathroom and bacon dragged him up and out of bed.

Amy must have heard Luke coming because she handed him a mug of coffee as he walked into the kitchen.

"'Morning," she said. "Anything in your coffee?"

"Hey, thanks. No, just black. Where're Finn and Jennifer?"

"Oh, they took the skiff out fishing about twenty minutes ago."

"Are they, I mean… actually speaking to each other this morning?"

"I know, it's weird. They seemed fine."

"Hmm, must've worked some things out last night."

"I guess. Hey, want some scrambled eggs and bacon?"

"Sure. Thanks for making all this. How're *you* feeling?"

"Me? Oh, I'm fine. I just couldn't talk myself into going back out on the lake this morning."

"Of course," Luke nodded, blowing steam off the top of his mug. "I'm sure I couldn't either, if I were you."

Amy smiled and dished up a plate for each of them. She had pulled her blond hair back into a bun and all the color was back in her pretty face.

"You look great this morning," Luke offered. "Must be feeling a lot better."

She looked up with a warm smile. "Thank you. I am."

"So… after breakfast, why don't you and I do a little fishing right off the dock? How does that sound?" Luke asked.

"Sounds safe, sounds perfect."

After helping Amy with the cleanup, Luke collected some essentials from his room: two fly rods loaded with 6-weight floating line and tippets, two vests, a net, and a set of dry flies he kept together as a kit for newcomers. The two walked together down to the dock, where Luke quickly discovered that Amy's one previous fishing experience actually had nothing to do with fly fishing. She and a friend had apparently spent a day fishing for bluegill, casting lures into a pond with spinning reels. So they dedicated most of the morning to working on casting techniques and learning about selecting flies. The dock was long enough to allow for back-casting without snagging shore vegetation, so they practiced a basic two-stroke overhead technique and Amy seemed to enjoy it all, even the many failed casts. She had the patience needed for fly fishing and that counted for a lot, the way Luke saw it. Finally, she was rewarded with a near-perfect cast.

"Nice cast," Luke said, as Amy's line unfurled across the water. "See how the fly just dropped easily into place there? That's exactly what you want. As natural as possible. You want the fish to see the fly first, not the line."

"Thanks, Luke. You're a good teacher. Whoa!"

A fish struck hard, and Amy's line started to run out.

"Okay, pull back a bit and set the hook. Keep tension on the line. That's it. Let him run with it a little but keep that tension on. That's a barbless hook, so it's easy to lose him. Good, you're doing great."

"What do I do now?"

"Okay, start bringing in a little line. Reel him in a little. Good, now let him run again, but not as far this time. Keep that tension in the line. Use the rod. Nice. Now, bring him in a little more and we'll have a look at him."

Amy worked the fish for nearly a minute and slowly brought it in close to the dock. Luke got his net under it.

"Nice going, Amy! That's a beautiful brookie – a brook trout. See that brilliant yellow-orange and the white spots? He's got to be a good sixteen or eighteen inches. We don't see a lot of those here in the lake. Mostly rainbows."

They kept the fish netted in the water and Luke showed Amy how to remove the hook. Luke gently massaged the tired brookie and let him go. The fish swam easily back into the depths and disappeared.

"That was so great, Luke! Thank you!" Amy threw her arms around Luke's neck and gave him a quick kiss. They pulled apart, looked at each other and laughed.

"A near death experience and a brookie," said Amy. "Two firsts for me on this trip already!"

"I'd go for seconds on only one of those, if I were you," Luke replied. "Hey, enough fishing lessons for the day. Want to head back up to the cabin?"

"Sure. What did you have in mind?" Amy asked with a sly smile.

"Well…"

One Year Later

Amy and Luke arrived at the cabin early on Thanksgiving morning, as they were the designated turkey-providers and needed to get the bird in the oven early. Finn and Jennifer had invited her sister, Maggie, and husband James, and were meeting them in Rockport to bring them up the mountain to the cabin. Maggie and James lived in Spokane where Maggie owned and operated a small environmental consulting company and James was an Associate Professor of Philosophy at Gonzaga University. He was the first person of color to hold that position in the department.

"I'll fire up the generator; be right back," Luke said, after lugging the turkey in from the truck.

"Can't hear you, honey!" he heard Amy shout, probably from the bathroom.

When did I become a honey? Luke wondered. *Makes me feel old, or tired, or something, I don't know. Also sort of settled, and maybe that's not so bad. But I'm not even thirty yet. And, crap, I'm almost thirty.*

The propane-fueled generator started immediately and settled into a smooth idle within seconds. Then, as Luke switched on a few breakers, he heard it lug down a bit, settling into its workhorse mode, providing the cabin with light, refrigeration, and heat. The downside, of course, was its noise. That was mitigated somewhat by the little shed the brothers had built to enclose it, and the low background droning was something one could eventually learn to ignore. But still, it was an unwelcome reminder of the artificial in an otherwise natural environment.

"Oh, there you are," said Amy as Luke walked back into the cabin. "Did you get the power on?"

Did you notice the lights? he wanted to say but didn't. "Yep, we're good. Let's get that oven pre-heating."

As they worked together preparing the turkey, stuffing and mashed potatoes, Amy seemed a bit on edge.

"Something on your mind?" Luke asked.

"Not really. I don't know. Maybe."

"So... talk to me. What is it?"

"I don't know. Sometimes I just feel kind of small. I mean, I'm sure Maggie and James are very nice but here I am, a lowly space planner, and they've got these important, exciting careers. I don't have any idea how to talk to a philosopher – I barely even know what that means. And Maggie, running her own company. I don't know, I've kind of got this weird panicky feeling, Luke. At least you teach at a university."

"Come here, I know." Luke held Amy close and stroked her hair. "I feel a little bit like that, too. After all, I'm just a writing instructor, not a professor. I get it. You know what I do when I'm feeling like that?"

"No, what?"

"Ask questions."

"Okay, like...?"

"Like, 'So, what is it about philosophy that drew you in?' or 'What kinds of companies hire environmental consultants? What are they usually looking for?' Anything to keep the spotlight off me, at least for a while. And, sometimes the answers can be really interesting."

"Okay, that might help. You're so smart."

"Not really. Just trying to avoid feeling awkward, I guess. Anyway, only Jennifer has actually met these folks and they haven't met us, so we're all kind of in the same boat," Luke added.

"You're right." Amy gave him a squeeze, a smile, and went back to work on the food.

It wasn't long until they heard the Jeep crunching up the gravel drive.

When the cabin door flew open and everyone came pouring in, they engaged in the common meeting rituals of "So great to finally meet you," and "I've heard so much about you!" and "Uh oh, I hope it wasn't too terrible," etc., etc., and all this was followed by the just-as-benign, "So how was the drive up here?" and "Did you run into any weather on the way over from Spokane?" etc., etc. Luke supposed that all this served its usual purpose, as most of the group quickly settled into some easy conversation on a marginally deeper level. But Finn quickly disappeared into a back room, ostensibly to dig out some sleeping bags and other necessities for the night ahead. When he didn't reappear after several minutes, Luke went to see if he needed any help.

Luke found him lying on his bed staring at the ceiling. "Hey, man, what's going on? You okay?"

"Yeah, just a killer headache."

"You want some aspirin? I've got some in my pack."

"Took some already, thanks."

"Sure. Need anything else?"

"Just apologize for me and tell everyone I'll try and make it out to dinner later."

"No problem. Get some rest."

When Luke returned, the group was talking about Amy's job and she seemed to be feeling comfortable with the conversation. James was friendly and inquisitive, and was giving Amy a chance to talk about the importance of her department in light of the company's rapid expansion.

"How many employees do you guys have now, and what's the name of the company again?" asked James.

"It's called Microsoft," said Amy. "And right now I think we've got almost a thousand people. We just opened a new production facility in Ireland, too."

"And we finally released the retail version of a new operating system called Windows," added Jennifer. "It's been a pretty big year and the place is starting to feel like a real company."

"Ever gonna go public?" asked James with a smile.

Amy returned the smile. "There're some rumors flying around. Maybe next year."

"So enough about Microsoft," said Amy. "What drew you into philosophy, James?"

Amy and Luke exchanged a look.

"I guess I was never any good at anything else," replied James. "I just sort of fell into it in school."

"Oh, come on," interrupted Maggie, elbowing her husband. "He's always been a thinker and always insists on asking the hard questions. His mother nicknamed him 'Y' because he started asking 'why?' as soon as he could talk."

"Yeah, I guess I was a real pain in the ass," chuckled James.

"Still are," added Maggie with a grin.

"So, to get back to Amy's question," Luke said. "What got you started?"

"Well, sometime in my teens I ran across that famous quote from Socrates; I'm sure you've heard it somewhere along the way: 'The unexamined life is not worth living.'" Well, I was in a pretty dark phase of adolescence at the time. We were poor, barely getting by in L.A., Dad had left us a few years earlier and I was trying to figure it all out. A couple of my friends drifted off into a gang and one got himself killed when he was only sixteen. I guess it was then I started to ask myself who I was as a black person and what I really wanted. When I first read that line from Socrates, the part that really caught my eye was the last phrase about life not being worth living. That resonated. It wasn't until later that the first part sort of became my salvation. I started looking hard at what my life had been about and decided to make some changes. And I guess my mother did too, bless her, because right about then she moved us out of L.A. and up to Spokane."

"So, did you go to school there?" asked Amy.

"I finished high school there and then left for college."

"And where was that? Luke asked.

"Columbia University. Did my undergrad work in math and philosophy there and then settled into their PhD program in philosophy."

"So how did you end up back in Spokane?" asked Amy.

"Well, unfortunately, Mom got sick and I came back to help out, best I could. And then Gonzaga University offered me a post-doc fellowship and it just all made sense."

"And your Mom? How's she doing today?" asked Amy.

"She passed away about two and a half years ago. Ovarian cancer."

"Oh, I'm so sorry," Amy and Luke said together.

"Thanks. That was a dark time for all of us."

"Yes," said Jennifer. "I think you had just met Maggie and she told me about the whole thing at the time."

"How *did* you two, meet, anyway?" asked Amy, probably trying to lighten the mood. Luke glanced at her, thinking that maybe they should have stayed with the current topic a bit longer, out of respect.

But Jennifer stifled a laugh and covered her mouth. Luke could see her eyes sparkling and felt some relief.

"Mags, is it okay if I ...?" asked James, looking at his wife.

"No, let me tell them. You can jump in if I miss anything important."

Everyone looked expectantly at Maggie.

"We met in a men's room at O'Hare airport." Maggie raised her eyebrows and let her statement hang in the air.

"Uh, okay..." said Amy.

Luke felt his mouth hanging open and Jennifer was laughing out loud, surely having heard the story from her sister before. James crossed his legs and seemed to be trying to maintain a serious demeanor.

"Yes, Concourse C, near Gate 18 if memory serves," he added, patting his wife on the knee.

"Alright, that's enough of that. I'm sure no one here is interested in our sordid past," continued Maggie, getting up from her chair.

"Uh, wrong! You can't just leave us hanging like that. Come on, sit down, this sounds like a great story. I promise I won't write about it, at least not without changing names and location," Luke said.

"Okay, okay," said Maggie, re-taking her seat. "Do you want the true embarrassing version or the sanitized boring one."

"Truth, truth, truth!" everyone chanted.

"Alright, you asked for it. It was late at night, sometime around eleven, I think. I'd been at a conference in Boston and missed my eight o'clock connecting flight out of Chicago back to Spokane. It's pretty much impossible to find flights directly to Spokane from anywhere on the east coast so I had to go through Chicago and I was waiting there for the next flight out. So, anyway, I got bored and sat down at a bar."

"Now, I'm not a big drinker at all," continued Maggie, "but the bartender was a great talker and, like I said, I was bored. So, after my third martini, I guess I was pretty wasted. And I really, really had to pee. So, I slapped some cash down on the bar, practically fell off the bar stool, and wandered off to search for a restroom. Luckily, I found one nearby and stumbled in, only to find a very attractive young black man in a three-piece suit washing his hands at a sink. He looked up and stared at me. I thought that was strange, but I was too far gone to question the situation. I turned to find a stall and noticed a row of urinals against the wall. Even that took me a moment to process. I just thought, wow, they do things a little different here in Chicago. Then, finally, I guess my pickled brain came around to understanding my mistake. But I was desperate at that point, so I turned to the man at the sink, nodded toward a stall at the end of urinal-row, and said, 'do you mind if I just…' He laughed, said 'be my guest,' shook his head, and walked out."

"So that was it? That's how you met?" Luke asked between bouts of laughter.

"That's not quite the end of the story," James said.

"Right," said Maggie. "So about an hour later, I was just barely emerging from my vodka haze, boarding the plane and trying to see the row numbers along the isle. It's funny the weird details you sometimes remember, you know? I found my row empty and settled into the middle seat, the only one I could get on the re-booked flight. I was feeling kind of numb and sorry for myself, knowing the flight was full and there'd be no chance of moving to the aisle or window, when I heard someone say, 'excuse me Miss, I'm in A.' I looked up to see the man from the restroom and I think I said something stupid and much too loud like, 'Holy shit, you're that guy from the restroom!' He nodded and said, much more quietly, 'Yeah, I'm that guy,' and slid past me to the window seat. I didn't even think to get up and make it easier for him to get in. People were staring at us and I wanted to slither down and stow myself under the seat in front of me."

"I can't imagine how the conversation went from there," Luke said.

"Well, I won't bore you with the details, but things started out in dead silence for the first twenty minutes or so. I was too mortified to speak. Then, after I just couldn't stand the situation anymore, I turned to the left and worked up the guts to say something like, 'Look, I'm sorry. I'm so embarrassed.' My seatmate nodded, smiled, and I remember exactly what he said. He said, 'Hey, it's okay; when you gotta go, you gotta go.' What a romantic beginning, right? The conversation got a lot better after that."

"So, do you like, look for new men's rooms to celebrate your meeting anniversary each year?" asked Amy with a grin.

"Sort of," replied Maggie. "We've decided to shake things up a little – you know, keep the marriage fresh: men's rooms in even years and lady's in the odd ones, and new venues too. I'm pushing for Denver International next year, but James is kind of holding out for Washington Dulles."

"Whatever you choose, I'm sure it'll be lovely," laughed Amy.

The Thanksgiving conversation was easy and fun after that, and Luke remembered it as a great beginning to a wonderful set of friendships. Not that everything was always perfect, or even that everyone remained in the circle. He only wished that Finn had been able to join in that day, and often wondered if anything would have turned out differently if he had.

The Stain

T he next morning, Luke woke early and followed the smell of freshly brewed coffee out into the kitchen, leaving Amy to sleep in. Maggie and James had insisted on sleeping in their tent outside and were showing no signs of emerging. Finn was sitting at the table, cradling a mug in his hands and looking down. The whole cabin was cold, and a white dusting of snow outside seemed to amplify the feeling.

"Hey," Luke said. "You never showed up for dinner last night. How's the head?"

"It's okay."

"Just okay?"

"I'm fine."

"Bullshit. I've never seen you miss a turkey dinner before."

"Just let it go, Luke, okay?"

"Okay, sure."

"I'm going for a hike." Finn got up, dumped the rest of his coffee in the sink, and headed for the door just as Jennifer emerged from their room, yawning, her dark hair down and disheveled. She wore a long T-shirt.

"There's some coffee ready on the counter," Luke offered. "I'm gonna get a fire going. It's freezing in here. Wait, here's a blanket from the couch to warm up with." He tossed it Jennifer's way.

As the new fire began to crackle, Jennifer came back into the living room, wrapped in the blanket and holding her coffee close. She sat down on the rug with Luke in front of the fireplace and managed a sad smile.

"So, what's going on with my brother?" Luke asked. "I've seen him a little down before, but not like this."

"Me either. He's been stewing for the past couple of days. I think it's about something at work, but he won't tell me. I mean, he's not the most open person in the best of times, but he's really shut down now. It worries me. *He* worries me."

"Yeah, if he won't talk to either of *us*, then I'm a little worried too. What about the headache? You think he's sick?"

"I don't know. I think the headache's real but maybe also an excuse to stay away from people. He was super quiet on the drive up the mountain yesterday, and now he's out walking around. It's just not like him."

Luke looked up to the sound of boots stomping on the front deck and saw Maggie walk in, shivering. James was right behind her.

"Hey, come on in and get warmed up," he said. "Coffee? Tea for you, James?"

"Absolutely, thanks. We'll be right back," said James with a frozen smile. They both headed toward the bathroom.

When they returned and sat down with everyone at the fire, hot drinks in hand, James said, "So, where're Amy and Finn?"

"She's still sleeping and he's out for a hike," Luke replied.

"Is he okay?" asked Maggie.

"We were just talking about that," Luke said. "I think so, but he's not usually like this."

Jennifer nodded. "I'm kinda worried about him. Normally, he'd be out fishing with somebody right now, not just hiking alone."

"Maybe if I offer to throw my line in the water with him later on? What do you think?" James asked the room.

"Maybe," said Jennifer. "Worth a try, I guess."

Amy was finally up and the rest of the group was just finishing breakfast when Finn returned. He shook the snow off his boots, left them outside, came in and sat down by the fire.

"Cold out there," he said. "Any breakfast left?"

"There's some scrambled eggs, sausage and a couple of pieces of toast, I think. Help yourself," said Jennifer, nodding toward the kitchen.

"Guess I'll have to."

"I'm headed that way anyway," said Amy. "Let me fix you a plate."

"No, get something for yourself if you want, Amy, but Finn's perfectly capable of getting his own," said Jennifer.

The room went silent and Finn stared down at his hands. Finally, he spoke.

"Sorry. I guess I'm just a little pissed off at the world right now."

"So, what's going on?" Luke asked.

"I got fired."

"What? When?" several people asked at once.

"Day before yesterday. They actually offered me a lower-level job and gave mine to a new guy. But I was so fucking mad that I told them to shove it and walked out."

"So, what're you gonna do now?" Luke asked.

"I don't know. I could probably go back, apologize, and maybe still get that other job, but I really don't want it and I won't apologize. I don't think I'd even take my old job back if they offered it. They won't anyway. It's all because of that Affirmative Action bullshit. Sorry, James, no offense, but it's all bullshit. The most qualified guy should get the job, not the guy with the darkest skin. It's reverse discrimination. America used to be all about working hard and getting rewarded for it."

"Whoa, hey, I get where you're coming from," started James. "And I'm truly sorry about what's happened, but I can't sit here and pretend to agree with your assertion."

"What assertion?"

"That Affirmative Action amounts to reverse discrimination."

"Well, what the fuck is it then?! Just look at what happened!" Finn was up out of his chair.

"First of all, you can't know for sure that this new guy was only hired to meet a quota," said James, staying seated. "I hesitate to say it, but it's possible that he's just a better fit for the job. And second, the whole point of Affirmative Action is to level the field of opportunity, not replace people. You know as well as I do that black and brown people in this country have been denied a chance to succeed since the beginning and still are today. You know that. Affirmative Action is just one small attempt to address that problem."

"So now it's my problem? Me and a bunch of other white guys across the country!?"

"Welcome to my world."

"Really? That's all you can say?"

"No, I could say a lot more, but it's pretty clear you wouldn't want to hear it."

"You're goddamned right about that. The rest of you – are you just gonna sit there and listen to this shit?"

Luke was stunned, and everyone else was silent. He wanted to come to his brother's rescue, but at what cost? He had never heard anything like this from Finn before. Jennifer got up and strode into the kitchen, followed by Amy. James had not moved, and Maggie was holding his hand, looking at the floor.

Luke finally found words, inadequate as he felt they were. "Look, Finn, I get that you're pissed. I probably would be too. But I think you owe James, and all of us, an apology."

"What the hell for!?" shouted Finn. "I'm the one who got the shaft here!"

James intervened. "Hey, it's okay, Finn. I think I know something about what you're feeling. Believe me, I've been there."

"I don't think so. I really don't think so," said Finn. He picked up his coat and turned toward the kitchen. "Jennifer, get out here! We're leaving!"

Jennifer stepped back into the room, head slowly shaking, jaw set, eyes glaring. "You may be leaving but I'm not. I'm staying right here with my family and friends. Get your stuff and go."

"What're you gonna do, woman – throw me out of my own cabin?"

Finn was smiling with a strange malevolence that Luke had never seen in him as he lurched across the room toward Jennifer. Without thinking, Luke stepped between them.

Luke had never been in a serious physical fight before, let alone one with his own brother. Fortunately for him, he lost quickly. Fortunately for Jennifer, Finn seeing the bloodied face of his brother seemed to drain the intensity out of him. As he pulled back for another punch, something stopped him mid-way, and, through the haze, Luke saw his eyes soften. He backed away, looked around the room as if seeing the people there for the first time, muttered a vague apology, turned, and walked out the door. No one tried to stop him.

James brought in the first-aid kit and patched Luke up – his nose, one corner of his mouth, and his pride the main injuries. Luke was surprised at the amount of blood on the floor and, even after Amy's good efforts at cleaning it up, a dark stain remained in the wood. But he remembered little else of that day. He slept through most of it, not so much because he was tired but because he wanted to escape from its implications, from the confusion and sadness of seeing his brother in this new and disturbing light, and from the thoughts of relationships damaged. He hoped for reconciliation. At the same time, a new anger was taking root in him – not because of the physical fight but because of its cause. Luke believed Finn was giving in to something, that he was allowing external circumstances to dominate him and to impact the rest of the group. He began to understand that his anger was directed at that, whatever it was, as well as at Finn himself.

And what about Jennifer? Luke didn't remember a single word from her, not that he expected any thanks for his mindless intervention. He knew she would've held her own without him and doubted that Finn would have done more than grab her by the arm anyway. She would have resisted him with her strong eyes and relentless will. Still, Luke found himself circling back around to her, again and again, in his semi-sleep.

When Luke emerged later that afternoon, Amy was the only one left. The others had said their goodbyes and departed. The fire had gone out, and the cabin was cold again. "Let's pack up and get out of here," he said.

"And maybe get some stitches for your mouth. That looks pretty deep right there in the corner," said Amy.

"No, I'm fine. It'll heal. Let's just get home."

Truth Over Coffee

A week later, Luke was grading papers in his office near the end of the day when he got a call. He jumped at the phone, hoping it was Finn because he'd been trying, without success, to contact him after the fight at the cabin. But it was Jennifer. She sounded worried and asked if Luke could meet for coffee around five at the new Starbucks in Redmond. He accepted right away and began stuffing student papers into his briefcase. The traffic across the 520 floating bridge was known to be painfully unpredictable, and he wanted to leave enough time.

Rain, on the other hand, was much easier to forecast. When Luke left the university just before four-thirty, the sky was darkly overcast, and, crossing Lake Washington on the floating bridge, he noticed a light chop on the south side and smooth water on the north. That, along with the unseasonably mild evening temperature, almost certainly meant rain.

By the time Luke rolled into the Starbucks parking lot in the small town of Redmond, streetlights were on and the storm was gathering force. The black asphalt danced with little pawn-shaped rain strikes and Luke made a run for the door, anticipating warmth and the inviting smell of coffee within. He spotted Jennifer next to a cozy fireplace on the far side of the room, waved, and went to order his drink. Minutes later, as Luke made his way back to the fireplace with coffee in hand, Jennifer patted the leather chair next to her and smiled, inviting him to sit. Her dark, shiny hair was pulled back into a ponytail and Luke noticed she was wearing a striking pair of small silver dolphin earrings with pinpoint diamond eyes that caught the light when she turned her head. The early evening crowd was light, and Luke felt grateful for the privacy of the little nook by the fire.

"Thanks for coming, Luke. I hope I didn't interrupt anything too important at work. I know you sometimes stay around late."

Luke smiled. "Are you kidding? I am *so* glad not to be grading papers."

"Good. Listen, I hope you don't mind but I really need to talk about what happened last week."

"Sure," said Luke. "Absolutely."

Jennifer turned toward him. "Luke, that was a wretched Thanksgiving."

"You're welcome!" he responded with a laugh, not sure of her intent.

"No, really, I mean it. Don't you agree?"

"Yes, of course. The absolute worst. I'm so sorry."

"No, it wasn't your fault, and thanks for trying to fix things. But how do you fix something like this? How's your poor nose, by the way? And that cut in the corner of your mouth looks painful." Jennifer reached out to touch Luke's face but stopped part way.

"Oh, it's coming along. Amy keeps telling me I need stitches, but I'm fine – physically anyway. Have you talked to Finn? I haven't been able to reach him and was going to call you next but I wasn't sure I should."

"That's why I wanted to meet you here today; well, mostly."

"Okay, sure. Talk to me."

"Alright. Well, when James, Maggie and I left the cabin, we all drove down together in their car and they came here to stay with me for the night, which was thoughtful and I really needed it. On the way down, I found myself apologizing and making excuses for Finn. But pretty soon I realized that the excuses were ridiculous, and I got more and more upset with myself and angry at Finn. Both James and Maggie were gracious and understanding, but I kept feeling worse. By the time we got home, I wanted to call Finn and have it out with him right then, but Maggie convinced me to wait until morning, until I'd cooled down a little."

Jennifer paused for a sip of coffee.

"So did you? Did you wait?" Luke asked.

"Yes, and that was probably a good thing because I was still pretty much a mess when I did call. I can't imagine what the conversation would've been like the night before."

"So, how'd it go?"

"Not great. I mean, it was civil enough, I guess. It was just a shock to hear some of the stuff coming from the guy I thought I knew so well. Has he ever mentioned a bunch of friends he has up somewhere in the northeastern corner of the state?"

"Uh, no. What friends?"

"He wouldn't say much about them, but apparently he's been talking with this group for a quite a while. They seem to share his ideas about things like Affirmative Action and I guess they've been giving him lots of moral support since he lost his job. Finn seems to be stuck in a kind of binary thinking where white people lose anytime black people win, and I think he must be getting this from them. He sounds like a victim half the timeIts like a victim mentality."

"Has he been up there to see these guys? Are they, like, an organized group or something?"

"No, and I don't think so, but I wouldn't swear to it. There's a lot of stuff I just don't know and it scares me."

"Sure, I understand. It does me, too."

"Has Finn always been like this? Hateful? Vindictive? Blaming everyone but himself?" asked Jennifer.

"No, I would've talked to you a long time ago if I'd had any clue about this. He's always been conservative, but this isn't conservatism, at least not the way I think of it."

"No, me either. So, what can we do?" Jennifer asked, her eyes pleading in a way Luke hadn't seen before.

"I'll talk to him. Maybe you can convince him to pick up the phone. Or, better yet, maybe I'll just drop by his apartment."

"That'd be great. Thanks."

"So, when I see him, what should I assume about… are you guys still…?"

"I don't know, Luke. I just don't know," Jennifer sighed. "A lot has changed."

"Of course; sure."

"So, how're you and Amy doing?" Jennifer asked. "About all this, I mean."

"Well, like you, I didn't see it coming. I'm confused and pissed off at both Finn and whatever this is that's gotten ahold of him. And Amy? I don't know. She's just kind of shut down. She doesn't seem to want to deal with this at all. I don't know why, but I *do* know it's damn frustrating. I don't have anyone to talk to."

"Yes, you do. I'm right here."

Jennifer reached out to touch Luke's hand, and this time she didn't pull back. He looked up and saw a softness in her eyes that stirred him.

Friends Up North

Finn finally picked up the phone during one of Luke's many attempts to reach him, and they agreed to meet at Finn's place on Sunday in east Bellevue, up the hill near Redmond and the nascent Microsoft campus. Luke arrived at about nine in the morning and found Finn dressed in shorts and a sweatshirt, looking as though he hadn't shaved in days. An empty pizza box lay open on the coffee table and beer cans were strewn about, looking like they'd been angrily crushed. The TV was on.

Luke decided to open on a brotherly note. "Hey, man, you look like shit."

"Yeah, well, you shoulda seen the other guy. Wait, you *are* the other guy."

They shared a nervous laugh, then Finn made an attempt to apologize.

"Sorry about the nose and that cut. Looks like that could use some stitches. I, uh, probably shouldn't've gone that far."

"Nose's okay. It's not broken. I guess I was just trying to help." Luke felt his tongue move to the cut at the corner of his mouth.

"Want a beer?" asked Finn.

"No, I'm good. You know it's nine o'clock in the morning, right? Got any coffee?"

"There's some instant in the kitchen. Help yourself."

Luke microwaved a mug of water, stirred in some miserable brown crystals, and brought it back to the living room. The brothers continued their banter for a while, until it ran out of energy and the underlying tension once again surfaced.

"So, I get that you were trying to help," began Finn. "But, hey, when you put yourself between a guy and his woman, that's not cool. It's humiliating. I couldn't let it stand."

"When the hell did you start talking like that? What do you even mean?"

"What I mean is she's mine and I'll deal with her however I choose."

"Yours? Deal with her?! What the fuck are you talking about? You can't be serious."

"I'm absolutely serious. Maybe it's time you wake up and stop mindlessly following this weak-ass feminist society we're suffering through today. Grow some balls, man!"

Luke sat there, staring at the brother he thought he knew, and finally muttered something inane about his balls not being the problem.

Finn continued. "Look, there're some good people out there who're starting to see things clearly. They're breaking through all this political correctness bullshit and telling things the way they are, or the way they should be."

"Things like?"

"Things like we were just talking about, man! Be honest with yourself for once. Look at nature. Males are meant to capture females, not beg for their favors like whipped dogs. And we're meant to go out and get ones of our own race. Otherwise, we're looking at racial extinction, and then where would our country be?"

Luke stared at his brother. "Where are you getting this horseshit? I mean, this doesn't sound like you. I'm just wondering what's changed here."

"I think I've always known this. And I bet you have, too, if you'd be honest with yourself. I just got a few reminders from some friends up north."

"What friends? Do I know these guys? I'm just assuming they're guys, based on the opinions they seem to have."

"No, you don't know them. If you did, we'd probably be having a much different conversation. There was a guy at work,

45

Jeff. I've probably mentioned him before. He thinks a lot like I do and he hooked me up with this group one day after work over a few beers – gave me their phone number. I've been talking with their leader on and off ever since."

"Is this an organized group or just a bunch of guys hanging out around a campfire?"

"Loosely organized, I guess. Do you remember that guy who got killed in an FBI raid on Whidbey Island in December a year or two ago?"

"Vaguely. I think I remember seeing an article in the Times."

"He was one of the originals. His group is gone now but there're a bunch of spin-offs."

"Holy shit, man! Wasn't that guy a neo-Nazi or something?"

"That's not a label we like to use a lot. But okay, sort of. It's really much broader than that. It's more about getting back to the natural order of things. And part of that's about purity and preserving our race. It's about family."

"Family. Really. How narrow a definition of that word are you using?" Luke asked.

"What do you mean?"

"I mean, like, for example, do you consider Maggie and James to be a family?"

"Hey, those two made a choice, okay? Not a good one, or a right one, in my book, but as long as they don't procreate, I'm not gonna make a lot of noise about it. They'll probably break up before long, anyway."

"Wow. I can't believe I just heard that. Isn't it possible that we're still evolving as a species? Isn't it possible that we're making progress toward a more unified society, that we're not static, that we're actually learning, however slowly and painfully, to really live together? Isn't that possible?"

"That's just a bunch of liberal Kumbaya crap, Luke. Listen to yourself! It sounds like something James would say. We're just not wired that way."

"That's exactly what I'm challenging! I don't think it's all wiring. I think a big part of it's like writing or software — malleable, evolvable. Can't you see there's hope in that?"

"I don't call that hope. I call that giving up; I call that defeat."

"Well, I'm not giving up, and I'm not giving up on you."

"Thanks, I guess, but you sound like a woman," said Finn with a thin smile.

"I'll take that as a compliment."

"See, that's what I'm talking about! Like I said, grow a pair."

The Library

L uke had been living with Amy in a small rental home on Queen Anne Hill just above downtown Seattle for about six months, and when Luke returned from his unsettling meeting with Finn, she was there.

"You feel like a walk around the neighborhood?" he asked.

Amy agreed, saying the exercise would be good and the sun was out, so why not? This wasn't exactly an enthusiastic yes, but Luke tried to take it that way and he needed to talk to her.

The pair had been lucky enough to rent the house from a friend, a tenured professor of English Literature at the university, and at a bargain rate compared to most others on the hill. They had gotten into the habit of walking a particular route that had a stunning view of the Seattle skyline – the Space Needle at the base of the hill in the foreground with the rest of the downtown area and Elliott Bay spread out beyond. On many days, the scene was partly obscured by clouds and fog, but this day brought the Emerald City into beautiful focus and, as a special bonus, Mount Rainier pushed its snowy peak up into view beyond the city.

"So, after stopping at the office this morning, I went over to see Finn," Luke said as they began their walk.

"Oh? How is he?"

"That's hard to answer. I guess my summary would be 'not good, probably worse than you can imagine.' And I'm sure he'd say the same about me."

"Did you two argue about politics again? I keep thinking maybe it's time to just agree to disagree. Move on, you know?"

"No, it's beyond that, Amy. It's way beyond that."

Luke spent the next half mile telling Amy everything he could remember about the conversation, answering her questions and listening to her comments about his relationship with Finn.

As they made the turn to come home, Amy said, "Look, a lot of that stuff is just testosterone-charged BS. I've heard it before in my own family. His pride is hurt from losing his job and he's taking it out on everyone around him. He'll get over it; you'll see."

"I wish I could agree, but I think it's more than that."

"He's your brother, Luke, and it's just stupid politics. I think you guys should try and work it out."

"I'd love to work this out if I could, Amy, but it's not one of those things that you can just avoid discussing at family events. And it's not just politics. It's more like hate. Finn's into something that sounds like a cult to me."

"Well, I don't know about that, but I need to ask you about something else," said Amy.

"Sure, go ahead."

Amy paused for a second and then looked up. "So, when were you going to tell me about your little get-together with Jennifer?"

"Oh, that? The Starbucks thing? She wanted to talk about Finn – the same kind of stuff. Not that it matters, but how did you hear about this?"

"A friend from work was there."

"Okay. Well, that's what led to my meeting with Finn today and I wanted to wait 'til after that to give you the whole story."

"But you didn't."

"I was just about to."

"Hmm."

"Look, I also knew you'd get weird about it, like this, and I just didn't want to deal with that right now, not with everything else."

"Weird about it? Really? My boyfriend hides a date with another woman, I get concerned, and you call that weird?"

49

"Come on, it wasn't a date!"

"Well, you set up a time and a place, you met, and you didn't tell me about it. I call that a date."

"It wasn't a date. It was a serious meeting about her boyfriend, my brother. It wasn't a fun time. I don't know what else to tell you."

As Luke and Amy rounded the corner to head back to the house, a marine layer of clouds was starting to push across the water from Bainbridge Island. Then, by the time they walked up to the front porch, the sun had disappeared and Luke had made up his mind about what to do next.

"Go on ahead inside. I'm going out for a couple of hours." he said.

"Oh, and do I have the right to ask where and with whom?"

"Of course. To the library, and by myself."

"The library. That's original. What are you, thirteen?"

"Come on, Amy, I don't want to fight with you any more today. And yes, I'm going to the library."

On the drive downtown, Luke mentally replayed his conversation with Amy and was feeling more and more unsettled. When he pulled into the parking lot near the Seattle Library, he realized that he didn't remember making any of the turns, stopping at lights, or dealing with the traffic. The process had been almost unconscious.

Once in the building, Luke made his way to the reference desk and requested access to all December issues of the Seattle Times from 1984. He was handed several sheets of flat transparent film and sent to a microfiche reader where he began his search.

It didn't take long to find what he was looking for. The front page of the Times on December 9 included an article about an FBI raid and shootout on South Whidbey Island which had occurred the day before. Over seventy agents had been involved, and a man named Robert Jay Mathews had been killed. Reading further, Luke discovered that Mathews had been identified as a neo-Nazi and the founder of a gang called The

Order which had recently beaten up a black disc jockey in Lynnwood. The gang had also been involved in several bank robberies and had assassinated Alan Berg, an outspoken Jewish radio talk show host in Denver.

Luke read on, but his focus was gone. His thoughts had already leapt to Finn, and then immediately to Jennifer.

Departure

L uke's first move after leaving the library was to find a phone booth. He called Jennifer at her home in Redmond, but after ten or twelve rings gave up and called her office, as she often worked weekends during project crunch times. No answer there either. He left a voicemail on the new Microsoft corporate answering system, asking her to call his home number, then drove back as fast as he could.

When he arrived at around four-thirty, Luke found Amy in the living room, reading a book and sipping a glass of wine. She smiled briefly and asked if he would like one, too. The bottle and another glass were ready on the coffee table. Feeling both surprised and relieved at Amy's calmer demeanor, Luke almost didn't ask her if any calls had come in. He didn't want to disturb the domestic equilibrium but knew he had to.

"Sure, wine would be great. By the way, were there any calls while I was gone?"

"No, it's been pretty quiet around here. Do you want to tell me about your afternoon?"

"Well, it was disturbing, to say the least."

"Oh?"

"Yeah, I went to the library to try and track down some information about that group Finn mentioned."

"So you actually *did* go to the library?"

"Come on Amy, yes! I wouldn't lie to you about this, or anything."

She looked away and took another sip. "Okay, I think I believe you."

"Well, thank you for that, I think."

Luke wanted to launch into a full-fledged fight about trust but felt the edges of hypocrisy closing in and quashed the urge before it had a chance to take hold. He flinched at a jolt of pain coming from the cut in the corner of his mouth and instinctively reached up to touch it.

"Look, what I found is damn frightening. I think Finn's somehow involved with a bunch of guys who were directly influenced by a white nationalist group called The Order which started out in Metaline Falls a few years ago. I vaguely remember hearing about those guys in the news back then, but what I didn't know is that The Order carried out at least two assassinations and tried to fund their activities via bank robberies and counterfeiting. Amy, they beat up a black DJ in Lynnwood, killed a Jewish radio talk show host in Denver and shot one of their own members. Almost all the original members of the gang were convicted of various crimes and are now in prison, and their leader, Robert Mathews, is dead. But their influence is still strong. In fact, it's probably stronger now that they have a martyr."

"Oh," said Amy. She put her glass down and looked up. "Luke, you've got to stay away from this. This is bad."

"That's what I've been trying to tell you! It's worse than bad. But I can't just walk away, Amy. I tried to call Jennifer but couldn't reach her. I left her a message to call here."

"Jennifer again."

"Yes, Jennifer again, and Finn too. I'm worried about both of them, Amy. This is serious."

Amy didn't respond and, as Luke turned away in exasperation, he noticed a dimly flashing red light across the room. The answering machine.

"Amy, there's a message on the machine. You said there were no calls!"

"I'm sorry; I didn't think there were. It must have come in when I was in the tub. I didn't hear anything."

Luke ran over to the phone and played back the message.

Hey, guys, it's Jennifer. Just wanted to let you know that Finn took me up to the cabin for a little getaway, kind of spur-of-the-moment. We're calling from a pay phone in Rockport before we head up the mountain to let you know we're fine and not to worry. One thing, though: I'm going to be away from a phone for a couple of days, so could one of you please call my group's Admin, Karin Barkley, at work on Monday morning to let her know I'll be gone for a few days? I don't really trust the new voicemail system yet and I need to be sure she gets the word. Should be back around mid-week. Amy knows her number. Thanks, guys."

"There's something weird about this," said Amy as Luke walked back across the room.

"No kidding. She'd never say things that way. She'd never say 'Finn took her' to the cabin. She'd say something more like, 'we're headed up to the cabin.'"

"Yes, and there's something more. Karin Barkley is *my* group admin assistant, not hers. And, on top of that, Jennifer trusts voicemail with important messages all the time. It's something else, or someone else, she doesn't trust."

"Shit!"

"And I bet Finn was standing right there next to her, listening, but he wouldn't have had a clue about this. She's trying to alert us behind his back. Maybe we should call the police?"

"I don't think that'd do any good," said Luke. "They won't lift a finger for something like this and it'll just waste time. We don't have any real proof of anything and, as far as they're concerned, this would just be a domestic squabble at worst. I've got to get up to the cabin."

"Right now? Tonight?" asked Amy.

"Yeah, right now. I've gotta go. Would you please call in sick for me in the morning?"

"Sure. Look, I'd go with you but I'm giving a presentation tomorrow about office space for the big move next year. I'm really sorry."

"That's okay. I understand. I'll take the truck." Luke stuffed a few things in a backpack, kissed Amy, and left.

In the Dark

By the time Luke merged onto Mercer Street heading toward the freeway, the sky was darkening and he had no real plan. He hadn't thought this through and hoped that Finn hadn't either. All he knew was that he needed to get to the cabin as quickly as possible to try to defuse whatever situation he might find there. Beyond that, he would have to let things play out, much as he did with his writing.

As Luke often told his students, some writers of fiction are meticulous planners – outlining their plots from beginning to end so the act of writing comes down to following the plan and creatively filling in details. Others, like himself, begin with a general concept or a set of characters and then let things flow. The downside of that, he had told them, is that sometimes the concept isn't enough and the flow doesn't flow or isn't of any interest to anyone beyond its self-deluded author. The upside is that sometimes that flow feels like real life and opens up possibilities that simply can't be seen at the outset. Luke hoped his situation that night would be more like the latter.

Musing about writing then led him to think about missing work the next day. Luckily, Luke didn't teach on Mondays, so at least his students wouldn't miss class, not that most of them would see that as a negative anyway. He did have office hours though, he reflected. *...and some lost soul just might drift in, seeking my literary wisdom, and I won't be there with that one brilliant flash of insight that would ultimately launch their extraordinary writing career, propelling them toward a well-deserved Nobel Prize in Literature. And, sadly, I won't get a free trip to Stockholm to share in their glory. Oh well, these things happen.*

Luke chuckled, feeling a bit of relief from the reality of the night. The traffic eased up as he left Everett behind and continued up Interstate 5 towards Burlington and the North Cascades Highway. He arrived in Rockport about three hours into the trip, pulled over to flip the front hubs and put his old truck into four-wheel drive for the last stretch up the mountain.

It had been a while since Luke had driven up the long dirt trail at night and he'd forgotten how dark it could be on a moonless night. He crawled along, watching for potholes, rocks, and downed branches. About halfway up, he saw the glowing eyes of a racoon family as they crossed the trail in front of him. They took their time, the leader pausing to briefly challenge the noisy bright-eyed monster that dared to invade its territory.

Then, as Luke approached the old steel cattle gate which marked the boundary of the Mason property, he decided it would be best to leave the truck parked just off the trail and walk the last quarter mile to the cabin. He didn't know what to expect ahead and decided to approach carefully. Slinging his pack over a shoulder, he grabbed a flashlight and began the short trek, only using the light when the stars failed to penetrate the forest, or the soft-edged shadows masked the edges of the trail and sent him stumbling into the woods.

Luke picked his way along slowly, keeping his eyes on the ground just in front of him. But when he finally did look up, he was surprised to see something large and dim, looming just ahead. It took a moment to let the adrenaline drain away, to abandon the alarming thought that he was lost, and to recognize the cabin itself, dark and quiet in the clearing ahead. No Jeep parked next to it, no lights on, no signs of life.

He approached the building quietly and peered into the living room window from the side. He could see nothing inside; it was just too dark. The only option he felt he had was to announce his presence and go in. He stepped up onto the front porch, knocked on the door and shouted, "It's just me, Luke!" Nothing. He unlocked the door and slowly walked in, and, as sometimes happens when one walks alone into a house, it became immediately but inexplicably clear that no living soul was present. Maybe it was the dead quiet, perhaps a smell, the lack of a smell, or maybe something bordering on the metaphysical, but Luke just knew.

He switched on his flashlight and played its beam around the room, looking for anything that might help him understand what had happened. Everything seemed to be in place and, thankfully, he could see no signs of a struggle, other than his old Thanksgiving bloodstain in the floor. The fireplace was empty and cold. He continued the search in the kitchen, the bathroom and the bedrooms, all yielding the same results.

Not knowing what to do next, Luke sat down to think. Had they been here to pick up something and then left right away? Had they gone somewhere else instead? Had Finn never intended to come here and tried to throw Luke off the scent by having Jennifer mention the cabin in her phone message? Maybe Jennifer had really believed they were going to the cabin. Maybe she was actually okay with the trip. Maybe not. None of this speculation was helping Luke get closer to a plan and he wished he could talk with someone about it.

Luke regretted not getting one of the new mobile phones that were just coming on the market, but he hadn't been able to stomach either the cost or the image. He knew that it was an irrational bias, or maybe his own projection, but drivers on their car phones, speeding along in their BMWs and Mercedes, always seemed so arrogant to him. But now, one of those new phones would be just the thing. He consoled himself with the idea that maybe they wouldn't work up there in the near wilderness anyway.

Somewhere in that tangle of thought, Luke resolved to stay overnight in the cabin, just in case Finn and Jennifer showed up later. He decided to build a fire but leave the generator off. After all, he'd just be going to bed soon, so why waste the propane? He went outside, forgetting his flashlight, felt around in the dark for firewood, brought back a small load, and started the fire.

Then, as Luke backed away from the fireplace to sit on the rug in front of it, a tiny glint of firelight sparkled off something near the edge of the brick hearth and caught his eye. He moved forward to get a better look. There, lying along a grout line in the brick, was a small dolphin-shaped silver earring with a pinpoint diamond eye.

Missing

Now at least Luke knew that Jennifer had been there, but the big questions remained. Why had they come up in the first place if they didn't stay? Where had they gone now? Was Jennifer a willing participant in all this? Luke was almost certain she was not, and that she had purposely left that earring as an indicator. But how was he to interpret it?

One other question was at least answerable: should he stay the night or drive back to Seattle immediately? By this time, Luke was getting tired and wasn't sure that the long drive back would be a good idea. But then, how could that little problem possibly compare to the ones facing Jennifer? And, at least he would be able to make phone calls if he were back in Seattle. In the end, he decided on a compromise. The small diner down in Rockport would almost certainly have coffee and a pay phone. He could make a few calls, get caffeinated and then decide whether he was awake enough for the trip back. He grabbed his pack and flashlight, then hiked back down the trail to the truck. From there, the drive down the mountain was relatively easy and he arrived at the diner at around eight o'clock.

Unfortunately, he had forgotten to consider the fact that this was a Sunday night in a very small town and, according to the sign on the door, the diner had closed an hour ago. The good news was that an old pay phone was mounted on the outside wall of the darkened building at one end. A tattered phone book hung from a rusted steel wire, its white and yellow pages fluttering in a cold breeze. Luke dug through the truck's glove compartment for change and vowed to reconsider the whole mobile phone idea.

He called James' and Maggie's place first. James picked up on the third ring.

"Hello?"

"James, it's Luke. How're you doing tonight?"

"Fine, hey, good to hear from you! What's up? Everything okay?"

"I'm not sure. That's why I'm calling. Sorry to bust in on your Sunday night. Have you and Maggie got a few minutes to talk?"

"Sure, absolutely. I was just reading student papers and a break would be great."

"I know how that is," said Luke.

James must have tried to cover the phone with his hand but Luke still heard his muffled shout to Maggie: "Hey Mags, it's Luke! Can you pick up the other phone?"

Then they were both on the line with Luke. Maggie and he exchanged greetings, then James said, "So, Luke, what's going on? How can we help?"

"I wish I knew the answer to either of those questions. I just need to tell you what's happened today and bounce some ideas off you."

"Of course, go ahead," said James.

"Oh God, this doesn't sound good," added Maggie.

Luke spent the next few minutes describing his meeting with Finn, his findings at the library, Jennifer's phone message and his trip up to the cabin. Maggie interrupted several times with questions, most of which Luke was unable to answer.

When Luke was finished, he could hear Maggie crying in the background.

"I'm so sorry," he tried. "For what it's worth, I can't imagine my brother actually hurting Jennifer, physically I mean."

"But he went after *you*..." Maggie sobbed.

"Yes, but I think that was different. It was a stupid macho thing. I'm not saying that Jennifer isn't in trouble, just that I'm pretty sure she's not in any mortal danger. And she's smart and resourceful."

"So, what should we do? What can *we* do?" asked James.

"We should call the police right now," interjected Maggie.

"I agree, Maggie," Luke said. "I was reluctant at first but now that Jennifer's not where she said she'd be, I think it's time."

"I'll call and file a missing person report right away when we get off the phone," said James. "When and where did you last see her?"

"I saw her in Redmond at the Starbucks a week ago but I got the phone message from her this afternoon. My guess is they're headed for somewhere up in the northeastern corner of the state. Oh, and don't forget about the earring I found at the cabin."

"About that – do you think she might have lost it when we were all at the cabin at Thanksgiving?" asked James.

"Not unless she's got more than one pair. She was wearing those earrings when I met her at Starbucks."

"Right, okay. Oh, and do you happen to remember Finn's license plate number?" asked James.

"No, sorry. Oh, wait a sec. I've got a picture of him in my wallet standing next to his jeep. Hold on, let me see if I can make out the license number."

Luke pulled out the picture and squinted at it in the semi-darkness of the parking lot.

"Damn! He's standing in front of the last three numbers. Wait, let me at least give you the first part I can see. Hold on."

Luke went back to the truck, examined the photo in the light of the cab and returned to the phone.

"Okay, here it is." He gave James the partial plate information. "Also, the Jeep's a 1980 CJ-7, dark green with a tan hard-top. It has a winch on the front. Oh, and sometimes Finn tows an open trailer when he's moving stuff."

"Okay, that's good info," said James. "I'll call it in now and ring you right back. What's the number of the phone there?"

Luke provided the information, hung up, and paced back and forth across the empty parking lot. In a few minutes, the phone rang and he ran back to pick it up.

"James?"

"Yes, it's me. Okay, the report's in but they weren't very encouraging about doing anything about it tonight since she's only been gone for less than a day. They seemed to think that her phone message marked her last-seen time. I argued with the guy but he wasn't budging. Anyway, it's probably better than nothing right now."

"Okay, thanks. How's Maggie doing?"

"Not well, she's really upset. Honestly, I am too, but I'm trying to hold it together for now."

"Yeah, me too."

"Look, Luke, if I were you, I wouldn't make the long drive home tonight. There's nothing more you can do right now. Just get some rest and we'll re-group in the morning, alright? Everything'll be okay."

"Alright; thanks, James."

Luke hung up, called Amy, gave her a quick summary of the situation, then drove back up the mountain.

This time he drove all the way up to the cabin and parked alongside it. But as he was pulling in, something didn't look right. It didn't feel right, either. Luke left the headlights on, got out and had a look around. There in the brightly lit gravel was the long mark of something being dragged from under the crawl space out onto the parking area. He peered under the house. Finn's kayak was missing.

Point of View

"I think he's gone," Luke said to Amy when she got home from work Monday night. Luke had arrived a few hours earlier and had dinner ready. They sat down to eat.

"I think Finn's decided to move somewhere," Luke clarified. "He's never taken that kayak off the property before. Not once. He'd only do that if he wasn't planning on coming back. He built that boat and it's his prized possession."

"And Jennifer's with him," Amy added. "Another prized possession."

"Yes, probably."

"You don't think they just took the kayak out to the island, do you?" Amy asked.

"No, remember, the Jeep's not there. And besides, it's winter and the lake's mostly frozen."

"Oh, right, of course. So what should we do now?"

"Well, at least we've got the police report in," Luke said. "Other than that, I know one thing I want to do. Tomorrow when I'm back at the U, I'll use the library there to dig into this whole white nationalism thing. I want to find out more about these groups – where they are and what they're up to. It seems pretty clear that Finn's gotten himself mixed up with them, at least to some degree."

"I'm worried that they don't think in degrees," said Amy.

"That's probably right, and that's one of the scariest things. You're probably either for or against, in or out, right or wrong and, literally, black or white. Not much gray in between, if any, I'm guessing. Finn was starting to sound that way, too."

~

The next morning, the subject for Luke's Creative Writing 101 lecture was to be the all-important topic of Point of View. He walked into class only marginally prepared and seriously distracted. In the middle of his discussion about the common Third Person Limited mode of writing, he saw a hand fly up in the front row.

"Yes, Ms., uh, Carter?"

"So are you saying that the narrator can only, like, be in the head of one character for the whole story?" Luke's student asked. He loved it whenever he found some evidence, however slim, that his students were actually listening.

"Almost," Luke replied. "The key is that the narrator can only 'be in the head of' – as you say – one character *at a time*. And what I mean by 'at a time' can vary a little, but a good rule of thumb for long-form fiction is that the time period should be no shorter than one chapter and often longer, sometimes the entire book. For a short story, the viewpoint character should never change – again, a common rule of thumb, sometimes ignored. And, once we've established that viewpoint character, our narrator can only describe what can be seen, felt, heard, or in any way experienced by that one character. If we allow our narrator to somehow see through more than one pair of eyes at a time, we're writing in a mode that's aptly called Omniscient. That can and has been done well, but it forces the reader to deal with a god-like narrator hovering over the whole landscape and this can easily lead to confusion."

"This all sounds really restrictive. What happened to creativity?" asked another student in the back of the room.

"Well, it is restrictive, yes, but I'd argue that it's a restriction in the service of realism. As writers, we want our audience to become caught up in our stories. We want them to feel that the world we're offering them is real. So, we try to reveal that world in a way that matches the human experience. Each of us perceives the world only through our own eyes; we don't look down on a room full of people at a party and magically know what everyone is thinking or feeling. We infer those things based on what we alone perceive – by participating in conversations, observing body language and making guesses about others' states of mind. We are always the *only* viewpoint character in our lives. So, to keep things real for our readers, we usually try to mimic that experience. We either try to establish and maintain a single primary viewpoint character, or, if we feel we must describe a major piece of the action from another character's point of view, we do that very intentionally, very clearly. Our readers can shift with us into another viewpoint if that shift is done skillfully, but he or she won't stay with us if we do that clumsily or too frequently."

The rest of the class went better than Luke had expected, given his preoccupation with current events, and he left the lecture hall pleased but wondering why. On his way over to the main library, he stumbled onto the answer: he had actually been interested in his topic, and not only from an academic perspective. He'd been interested because he'd been struggling with the frustration of not knowing what was really in the head of his brother, especially now that he couldn't just sit down and talk with him. Luke longed to be an omniscient narrator in his own story.

But, of course, the best he could do was to learn everything he could about what he imagined to be Finn's situation and then make some relatively intelligent guesses about what Finn might do, where he might go, and how he might treat Jennifer. Luke could, in effect, create a story which he hoped would be as close to reality as possible – something he could then act on. But at the same time, he had to understand that it was just his story and would necessarily be incomplete and probably even wrong.

Luke spent the rest of the day in the library, knowing that would mean a few hours spent at home that night catching up on his real job. He chewed through newspaper articles related to white supremacism, and academic papers on topics of nationalism, racism, misogynism, confirmation bias, and similar subjects. Finally, he checked out several books on the history of slavery in the U.S., the Post Civil War era, the Civil Rights movement, and cult psychology.

All this made for a very long day and Luke left campus at around seven o'clock. When he arrived home, he found a message on the answering machine from Amy. She was working late and would get something to eat at her desk. Luke felt himself relax as he headed for the refrigerator. The evening would be easier now – quieter, and without conversation that might lead to another fight. Luke had noticed this feeling of relief several times before when alone in the house but hadn't allowed himself to think much about the implications. Even now, he pushed the thought aside.

A Few Days Earlier

"I thought we were staying at the cabin," said Jennifer.

"Change of plans," replied Finn. "We're headed over to Colville, to that place I told you about."

"And does my opinion about this matter to you? At all?"

"This is what's called an executive decision."

"Oh, and you're the executive? This is not going to work, Finn."

"This is how it's supposed to be – the way it works." Finn was maneuvering the Jeep and its cargo down the rutted trail from the cabin and was glancing over at Jennifer as he spoke. She was staring straight ahead, neither smiling nor frowning. Her mouth was set in a frozen line and her eyes were squinted as if she were peering into darkness. She said nothing more.

"Hey, talk to me. Come on! What're you thinking?" Finn reached out to touch the side of her face.

Jennifer batted Finn's hand away. "What am I thinking? You can't be serious. What would you be thinking if you were being abducted?" she spoke through clenched teeth, her gaze still locked on the trail ahead.

"Jennifer, no. That's not what this is. This is the best way for us, for you. You'll see. I need a woman and you need to finally *be* one – for me, for our future children. It's the natural order of things. It's right."

"Stop the Jeep," Jennifer groaned, rolling down her window.

"No."

"I'm going to be sick."

"Yeah, right, you never get carsick. Just deal with it. We'll be down the mountain in ten minutes."

"No, I'm really gonna be sick, you asshole."

Finn felt a sudden hot surge of anger and raised his hand to strike. But before he could follow through, Jennifer vomited explosively onto the center console and the floor in front of her. She hung her head out the window to spit out the rest.

"Oh, nice, really nice!" said Finn, coming to a stop. "What the hell is wrong with you?!"

"You are. I'm getting out now." Jennifer opened the car door.

"You're damn right about that. Get a rag out of the trailer and clean up this mess. I can't believe you did that!"

Jennifer sank to her knees in the dirt and threw up again.

Finn got out of the Jeep and came around to Jennifer's side. He looked down at her, hunched over in the rocky dirt trail, defeated, defenseless, shivering from the cold. Her dark hair hung down in strands along the sides of her face. Not a pretty sight, disgusting actually. But also his responsibility. She would be beautiful again and he would want her again. She would learn from this.

"Okay, okay," said Finn. "I'll take care of it. Just rest for a minute and you'll be fine. Here's some water."

Finn held out a bottle and Jennifer took it without looking up.

When Jennifer finished with the water, Finn took it back and cleaned up the inside of the Jeep as much as he could. *I'll never get rid of the smell,* he thought. He made several passes with three separate rags, then tossed them into the woods. He opened the windows and turned the fan up all the way.

"Here," said Finn, offering Jennifer his hand. "Let's get going."

Ignoring the hand, Jennifer stood up unsteadily and spit in the dirt. "I'm not going anywhere with you."

"Yes, you are. It's your duty and you're my responsibility now. You'll look back on this and thank me someday. Just get in the Jeep."

Finn saw his captive turn to look into the forest and thought he'd have to chase her down. There'd be no contest in her weakened state, though. In fact, it would feel good to quickly dominate her, tie her hands and bring her back. Finn grabbed a rope from the trailer. *Just try it, girl. Go ahead.*

But she didn't. Finn saw her shoulders drop and knew her will was depleted. She climbed back into the Jeep and stared silently ahead.

Finn used the rope to tie Jennifer tightly below the waist, knotted behind the seat, out of reach. She offered no resistance.

"It's for your own safety. I don't want you trying to get out while we're moving. Don't worry – I'll take good care of you."

Silence.

Finn drove down the mountain and paused at the main road in Rockport. He knew that the North Cascades Highway was closed for the season but there hadn't been any new snow since the closure. The Jeep would probably make it through. Probably. Who knew what the conditions would be like ten miles east, but the other route, down south and then back east on Highway 2 over Steven's Pass? That was a hell of lot longer and would expose them if anyone was searching for Jennifer. *I'll have to risk getting stuck.* Finn turned left and headed east on the highway he knew would be closed only a few miles ahead. He thought about stopping to top up the gas tank but rejected the idea as too risky. He had four five-gallon reserve tanks in the trailer. Those should be enough.

When he got to the road closure, Finn was relieved to find no one around. No State Patrol, no other vehicles. It didn't look too bad, and with just a little shoveling, he was able to get around the barrier. On the other side, he stopped on the packed snow and put chains on all four tires. He pressed on, feeling more confident.

Into the Night

J ennifer awoke to a sudden jolt and looked out the Jeep's side window. It was alarmingly tilted downward. Snow reached up and over the first third of the glass. She looked the other way toward Finn as she heard him curse.

"Where are we?" she asked, feeling as if she had awakened into a bad dream instead of from one.

"Near Ross Lake. Came around a tight turn and slid into the ditch."

"Great. What now?"

"I'll take care of it. Just stay where you are."

"Like I have a choice?"

Finn mumbled something and struggled up and out of the Jeep. Jennifer watched as he made his way around the front of the vehicle and seemed to be taking stock of their situation. Then he bent down and disappeared for a few moments. Jennifer heard the sound of something metallic and saw Finn reappear with a heavy metal hook in one hand attached to a steel cable. He was pulling it out and away from the Jeep. He slogged through the snow ahead and over to the other side of the road where he wrapped the cable around a large tree, securing it with the hook. He walked back to the Jeep, started it, then stepped out again and moved to the left front side of the vehicle. He had something in his hand with buttons and a long black wire.

Jennifer felt another jolt and heard a whining electrical noise as Finn pressed one of the buttons and the Jeep began slowly rising up and out of the ditch. Up on the snow-covered road again, it lurched back into a fully upright position and tracked toward the tree on the opposite side of the road. Finn pressed another button on the device in his hand and the Jeep stopped. He detached the steel cable from the tree, retracted it, and got back into the driver's seat.

"Nothing like a good winch when you need it," said Finn.

Jennifer fought back the urge to feel rescued. But Finn had only fixed a problem of his own making and nothing had changed about their relationship or the stark reality of her captivity.

"Yes," she said. "Nothing like it."

"What? You're not even going to thank me for getting us out of that mess?"

"*Your* mess. No. And, by the way, I've got to go to the bathroom."

Finn grumbled but got back out of the Jeep and opened the door behind the passenger seat to untie Jennifer's rope.

"There. Go ahead."

"You're just gonna let me out?"

"Look around, Jennifer. There's no one for miles, it's well below freezing and getting on toward sunset. You wouldn't survive thirty minutes out there."

"I'm touched by your compassion."

Jennifer got out and shuffled across the icy road toward a thick grove of cedar trees with low-hanging branches on the opposite side. When she came back, she found Finn studying a map.

"So," he said, "there's not much point in going any farther tonight. Too risky in the dark. We'll camp here for the night. I'll pitch a tent for us over there in the clearing." He nodded down the road to the left.

"For you, maybe," said Jennifer. "I'm not sleeping anywhere near you. I'll stay right here in the Jeep."

"Suit yourself, but that attitude's gotta change."

"Really? Or what?"

Finn just shook his head and took the keys out of the Jeep's ignition switch, then walked around to the trailer to dig out the tent. He tossed two blankets at Jennifer and headed down the road toward the clearing.

"You're not even gonna let me run the heater for a while?" asked Jennifer, staring at the keys in Finn's hand.

"Your choice, girl. You wanna warm up? Come see me in the tent."

Jennifer rolled up her window and glared at the retreating back of the man she once called her boyfriend. A boy, yes. A friend or lover? Never a more disgusting thought. Jennifer took a drink from her water bottle, put on a hooded down jacket from her bag, and wrapped herself in two layers of blankets to face the night ahead. She let her anger carry her through these steps, and frustration at her helplessness refueled the anger.

Then, as darkness crept into the forest and the last glow of sunlight faded from the horizon, Jennifer tried to use the energy of her anger to make plans, to think rationally about her situation, like she did at work when the challenges seemed overwhelming.

Escape was not an option at this point. For now, the goal had to be simple survival. She thought about the moment earlier in the day when Finn had raised his hand to hit her; she was convinced he would have followed through if she hadn't gotten sick right then. She was strong but knew she had no hope of winning a physical fight against him. This argued for appeasement, the thought of which almost turned Jennifer's stomach again. But it would have to be. She would need to hold her own against Finn psychologically – never let him see weakness – but at the same time avoid pushing him to the point of violence. Just get through the next couple of days unharmed, then do anything necessary to escape once they reached civilization again. And do this before reaching the compound Finn kept talking about. That, Jennifer felt, was essential. Who knew what would happen if she found herself in that environment? One guy, this guy in particular, she could handle. But a group of them? No.

Jennifer pulled the blankets more closely around her and adjusted the seat as far back as it would go. She pulled the jacket's hood over her head, leaned back and stared out at the darkening sky. How had she allowed herself to get to this point? It was stupid to agree to go to the cabin with Finn in the first place. But that was all in the past; this was now. What could she do in the next couple of days to get away? Maybe she could even think of something to make Finn want to leave *her*, to push her away. What could she do or say that would make her so repulsive that he might do that? She would give the idea more thought. But if she found such a thing, she would have to use it when they were out of the wilderness – not here where survival on her own was nearly impossible.

On my own, she thought. *On my own.* She glanced over her shoulder toward the back seat and thought about Luke and their first real conversation in this same vehicle. She had felt a connection then, and again more recently at the coffee shop. He was so different from his brother. So very different.

But these thoughts only brought Jennifer back around to her original non-productive question: *how did I get to this crazy place in my life? This isn't like me at all. I usually make good decisions, don't I? What's going to happen to me now?*

The sky was now completely dark, and Jennifer's eye caught the ephemeral line of a meteor as it slashed the blackness through a blur of tears. She had never felt so alone.

History

Luke spent the next couple of days without any word from Jennifer or Finn, and frequent calls to the police yielded nothing new either. To deal with his increasing anxiety and sense of dread, he used virtually all his spare time for more research. He wanted to feel, whether justified or not, that he was doing something.

He began to see how the blatant racism expressed by the modern-day white supremacy movement was largely a continuation of the corrosive attitudes which had been in play since the beginnings of slavery in the U.S., and even long before that. Luke was shocked to learn that President Lincoln, as effective as he had been in preserving the union, did not do nearly enough to begin the process of integrating freed slaves into society after the war. "I am not," Lincoln had said, "nor ever have been, in favor of bringing about in any way the social and political equality of the white and black races." And President Andrew Johnson, who followed Lincoln after the assassination, was actually destructive, commanding the army to throw tens of thousands of freed black people off their newly-leased land and actively promoting his previously championed Homestead Act providing free 160-acre parcels to poor citizens, which would exclude black people because they were not granted citizenship. Much to the satisfaction of many southern states, Johnson declared, "This is... a country for white men, and by God, as long as I'm President, it shall be a government for white men." The state of Mississippi undoubtedly felt a certain permission granted by the President and immediately passed a series of laws applicable only to African American people which undercut any chance or hope for civil rights, economic independence, or even the reestablishment of families ripped apart by slavery. These laws were called the Black Codes and were quickly adopted by other southern states. All of this sparked the advent of white supremacist groups which began to spread across the south, culminating in the most visible and enduring of all: the Ku Klux Klan.

As Luke continued to look at history, including the Jim Crow laws in effect until 1965, the Separate But Equal justification for discrimination, the horrific lynchings, the halting progress of the Civil Rights Movement, and the assassination of Martin Luther King, Jr., the burning hate at the center of it all was obvious, but the reasons behind that hate seemed more obscure. Luke was sure there were multiple contributing factors, but the one that stood out above all others was fear – fear of displacement, fear of "the other," fear of the unknown.

Luke had never thought of Finn as a particularly fearful person, and yet he felt that Finn's extreme reaction to being displaced at work must have been primed by something. Surely it couldn't have sprung out of nowhere. People got fired all the time and rarely did they act like this. Would Finn have reacted similarly if his displacer had been white? Sadly, Luke doubted it. How would he, himself, have reacted if he'd been the one who'd lost his job? Very differently, he hoped, but he also knew that this hope was grounded in something untested in himself.

And what about the other disturbing element of Finn's world view? What about his apparently new attitude toward women? It was just flat-out misogynism; Luke couldn't interpret it any other way. And was this truly new for Finn or had he successfully hidden it before? But most importantly, what did this mean for Jennifer? Questions far outnumbered answers, and Luke's bewilderment, his dread, and his feelings of helplessness seemed to increase by the hour. He reached up to feel his slowly-healing cut. The pain was receding but a spot at the right corner of his mouth was numb.

Meanwhile, Amy continued to spend a lot more time at work and mostly left Luke to his educational but otherwise fruitless investigation. He knew she was heavily involved in planning the big move to the new Redmond campus, but wondered if she was also avoiding him. He supposed that if he'd been in her shoes, he too would want to take a break from the obsessed boyfriend papering the walls of the spare bedroom with articles, maps and notes. He couldn't really blame her, and in moments of more honest introspection, he realized that her absence didn't really bother him anyway.

So, life limped along. Until the third day, and on that day everything changed.

Luke was in his office at the university, half-heartedly putting together a plan for his next lecture, when the phone rang. An operator came on the line and asked if he would accept a collect call from Jennifer Lassiter. He said 'yes' immediately.

"Luke?" he heard her say.

He fought back tears and this took him completely by surprise.

"Luke, are you there?"

"Yes, yes, I'm here Jenny! I'm sorry, I just couldn't believe it was you. Are you okay? Where are you?"

Luke had never called her 'Jenny' before, and this also took him by surprise.

"Oh, Luke, I'm so glad you were in the office when I called! I'm okay now. I'm in the little town of Quincy, just off I-90 a few miles from the river."

"Okay, I know roughly where that is. Is Finn with you?"

"No, thank God. I'm so sorry to ask, but can you come and get me? I thought of calling James and Maggie first because they're closer but then I realized that I'd be putting them in danger because, you know…"

"Yeah, I think I do. And, yes, of course, I'll leave right away. Where in Quincy will you be?"

"There's an old motel right around Fourth and F streets. It's the only one nearby. I'll tell you everything when you get here.

And Luke? Don't tell anyone else where I am, okay? I just can't take the chance that Finn will find out."

"I hope he's not anywhere nearby. He's not, is he?"

"No, I got away from him about a hundred and fifty miles northeast of here last night. I'll tell you everything later. Oh, I'm checked in here under another name but you can find me in Room 3. Thank you so much, Luke, thank you!"

"Of course! I can't tell you how glad I am to hear your voice. I'm on my way – should be at your door in about three or four hours. Be safe."

Luke hung up, grabbed his keys and ran out the door.

~

It wasn't until he started to get into mountainous terrain, climbing into the Cascades on I-90, that Luke thought to call Amy to tell her he wouldn't be home for dinner, or maybe not at all that night. He pulled off at the next rest stop and pumped coins into a phone there. It was about three in the afternoon and he hoped Amy was in a meeting so he could just leave a message. But that wasn't to be.

"Microsoft, this is Amy Carpenter."

"Amy, it's Luke, hi."

"Hi, what's up? I'm just about to leave for a meeting."

"Listen, I'm probably not going to be home tonight. But the good news is that Jennifer called and I'm on my way to pick her up."

"Of course you are."

"Amy, hey what's wrong with you? Aren't you glad she's okay?!"

"Yes, I'm glad, Luke. But I'm sorry – why exactly can't she get home on her own?"

"You don't sound glad."

"Well I am. Where is she?"

"I can't tell you. It puts her at too much risk."

"Right, well, I'm at risk of being late for my meeting. Goodbye."

Luke stood listening to the dial tone for several seconds before replacing the handset and walking back to the truck. He sat behind the wheel feeling numb. He wanted to feel either more than that or less than that, but numb was where he had landed, and he eventually accepted the emotional purgatory. He started up the truck and continued east.

The beauty of the dense evergreen forest on both sides of the highway helped divert him, and the winding trip down the other side of the Cascades focused his attention. At about four o'clock, the sun dipped below the distant mountains behind him as Luke crossed over the Columbia River and headed northeast toward his goal.

He took the state route off I-90 a short distance into the town of Quincy, a small community amid the massive agricultural expanse which defined most of Eastern Washington. The landscape had changed dramatically from the lush evergreen forests of Western Washington to the beautiful, rolling plains of the east. Silos, tractors, irrigation systems, and seemingly endless vistas were the hallmarks of this area.

As he turned into the parking lot of the aging motel, Luke noticed a dried-up, seemingly long-abandoned swimming pool, a "Free Color TV" sign in multiple faded colors, three cars and little else. He hid the truck behind the building and walked around to the door marked 3. He knocked.

It took a few seconds but then he heard Jennifer's poorly disguised voice say, "Who is it?"

"Nice try. It's me, Luke."

She opened the door, a crack at first, then all the way. Luke stepped in, Jennifer locked the door behind them and turned to face him. Her long dark hair was down and she wore jeans with a loose long-sleeved T-shirt. Her eyes were wide and wet. Luke took her in his arms and held her gently.

"Jenny," he said, and all other words failed.

Quincy

L uke and Jennifer held each other as if separating would be unthinkable, slowly rocking side to side. But when they did eventually let go, Luke felt the connection remain. And, for him at least, that connection wasn't new. He felt it the moment Jennifer turned around to speak with him in the Jeep on that first trip to the cabin over a year before.

Their smiles were soft and unabashedly tearful as the two of them sat down facing each other on the carpet at the foot of the bed. Luke held both of Jennifer's hands in his and, after a time, words returned.

"I love that you called me Jenny," she said. "Would you keep doing that?"

"Always," said Luke.

He pulled her close and they embraced again. Luke looked deeply into Jennifer's soft brown eyes, then, seeing clearly that the connection was shared, he kissed her long and soft, their lips meeting again and again as if to make up for a lost year.

But, against all instinct and building desire, Luke forced himself to stop.

"Jenny," he said. "Let's get you out of this place. We need to get you home and safe."

"But I feel safe, right here with you... Oh, it's because of Amy, of course. I'm sorry. I'm a terrible person. I don't want to..."

"No, no, stop. It's definitely not because of Amy. It's because of us. I don't want our first time to be spent in a rat-hole like this. I'll tell you my story on the drive home if you'll tell me yours."

Jennifer packed up the few things she had taken with her, they left the key at the front desk and set off into the night together. Luke's old truck had a single long bench seat, and Jennifer snuggled up close to him, creating a scene reminiscent of the nineteen fifties. Her warmth seemed to make the cold world outside irrelevant.

As Luke merged onto I-90, heading for the Columbia River, he turned to Jennifer and said, "Are you ready to tell me what happened? I can wait if you're not."

"Could you start, Luke? Tell me what's going on with you?"

"Yes, definitely. Well, the main thing is that Amy and I haven't been close for quite a while. Honestly, at least from my perspective, we never really were. Maybe from hers we were, I'm not sure. I guess I always felt a sort of sad sense of obligation; I can't think of a better word for it, and that's no basis for a relationship. I just couldn't admit it to myself for the longest time. I think it started during our blind date at the very beginning. And then, the whole lightning thing seemed to carry it forward on automatic."

"You saved her life. That's a wonderful and powerful thing."

"Of course I'm glad it turned out that way. But, again, if that's the heart of it all, it's just not enough."

"Yes, I get it. It wasn't the same thing with Finn and me. It was worse, I think, in many ways. I'm so disappointed in myself for not seeing things clearly. I think I really cared for him until I began to see who he really was. I don't think even he knew who he was, or that he knows even now. I can't imagine us together now."

"Don't kick yourself. He's my brother and even I didn't see this coming. Looking back, the signs were there, but I obviously didn't interpret them well, or at all. I think our minds sometimes hide things from us that we don't want to see, if that makes any sense."

"Of course it does. It probably happens more than we'll ever know. You don't think it's happening to us right now, do you Luke? That we're just drawn together in the moment for the wrong reasons?"

"No. This has roots that, at least for me, go back way before any of this chaos began."

"Me too." Jennifer snuggled in even closer. "As much as I wanted it, I just didn't see a path for us back then."

They drove on in easy silence for a while before Jennifer spoke again.

"So, how is Amy now?"

"She's okay. Really busy at work. Pissed as hell at me."

"Really? Why?"

"She knew, even before I would admit it to myself, that I was thinking way more about you than her. She knew things weren't working."

"And now?"

"I think she broke up with me this afternoon."

"You think? What do you mean?" Luke had seen Jennifer pushing people to get to the point of things before, and knew she was good at it.

"She said 'goodbye' and hung up in the middle of a very tense call when I told her I was going to pick you up and wouldn't tell her where. She never uses that word, 'goodbye.'"

"Sounds to me like you need to finish that conversation. I mean, if that's what you want."

"That is without question what I want."

Luke drove on across the river, past the desolate Ginkgo Petrified forest, and on up the road to Ellensburg.

"Are you ready to talk to me about your ordeal?" he asked.

"I'll try."

"Only if you're ready."

"I'm ready. It's just hard."

Luke took one hand off the wheel to hold Jennifer's.

"It started at my apartment last weekend when Finn came by unannounced. He told me he wanted to take me to the cabin to get away for the weekend and talk things over. I wasn't at all sure I wanted to go and suggested we just talk there, in the apartment. He wasn't into that idea and made it clear very forcefully at first, then emotionally. It was a weird sort of a switch and it put me even more on alert. But, in the end, against my better judgement, I agreed. I packed a few things and left with him. He had a lot of bags crammed in the back of the Jeep and he was hauling the trailer."

"Damn," was all Luke could manage.

Jennifer nodded. "So when we got to Rockport, he told me we were only going to the cabin to pick up his kayak and that we'd go from there on over to Colville where he wanted me to meet some friends. When I asked him why, about both the kayak and the meeting, he said he was moving to a place near Colville and the kayak and I were the only things he had left. At that point, I panicked."

"Yes, of course."

"That's when he forced me to call and leave that message for you. I can't even talk about how he did that. It's too demeaning."

Luke nodded and decided not to pry further. "And you put us on alert with the wrong name for your admin. I've got to give Amy credit for noticing that. I immediately drove up to the cabin and found your earring on the hearth. I'm so glad you left that. You did leave it on purpose, right?"

"Yes. I put it there while Finn was loading the kayak into the trailer. I didn't have time to write a note and figured he'd find it anyway. I thought about running but knew I'd never make it through the woods with all the dense growth. And if I kept to the road, he'd find me easily. So I played along for a while longer. What did you do when you found the earring?"

"I recognized it from our time at Starbucks and then I knew you'd been there and something was wrong. That's when I drove back down the mountain. I called your sister and James from the diner in Rockport and we decided to file a report with the police right away, not that it did any good. Oh, I've got to remember to cancel that tonight! So what happened next with you?"

"That's when the worst part began, Luke. It was horrible."

"You don't have to tell me."

"No, I want to tell you at some point, and it might as well be now. I think it might be best for me to get it all out."

"Okay." he squeezed her hand.

"The highway over to Winthrop was already closed for the winter but Finn insisted that we go for it anyway. We went around barriers, got stuck several times, and had to camp alongside the road two different nights. Finn had a tent in the trailer but I insisted on staying in the Jeep. I really wasn't sure we'd ever make it all the way over to the Methow Valley, but we eventually did. I guess the winter's been unusually mild and the snowpack is much lower than normal. Still, it was an incredibly stupid thing to do.

At the end of our long slog, Finn wanted to stay the night in Twisp so that's what we did. By that time, it was clear I had no say in the matter. He found little rental cabins along the river and got us moved in for the night. I insisted on one with two beds and wouldn't let him come near me. This enraged him and, at one point, I even thought he'd try to rape me. But then he got all quiet again and started talking about the urgent need to preserve the pure white race, trying to convince me that I had a duty to help him with that. Everything about that disgusted me and I told him so.

Then the rage started again and I was more frightened than I think I've ever been of anything or anyone. But his lecture about the preservation of the race gave me an idea. I knew it was risky but at that point everything felt that way. I hoped telling him the truth might save me."

"The truth about what?" Luke asked.

"My heritage. You probably don't know this either, but I'm a quarter Native American. My maternal grandmother was pureblood Cherokee."

"That's beautiful. How did he react?"

"He went completely silent, and that scared me more than his tirades. He just looked down at his hands and shook his head slowly back and forth. I thought I'd made a huge miscalculation and that, at any moment, he'd boil over and attack me. But he didn't. He just slowly walked across the room, picked up my bag, took it over to the door, dropped it there and said, 'Get out. I never want to see your face again.' I was stunned and said something stupid like, 'Where?' I think he replied that he didn't give a shit and opened the door. I walked out."

"That bastard, my own damn brother."

"You know, his were the most hurtful words anyone has ever spoken to me, but they were also the most liberating. I was free."

"So, how did you end up way down in Quincy?"

"Well, I walked out of the cabin and then ran all the way to the main road before I even dared to stop and put on the winter coat from my bag. I headed south, hoping to find a way to put as many miles between me and Finn as I could, worrying that he might change his mind and come after me. I found a gas station not much farther down the road and a big semi was there filling up. The door to the cab was open and, as I walked by, I could see a photo taped to the dashboard – a picture that looked like it was probably of the driver's wife and kids. I decided this was as good an indicator as any, so I waited there by the truck until the driver came out of the convenience store.

It turned out he was heading down to Yakima that night and I don't know if he saw the desperation in my eyes or heard it in my voice, but he offered to take me wherever I wanted to go along the way. He was a kind man and didn't talk much, which was just fine with me. I decided to get out in Quincy because I liked the idea of being in an obscure place off the main highway and far away from Finn. I walked down the street to the nearest motel, got a room, locked the door, called you, and went to sleep."

"Jenny, you've been through hell."

"But now I'm out."

"Yes."

"And I'm with you."

"Yes."

"And I don't want to go home tonight. Do you know anywhere along the way we can stay?"

"Yes, I know just the place."

The Lodge

B y the time Luke and Jennifer left the freeway near
North Bend, it was well after eight and a cold snow was
beginning to fall, but ten minutes later they found
themselves surrounded by the warmth of the Salish Lodge,
perched high on a rock ledge overlooking Snoqualmie Falls.
Luke called James from the lobby while Jennifer finished
checking in.

"James, it's Luke. I've got good news."

Luke gave him a quick summary and asked if he would call
and cancel the police report since he was the registered contact.
Luke could hear him excitedly giving Maggie the news as she
apparently ran into the room. He put her on the line and Luke
handed the phone to her sister. Smiling, he walked across the
lobby and overheard Jennifer's end of the call.

"Yes, yes, I'm fine.... No, he didn't... No... I have no idea
and don't really want to know... What?... Yes, I'm sure he will...
No, I've got Grandma to thank for that... Uh huh... Yeah, no
doubt... No, not the kind of adventure I ever want to repeat...
I know, they're so different – he's the best..."

The conversation went on for several minutes before Luke
heard it finish.

"Okay... Yes, definitely. When I get back I'll call you and
we can talk more privately, okay?... Tomorrow, yes... Thank
you, Sis... Yes, I promise... I love you too. Bye."

The pair made their way up to the room and found it to be
a welcome contrast to the old motel in Quincy. It had a large
soaking tub, a king-sized bed, a window overlooking the river
just above the falls, and a fireplace. Luke started the fire while

Jennifer took a hot bath and changed into clean clothes. Even with the window closed, they could hear the muffled sound of the falls outside, pouring masses of water into a rock pool more than two hundred fifty feet below.

They sat together in front of the fire and mulled over the events of the day and the uncertainties that lay ahead. At first, the conversation centered around the two people most obviously missing from their imagined future. Luke could tell that Jennifer was uncomfortable with the way he and Amy had left things. Jennifer talked about her friendship with Amy and the sad likelihood of its demise, and Luke opened up about his hope of somehow helping Finn leave the horrific path he was on, as thin as that hope was. Luke despised Finn's recent words and deeds, and tried to make that clear to Jennifer, but at the same time, Finn was still his brother. He didn't want to give up on him but had no idea how to live with that. The only thing Luke knew for sure was that he would never let his brother hurt Jennifer again.

Then they turned to their own future together and Luke got his first real taste of Jennifer's pragmatic nature. While she went on about the uncertainties of relationships and the need to build a strong base of understanding and trust, Luke was ready to marry her on the spot. It wasn't that she didn't want to move forward – she also made that clear – but Jennifer was very much the designer-of-software to Luke's writer-of-fiction.

Inside, Luke smiled wistfully, rationalizing his more romantic tendencies by reminding himself that he had been thinking of her in this way for well over a year. *So this isn't really so spur-of-the-moment now, is it? No, of course not. I'm being completely rational...*

Right, sure. Luke had to smile again, this time outwardly.

Jennifer must have noticed because she asked what he was thinking.

"Oh, I was just thinking about how much sense you're making and how beautiful you look in the firelight."

Jennifer laughed and moved closer. Luke was sitting with his back against the hearth and she snuggled into position in front of him, taking his arms and hugging them across her chest. Luke kissed her neck and breathed in her clean, feminine scent. They sat together in anticipatory silence.

Then she turned to face Luke and took both of his hands in hers. "Luke, when we first got here tonight, I wanted to make love with you more than anything in the world. But now I realize that I'm just not ready. The last few days are weighing on me and I know I just wouldn't be all here for either of us. I'm so sorry."

Luke brushed the hair back from her forehead and took a deep breath. "No, Jenny; of course. We both have our stuff to resolve. It's going to take time to work through it all – some of it together and some alone. I want to work on us more than anything in the world. You?"

"Yes, definitely yes," she said, nodding each time.

"Oh, here, I almost forgot," Luke said, reaching into his pocket and pulling out the little silver dolphin earring. He helped Jennifer put it back on.

They held each other in front of the fire and listened to the rumble of the river meeting its destiny, stretching thin and quiet toward the edge, then suddenly losing its footing and yielding to empty air in a beautifully dangerous cascade before recreating itself as a new river far below.

Amy

The next morning, Luke dropped Jennifer at her apartment, convincing her to spend the day getting the lock changed and taking it easy instead of going back to work, then drove across Lake Washington to Seattle. When he arrived home, he expected to find either an angry note or a message on the machine. Instead, he found Amy.

She sat at one end of the couch in the living room, her eyes red, her shoulders sloped. The couch was covered with a blanket and pillow. An empty wine bottle and nearly empty glass stood together on the coffee table.

"You were with her last night, weren't you?" she said, looking up at Luke.

"I told you I was going to get her, yes," he replied, sitting down at the opposite end of the couch.

"You know what I mean. You were *with* her."

"No, Amy, I wasn't *with* her."

"Liar!"

"No, I'm not lying about that."

"Then what *are* you lying about?! You're not telling me something."

Luke couldn't answer.

"You bastard! You love her!"

"Yes."

Amy pounded the table, knocking over the wine glass, and began to cry. "You're as bad as your brother! You're both the same, you asshole!"

"Amy..." Luke reached out for her hand.

"Don't touch me! Don't ever touch me again!"

Luke pulled back and searched for any words that might help. There were none. He just let her sit there and sob. He knew he had hurt her badly and felt like a wretch for doing it, but his own tears wouldn't come. He could do nothing but wait.

And the wait seemed like hours. Finally, Amy got up without a single glance back, and walked into the bedroom. Luke stayed right where he was. Minutes later she emerged with a carry-on bag, her hair still unbrushed.

"Where are you going?" Luke asked.

"To work."

"Like that?" Luke asked, immediately regretting the implications.

"Yes, like this, you bastard."

"And then what?"

"And then I'll have someone come pick up the rest of my things."

"Amy, look, you don't have to give up the house. You can stay here. I can move out."

"Are you fucking kidding me? I'm not staying anywhere you've been even close to."

"But I can't afford the rent on my own." Again, Luke immediately regretted the impulsive transparent selfishness and stupidity of his remark. *What a complete ass I am!*

"Not my problem," said Amy, and slammed the door behind her.

After silence descended upon the room, Luke's first thought was to call Jennifer, but he rejected the idea right away. She needed time alone and he needed to get himself together. So he began, whether or not he understood or appreciated the metaphor at the time, by cleaning up the house.

He mopped up the spilled wine, tossed the empty bottle in the trash and removed the blanket and pillow from the couch. He pulled sheets off the bed and washed them, did the dishes and vacuumed the entire house. Finally, he sat down to think.

This was inevitable, Luke reflected. *Even if Jennifer hadn't been in the picture. But still, I should have acted earlier instead of letting Amy*

*think things were okay for so long. I knew they weren't. I just didn't have
the guts or the insight or the kindness — whatever it was — to sit down and
talk with her months ago. It wouldn't have hurt her so much then. Why
did I hang on like that? Maybe I liked the stability. Maybe it was the sex.
That was probably it. What an ass I am.*

Luke continued to berate himself well into the afternoon
and started drinking whiskey somewhere around four.
Fortunately, he was interrupted by a phone call from Maggie.

"Luke, hi, I just wanted to call and thank you for rescuing
my sister yesterday."

"Oh, hi Maggie. Thanks, but there was no rescuing – not on
my part anyway. I just picked her up and brought her back.
Jennifer did all the rescuing herself."

"Well, whatever, but you were there for her and we all
appreciate it so much. I know that she does. She couldn't stop
talking about you when I spoke with her earlier today."

"She's an amazing woman, Maggie, but I'm sure you've
known that for a long time."

"Yes, I certainly have. Listen, Luke, I don't mean to pry, but
Jen told me about you and Amy. I'm so sorry. Think you'll be
able to work things out?"

"Uh, no. I really don't. We split up this morning. For good."

"Oh, again, I'm so sorry."

"Well, thanks, but you don't need to be. I regret not being
honest with her a long time ago. I regret the pain I caused her
by not confronting things then. I feel terrible about all that. But
the breakup is the right thing for both of us in the long run, I'm
convinced. So there it is."

"Still, I know it's got to be difficult. Just let me know if
there's ever anything James or I can do for you, okay?"

"Okay, I will. Thank you, Maggie. I think you just did."

After saying goodbye, Luke put the cork back in the whiskey
bottle, poured a glass of water and called out for pizza.

Patriots' Pride

F inn stared at the back of the door and convinced himself that he'd done the right thing. *How could Jennifer have hidden this from me? Her skin wasn't red or brown. Sure, it wasn't pale white either, but she seemed like any other pretty, brown-eyed, dark-haired girl in her late twenties. And she was smart. Was she lying?* Finn wanted to believe that Jennifer had fabricated the story of her Native American heritage because she didn't fit with his concept of inferior races. *But, on the other hand...*

No, there is no other hand, Finn decided. *She must have lied. She was definitely a white girl, just a deceptive one. One not worth keeping. She resisted me on so many fronts and she would never submit. What a pain in the ass. She's gone now and that's for the best.*

Finn resolved to find someone more in line with his thinking, someone who wouldn't argue with him all the time. He knew there were plenty of girls like that out there, ones who wouldn't demand to be called 'women' all the time, ones who were proud of their white race, proud to be True Americans, and would feel lucky to be his. The thought brought a smile to his lips, the first in many days.

With that in mind, Finn packed up the Jeep, checked out of the room and headed northeast. His route took him up through the Okanagan Highlands, east over to Kettle Falls and finally down to Colville. It was there, in the hills northeast of Colville, that Finn's new friends had established their compound.

The rocky dirt road up to the compound was no challenge for Finn's off-road skills, but his trailer, loaded with the kayak and a few other heavy items, forced him to take it a bit slower than he might have otherwise. Brad Thoreson's directions had been good, and Finn navigated the many unmarked twists and turns easily, arriving at the gate before dark.

The metal gate was set into a crude wooden frame typical of a ranch entrance and was adorned with an American flag. A large sign, mounted high above the unlocked gate, read "Patriots' Pride." Finn swung the gate open, drove in, and closed it behind him. The road from there wound through acres of Douglas Fir, Western Hemlock and old-growth Cedar, ending in a gravel clearing.

At the far edge of the clearing stood a sprawling single-level building with a green metal roof, several windows built high on the walls, and a large sliding barn door, open. The land gently sloped up behind this building, and, set randomly among a sparse grove of fir trees in the distance, Finn saw several small cabins and other structures, all against a backdrop of higher, denser forest. The structures all had the same green roofs and were all linked by gravel trails.

A tall, fit-looking bald man of about forty with a large tattoo of a lion on his neck approached Finn's Jeep, carrying a rifle at his side. A few other men and one woman appeared to be hard at work around the main building, some doing construction, some tending the grounds. Finn parked near the armed man and got out.

"Can I help you with something?" asked the man, unsmiling.

"Finn Mason. I've been talking with someone here named Brad Thoreson?"

"That'd be me. Good to finally meet you, Finn." Brad offered his hand and Finn shook it.

"Good to meet you, too. You've got quite a place here. How much land do you guys own?"

"Right now you're standing in the middle of about two hundred acres. We like the solitude, if you know what I mean."

"Sure; I think I do."

"So, Finn, come on in. Let's talk. But first, we can't be too careful."

Brad led Finn over to the large building and patted him down.

"He's clean!" Brad shouted to a man with a dark beard standing nearby.

"You ever carry?" Brad asked.

"No, I don't even own a gun."

Brad laughed. "That'll need to change. Come on in. Have a seat. Beer?"

"Sure, thanks."

Finn glanced around the interior of the building. He was sitting at one of two long tables with chairs for twelve. In one corner and stretching along part of one side of the building, a large roughed-in kitchen dominated the scene. A few other chairs hovered around a massive brick fireplace, and a partially erased whiteboard stood on an easel near that grouping. The floor was dusty plywood. Finn found himself thinking about how he would finish the carpentry in the room if it were his.

Brad reappeared with two bottles of beer and introduced Finn to the stocky, heavily bearded man he had just seen outside.

"Finn, this is Cal Shorten. Cal's our security officer and I've asked him to sit in on our discussion. If you end up joining us here at Patriots' Pride, you and Cal will probably get to know each other pretty well."

Finn stood to shake Cal's hand, noticing the small black handgun at his side. Cal nodded without a word and everyone sat back down to talk. Finn also noticed that Cal was the only one without a beer.

"So, Finn, the way this works is you tell us about your background, why you want to be here and how you think you can contribute. Then, if Cal and I like what we hear and it all squares with what we already know about you, we'll tell you more about us. We'll all have the night to sleep on it, and then tomorrow we'll make some decisions. But that isn't the end of it. If we want you and you want us, then there's kind of a trial period, for about a month. You're not really in until that's over. Understood?"

"Understood."

"Good. Now, why don't you start by telling us more about your real estate work."

"Sure, well, as I've told you on the phone, I'm in commercial real estate, or at least I was. I've handled the purchase and sale of everything from small office buildings to shopping centers to boatyards. I've even done a couple of medium-sized manufacturing centers. I like the work. It's different from the residential side — more demanding because you're dealing with hard-nosed businessmen who know how to negotiate. But the people who run my old company are a bunch of bleeding-heart liberals. Guys like that are gonna destroy their business and this country if they have their way."

"Tell us more about that."

"You know what I'm talking about, right?"

"We want to understand your personal viewpoint," said Cal.

"Personally? Yeah, it got personal when they gave my job to that black guy and offered me a really shitty position. I told them to fuck off and left. I lost one deal and that's how they treated me. One deal!"

"What if the guy who took your job had been white? Would you still be pissed?"

"Sure. Maybe not as much. But I didn't deserve that treatment no matter what."

"You know, I get what you're saying, but we're looking for someone who's got some real fire in his belly about what the blacks and Jews are getting away with in this country."

"I've got that. You just haven't seen it yet. And about the Mexicans and Indians, too. This used to be a white country run by white men. Now all that's in danger and nobody seems to care. We need to fucking take it back," said Finn, after taking another pull on his beer.

Brad nodded to Cal before looking back at Finn. "That's what we're talking about, brother. That's what we're talking about."

"You got a girl back home?" Cal asked.

"No, not anymore. She pissed me off and I kicked her out."

"White girl?" asked Brad.

"Of course."

"Too bad. We could've used another girl around here."

"Sorry, I can't help you there. At least for now."

"Ever been arrested?" asked Cal.

"Nope," replied Finn, wondering if they were trying to catch him off guard by changing the subject so abruptly and often.

"Alright. Ever been fingerprinted?" Cal continued.

"Not that I remember."

"Not that you remember?"

"No, I'm sure I haven't."

"You willing to work your ass off?" asked Brad.

"That's what I've always done. Looks like you need some construction help. I've done carpentry, electrical, plumbing, you name it. My brother Luke and I built a cabin from the ground up."

"Good, that'd help, but we're more interested in your real estate skills," said Brad.

"Oh?"

"Yeah," said Cal. "So, your brother, what did you say his name is?"

"Luke."

"Right, Luke. How's he feel about what you're doing here?"

"He doesn't know I'm here. He knows how I feel about things, though."

"How does he feel?"

"He's not like me. He doesn't get it."

"Is he gonna be a problem for us?"

"No, he's a good man at heart but he's kind of a candy ass. We don't have to worry about him."

"Parents?"

"They're both dead."

"We okay for now?" Brad looked to Cal.

"Sure, but let's hold off until tomorrow on all the rest, okay?"

"Right, that makes sense. Let's you and I talk more after we find Finn here some food and a bunk for the night."

First Test

Finn finished up a simple dinner of roast chicken and salad prepared by a thin, blond young man named Steven who said he was the cook. Finn wondered about Steven because he said almost nothing else, and the few words he did offer seemed directed not so much at Finn as at some other unseen presence in the room. But Finn was hungry and the food was welcome.

After dinner, Brad reappeared and escorted Finn out to get his bags from the Jeep. Finn noticed that everything in the Jeep and the trailer had been opened and moved around but he decided not to complain to Brad, guessing that it was just a necessary part of the protocol when someone new arrived.

Finn followed Brad up the hill behind the large building and through the firs to a smaller structure which turned out to be one of three bunkhouses on the property. Inside were four beds, two uppers and two lowers, with two men in the lower ones, both propped up and reading.

"That's yours," said Brad, pointing to an empty bunk on top. "There's a latrine outside about twenty yards away. Meet me in the morning at oh seven hundred for breakfast and we'll talk some more, okay?"

"I'll be there," said Finn.

"So I'm Ted and this here's Jonathan," said one of the men after Brad left. Jonathan nodded but neither man offered a hand.

"I'm Finn. Good to meet you. How long have you guys been here?"

"About a year for me," replied Jonathan.

"Year and a half," said Ted.

"So, what's with that guy Steven?" asked Finn, trying to break the ice that seemed ten feet thick.

"You don't want to talk about him," said Ted.

"What do you mean? Why not?"

Ted looked at Jonathan and Jonathan at Ted. Finally, Ted responded. "He's kind of a retard but he can cook, a little."

"Is that the only reason he's here?" Finn persisted.

"He's Brad's adopted kid, okay? Enough said," replied Ted.

"Oh, okay. I was just wondering."

"Yeah, well, if you like the idea of staying alive and healthy, don't let Brad hear you talk about him, ever," said Ted. Jonathan just nodded.

"Okay, good tip. Thanks," said Finn. He began to wonder about the wisdom of the choices he was making but pushed the thought aside. He felt a certain pride in the fact that his professional experience seemed of value, and this overrode everything else. *I think these guys might have the right idea about America and maybe I can help them push it back on track, he thought. Maybe I can make a real difference here.*

~

Finn woke several times during the night and checked his watch each time. He didn't want to be late for his breakfast with Brad. The last time he looked, he discovered it was six-forty and crawled out of bed to a cold morning. He got dressed, paid a visit to the latrine and walked down through the woods to the big building he would soon learn was called The Capitol, where he had met with Brad and Cal the day before.

When he arrived, Finn found Steven in the kitchen mumbling something into a large cast iron skillet containing scrambled eggs. Another pan sizzled with sausage. The smell and the building itself reminded Finn of a summer camp he'd enjoyed for a few days before his father arrived unexpectedly and yanked him out as punishment for a mediocre report card which had arrived in the mail that day. He had never forgotten the shame he felt when his father yelled at him in front of his new camp friends and dragged him out of the mess hall, crying. Why couldn't he have waited until Finn got home? Finn would've preferred the usual beating. He knew he deserved some punishment, but that? His next report card had been better.

Brad walked in at precisely seven o'clock and Finn stood to greet him.

"Morning," said Finn.

"Congratulations, you passed the first test." Brad glanced at his watch and smiled.

"Thanks. Being on time is important to me."

"As it should be."

Steven brought two plates over to the table, with ample portions on each. He mumbled something Finn couldn't interpret.

"Coffee?" asked Brad.

"That'd be great. Thanks." Finn made a point of directing his answer to Steven with a smile.

Brad seemed entirely focused on his meal, so Finn decided to do the same and wait for his new boss to break the silence. When he did, it was with a subject that Finn didn't expect and was somewhat disappointed with, given the focus of the previous day's discussion.

"Finn, what do you think of this room we're in?"

"What do I think of it? Uh, well, it seems like a good all-purpose kind of space."

"But, specifically, when you really look around, what are your first impressions?"

"Okay, honestly? The structure looks sound but there's no finish work. Maybe that's not important right now but that's what stands out to me."

"Good. What would you do if you could?"

"I'd tape the drywall seams, paint the walls, trim out the windows and the fireplace, get some decent countertops for the kitchen, put some better ceiling lighting in and do something with the floor. You can't just have plywood. With enough traffic in here, you'll wear it through in no time. Besides, it looks like shit. No offense."

"No offense taken. In fact, that's the kind of thing I was hoping to hear."

"Okay…"

"Don't worry, I didn't ask you to come here because of your construction skills. That's just a bonus. I asked you to come because of your professional experience. The question about the room was really about honesty and attention to detail. And, by the way, I agree with you. But none of that is a priority right now, for two reasons. One, we don't have the cash, and two, we need to focus on strategy. I think you might be able to help with both."

"Sounds good to me."

"Okay, so let me tell you more about us. First, our name, Patriots' Pride. I think names are important. They say something about identity – who a group really is. There're three ideas I wanted to bring out in this name. Can you take a stab at what they are?"

To Finn, two ideas seemed obvious: the concept of real patriotism – loyalty to America as it was meant to be – and the notion of personal fulfillment that can come from working toward an important goal. He described these to Brad but admitted to missing out on the third idea.

"The third idea is hidden in the word 'pride' and it's every bit as important as the first two, maybe even more important because it's so fundamental. It's the idea of family. I think of us as a tightly knit family. A family group of lions is called a 'pride' and that's how I think of us," said Brad, pointing to the tattoo on his neck.

"So what makes a family a family?" he continued. "Well, there's the biological relationship, but that's not essential. Beyond that, a family has a shared value system, it has a hierarchy of control and discipline, and it replicates itself, moving its value system forward into the world. It defends itself from enemies and provides for its members. And it keeps itself pure, even to the extent of expelling members if they don't share the family values or don't pull their own weight."

"So, what are the values of *this* family?" asked Finn.

"Pretty simple, really. We believe in freedom from excessive government control. We believe in the basic value of hard work. We recognize that the Caucasian race is the clearly superior one but is currently losing control in this country. We are adamant about the traditional family. The man is the head of the household and should be firmly in control of it. We believe that Christianity is the one true religion, but we don't insist on all members outwardly practicing it. And, as a key part of that, we believe that Caucasians in Europe were God's original chosen people but were cleverly displaced by the Jews in mythology they created very early on."

"So... what do you think should happen to the other races?" asked Finn.

"Let me put it this way. We believe all other races will eventually die out on their own. We don't hurry that along unless they get in the way of our progress or try to mix with us. Personally, I'd be fine with all the blacks going back to Africa and living there in peace. Same with other races, all to their own places. We're not meant to live together. It just doesn't work. This is America and we need to get back to our white roots."

"So what's your strategy?" asked Finn.

"Let's leave that one a little vague for a while," said Brad. "For now, let's just say it's about waking up the white population of America with education and action."

"No problem. How can I help for now?"

"Here's what I'd like you to do. We need to raise some cash, not just to fund our operation here, but also to extend our reach and take some action. I think you can be the missing piece of a team to do that. You know the real estate world. Cal was an investigator for a law firm and a cop before that. There's a third guy you met last night, Jonathan. He used to run a print shop and has gotten really good with counterfeiting. In fact, we tried that whole racket for a while, but it's getting harder and harder to do without getting caught. Jonathan's skills will be useful in other ways."

"So basically, fraud," said Finn, frowning.

"Well, if you want to put that kind of government label on it, sure, I suppose so."

"But how do you square that with your value system?"

"Finn, when you live under a corrupt government, you can exploit its flaws to bring about a greater good. We might have to break a few laws in order to fight for higher, more important ones."

"You're saying the end justifies the means."

"You make that sound like a bad thing. Yes, of course it does. We've got to keep our eyes on the big picture. If some wrong-headed laws, institutions or people have to suffer in the process, then that's just part of the necessary cost. It's called leadership, Finn. Real leadership."

"Okay, so I'm still not clear on exactly what you want me to do."

"Let me lay out the opportunity for you, then you can come up with a detailed plan, okay?"

"Yeah, sure. Go ahead."

"We own a piece of commercially zoned property down in Spokane. It's about ten acres in size and, on the surface, it looks like an ideal spot for a light industrial park, a strip mall, or maybe even a hotel. I'm sure there are lots of potential uses. And it's got a nice view of the Spokane River."

"On the surface, you said?"

"Right, literally. The problem is that it's pretty much worthless because there are several large diesel fuel tanks buried there, and they've been leaking for years. It used to be a big truck stop that went bankrupt back in the early seventies, but all the old buildings have been scraped off. The damned environmental cleanup would probably cost more than ten times what the property's worth. Still, it looks great on the surface and its problems can be hidden, at least up front. So, the challenge is this: how can we make some serious money off this without actually closing a sale and exposing the property's real problems?"

"That sounds close to impossible if you ask me," said Finn.

"Just close, or actually impossible?"

"Close, very close. But let me work on it and get back to you in a day or two."

The Plan

L ater the same day, Finn sat down to think about the challenge facing him. Applying his expertise, even in this way, felt good, and it had the convenient side-effect of keeping his mind off the deeper issues involved. But at some level of consciousness, those issues threatened to surface, and Finn felt them there, begging for consideration, or at least rationalization. He successfully ignored the begging.

Thinking about the skills he could leverage in Jonathan and Cal, Finn began to put together the basics of a plan. As part of his training as a commercial real estate broker, Finn had studied various forms of criminal activity that the federal government called CREF – Commercial Real Estate Fraud – and one of the schemes sometimes used by criminals was called "Advance Fee." He began to think, with help from Jonathan and Cal, he just might be able to do something similar. He set off to search the compound for the two men.

Finn found Cal working on the roof of another bunkhouse and, after assuring him that Brad wanted them to work together, he was able to convince Cal to postpone his job and help find Jonathan. Cal knew just where to look, and they all sat down together in a small building which was to serve as the compound's future print shop. Jonathan had been working to restore an old offset printing press and some silk-screening equipment. He seemed glad for the break.

After reviewing Brad's goals, Finn outlined his own plan for the newly formed team.

"Here's the basic idea for a scheme that's been used before. A broker looks for clients who want to buy property but are having difficulty getting financing. The broker promotes himself as someone who specializes in obtaining financing from special investors who are less risk-averse than typical lenders. But because the situation requires special expertise and involves some risk, the broker must charge an up-front fee which is a reasonably large percentage of the intended loan down payment. This fee is guaranteed to be ninety percent refundable if and when the financing comes through and the client remains in compliance with all other elements of his contract. The scheme works because the broker always finds a reason for non-compliance; something in the client's background causes the fictitious lender to back out. The broker keeps the full fee.

Now, before we go any further, I need to ask you guys about this property in Spokane. How's it titled? Does the title identify Patriots' Pride or any individual here?"

Cal jumped in. "No, Brad's been real smart about this from the beginning. The property's held by a shell company somewhere in the Caribbean."

"Good," continued Finn. "Do we have any other real estate to work with?"

"No," answered Cal. "Other than this compound, that's it."

"Okay," said Finn. "So we've got to leverage the Spokane property as much as possible if we're going to get any decent cash out of it."

"What do you mean by that?" asked Jonathan.

"The key is to get multiple buyers on the hook and make sure that none of them spook the others when their deals fall through. That's where you guys come in," said Finn. "Cal, how good are you at digging up dirt on people?"

"Pretty damn good. That's a big part of what I did for the law firm. What kind of dirt?"

"Two kinds," answered Finn. "First, financial. We need to find clients who've defaulted on loans in the past or have other serious money problems that would make a lender uneasy. And second, we need those same clients to have something deeply embarrassing or seriously illegal in their backgrounds that makes them vulnerable to blackmail. We need to be able to keep them quiet after we keep their fees."

"Where do I come in?" asked Jonathan.

"We're going to need some official-looking documents. I'll create the content, but we need you to make all the paperwork look right – letterheads, logos, notary stamps, things like that. Can you do our marketing brochures, too?"

"No problem," said Jonathan.

"What about lenders? How do we get them to cooperate and keep quiet?" asked Cal.

"We don't need any actual lenders," Finn answered. "I'll act as a mortgage broker, appearing to search for financing. At the beginning of each deal, I'll be very encouraging about being able to locate the perfect lender for the client's special needs. Then, as we go along, I'll start to report one or two lenders backing out. Finally, I'll have to deliver the bad news that none of them will come through. That's when we'll use the dirt we've found, blaming one or more of the lenders for finding it. We've got to make sure that the stuff we find is powerful enough to make the client disappear and stay quiet. If just one client goes to the press or tries to sue us, we're screwed."

"Sounds pretty damn risky," said Cal. "Plus, how the hell are we going to find enough clients that are like this?"

"Sure, there's risk," said Finn. "But we do all this as a new company, an LLC, that we'll set up in Spokane. Patriots' Pride doesn't get exposed."

"What about finding all these clients, like Cal said?" asked Jonathan.

"I'll take the lead on that," said Finn. "But with a lot of help from Cal. They're out there, believe me. We've just got to find them and be really, really careful doing it. The people we're looking for will think of themselves as entrepreneurs, risk-takers, deal-makers, but they've also got to be egotistical, maybe even narcissistic, and more than a little desperate, but with enough cash for our fee. Our best targets are people who act like they're wealthy when they're actually not. They need to see our property as a way to finally fulfill their dreams or get out of a hole. Some will probably want to re-sell it fast, so we've got to price it low, but not suspiciously low. It's got to look like a genuine opportunity."

"I don't know..." began Cal.

"Come on, man, grow some balls! We can make this work," said Finn.

"Fuck you," smiled Cal.

"That's the spirit!" said Finn.

The team talked for another couple of hours, working out details and trying to poke holes in the plan. They found a few and filled them. In the end, all three men were on board.

~

The next morning, Finn met with Brad at The Capitol to discuss the plan. Brad listened as Finn outlined the idea on the whiteboard, then listed the steps necessary to get started. Brad nodded several times during the presentation and was smiling by the end.

"Good job, Finn. I like it. I just have a few questions."

"Shoot."

"First, I think we've got one big problem. What happens when a buyer goes to the county requesting records and finds evidence of the diesel tanks?"

"Your man Cal has that one covered. Remember that corruption case against a couple of guys at Spokane County a few years ago?"

"Didn't that just finish up last year?" asked Brad.

"It might have, I'm not sure. But here's the thing. The law firm that Cal was working for at the time was defending one of the guys involved. They lost the case, but along the way they turned up evidence against another guy named Sherman Taylor, but it was too late in the process to use it. That guy is still there. Cal was the investigator who interviewed him, and he made sure that Taylor knew what he had on him. Luckily for us, Taylor runs the Records department for the County Assessor. Cal's got good leverage on him. We can feed him some replacement records that Jonathan and I will produce."

"Excellent. Now, what's your marketing plan? How're you going to make sure that only the right people hear about the offering and no one else?"

"We used to do something similar all the time in the business, legitimately. We do our homework up front – that's gonna take time, probably months – then we only send personalized marketing materials to our selected clients and we make sure that each one feels like part of an elite group. Narrowly targeted marketing."

"What if they send the materials along to someone else?"

"That can happen. But if we choose our targets carefully, they won't want to give anyone else a chance to bid against them. It's still a risk, though, I admit. And the only way I know to keep it under control is to limit the timeframe of our scheme – spend most of our time carefully selecting target clients, then get them the materials all at the same time. That's when our risk begins. If an inquiry comes in from someone else, we tell them we've already got a sale pending and hope they go away. And, we don't leave the scheme open for long. If there's any hint of a problem, we shut it all down, take the property 'off the market' and dissolve the LLC."

"It's kind of a one-shot deal then, isn't it?" Brad commented.

"Yeah, it is. We can't repeat it again, at least not for a long time."

"How much can we net out of this?"

"Well, that depends on how many targets we can find."

"Rough guess on the dollars?"

"Up to maybe a quarter million."

"Why should I trust you?"

Finn didn't expect that question, at least not at that moment. "On that estimate?"

"No, in general. Why should I trust you?"

"Uh, well, I don't know exactly. But I'm sure you must've had Cal dig into my past. Hell, tell him to keep digging. All he's going to find is a guy who's pissed off with the direction the country's headed, who's lost his job, lost his girlfriend, and probably lost his brother, too. A guy who wants to get America back to its white roots at any cost."

"Your girlfriend's sister married a nigger."

"He wasn't one of the worst, but it still disgusts me."

"It should."

"It does."

"Okay. Let's move on this. You've got six months to get me the marketing materials and a list of targets. Then I'll decide whether to pull the trigger or not. All proceeds go to Patriots' Pride. You'll get an allowance, but only when it's all done and the money's in the bank. In the meantime, you get free room and board here."

Finn nodded and the meeting was over.

Elsa

F inn couldn't have felt more energized if he had just left the boardroom of a Fortune 500 company after a successful presentation. Someone was finally listening to him, respecting him, giving him a chance to use his expertise. And it was all in the service of something he believed in. Breaking the law to lay the groundwork for a new order – no, to restore the *natural* order – was a necessary and insignificant price to pay. It was, in fact, a moral duty.

As Finn rounded the corner of the Capitol on his way back to the bunkhouse to start the next phase of planning, he collided with a young woman coming the other way and carrying several bags of groceries. One bag fell to the ground, and a six-pack of beer became shards of glass and a dark stain on the concrete walkway.

"I'm sorry," said Finn, squatting down to pick up the pieces and collect the other spilled items. "I wasn't looking where I was going. You okay?"

He looked up to see a strikingly beautiful, blond, blue-eyed woman, probably in her late twenties, wearing faded jeans and a loose cotton sweater. A wedding band graced her left hand.

"Yes, I'm okay, I'm sorry. It was my fault. I shouldn't have come around the corner so close. Brad's gonna kill me."

"No, no. It was me. I was preoccupied. I'm sure Brad will understand. I'm Finn, by the way. New around here."

"Elsa," said the woman, offering her hand. "So I guess you don't know Brad very well yet, do you?"

"I don't know – seems like a pretty reasonable guy to me."

112

"Don't get me wrong, I think he's a great leader. You just don't want to get on his shit list."

"No?"

"No. That's all I can say. Just don't do it."

Finn finished putting all the broken glass into a bag. "So, Elsa, is he going to be pissed about this? Was this his beer?"

"Yes." Elsa stared at the wet concrete.

"What'll he do when he finds out?"

Elsa was silent, still looking down, slowly shaking her head.

"Okay, look, I'll go talk to Brad and straighten this all out. It'll be fine," offered Finn.

"No, don't. It won't work. He'll still punish me and then you'll be in trouble, too. Might as well be only one of us."

"Well, wait, can't your husband talk some sense into Brad?" said, Finn, glancing at Elsa's ring. "I haven't met him yet but I'm sure he'd stand up for you."

"He's gone."

"But he'll be back soon, right?"

"No, he's gone. Jim's dead."

"Oh, damn, I'm sorry."

Silence.

"Look," said Finn. "I've got to run into town for some paper and printer's ink in the next few days anyway. So I'll go now and pick up another six-pack while I'm there. Can you wait a couple hours before you deliver the rest of this stuff?"

"He expects me to be cleaning the kitchen right now, but I don't think he'll miss his beer until this afternoon. Thank you, Finn. Thank you." Elsa reached out and touched Finn's arm.

"No problem. Where can I find you when I get back?"

"I'll be right here, in the Capitol. If I'm not in the kitchen, I'll be cleaning the toilets."

"Okay, good. I'll see you then."

Finn checked in with Cal before getting his keys from the bunkhouse. One of the things he'd learned recently, to his surprise, was that anyone traveling outside the compound had to log the trip with Cal, noting the time out, time back, and reason for the trip. Finn felt a little constrained and offended by the process, but dutifully complied. He unhooked the trailer from his Jeep and headed down the long dirt road to the gate and then into town.

Colville was a small place, so finding the print shop and liquor store was easy. Finn was careful to get the same brand of beer he'd seen smashed to bits on the concrete – Coors, in bottles, not cans – and picked up some for himself and his bunkmates as well. It wouldn't stay cold in the bunkhouse, but what the hell. It'd be better than nothing and it wouldn't hurt to stay on the good sides of Ted and Jonathan.

With his errands complete, Finn drove back to the compound and arrived a few minutes before eleven. He logged back in, took the printing supplies over to Jonathan's shop, stashed his own six-pack in the bunkhouse, and made his way back to the Capitol with the other one in a bag.

Opening the door, Finn was relieved to find the main hall empty. He put the beer in the refrigerator and turned to leave when he heard a toilet flush. He walked over to the other side of the dining hall and found the door to the single restroom. "All done, Elsa!" he shouted through it.

"All done with what?" answered a man's voice from within.

Brad walked out, looking quizzically at Finn.

"Oh, sorry, I thought Elsa was cleaning in there."

"She is. Done with what?"

"She, uh, wanted me to look at the hot water faucet in the kitchen. Didn't have enough flow, she said."

"Huh, I hadn't noticed that."

"Yeah, no big deal. The valve under the sink just wasn't on all the way. It's fine now."

"Okay, thanks."

Finn left the building and heaved a sigh of relief. *That was close! And what was Brad doing in there with her, anyway?* Finn tucked the question away and went back to work.

Don't Lie to Me

The next day, Finn walked over to Cal's cabin to brief him on the plan to find potential clients. There were three small individual cabins on the compound – one occupied by Cal, another by Brad, and the third, Finn guessed, by Elsa. The bunkhouses were used for everyone else with extra space ready for future members. Cal needed privacy because of his security work and Finn supposed that Brad just wanted his own space and took it. Ironically, thought Finn, Patriots' Pride was no democracy.

Finn knocked on the cabin door.

"Come on in," shouted Cal.

Cal finished locking up his safe and gestured toward one of two wooden chairs at a small table. "Have a seat and I'll be right with you."

Finn glanced around the two-room cabin. A made-up bed in one corner by a small window, a sink and hotplate on a tiny counter, the single table, and a partially open door leading to what was probably a minimal bathroom. A phone sat on the table, the only one at the compound, Cal had proudly mentioned. A FAX machine lay on the floor, still in its box.

"Oh, before we get going, Brad asked me to tell you he needs to see you after we're done here. He suggested around two this afternoon," said Cal.

"Did he say what it's about?"

"Nope."

"Did he say where?"

"His cabin."

"Hmm. Did he seem pissed about anything?"

"Couldn't tell. I'm sure everything's fine. Why?"

"No reason. Let's get started."

Without revealing names, Cal laid out a list of contacts by title that he thought might be of use in locating potential targets. A detective in Spokane, a couple of guys at the County there, three cops, two in Sandpoint Idaho and one in Walla Walla, an insurance agent in Coeur d'Alene, and several others scattered around the general area. One, a real estate agent, was up in Roundup, Montana. Another was a private investigator all the way across the country in Virginia.

"I'm impressed," Finn remarked. "So how do we get these guys to work for us? Do you have something on them or what?"

"On some, yeah. And a few favors I can call in. The others need money."

"So, where does that come from?"

"Brad's got a fund stashed away from the old counterfeiting days. It's there for emergencies but he said we can use some for this. He knows we can't do all this for nothing."

"How much does he have?" Finn asked.

"Not for us to know. We just ask for it when we need it."

"Okay, well, let's get started."

The two men worked up a general plan. In looking for targets, they would instruct their contacts to avoid the Spokane area and concentrate on more remote geography. The farther away the better – local knowledge could be a problem.

Cal and Finn narrowed down the contact list to people they felt would be most trustworthy and most able to help. Then they put together a general script to use when calling these people, but in the end they decided that Cal would need to make all the calls. Finn would sit in and listen so he could help make choices and refine the plan. There would be nothing in writing until they were dealing with actual clients.

Then there were contingencies to consider. What if one of the contacts asked too many questions or balked when asked to assist? Discussion on this and related topics went on for over an hour, resulting in agreement on a general escalation plan

116

beginning with calm persuasion, proceeding to carefully orchestrated blackmail, and ending with threats of material and physical violence. Finn hoped they would never have to escalate fully, not because he opposed violence in the service of a greater good, he told himself, but because that kind of action would complicate things and lead to exposure.

The meeting was over at one forty-five and Finn took the long way over to Brad's cabin. Still, he arrived about five minutes before the agreed time and waited four of those minutes before knocking at the door.

"Come in," said Brad. "Pull up a chair."

"What can I do for you?" asked Finn, noticing the veins standing out around the lion tattoo on Brad's neck.

"I'm glad you asked," began Brad. "It's really pretty simple. You can stop lying to me."

"About…?"

"Come on, Finn, don't insult me. You know exactly what I'm talking about."

"Elsa?"

"Yes, Elsa."

"That seemed like such a small thing. I was just trying to protect her."

"Goddamnit Finn! No untruth around here is a small thing – you need to learn that right now! And the girl doesn't need your protection, especially not from me! I'll protect her and I'll discipline her when she needs it. From now on, I want you to stay the hell away from her. If you see Elsa walking toward you, take a long detour. And if I ever see or hear about you talking with her – and I hear about everything around here – it'll be a very bad day for both of you. She knows what that means for her. If you really want to protect her, stay the fuck away from her! Is all that clear?"

"Yes."

"Then get the fuck out of my office and get back to work!"

Walking back to the bunkhouse, Finn felt like a child again, and he hated it. Even though he'd only been given a warning, it felt like a beating, a humiliating beating, like the ones he'd received at the hands of his own father for things Finn felt were mostly minor infractions.

Finn didn't think his little brother had ever seen the darkest side of the Mason family. In fact, Finn had tried to protect Luke from all that. He'd been the wild kid while Luke had always been the good one – never, or rarely, in trouble. Always trying to please everyone. Good grades in school. And the few times that Luke *had* stepped over the line, like the time he "borrowed" the Mustang for a date and accidentally scraped off one of the side mirrors on a post in a parking garage, Finn had stepped in and taken the blame, lying to say he had dared his brother to take the car without permission. Luke got grounded and Finn got a beating, one of several that he never told his little brother about.

So with Luke's generally good behavior and Finn's protection, Luke had probably remained blissfully ignorant of the Mason family dark side. That, at least, had been Finn's goal. But his efforts had other consequences as well. Over time, Finn began to chafe at the unfairness, self-inflicted as much of it was, and gradually developed a kind of latent anger and resentment, seasoned with a competing desire for approval and acceptance.

And now, as he walked back to the bunkhouse, Finn struggled to cool the familiar simmering in his gut. *I was just trying to help. I was right to do what I did and Brad blew it all out of proportion. But, what the hell, he's got to maintain discipline around here. I get that. I'd probably do the same thing if I ran this place. I'll get his respect back.*

The Launch

Over the next several months, Finn, Cal and Jonathan worked their contacts, developed a final list of fifteen target clients, and completed the template for a detailed marketing document to be customized for each one. Finn created a Limited Liability Corporation called "Northwest Premier Properties," Cal successfully sanitized the property records at Spokane County, and the scheme was ready to launch. Brad's approval was all that remained.

Finn was acutely aware that the launch would begin a period of maximum risk for Patriots' Pride and he worked to control his anxiety as he and his team made their way over to the Capitol to meet with Brad.

They arrived early and Elsa was the only one in the building. She was busy cleaning the kitchen and Finn managed to avoid eye contact as he had many times since Brad's warning. Many times, but not all. There had been two or three moments when Elsa and Finn had passed each other on one of the compound's several trails. They hadn't spoken but they had exchanged smiles. Finn was certain that Elsa knew his aloofness was forced and that she knew exactly why.

Brad walked in at nine o'clock, and the four men took chairs in front of the unlit fireplace.

"Should we ask her to give us some privacy?" suggested Cal, nodding back toward Elsa.

"Don't worry about it," replied Brad. "She can't hear us way over here. And even if she could, she wouldn't understand a word of it."

"Are you sure?"

"I said, don't worry about it."

"Right, okay. Should we get started?"

"That's why we're here, boys. What've you got for me?"

Finn cleared his throat. "The bottom line is we're ready to launch. All we need now is your okay. Since you've been in the loop all along, we didn't want to waste your time this morning going back over everything but we expect you've got some questions for us."

"Good. I've got a few. First, how many targets did you end up with?" asked Brad.

"Fifteen," replied Finn.

"Okay, and out of those fifteen, how many do you think will get to the point of actually wiring the fee to us?"

"Cal?" Finn deferred to his teammate.

"Based on all the background work on these guys, our best estimate is ten."

"Ten, alright," said Brad. "And we net how much on each?"

"After expenses, we're looking at about twenty-eight thousand each," replied Finn.

"Good. That's good. More than you thought at first, right? How confident are you in that number?"

"Pretty damn confident," said Cal. "All our targets are actively looking for property of this kind and in this price range. These ten have plans or obligations that make a purchase urgent and they've already been turned down for financing at least twice, most of them more. All fifteen have deep dark secrets, except from us."

"Okay, great. Now, suppose one of these poor suckers gets suspicious and backs out early, before we get our hooks into them. Couldn't they piss in our punchbowl? Spoil the whole party?"

"It's possible," said Finn. "But that's when we bring out the dirt."

"And if that's not enough?"

Cal jumped back in. "The shit we've got on these guys really stinks, believe me. But okay, let's assume it isn't enough and the target starts talking publicly or something. That's our worst-case scenario. That's when we shut it all down."

"What if that happens when we've already taken cash from other targets but we haven't given them the bad lender news yet? What do we do with those guys?" asked Brad.

"We've talked a lot about that one," said Finn. "At that point, we'd have to weigh the potential exposure against the amount of cash we've taken in. In the worst-worst case, we'd refund the money to everyone and disappear fast. If we thought we could really minimize or manage our exposure, we'd keep the cash, give everyone their bad news, along with our knowledge of their dirt, and then shut down. No matter what, we'd need to decide and act fast."

"Let me have a look at your final marketing material," said Brad.

"Here you go," said Jonathan, handing over a multi-page packet. "You can see where we'll fill in the details on each target before these go out."

Brad studied the full color document from Northwest Premier Properties. Because of Finn's experience and Jonathan's aesthetic touches, it appeared more like a serious investment prospectus, including the usual caveats, than it did a sales tool. The photographs of the property and surroundings were compelling.

"Excellent," Brad finally said. "Here's what I want you to do. Go with your big ten. Toss the other five. I don't even want you to think of them as backups. Just toss 'em."

"You got it," said Finn. "We'll get the materials in the mail by Friday and then I'll personally follow up on the phone with each target late next week."

"Okay, go! Get out of here! Do it!" Brad smiled and waved the men out.

Finn left the meeting with a sense of pride. He and his team had put together a good plan, a solid plan. Brad seemed proud of them too, even though he hadn't exactly used those words. Now Finn knew they would have to deliver. Planning was the easy part. Execution would require relentless attention, energy and professionalism. That's where he would really shine, and everyone would see it.

First In

T he marketing packet went out to all targets on Friday, as Finn had promised. But even with his growing sense of optimism, he wasn't expecting results as quickly as they came in. Cal had set up an answering machine on their unlisted phone line with a greeting from Northwest Premier Properties, and on Wednesday its light was blinking. Finn listened to the message.

"Hello, this is John Markham, CEO of Markham Enterprises in Bozeman and this message is for Finn Mason. We've been looking for commercial land to develop in or around the Spokane area and, uh, we were closing in on several good prospects when we got your materials in the mail yesterday. We'd like to add your property to our list of potentials and I need to get a little more information from you before we do that. So, when you get a chance, I'd appreciate a call. Thanks."

Mr. Markham left his number and hung up. Finn stared at the machine. A blinking light signaled a second message. *Holy shit,* He thought. *This is really happening.* He pushed a button to save the first message and then played the second one.

"Mr. Mason, this is Carl Stepton. I run an investment firm out of Lynchburg, Virginia and we'd like to consider adding your property to our real estate portfolio. We could also use some assistance with financing, and it sounds like your company has some creative solutions that might fit our needs. Call me."

Hmm, Finn *thought. I wouldn't have pegged these two as first in. Interesting. And Carl seems dumber than I expected from Cal's research.*

An investment company that admits up-front to needing assistance finding financing? Really?

Finn reviewed Cal's files on each of the two companies, made a few notes, and then called them back. He thought both conversations went reasonably well and, after asking a few questions carefully crafted to communicate both authentic business conservatism and guarded optimism, he promised to open a financing search for each company immediately upon receiving their fees. He faxed each of them a detailed contract outlining mutual responsibilities, then called back to verify receipt. As Finn expected, both companies asked for several days to review the contract with their "legal teams" and perform other due diligence before proceeding. Dates were set for follow-up phone meetings the next week.

Legal teams, my ass, Finn laughed to himself as he finished up his notes. *So far, so good.*

Reacting to this unexpected early encouragement, Finn considered calling the other eight targets right away but then rejected the idea as appearing too eager. The original plan would do just fine. He reminded himself not to change course arbitrarily.

By the end of the week, three more of the targets had called. One had already seen the property on a recent visit to Spokane and raved about its location and potential. All three began the process with Finn. Then Finn called the remaining five. Three sounded interested and promised to get back to him in the coming week to explore the opportunity, one sounded guarded and the other didn't answer repeated calls.

Finn went into the weekend feeling a bit more subdued but consoled himself with the realization that the early results were still looking much better than those expected from most legitimate marketing campaigns. He traded his initial euphoria for optimistic realism and decided to take advantage of the beautiful morning for a hike in the woods.

The early morning air held a slight chill, a reminder that fall was just around the corner in the Pacific Northwest, and Finn welcomed the change. He hadn't taken the time to explore the local forest since his arrival at Patriots' Pride because it had been so important to focus – to demonstrate his work ethic and dedication to the mission. Finn was doing both of those things, he felt, and doing them well. It was time for a short break.

Finn followed a narrow trail cut into the forest behind the compound. It wound through stands of hemlock and cedar, up a hillside bathed in the warming but slanted rays of late August, then back down again into the cool of the woods. It ended at a small stream. The sound of the water tumbling over rounded stones was mesmerizing, and Finn sat on a mossy log to enjoy it.

I've missed this, he thought. *I need this.* For the first time in months, Finn let his mind drift. It wandered around the nearby scene – the shaded stream bank, the soft moss underneath him, the sounds of the water, from the treble splashes to the bass gurgles, little eddies forming under the influence of two larger rocks. And then to thoughts of fishing as he saw a trout tuck under a ledge along the far side and turn to face upstream.

Why do they do that? he wondered. *Easier to hover in one place? To see what the oncoming water has in store for them? Yes, to see the future.*

Unlike the trout, Finn had not allowed himself to look upstream for several months, at least not very far upstream. His focus had been on immediate tasks. Yes, he had done a lot of future planning, but the plan itself was the focus, not the anticipated results. And now, sitting on the log, taking in the serenity of the place, Finn allowed himself to squint into the darkness ahead, if only for a moment.

What would his role be after his scheme succeeded and Patriots' Pride had some cash to work with? What did he *want* his role to be? It occurred to Finn that those two things might not be identical.

As Finn's plan started to show signs of success, Brad had begun to open up about his vision for Patriots' Pride. Finn reflected on a recent meeting in which Brad had painted a broad picture of Patriots' Pride fitting into a mosaic of other such groups in the Northwest, a few of which he was already working with. Brad had gone on to describe this mosaic as evolving into a more organized hierarchy, and eventually becoming a kind of state in its own right, a state with only white leaders and white citizens. Brad hadn't been optimistic about seeing this come to fruition in the next several years, but he had expressed a fervent desire to be a major player in paving the way for it. In general, Brad professed to be a nationalist, wanting to see all of America become a white homeland and regain the greatness he believed it once had, closing itself off from the outside world if necessary.

But Finn had also come to know Brad as a practical man, willing to take small, realistic steps on his way to larger goals. And the next steps, as Finn understood them, involved plans to cooperate with other Northwest groups by doing everything possible to make it uncomfortable for non-whites to live and work within their local geographies. The exact definition of "uncomfortable" was unclear to Finn but he had heard talk of tactics ranging from subtle job discrimination, to harassment and threats, to destruction of property, all the way to violent attacks. Brad clearly knew how to use fear as a tool, and he planned to employ it in two distinct ways. Not only would he use it directly against the outsiders, but he would also use it to motivate whites in the local communities. If he could help engineer and then publicize situations in which people of color became violent or otherwise threatened the God-ordained supremacy of whites, he could paint a picture of an increasingly dangerous world which must be set right. He could unify his white brethren behind a wall of fear.

Finn looked up from his thoughts, and his eyes once again focused on the stream in front of him. So, the original question remained: what next? He realized, over the course of the last several months, that his anger – the primary reason he had first come to the compound – had subsided. He had been accepted, his skills had been recognized, and his sense of unfairness had abated. So, again, what next?

When he allowed himself to skim the surface of the subject, Finn wasn't certain he was fully invested in Brad's long-term plans, let alone his philosophy. Would he be willing to harass a black man or woman, or even kill someone to advance these plans? He wasn't at all sure, and this realization scared him. Was he the Finn of Patriots' Pride or the Finn of two years ago? Were they really any different? What about the Finn of next year? Who would that be?

And this bothered him for other, less existential reasons as well. He had carved out a niche for himself at the compound and it felt good. It felt safe. No one else there could do his job as well as he could, and no one could steal it from him. He had earned the trust of everyone, probably including Brad, and he could easily continue down his current path if he didn't think too much about the future implications.

Then there was Elsa. Elsa confused him. He thought about her constantly but wondered if part of the attraction was the forbidden fruit situation Brad had created. Finn had followed the letter of that law up to the present but was frequently tempted to violate it. How did Elsa feel about the whole thing? Finn had no idea. But the mix of danger, uncertainty and desire created a strong cocktail.

On his trek back to the compound, Finn tried to re-focus his thoughts on the work ahead. *Don't overthink everything. Just do what you're good at. Everything else will fall into place.*

Labor Day

L uke stopped the truck at the old cattle gate and turned to kiss his smiling new wife. He and Jennifer had started this little tradition on their recent honeymoon trip to the cabin and neither had any intention of letting the moment pass unobserved.

"I love you, Jenny Mason," said Luke as he stepped out to open the gate.

"I love you, too, Luke Mason!"

The midday air held the promise of a warm afternoon and a dry, crisp evening. The lake sparkled under the influence of a light breeze as the two made their way down to the dock. This had become another part of the tradition – visiting the lake once before entering the cabin. Luke, and he imagined Jennifer too, valued these little rituals as ways of making the place their own.

For months they had talked about the problem of Finn – that his unseen presence at the cabin, and in their lives, still lingered – but Jennifer had insisted that discussing it openly would be the key to dealing with it. She said that her memories of moments there with Luke far outweighed all others and that all relationships outside of fairy tales had their imperfections and challenges. That made them real, she said, and she wanted theirs to be as real as the lake and the forest around it.

The couple talked about the afternoon ahead as they walked back up the trail to unload the truck. They had invited Maggie and James to the cabin for the long Labor Day weekend and looked forward to their arrival in a few hours. But they also had unspoken plans for those intervening hours of privacy. Luke's old room had become their room and that is where they went right after the truck was empty.

Without a word, Luke took Jennifer's hand and led her in. As the last piece of clothing found the floor, they fell onto the bed together, laughing.

A little over an hour later, the crunch of gravel outside woke Luke with a shot of adrenalin. He tumbled out of bed and went to the window. Jennifer just rolled over. Luke was amazed at his wife's ability to sleep through almost anything. He, on the other hand, would spring to consciousness at the mere sound of an owl hooting a half mile away in the forest. He pulled back the curtain far enough to peer out. He had expected to get a call from Maggie down in Rockport when they were ready to be taken up the mountain in the truck. But instead, there they were, getting out of a new Ford Bronco outfitted with large off-road tires, brush guard and winch. Luke quickly grabbed his clothes off the floor, put most of them on, and made sure Jennifer was awake before scrambling out to meet their guests.

"Well, look at this!" said Luke as he stepped outside. "Doesn't look like you had any trouble getting up the road. So good to see you guys!"

"So good to be here!" returned James. "And you're right; this little rig is amazing. No trouble at all."

"Maggie!" said Luke, hugging his sister in law and then turning back to James for the same.

"Come on in. Here, let me help you with your stuff."

"So, what made you decide to get something with four-wheel drive?" asked Luke as everyone came through the front door.

"Well, you know how the winters can be around Spokane," said Maggie. "We just thought it was time we had something that would let us get out to stores, the doctor, you know, whatever, during one of those big snowstorms. And, it gets us up here without having to bum a ride from you guys!"

"Well, it looks like a great choice," said Luke. "Jenny, they're here!" he shouted back toward the bedroom.

129

Jennifer ran out to meet her sister and brother in law, not looking at all like she'd been asleep only minutes before. After more hugs and some settling in, the foursome decided to pile into the skiff and take a short cruise on the lake.

The late afternoon air was warm with not even a hint of a breeze, and the water looked like dark blue glass. The skiff sliced easily through it on the way out to the island as talk quickly turned to careers.

"So," said James, looking at Jennifer. "Are you moved over to that new campus in Redmond yet?"

"Yes, we actually got in a little earlier than expected. I'm in Building Two out of four. I even have a window looking out onto Lake Bill!"

"Lake Bill?" said James with raised eyebrows.

Maggie jumped in. "You, know. I told you about that before. We just didn't know Jen would be able to see it from her new office. It's named after their fearless and geeky leader."

"It's actually just a pond," added Jennifer. "But nice to look at while coding for ten hours straight."

"Oh, right," said James. "That is so cool – congratulations!"

"And one other thing," added Jennifer. "Remember the company went public this Spring? Well, they started making stock options part of our compensation packages. But, you know the old joke about wallpapering your bathroom with worthless options."

"I've got a good feeling about this one," said James.

Jennifer just shrugged. "We'll see. And what about you? What's going on at the university?" she asked.

"Not much change really. I'm teaching a few classes – a survey of western philosophy, an ethics class, things like that. And then I'm collaborating with someone from the Anthropology department on a paper looking at cultural diversity and the notion of tolerance."

The discussion moved from there to Luke's teaching job. He told a couple of tales about his students and mentioned his ongoing work toward a collection of short stories which he hoped to have published. He pivoted back to Maggie.

"So, Maggie, how's your company doing?"

"Oh, things have been kind of slow lately. Environmental consulting isn't something most people are itching to spend money on these days. But still, business is okay. In fact, just a couple of days ago I got a call from an investment firm in Virginia of all places. I don't think I've ever had a client outside the Pacific Northwest."

"What in the world are they looking for?" asked Luke.

"I don't think it's gonna amount to much. They're just looking for advice on some land they're thinking about buying in Spokane. Personally, I wouldn't touch that parcel with an eleven-foot pole."

"Why not?" asked Jennifer.

"Remember, when we were kids, that ugly old truck stop down by the river?"

"Oh yeah. What a dump."

"Well, that's the place. There's nothing on the land now but it's got to be an environmental nightmare below the surface. I'll just pull the records from the county and that'll be the end of it. It'll all be over and I'll be able to bill for what, maybe three or four hours? Anyway, there're a few other things in the pipeline, so we'll be fine."

Luke guided the boat around the island, stopping to look at an eagle soaring over the water along the shore looking for supper. They all decided to head back as the sun dipped below the trees behind the cabin on the western shore.

An Announcement and a Paradox

Back at the cabin, Luke opened a bottle of Cabernet Sauvignon from a winery in Woodinville that was starting to get some national exposure. He brought four glasses into the living room and set one in front of each person. As he began to pour, Maggie covered hers with a hand.

"None for me, thanks. I'll just get some water."

"Really? You sure? This is a great vintage," implored Luke with his best bartender smile that partly hid the scar on the right side of his mouth.

"Yep, I'm sure."

"You feeling okay?" Jennifer asked her sister.

Maggie exchanged a look with James and then said, "Yes, I'm totally fine. We weren't going to tell you guys just yet, but what the heck, here goes. I'm pregnant! Yaw!" Maggie threw her hands up in the air and beamed.

"Oh Maggie!! What wonderful news! I can't believe it – I'm so happy for you both!" Jennifer jumped up to hug her sister and James. "When are you due?"

"Thank you! Should be around the end of March."

"Congratulations!" said Luke. "You'll be such great parents. This is the best news I've heard since Jenny said yes!" He ran into the kitchen to fill Maggie's glass with water and a slice of lemon.

Luke returned to a lively conversation about baby names, plans to expand the house, and how Maggie expected to keep the company going in her absence for a couple of months after the baby arrived.

Later, over dinner, the conversation turned to Finn.

"So," Maggie said. "I don't want the whole weekend to be about the baby – well, I sort of do! But, no, I want to know how you two are doing with, you know…"

"With Finn being gone and all?" asked Jennifer.

"Yeah, that."

"I think it's much harder on Luke than it is on me," began Jennifer. "Honestly, I'm glad he's not around but I also worry about what he's up to. I know Luke does." She glanced toward her husband.

"It's hard," said Luke, looking down at the table. "It's really hard. He's still my brother and I care about him. But I'm also confused, revolted, scared – you name it. It's such a damned mix of things."

Jennifer put a hand on Luke's shoulder as he looked up and continued.

"Sometimes I just try to put it all out of my mind and get on with life. But then the next day I'll find myself trying to figure out how I can help pull him out of this hole. And then I get completely pissed off when I realize he probably doesn't want my help, or anyone else's."

"That's a tough spot to be in," offered James. "I think we all feel pretty helpless."

"That's it – helpless, frustrating," said Luke. "You know that paper you're working on? You mentioned tolerance. I've been thinking a lot about that subject lately and the big question for me is how far we should take it. I mean, look, if I'm having a conversation with someone about, oh, I don't know, let's say taxes. And let's say I disagree with this person. He says we need to reduce taxes on the wealthy so they'll create more jobs for everyone else and I say, no, we need to help lift people out of poverty directly because the whole trickle-down thing doesn't work. Okay, well, I can listen to his viewpoint and try to learn more about why that might be a compelling idea for some. I might even be open to changing my own position. But at very least I can be tolerant and civil about something like that. But what if the conversation moves down the path of letting poor

133

people suffer until they decide to take more initiative? What if it goes from there to assertions that black people are the problem, and from there to support for their persecution and maybe even a horrendous joke about reviving lynching. At what point does tolerance become unethical or immoral?"

"That's such an important question, Luke," said James. "In some ways, I think life is easiest for binary thinkers – those for whom issues are always black and white. It's harder for those of us who live in the gray zone, who want to be tolerant of other views, who try to be compassionate. As much as I disagree with most of what Oliver Cromwell said and did, I do like one thing he's often quoted on. He said, *'I beseech you, in the bowels of Christ, think it possible you may be mistaken.'* I think that's great advice in general, staying open to the possibility, even the likelihood, of one's own fallibility. If we can do that, we can genuinely listen, and sometimes that's the best we can do."

"But shouldn't there be a limit, even to that? Shouldn't there be a point where we just say, 'No, you're wrong?'"

"In my opinion?" said James. "Yes, absolutely. I think Karl Popper had an important angle on this and I've used a quote of his in my paper, so it's on my mind right now. He said, *'Unlimited tolerance must lead to the disappearance of tolerance.'* He called that 'the paradox of tolerance' and you can see why."

"Yes, definitely," said Luke. "I can't help but think though, that the truly difficult, real-life problem here is knowing when you've reached that point – knowing when to stop tolerating someone's intolerance."

"Uh huh, I think it probably comes down to individual beliefs and convictions and how strongly held those are. One person's breakpoint might be different from another's. But wherever that point is for someone, the next question is what to do when it's reached."

"That kind of comes back around to my original comment – sometimes I just shut down and try to ignore the whole thing and sometimes I want to jump in and 'fix' it. You know what I mean?"

"I think I do," said James, nodding and smiling. "And I think that the desire to 'fix' it is a noble one, and one that should be encouraged. But what does that mean? It might mean active listening mixed with rational, non-emotional argument where possible. It might mean direct confrontation. It could include helping someone clearly see the potentially devastating consequences of their choices. It might even mean ignoring the intransigent individual and giving your perspective a larger audience – working on the problem more broadly and not just with that single person. But no matter what, I think real solutions almost always come down to personal relationships – if not with that original person, then with others."

"Hmm, food for thought."

"Well, the good news, as I see it, is that you're asking great questions – that you recognize the situation for what it is. You're not caught in one of those 'slowly boiling frog' traps where you can't even see the danger approaching. For better or worse, Finn isn't being real subtle about this."

"That's for damn sure."

Spokane

Maggie was settling back into work after the long weekend and was on her way to the Spokane County Courthouse to pull the records on the old truck stop property that Stepton Financial Services seemed so interested in. But before she took the bridge over the river, she decided to take a quick detour and have a first-hand look at the site. It had been years since she'd been over that way and she was curious if it had changed much. She was sure that Carl Stepton wouldn't be so enamored with it if he knew about its fuel-soaked past. But the location was prime, and Stepton had said the price was 'better than right' when he talked to Maggie's assistant a week before.

Maggie pulled over and parked the Bronco alongside a large vacant field overgrown with weeds and dotted with a few small trees. The land sloped gradually down to the river and offered a first-class view. But Maggie knew that its proximity to the river would make any necessary environmental cleanup even more complex and expensive than usual. If she had spoken with Carl Stepton in person, she might have warned him right up front. Still, it was possible that some work had been done in the last few years that she wasn't aware of, and her trip to the county records department would clear that up.

Maggie walked the rest of the property, finding several old footings under the weeds and a large concrete pad with rusted pipes protruding up a few inches. The remains of a building's foundation were largely hidden under a tangle of blackberry vines. She walked back to the Bronco and drove across the Monroe Street bridge to the courthouse on Broadway.

Once inside, Maggie went to the Assessor's office and asked to see all property records for the parcel. What she expected to find was commercial zoning, tax records, and some detailed environmental impact statements revealing a dark past and portending a difficult future. What she found instead confused her. Property taxes had been consistently paid, so that was good. But the parcel was zoned much more flexibly, for Retail/Residential Mixed Use. And if that wasn't strange enough, historical records showed that it had once been the site of a general store, not a truck stop. No environmental issues were noted.

Maggie shook her head and double-checked the parcel number and address. It was correct, and an aerial photo showed the weed-covered field she had just visited. She checked on the current ownership and found that the title identified a corporation in the Cayman Islands. That was a bit unusual for a property like this, but not unheard of. Still, the rest of the information just couldn't be right. Maggie decided to check with the manager in charge of records.

A secretary ushered her into a small office where she found a middle-aged, balding man behind an old gray steel desk, pouring over a document. He looked up and introduced himself.

"Hello, I'm Sherman Taylor, manager of the department. How can I help you today, Miss, uh…"

"Margaret Reynolds, Fairwood Environmental Consulting."

"Nice to meet you. Please, have a seat. What can I do for you?"

"Well, I'm doing some research for a client on a parcel here in Spokane and the records just aren't making sense to me."

"Okay, let's see if we can shed some light. What's the parcel number?"

Maggie consulted her notes and read off the number.

"We've just started computerizing our operation here so maybe that's causing some problems," said Taylor. "We're

137

replacing all those paper documents you've been digging through with digitized versions. Let me see if I have that particular parcel in the system yet. Just give me a sec."

Taylor tapped some information into a terminal on his desk and waited a few seconds. Maggie thought she noticed his eyes widen as he stared at the screen for a moment. Then he looked up.

"Hmm, that one's not in yet. All I'm getting is the site address, nothing more. What was the confusion you were having?"

"I've lived here all my life, Mr. Taylor, and I remember that property being a truck stop back in the sixties. Unless some major work has been done that I'm not aware of, there are still some large fuel tanks buried there. And if there'd been a cleanup operation, there'd be records describing it, and I would almost certainly have heard about it. That kind of work is very visible and takes a lot of time and money."

"Look, I don't know what else I can do for you right now. Maybe the records system changeover has caused a mix-up of some kind. Maybe the paperwork got shuffled in the process of digitizing. Or maybe you're remembering another property nearby?"

"I don't think so. I'm sure this is the one."

"Okay, no problem. Why don't we do this: I'll dig into it further and give you a call by the end of the week. By then we should be able to sort this all out. How's that sound?"

Maggie noticed that Taylor's forehead was beaded with sweat and the room was barely warm. "Thanks, but my client is pushing pretty hard on this," she fibbed. "Any chance you could have something sooner?"

"I'll do my best but can't promise anything. How can I reach you?"

Maggie recited the phone number, repeated the name of her company, thanked Taylor, and left the building.

On the way back to her office, Maggie thought about the encounter with Sherman Taylor. Something wasn't right. He

138

didn't even offer to look at the paper file himself. And he was obviously nervous. *Will he even call me back on this? Is he trying to hide something about this property?*

When Maggie arrived at the office, she checked the time. It was still within regular business hours in Virginia so her client would probably still be there. She decided not to share her specific concerns yet but at least wanted to let the client know she was on the case. She looked up the number and made the call. It was picked up on the second ring.

"Good afternoon, Stepton Financial Services. How may I direct your call?"

"Yes, hello, this is Margaret Reynolds from Fairwood Environmental. Is Mr. Stepton available?"

"One moment…"

"Stepton here. How can I help you?"

"Mr. Stepton, this is Margaret Reynolds from Fairwood Environmental in Spokane. I believe you spoke with my assistant Jessica a few days ago?"

"Yes, yes, thank you for checking in. Have you had a chance to look into that property yet?"

"We've made a start, yes. But Spokane County is in the middle of computerizing their property records and the information I'm looking for doesn't seem to be available right now. So, I'm sorry to say that it'll be a few more days before I can give you what you need. I hope the delay isn't going to inconvenience you too terribly much."

"We'll manage. But do you have any idea how this is going to go, just a gut feeling?"

"Right now I'd have to say things look a little questionable. I wish I could be more definitive but it looks like we're just going to have to wait for the data."

"So you think we'll know more by the end of the week?"

"That's what I was told this morning by the county. I promise you I'll stay on them."

"Okay, thanks. Call me when you learn anything more, will you?"

"Absolutely. You have a good afternoon, Mr. Stepton."

Maggie put down the phone, made a note in her planner to call Sherman Taylor in two days, and turned to other business.

Exposure

Cal Shorten put down the phone and cursed at it. He had just taken an early morning call from his man at Spokane County and the news wasn't good. Some damn consulting company was digging into the falsified records, someone who wasn't on the target list, someone who knew something damaging.

Shit! And just when we were starting to get some traction with this thing!

They had already managed to pull in three healthy checks from other targets, and now this little incident threatened to cut off the cash flow and drive the whole damn thing into the ground. Cal thought about pulling Finn in for some brainstorming on the problem but then decided it would be wiser to keep him out of it for now. *The fewer people involved at this point, the better.*

Cal put together a rough plan. He wouldn't recommend shutting down the whole scheme over this one fucking problem. Not yet anyway. Instead, he'd find the consulting company down in Spokane and help them understand why they needed to back down. He would convince them to drop their client immediately. No time for research or subtle methods. This would have to be an old-fashioned deal.

Cal slipped his weapon into his shoulder holster, put on a coat, signed himself out of the travel log, and drove out of the compound.

The office of Fairwood Environmental Consulting was outside the city of Spokane to the north, so the trip from Colville was an easy one, straight down highway 395 and taking only a little over an hour. Cal parked his truck a block away and glanced at his notes. *Margaret Reynolds. Why does that name sound familiar? I just can't place it and it bugs the hell out of me.*

Cal double-checked the address as he walked up to the neatly kept craftsman-style house. A small sign on the front door confirmed that this was indeed Fairwood Environmental Consulting, so he opened the door and entered.

The entryway had been converted into a reception area, complete with desk, potted plants, and two guest chairs off to one side. A smiling young woman with dark brown skin sat behind the desk and had just hung up the phone.

"Good morning, sir. How can I help you?"

"I'm here to see Ms. Reynolds," announced Cal.

"And your name?"

"John Tucker," lied Cal without hesitation.

"Do you have an appointment, Mr. Tucker?"

"No, but I'm here on a rather urgent matter. If she could spare just a few minutes, I'd really appreciate it."

"Her schedule is pretty tight this morning, Mr. Tucker, but let me check with her. Have a seat right over there and I'll be back in a moment." The receptionist motioned toward the guest chairs and a small table covered with magazines.

Cal didn't waste a second. He scanned the reception desk and located a day planner, opened it to the current month and looked for anything that could be helpful. He found an entry at the end of the week which read "Status call: Stepton Financial." That was confirming but not unexpected. But then, on the following Wednesday, Cal found an interesting note: "Maggie OB appointment, Dr. Marshall." He replaced the day planner on the desk and went back to his seat.

Moments later, the receptionist re-entered the room followed by a pretty and professional-looking young woman with her brown hair pulled back into a French twist. She extended her hand.

"Mr. Tucker, I'm Margaret Reynolds. Jessica tells me you've got something urgent to discuss and I've got a few minutes before my next meeting, so why don't you come on back and we'll talk. Coffee?"

"No thanks. Appreciate your time."

Cal followed Maggie down a hall and into her office at the back of the building, taking note of an adjacent door to the outside. He closed the office door behind them.

"Oh," said Maggie, looking at the door. "This must be a very confidential matter."

"Yes, very."

"Okay, well, tell me what's on your mind. I've got about ten minutes."

"That's fine. We should only need about half that. Here's the thing…"

Cal was interrupted by the intercom on Maggie's desk. "Maggie, I'm sorry to interrupt, but James is here with bagels. Would you like him to bring a couple back?"

"Sure, send him back Jessica. Thank you."

"I'm sorry, Mr. Tucker, this'll only take a second and you'll get a free bagel out of the deal."

The door opened, and in walked a tall, smiling black man with a bag.

Cal tried to hide his surprise and fought back revulsion as the man leaned over the desk to kiss Margaret and then turned to be introduced. And in that moment, Cal made the connection. *Oh, shit. Margaret/Maggie, James, Finn. Fuck!*

"John Tucker, this is my husband James," said Maggie.

"Pleasure to meet you, Mr. Tucker," smiled James, offering a hand.

"Hmm," said Cal, ignoring the outstretched hand.

"Is there a problem here?" asked James.

"You might say that," replied Cal. He reached under his jacket, pulled out his Ruger 9mm semi-automatic and waved it at Maggie and James. "Have a seat, both of you. We need to chat for a minute." He kicked the door closed again.

Maggie sank slowly into her desk chair and James backed into a chair in front of the desk. Cal remained standing and noticed both of his captives were staring at his gun. *Good. I've got their attention.*

"Okay you two, I'm probably not gonna shoot you, not today anyway, so relax. Have a bagel. You've got a client called Stepton Financial, right?"

Silence.

"Right!?" Cal repeated.

"Yes, I do," replied Maggie in a hoarse whisper.

"Look," said James, starting to get to his feet. "Whatever this is about, I'm sure we can…"

"Sit the fuck back down, bagel boy!" snarled Cal, swinging the gun back to point directly at James' forehead.

James sat.

"Here's what you're going to do with your client," said Cal in a quieter voice, moving his gun arm down to his side again. "I want you to follow my directions exactly, do you understand?"

Maggie nodded. "Yes."

"Good. I want you to call Mr. Stepton after I leave today. Tell him that you do routine background checks on all clients and that you found something in his background that will make it impossible for you to continue with him as a client. Tell him – and this is important – tell him you know about his relationship with The Syndicate in Newark. Then, if he doesn't immediately hang up or if he tries to ask you anything, tell him you also know about another relationship – the one with Crystal Duncan. Then just tell him never to contact your company again. Okay? Have you got all that? Now, repeat it back to me."

Maggie stammered her reply.

"Okay, now write it down and tell me again."

Maggie followed directions.

"One last thing," said Cal. "I'll know if you don't do this, or if you don't do it exactly right. I've got your line tapped and I'll be listening from my truck. And I'll know immediately if you contact the police, no matter how you try. I have lots of friends in law enforcement all over the country. So don't fuck with me.

Oh, and congratulations, Maggie. I'm sure your baby would really like to grow up with two parents." Cal glanced over at James as he finished his sentence.

"Who the hell *are* you?" shouted James, getting up.

Cal moved quickly, putting James into a choke hold in front of him with the gun at his back. "Come on, nigger; we're gonna take a little walk out to the alley."

Cal pushed James toward the door, out into the hall, and out the back door to the alley behind the building. Then, without warning, Cal struck James hard across the face with the pistol, punched him in the gut and gave him a few solid kicks after he went down.

"Like I said, don't fuck with me."

Cal holstered his weapon and walked out of the alley, whistling.

Black Eyes

Maggie ran from her office to the back alley, her heart pounding and tears clouding her vision. "James! James! Where are you?!"

She spotted his legs on the ground, the rest of his body hidden by a dumpster against the building. She ran to him.

"James! Are you okay?"

He was groaning and trying to sit up. Blood oozed from an ugly gash along the left side of his face and one eye was beginning to swell.

Jessica must have heard Maggie's cries because she burst into the alley from the back door.

"Where are you?! What happened?! Oh my god, James!"

Maggie and Jessica helped James to his feet and slowly guided him toward the door. "Come on, let's go inside and get you some help," Maggie said.

"What happened?" Jessica repeated.

James glanced at Maggie and managed to say, "I got mugged. Went out to dump some trash and the next thing I know, there was this guy."

"I'll call an ambulance," said Jessica as they settled James into a chair in the office.

"No, I'll drive him down to the hospital myself," said Maggie, remembering Tucker's threats. "It'll be faster. But if you could grab the first aid kit, Jess, that'd be great."

Maggie patched up her husband's face, stopping the bleeding, then got him out to the car with Jessica's help.

"I'll report this to the police while you're gone," offered Jessica.

"Thanks, but, you know, I think it would be better if I did that from the hospital," said Maggie. "I got a look at the guy as he ran away and they'll want a description. Why don't you just close up the place and take the rest of the day off."

"Are you sure? I'd really like to help."

"I know, Jess, and thank you. But I think closing up would be the biggest help right now."

"It wasn't that Tucker guy, was it?" asked Jessica.

"No, no. He didn't need more than a couple of minutes for a quick question then left out the side door. If you could just cancel the rest of my meetings today and lock up, that'd be great. Thanks, Jess."

Maggie got to the hospital in Spokane within fifteen minutes and walked James into the Emergency Room. They checked in with a triage nurse and sat down to wait their turn.

"So, what should we do about reporting this?" asked Maggie. "They're bound to ask us about it here."

"I think we're safe if we report it as a mugging," said James. "Might actually be good to call the police from here."

"I don't know, James. I'm scared for us and I'm scared for the baby. I think we should just say we already called it in if they ask."

"Any way we cut it we've got problems, Mags. But okay, let's go with that plan for now. What do you think this John Tucker thing is all about, anyway?"

"I don't know but it's got to be tied in with what I found at the county yesterday. I haven't even had time to tell you about that. When I got a look at the files... Oh shit!"

"What?"

"I forgot to call Stepton! Tucker's going to be waiting! I've got to go back to the office and call from there so he'll know it's done. Can you manage on your own here for a while? I'm so sorry, sweetheart, I'm so sorry!"

"Yes, of course, go. You've got no choice. I'll be fine. Meet you right back here in the waiting area. Go!"

147

Maggie kissed her husband gently and ran out of the hospital.

She got back to the office in record time and unlocked the door. Jessica was gone and all the lights were out. Even in the ambient light of mid-day, it felt eerie in a way that it never had before. Maggie turned on the hall lights and made her way back to her office. She shuddered as she opened her door and peered in. Of course her office was empty, and Maggie cursed John Tucker for making her feel so paranoid in addition to everything else. She sat at her desk, studied the note she had taken with the Stepton instructions, took a deep breath, and made the call.

"Mr. Stepton, Margaret Reynolds here."

"Yes, hello Margaret. Have you got any news for me?"

"Well, yes, but not the kind of news I'd hoped to give you. Mr. Stepton, my company does routine background checks on all its clients, as a precaution; I'm sure you understand. Unfortunately, in your case this has turned up some information that makes it impossible for me to continue working with you as a client."

"Oh?"

"Yes, I won't be billing you for work done to date. We've become aware of your relationship with The Syndicate in Newark."

Silence.

"Mr. Stepton?"

The line had gone dead.

Maggie replaced the handset in its cradle and stared at it. *Have I just opened us up to more trouble?*

She wanted to scream at the walls and kick the door Tucker had come through, but she knew that would have to wait. She had to get back to the hospital and James.

By this time, traffic had picked up and it took Maggie almost a half hour to get to the hospital, park the Bronco and run into the waiting room. James was there, leafing through a copy of Time Magazine and sporting a new bandage.

148

"Hey, how're you feeling?" Maggie asked, tenderly touching the uninjured side of her husband's face.

"Not too bad, considering," James replied. "Seven stitches and a pretty thorough exam. At first they were concerned about internal bleeding but now they say it's unlikely. Told me to rest for a few days and gave me these pain meds. Good thing tomorrow's Friday, huh?"

"That's one good thing I guess. Gives us a long weekend," smiled Maggie.

On the way home, James was quiet and Maggie knew that his pain was much more than physical.

"That was a vicious attack, sweetheart, and I mean the verbal parts too. I thought that was mostly behind us in this country, but I guess I was being naïve. I'm so sorry this happened to you."

"Mags, I see and hear things more often than I ever tell you about," said James. "Not usually this blatant, but it's there. Racism is alive and well in America, but sometimes you can only see it when you look at the world through black eyes."

Stepton Down

C al smiled as he drove under the Patriots' Pride sign back at the compound. Two birds with one stone. He had averted exposure of the scheme and had put another black man in his place. But he did have one worry. Even though Fairwood Environmental was one of only two such consulting companies in the greater Spokane area, what were the chances that Stepton would, first of all, go to a consulting firm at all, and second, that it would happen to be one indirectly related to Finn? Would Maggie see the connection and try to contact Finn? Could Finn learn about what happened to James? Was he becoming a liability? He vowed to watch Finn very carefully in the coming days.

There had been no wiretap on Maggie's office phone, but Cal had found this to be a credible threat in the past and expected it to be effective this time as well. Just to be sure, he placed a call to his detective contact in Virginia and asked him to check into Stepton's status and report back. Then he went to find Brad. He caught up with him at Jonathan's print shop and asked him to step outside for a moment.

"We had a close call today, but I've taken care of it," Cal began.

"What kind of a close call?" asked Brad.

"With one of our targets, Carl Stepton. He hired a consultant in Spokane to check into the property instead of going directly to the county. I have no idea why but, as bad luck would have it, this consultant knew about the property's history and went to the county herself. She found records that she knew couldn't be right and spoke to Taylor about it. Well, it's a good thing she went to Taylor because he deflected her and then called me to alert us."

"Shit. Sounds like we still have a problem."

"That's why I went down there this morning."

Cal filled in the details, including the potential link to Finn. But he downplayed the risk. Finn was just too valuable to their financial future, at least for the next few months.

"Do you think they have any reason to tie this back to us?" asked Brad.

"No, none. I took all the usual precautions, and then some."

"Good man. Keep your eyes and ears open, and with Finn too."

"Will do."

On his way back over to the Capitol for a snack, Cal ran into Finn coming the other way.

"Hey, Cal, I was looking for you earlier today," said Finn.

"I had to run an errand. What's up?"

"Just wanted to let you know we got another check in the mail this morning. That makes four now."

"Hey, that's great. Good news. Look, Finn, don't expect to get one from Stepton Financial, okay?"

"Sure, okay. Why not?"

Cal looked for any telltale signs and found none. *Finn really doesn't know.*

"I got word from my guy in Virginia. He found out Stepton's going under. He'll probably just drop off the map and we'll never hear from him again."

"I could call him, just check in?"

"Nah, it's not worth it. He doesn't have any money and he's nothing but a risk to us now. Just let it go."

"No problem. He seemed kind of flaky anyway. Should we look for a replacement – maybe go back to our other list?"

"Maybe; let's see how the others play out in the next week or two."

Not Even Part of Her Universe

"Microsoft Corporation, Jennifer Mason speaking."

"Jen, this is Maggie. I'm sorry to call you at work but I thought it would be safer. Have you got a few minutes?"

"Of course, Maggie. What do you mean, 'safer?' What's going on? Are you alright?"

"I'm okay, and James is, now, but, oh Jen, it was awful!"

"Wait, wait just a sec while I close the office door... okay, tell me what's going on."

Between sobs, Maggie told Jennifer she was calling from a pay phone at Gonzaga University. She described the terrifying experience with John Tucker, his threats, the attack on James, the trip to the hospital, and then backtracked to her research at Spokane County.

"But the way he talked to James and the horrific attack, Jen, it was pure evil. I can hardly believe it really happened and I know it must be ten times worse for James. I mean, that asshole Tucker came after me for something I did. But he came after James for who he *is!* And it was my fault!"

"No, it wasn't your fault, Maggie. You got caught up in the middle of some bad business and James just happened to be there at the time. But I get how you must feel. I'm so sorry, Sis. What can I do to help? Would you and James like to come stay with us over here for a while?"

"Thanks, Jen, but he's got to go back to the hospital for a follow-up in a few days. Maybe sometime after that."

"Any time at all. Are you safe, though? You think it's over?"

"I don't know. I think so. I did everything he said."

"And you didn't go to the police?"

"No, do you think I should now?"

"Probably not. Sounds too risky to me. How's James doing with all this?"

"You know him; he's been pretty stoic about the whole thing. I wish he'd talk to me more. He's probably trying to process it in his own way – writing about it, most likely. I hope he is. I just don't want to see him hold it all inside."

"He knows you're there for him, I'm sure. Let him know the rest of us are, too, okay? We love him."

"Thanks, Jen. I'll tell him. Jen?"

"Yes?"

"I don't mean to upset you any more than I probably already have, but it just seems so strange that this and the Finn stuff both happened within a few months. Do you think there could be any connection? I can't imagine Finn actually doing something like Tucker did, but still... I mean, doesn't it seem a little weird?"

"Yeah, it does. But you said your client's in Virginia, right? Still, I guess Finn and this Tucker bastard could still somehow be connected. I hate to even think about that possibility."

"It's probably nothing, Jen. I shouldn't have even mentioned it. Tucker couldn't have known James would just drop by that day. He wasn't there for him. He was there for me. I'm sorry, Sis."

"No, it's okay. This must be so horrible for you and James. Please, please let me know how I can help."

"I will, Sis. Thanks. I love you."

"I love you too, Maggie. Let's talk again tomorrow, okay? I just want to be sure you're safe."

"Okay, bye."

"Bye."

Jennifer put down the phone and stared out her office window. A great blue heron stood in the water along the edge of Lake Bill, patiently waiting for lunch to swim by. *So focused,* thought Jennifer. *The rest of the world is right there around her, with all its worries, its tragedies, its hate and its wars, but she participates in none of that. Those things are not even part of her universe.*

Waiting

Maggie woke with a start. She switched on the bedside light and found James doubled over, sweating profusely and moaning. The blankets and sheet were tossed aside.

"Sweetheart, what's happened? What's wrong?" Maggie gasped.

"Pain, lots of pain, and so hot."

"Where? Where's the pain sweetheart?"

"Here." James pointed to his stomach area. "And here." He put his hand to the side of his head over the stiches.

Maggie worked to control her panic. She felt his forehead. Hot. "Okay, stay there. I'll get you some sweatpants and a shirt. We're going to the hospital. You've got a fever and there's something wrong around those stitches."

Getting James to the car was much harder than Maggie had anticipated. He could barely keep his six foot frame balanced as he tried to walk and had to stop several times to rest. After several minutes of effort and increasing worry, Maggie finally got James into the Bronco and raced to the hospital.

At a quarter to three in the morning, the trip was fast. Maggie stopped in front of the Emergency Room, left James and ran in to get help. Fortunately, there were no other patients waiting and a young ER doctor raced out to the street with a nurse and gurney. They had James inside and on a bed in minutes. Maggie went back out, parked the Bronco and ran back in. James appeared to be sleeping and was hooked up to an IV drip and a pulse oximeter.

"I'm Doctor Swanson, and you are?"

"Margaret Reynolds, James' wife."

"Okay, Margaret. We're going to take good care of your husband. I'm glad you got him here as quickly as you did. Can you tell me what happened?"

Maggie fought back tears, described the original attack, the first trip to the ER, and the events of the night.

"He's going to be fine, right?" she stammered.

"We'll do everything we can to make sure of that, Margaret, but right now James is very ill. I think he's bleeding internally. His abdomen is distended and he was clearly in pain. There's blood in his urine. On top of all that, it seems that his head wound is infected. We've got him on some broad-spectrum antibiotics and a low dose of morphine for the pain. We'll need to get an MRI right away. That'll help us decide on next steps."

"Thank you," was all that Maggie could manage.

"You're very welcome. And this is Katie," said Doctor Swanson, nodding toward an attractive blond woman with a clipboard. "She's one of our finest nurses and she'll be here until eight o'clock this morning. I'll be here also, for as long as necessary."

"Try not to worry, Mrs. Reynolds," said Katie with a warm smile. "We'll take very good care of James. I'll be back in a couple of minutes to take him down to Radiology."

"Thank you, Katie. Thank you," said Maggie.

Maggie was left alone in the room with James. He was sleeping with no sign of pain, but Maggie's mind strayed to the worst-case scenario. What if he died? He was still so young, energetic and smart. He was the father of her unborn child. She loved him more than anything or anyone, more than she ever imagined being capable of. She couldn't lose him. But people *did* lose their loved ones, every day, in hospitals just like this one. Every day.

Katie stepped back into the room with a handful of forms, and Maggie signed them all without reading much of anything. Katie said Maggie could stay there in the examining room while James was getting his MRI and promised to be back within an hour. She wheeled James out of the room and pulled the curtain closed behind her.

Maggie waited. She looked at a clock on the wall: three thirty. For the first time, she noticed the quiet of the nearly empty ER. Occasionally, she could hear the muffled voices of two or three people working at the nurse's station outside. Once, a phone rang and a short conversation ensued. Someone walked up to the closed curtain of the room, paused, then continued on. Maggie waited.

When she looked up at the clock again, it was four thirty-five. *I must have dozed off. Shouldn't someone be back by now? Why is this taking so long?*

Minutes later, Maggie heard the sound of footsteps approaching. Papers shuffled outside as the footsteps paused. Then, "Knock-knock," and Katie pulled the curtain aside.

"Where's James?" asked Maggie.

"He's on his way to surgery; we're admitting him to the hospital. That's actually good news, because we know what's wrong. We can start helping him get better now."

"So, what is it? What's causing all this?" asked Maggie.

"James has some kidney damage that went unnoticed before, undoubtedly from the attack. It caused some internal bleeding and there might also be an infection there. His head wound is definitely infected, as we already knew. His temperature was dangerously high from his body's immune response, but we've got that under control right now. He's much more comfortable and Doctor Swanson says he's got a good chance for a full recovery once the surgeon does his work."

"A good chance? What do you mean? Could he…"

Katie touched Maggie's hand. "Doctor Ellis will be the surgeon. He's excellent, and he's done this kind of procedure many, many times with great success. James will be getting the best care possible."

"Okay, thank you… but… I'm scared."

"I know, I know. It's so hard to see someone you love go through this kind of thing. But the best thing you can do for James right now is to go home and try to get some sleep. He'll be in surgery for a couple of hours, then in recovery for a while. You'll be able to see him later this morning. You need to keep your energy up, for both of you."

"Can I just stay here instead?"

"Of course. Well, not here exactly, but over in the main hospital. There's a special surgical waiting area that's more comfortable and quieter. I'll take you over there and get you settled in."

Katie apologized for pushing more paper at Maggie while having her sign admitting and surgical consent forms, then walked her over to the surgical wing.

"Here's a blanket for you, and these chairs are actually pretty comfortable," said Katie as they entered a small, dimly lit room. "Can I get you some water, or coffee maybe?"

"No, thank you. You've been so kind. Thank you."

"Of course. Now try and get a little sleep, okay?"

"Okay, I'll try. Thank you."

But sleep never came. Maggie tossed her unread Newsweek back onto the pile. As much as she tried, neither that pile nor the aquarium in the corner could hold her attention for more than a few seconds. Her eyes had scanned the paragraphs and followed the fish as they explored their world for the thousandth time, but her mind refused to extract any meaning from these things. She glanced at the clock. Six eleven.

Time crept forward. The sky would show signs of morning soon, but Maggie would not see the first glow there alone in that windowless room. Outside, traffic would pick up. People would eat breakfast and go to work. Many would experience their day as nothing more than a series of "normal" events and would rue the boredom of it all. But Maggie craved normality. The mere idea of sitting across the kitchen table from James in the morning, she with her coffee and he with his tea, brought tears of longing to her eyes.

Maggie knew there were probably people in that very hospital, at that very moment, who would never again have such simple but meaningful times with their husbands, wives, or children. And there were undoubtedly others, down in the bowels of the building, who had already passed from normality, from life itself, into… what? And their families, their friends? How would they even begin to comprehend their losses? How would they continue living? For some, would it even be worth the effort?

As this darkening spiral of thought continued, the wise, wrinkled face of an older Native American woman on a National Geographic cover caught Maggie's eye. The woman reminded her of her grandmother, long gone but still very much present in Maggie's memories of warm embraces, kind words and simple advice. And one of those pieces of advice, which Maggie always valued and wanted to believe, was this: *if you wish to avoid having a bad dream about something, think about that thing, long and hard, before you go to sleep; you will only have nightmares about things you try to hide from yourself.*

That advice had seemed to work for Maggie as a child and she knew she would use it again in the coming days. She even caught herself imagining that thinking long and hard about bad things might prevent them from happening in real life, too. *But that's wishful thinking and its exact opposite at the same time!* Maggie smiled through her tears. *That's James talking. I can hear him saying those very words.*

Intensive Care

Maggie still hadn't slept by the time the door opened and an older doctor in scrubs stepped into the waiting room.

"Mrs. Reynolds?" he asked.

"Yes." Maggie rose to her feet.

"I'm Doctor Ellis and I've got mostly good news for you."

Maggie's heart both rose and sank at Doctor Ellis's use of the word "mostly."

"Please, tell me," she said.

"The surgery went very well. I was able to repair his damaged kidney; it should recover nicely, and the other kidney is fine. I don't think we're looking at a future of dialysis or anything like that. The bad news is there's some infection in the retroperitoneal space around the kidneys, and this has resulted in sepsis."

"What does that mean, sepsis?"

"It's a condition in which the body's response to infection causes injury to its own tissues and organs, and it can be serious."

Maggie sat down, speechless.

"But you shouldn't worry, Mrs. Reynolds. We've caught this early. Your husband's blood pressure is normal and that is a very good sign that things haven't progressed too far."

"Can I see him?" asked Maggie.

"Soon. We're transferring him to the Intensive Care Unit and giving him a more specific antibiotic and fluids. He'll be a little groggy from the anesthetic but he should be ready to see you in about an hour."

"The ICU? Is it that bad?"

"It's just that we can monitor him so much more effectively there and give him the best chance of a full recovery. He shouldn't have to be in the ICU for more than a few days."

"A few days?"

"Two or three, yes."

Maggie struggled to understand and accept the situation. This doctor was telling her that James had narrowly escaped death and would now be confined to a bed, hooked up to equipment designed to give him the best chance of completing that escape. *The best chance.* Maggie longed for certainty but the events of the last few days had forced her to face an unpredictable world, a world over which she had almost no control.

"Thank you, Doctor, for saving my husband's life," she finally said.

"My pleasure. I'll send someone back to get you when James is settled in. In the meantime, if you need a phone or a restroom, both are just down the hall from here."

"Thank you."

Maggie was once again alone with her thoughts. She glanced at the clock. It was late enough now to call Jennifer. But as she got up to do that, a middle-aged woman walked in the door looking distraught. Her red eyes betrayed her distress.

"Hello," offered Maggie.

"Hello."

"Are you okay? Here's a blanket if you need one," said Maggie.

"Thank you. That's kind. I guess I'm as okay as anyone who waits here. My husband had his third heart attack this morning."

"I'm so sorry. How's he doing now?"

"Not great, from everything they've told me. I'm afraid I might lose him this time."

"I think I know a little about how you must feel. My husband was mugged. They're taking him to the ICU after surgery."

161

"Oh God, how horrible. I'm sorry. Do you have kids?"

"My first is on the way," Maggie patted her belly.

"Congratulations, that's wonderful."

"And you? Kids?"

"I've got a daughter in high school and a son in junior high."

"Do you have any pictures with you?" Maggie asked, thinking the distraction might be good for both of them.

"I do, right here… here's the two of them together last summer."

"Oh, what beautiful kids. How are they coping with all this?"

"I don't know, they seem sort of shut down. I don't think they want to face what's going on with their dad. And I try to protect them but I don't know how, or how much to."

"That's got to be hard."

"It is. So, how did your husband get mugged? I hear there's a lot of blacks moving into the area now. Can't be good, right? Was it one of them?"

"My husband is black. And no, it wasn't 'one of them,'" answered Maggie with a frown.

"Oh, I'm sorry. I guess I just sort of assumed…"

"Uh huh. That's usually how it is."

"How *what* is? Are you saying I'm racist?"

"Well?"

"No! I'm the least racist person I know!"

"That's not terribly encouraging."

"Excuse me. I'm going to find somewhere else to wait." The woman started to get up.

"No, hold on," said Maggie. "I was about to go anyway. You stay here. I don't want to add to your troubles today."

"You already did."

"Look, I'm sorry, but when you said those things, it hurt. It hurt a lot. James, my husband, is the smartest, strongest, most caring person I've ever known. If he were here instead of me right now, he'd try to understand where you're coming from. He'd listen. You'd probably end up liking him."

162

"A man who listens? That'd be different."

"Yeah, well, I've got to go call my sister. I hope everything works out for your husband."

Maggie managed a short smile and walked away.

I handled that badly, she thought. *James would have done so much better. He might have even helped that woman see things differently.*

Maggie went to the restroom and then found the phone in the hallway. It wasn't the most private place for a conversation, but she managed to tell Jennifer what had happened without breaking down. Despite Jen's positive words, Maggie could tell how worried her sister was, and she drew strength from that combination of empathy and encouragement.

Then, just as the sisters were finishing up their talk, Maggie noticed a familiar figure walking down the hall toward her and smiling.

"I've got to go, Jen... Yes, thank you... I love you too. Bye."

"Katie, hi."

"Hi, Mrs. Reynolds."

"No, please, it's Maggie."

"Well then, hi Maggie. Glad I caught you. I just went off shift and thought I'd stop by and help you find the ICU. I've been following your husband's case."

"Oh, that's so sweet. Thank you. Do you have any news about James?"

"Probably no more than you've already heard from Dr. Ellis. I know he's been moved to the ICU and that he's stable. The surgery went well, and the most important thing right now is that we get his sepsis under control. Here, let's walk down there together. Have you ever been in an ICU before?"

"No."

"Okay, well, it can be kind of alarming if you're not prepared for it. There's a lot of technology around and you might feel a little overwhelmed by it. It might seem like James is the center of a big medical experiment, but all that equipment is there to help him get better as soon as possible. And the staff is wonderful."

"Thanks. I'll try to keep all that in mind."

"Oh, and don't feel that you have to be there all the time. Your presence will be a huge help to James, even when he's groggy or sleeping, but he'll need breaks, too. Resting will be a big part of his recovery. And you're going to need time away also, so take it. Never let yourself feel guilty about those breaks. They're important for you both."

"Thank you, Katie."

"You're welcome… Okay, here we are. You'll need to wash your hands before going in, and they might ask you to wear a surgical mask, too. I'll check on James over the next few days. Take good care of yourself, Maggie."

"You too, Katie. And thank you again. You've been a ray of light."

Brannon Enterprises

By the end of the year, Finn's scheme had netted over two hundred thousand dollars and he was beginning to think about shutting it all down. The risk/reward ratio was starting to feel a little heavy on the risk side. But in Finn's recent conversations with his boss, he had been pushed to continue. Brad had reminded Finn of his original quarter million dollar estimate and seemed hell-bent on getting to that number. He had directed Finn to go after one more target, this one from the lower-priority list of five that Brad had originally rejected. Finn and Cal both resisted, arguing that their current haul was secure and that another target would only put the existing money – and Patriots' Pride itself – at more risk with relatively little upside potential. They lost that argument and dutifully worked to send out one more marketing packet, this one to Brannon Enterprises in Boseman.

Having completed this task despite his own concerns, Finn decided to take another hike along his favorite trail. Since his first trek a few months back, Finn had tried to get out at least once a week, exploring the land around the compound, doing a little fly fishing, and feeling better physically and mentally because of it.

A light dusting of snow lay on the ground from a recent flurry as Finn set out. The winter landscape felt sparser and more open as the alders and maples were bare and allowed longer sightlines through the forest. Finn hiked up the now-familiar hillside and down into the valley toward the stream he had come to love. He could hear it ahead in the distance long before he could see it, playing a lighter, higher tune than it did in the summer when the water was deeper and the forest denser.

Arriving at the stream, Finn sat down to rest on his favorite log. Out there, two or three miles from the compound, Finn felt freer and more able to reflect. On his first hikes, those thoughts had been mostly confined to business tactics, maximizing revenue and minimizing risk. But then, as those tactics began to bear fruit and Finn's position solidified, he found himself straying into deeper territory. What, exactly, would they do with all this money? What impacts would Patriots' Pride have on the area, the state, the country? What impacts did he want them to have?

As Finn slipped deeper into thought, he caught some movement in his peripheral vision and turned to see what it could be. Far back along the trail, something showed itself for a fraction of a second as it passed between stands of evergreens. A deer maybe? Possibly a bear? Finn drew his handgun just in case, and waited.

Sounds. A snapping twig. Then footfalls crunching through icy snow.

When the creature finally emerged from the trees on the last bend in the trail, Finn laughed with surprise and relief. He lowered the gun.

"Elsa! What are you doing out here?"

"Following you."

"You know you could get us both in a whole lot of trouble, right?"

"I know. But Brad and Cal are both in Spokane on errands."

"And what about the others?"

"I was careful."

"I hope so."

Elsa stepped into the clearing. She was wearing jeans, hiking boots, a soft-looking sweater, and a parka. Her long blond hair was down, and it framed her pretty face perfectly. Finn felt a surge of desire, followed immediately by suspicion.

"Well, since you're here you might as well sit down. I was just doing some planning." Finn motioned to a flat space on the log near where he'd been sitting.

"Planning?" said Elsa. "Out here?" She sat, and Finn did the same.

"Sometimes if I get away from the compound for a while, things seem a little clearer."

"I do that too, not that I have a lot of planning to do," said Elsa, brushing back a lock of hair. "You know, just thinking."

"Have you been down here to the creek before?" asked Finn.

"I come here whenever I can get away for a couple of hours."

"Really? Right here?"

"My favorite spot."

Finn nodded and gazed out at the creek. "Mine too."

The presence of the rushing, gurgling water provided a welcome focal point, slowly defusing the competing tensions that Finn had begun to feel. A little eddy current along the shore seemed a stable presence amid the otherwise chaotic flow. A leaf was trapped in the circling water.

When Finn looked up at Elsa again, she was smiling with sad eyes.

"What? What're you thinking?" asked Finn.

"I need to tell you something."

"Okay…" Once again, desire surfaced.

Elsa continued. "You know the Stepton account?"

Finn's hopes deflated. "…Yeah?"

"You didn't lose it for the reasons you've been told."

"What? No, they're going out of business. They don't have the cash to do anything."

"That's what Cal told you," said Elsa, looking Finn straight in the eyes.

"Yes, that's what he said. Is he in the dark? Do you know something different?"

167

Elsa paused and looked away. "I'm afraid it's you who's in the dark, and you've been put there on purpose."

"What the hell?! What's going on?"

"I hear stuff in the Capitol sometimes. Stepton hired an environmental consulting firm in Spokane."

"Okay, so, did he learn anything? Did Cal shut him down? We've got plans to deal with stuff like that."

"Does the name 'Fairwood Environmental Consulting' mean anything to you?" Elsa probed.

"No, I don't think so... Wait, Fairwood? That's a little area just north of Spokane. That's where my ex's sister lives, I think. Oh, crap, is that the name of her little company?"

"That's it."

"Does she... does Maggie know anything about me, about Patriots' Pride?"

"Cal doesn't think so. But there's more."

"How could it be any worse?"

"Oh, believe me, it is," continued Elsa. "When Cal found out what Stepton was doing, he went down to Spokane to look into it. At first, he didn't know about your connection to the consulting company. He just went there to intimidate them and use them to shut down Stepton."

"Wait, is Maggie okay? He didn't...?"

"No, Maggie's fine. She's fine. But her husband decided to drop in during the meeting."

"Oh no."

"Apparently Cal attacked him. He was in the hospital for a while. He's out now, but still recovering. He almost died."

Finn struggled to understand what he'd just heard.

"But James is a peaceful guy. He's a philosopher, for Christ's sake. He'd never try to go after Cal, or anyone else, except maybe with words. Why the hell did Cal do this?"

"James is black."

"But still..."

"But what? James is black."

"Damnit, I get that, but aren't there other ways...?"

168

"Not here, Finn. Not at Patriots' Pride. Cal's proud of what he did. When I overheard him telling Brad about it, they were celebrating. Cal said his only regret was that he didn't kill the bastard."

"Oh."

"Finn, if this was some other black guy, if it wasn't James, would you still be asking these questions?"

"I don't know. Damnit, I don't know. Maybe. I'm so messed up."

"Yeah."

Finn and Elsa sat in silence. Finn listened to the creek and tried to hear something calming in it. But now it sounded more like noise – chaotic and confusing. A crow flew overhead, its raucous call like a rebuke.

"So, why are you telling me all this?" Finn finally asked.

"I need to know where you stand."

"Why?"

"I think we might be in the same boat. We're both getting screwed by Brad; it's just more literal for me."

"Elsa, what's he doing to you?"

"Sometimes he calls it discipline. Sometimes duty. I call it rape."

Hidden Plans

"**O**h, Elsa. I am so sorry. What is *wrong* with this place!?"

"Nothing."

"What?"

"Nothing, if you buy into the whole idea of Patriots' Pride. It's working exactly like it's supposed to," said Elsa as she stared off into the woods beyond the creek.

"Do *you* buy into it?" asked Finn.

"I did, at one time, yes."

"And now?"

"Not so much."

"What changed?"

"I guess *I* did. I followed Jim here. I thought we were doing something important, at least something important for him. I wanted to support him. And then, when he died, I started to see things differently."

"What happened to him?"

"Jim was a Vietnam vet, a Sergeant in the Marine Corp. But he saw some things, horrible things, and they changed him."

"What? How?"

"He had a friend named Stan, a First Lieutenant, and he was killed one night while Jim was on watch."

"The Viet Cong got him?"

"No, a black enlisted man in the same platoon. The guy tossed a grenade into Stan's tent."

"Another Marine? Why?"

"I guess it happened more than we've heard about. It was payback. Stan beat up another black man the night before. They were both drunk and Stan was known for his temper and racist jokes. Jim felt responsible. And then there were other things that got to Jim later on."

"Such as?"

"When the war ended, Jim came home convinced he'd be able to get a good job if he finished his degree after faithfully serving his country. He spent the next three years back in college and the year after that trying to land a job as a civil engineer. It didn't happen. He ended up working in construction."

"He never worked as an engineer?"

"No. I guess he wasn't great at interviews and he kept getting edged out by other people, some of them minorities. He became depressed, but I think it started long before that."

"I think I know how he felt," said Finn.

"Yes, I heard what happened to you."

"You know, I was so pissed off about that. But now, I don't know... So, about Jim – what happened? How'd he die?"

"Suicide."

"Damn. Why? How?"

Well, at the beginning, Jim fit right in. He and Brad would hang out drinking beer and making grand plans, sometimes into the early morning hours."

"At the beginning?"

"Yes, at the very beginning, a little over two years ago. I guess it was only about three or four months later when Jim's symptoms started to sneak back up on him. He ran out of meds a few weeks before that, and when Brad found out Jim had been on anti-depressants, he told him that 'men don't need that shit' and that Jim should just tough it out. He said that working harder toward the mission would give him all the focus he needed. Well, as a Vietnam vet, Jim knew a lot more about toughing things out than Brad ever will. But still, he let Brad get to him. Six months later, Jim was dead."

"I'm so sorry, Elsa."

"Thank you. Brad tells everyone that Jim was killed defending our compound from an intruder while he was out

171

hunting. But I know it was suicide. I watched him fall deeper and deeper into depression, but I guess I just didn't see – or want to see – how far it had gone. And besides, a combat-seasoned marine isn't likely to lose a firefight out in the woods."

"Right. So was it actually ruled a murder by the police?"

"Brad never reported Jim's death."

"What?"

"Never reported it."

"So, where is...?"

"Buried up on the hill where he shot himself – or, as Brad says, where he was killed. Brad even held a funeral for him and made him out to be some sort of martyr, which was ridiculous. But I kept quiet."

"Does he have any family?" asked Finn.

"Just his father, and he's deep into dementia, so no, not really."

"And what about you? Why did you stay here after that?"

"I didn't feel like I had any choice. I was afraid, and still pretty ignorant about what was actually going on here. When Jim was alive, Brad mostly ignored me, other than giving me cleaning and shopping orders. I'm sure he just saw me as Jim's dumb, obedient wife. I don't think he and Cal even bothered to look into my background. If they think I have half a brain, I'd be surprised. Anyway, after Jim died, I decided it was safest to keep that image going."

"What do you mean about your background?"

"I left school to come here with Jim. Not the best decision in my life. I was about six months away from a master's degree in psychology."

"Oh, I had no idea."

"Uh huh, that's the way I want it for now."

"Why?"

"It's safer, at least for a little while longer. I'm pretty sure the only reason Jim and I were accepted here was because Brad saw us as an ideal 'breeding pair.' Both of us blond, blue-eyed, strong. And now that Jim's gone, Brad still sees me that way. He

172

won't let me leave. Hasn't even let me go to the store since that last beer run."

"You mean... you and Brad?"

Elsa looked down. "It's bad. Brad's got some kind of physical problem which means he can never be a father, but that doesn't stop him from trying. He gets angry, and that makes everything much worse. You have to promise you'll never say a word about this to anyone."

"Of course not. Never."

Elsa rolled up the sleeves of her jacket and showed Finn her wrists. They were both red and bruised.

"What's this?" asked Finn, his eyes narrowing.

"Same with my ankles. He ties me down. Tells me I belong to him now. Sometimes he leaves me there for hours after he, you know, finishes with me."

Finn let out a long breath and looked away.

"Then he comes back all apologetic, with food from the kitchen. He sits there, berates himself and says not to worry, that he'll find me a real husband someday. I find that disgusting, but I try not to show it."

"A real husband?"

"Someone who'll give me babies – no, who'll give Patriots' Pride babies. It's not that easy to recruit new people from the outside."

"But little kids, living here?" said Finn, glancing back over his shoulder in the direction of the compound.

"Okay, listen to what you just said."

"What do you mean?"

"Come on, Finn, think about it."

"I don't know – I just have a hard time with the idea of kids growing up around people like..."

"Like who? Like Brad? Like Cal? Like you or me?"

"Okay, I get it."

"Finn, did you know that most of the money you've brought in is supposed to go toward building a school here?"

"What? No, Brad never mentioned that."

"There're a lot of things he's probably never mentioned. Brad wants to build a private school here so he can 'raise right-thinking kids from the get-go,' as he says. He wants to bring in kids from the local area and use the school as a recruiting tool. There'd be all the usual subjects and it'd be promoted as a conservative school with old-fashioned discipline. There'd be an emphasis on patriotism and what Brad would call 'traditional family values.' And, of course, running through everything would be the theme of getting America back to its roots, its white roots."

"So, why am I being kept out of the loop on all this?" asked Finn. He stood up, walked down to the creek and turned around to face Elsa.

"I don't know. Maybe Brad's just trying to keep you focused."

"Or maybe he doesn't trust me."

"Maybe."

"So why are *you* trusting me right now?" asked Finn.

"Well, remember that time you went out and replaced that six-pack of beer?"

"That was just a little thing. And what if I told you I was just hitting on you?"

"I'm not that naïve. I knew you were. But you were also kind, and I like to think that you actually cared about what might happen to me."

"I did. I do."

"And then there were the times you carefully avoided me after that. I know you were following Brad's orders, but I got the feeling you were also trying to protect me."

"Yes."

"And, just now, it was how you took the news about Maggie and James, and your concern about kids being here."

"Okay, but..." Finn walked farther down along the creek and kicked a rock into it.

"What?" said Elsa.

"I don't know what to think anymore."

"That's okay, Finn."

"It doesn't feel okay at all."

"Yes, I know," said Elsa with a warm and sympathetic smile. "Look, it's cold out here. Why don't we hike back down to my cabin and warm up. We can talk more there."

Fairwood

"Got your phone?" shouted Jennifer. "Wallet, keys?"

"Yep, all set," Luke replied as he loaded the last bag into the car.

A few days before, Luke had finally given in to the idea of owning a mobile phone and was looking forward to seeing how it would actually work on the road. He plugged its charger into the car's cigarette lighter socket and waited for Jennifer to lock up the house. It was just after dawn on a rainy Saturday morning and the two had decided to spend a weekend in Spokane catching up with Maggie and James. It would take them a good five or six hours to get there but Jennifer's car would make the trip much more comfortable than Luke's truck ever could.

"Do you think we should tell them about our Sunday night plans?" asked Luke as Jennifer slipped into the passenger seat beside him and buckled her seat belt.

Luke smiled at the thought. Cocktails, dinner, and a relaxing night's stay at a beautiful old hotel in Spokane might be just the thing for them right now. Besides, with James still recovering and Maggie pregnant, he rationalized, it would be too much of a burden on them to host anyone for more than one night.

"I don't know. I'm sure it wouldn't bother them one bit if we told them," Jennifer replied. "But still, sneaking around feels kind of fun, so let's not mention it."

"Right. That's obviously the way to go," laughed Luke.

Luke was the designated driver for the morning because, as he expected, the patter of the rain, the swish of the wipers, and the dark sky put Jennifer to sleep within minutes of their departure. He glanced over at his wife from time to time, smiling at her ability to simply check-out at will, and taking that as a sign of her trust in him.

As the car climbed up and over Snoqualmie Pass, Luke was grateful for the cloud cover. As stunning as the sunrise could be from atop the Cascade Range, it could also be blinding for east-bound drivers. Near the summit, the rain turned to wet snow and then stopped altogether as the road wound down off the pass by Cle Elem, through the thinning forest and onto the plains past Ellensburg. Then, as they crossed the Columbia River and the clouds broke, Luke couldn't help but reflect on the time, still less than a year ago, when he had driven this same route on the way to Quincy with an angry Amy receding into his past and a brave, beautiful Jenny waiting for him ahead. It seemed like both yesterday and a lifetime ago.

Some eighty miles farther down the road, Luke pulled into a highway rest stop. Jennifer stirred and opened her eyes.

"Where are we?" she asked, straightening up and looking out the side window.

"Ritzville, at a rest stop. I needed a bathroom break. You?"

"Yes, and maybe some coffee, too."

"Definitely."

Luke was in and out first. He stretched his back in the dry cool of the Eastern Washington morning and wandered over toward the free coffee kiosk. He poured two cups and gazed west across the plains back toward the distant mountains. But his thoughts were focused northeast on the trip ahead. Planning to spend some nice time at the hotel, he knew, was an attempt to step away from the painful confusion that both he and Jennifer now lived with. He knew that it wouldn't fix anything, but it wouldn't hurt, either, would it? Maybe it would give them a chance to talk, to process, to deal with the darkness and uncertainty. But first, they would need to be strong for their family.

Jennifer was good at that, maybe too good, Luke thought. In the last few weeks, she had thrown herself back into work, and in the evenings had come home with another task in mind

– one that Luke had recently come to think of as the "Even Keel Project." And he had been quite happy to participate at first. It did dull the pain of Finn's absence and the attack on James, but now he worried that, for all of Jennifer's talk about confronting things head-on, she was starting to do the exact opposite. Did she see this in herself and just decide it was best to plow ahead anyway? Or was she blind to it? Luke pondered these things but pushed them aside as he saw Jennifer walking toward him, smiling.

"Here you go, Jenny," he said, handing her the coffee and returning the smile. "Cream and sugar's right over there. I still don't know exactly how much of that stuff to put in for you."

"Thanks. Wow, what a beautiful morning, right?" said Jennifer, raising her hands to the sky. "Want me to drive the rest of the way?"

"Oh, sure. That'd be great."

The next hour and a half passed without much conversation as the road led gradually up through thin pine forests and finally into the streets of Spokane. To Luke, Spokane's Division Street seemed aptly named. It was such an unwelcome contrast to the natural geography of the area and seemed to pit the beauty of the high plains against the retail madness of Anywhere U.S.A.

But before long, the strip malls gave way to quiet suburbia as the road passed near Whitworth College and led up into the Fairwood area. Luke felt his shoulders relax and his blood pressure drop as Jennifer slowed the car and followed the tree-lined streets to their destination.

Maggie and James lived in a two-story contemporary brick home near the western edge of Fairwood, and its high-arched entry off the landscaped circular driveway felt welcoming as Luke walked up to it with a duffle bag slung over one shoulder and a roller-bag trailing behind him. Jennifer followed close behind carrying a bright bouquet of flowers for their hosts. Tall evergreen trees presided over the neighborhood but still let in enough light to make the place feel warm.

"James!" said Luke as his smiling brother in law opened the front door. "How are you man? How're you feeling?" The two men hugged.

"Better every day, I'd say. And you, how're you both doing?"

Jennifer interrupted as Maggie came into view. "Sis! Hey, that baby's really showing now! You look so beautiful! Here're some flowers to brighten up your dreary little hovel."

"We're good," said Luke, responding to James.

"Come on in, you guys. Make yourselves comfortable," said James. "I'd offer to take those bags up to your room but the doc would kill me, and that would probably make him feel bad about his Hippocratic oath and all, so it looks like it's up to you."

"Coffee? Tea? Maybe some lunch?" offered Maggie. "I'm so glad you're here!"

After a light lunch and a walk around the neighborhood, the four found themselves splitting up into pairs, with James and Luke outside on the back deck and the women together in the room that was to become the nursery. On the walk, Luke noticed that James limped a bit and he saw further evidence of pain as James winced while sitting down outside.

"Want a beer?" offered James. "Sorry, I should have asked earlier when we were inside," he said, starting to get up again.

"Sure, but let me get 'em. You stay put. In the kitchen fridge?" said Luke.

"Yes, thanks."

Luke returned with two opened bottles and set one down in front of his brother in law. "Cheers!"

"Cheers."

"So, are you back at the University full time again?" asked Luke.

"Almost. I'm at about two thirds now. Feels good to be back, though. My students have been amazing. I didn't expect so much expressed empathy. I don't know what I really thought would happen, but I've had so many of them come up after a lecture or during office hours and just want to wish me well, tell me how sorry they are about what happened and ask what they can do. And these are almost all white kids, too. All that, mixed with Maggie's love and care, and I'm a happy man. A little sore still, but a very happy and grateful man."

Luke nodded. "I really admire you, James. I don't think I've ever come right out and told you before, but it's true. I don't know if I'd be able to hold onto that kind of attitude if I were in your shoes."

"Well, you know, it isn't always a natural or easy thing. But the way I see it, it's about choice. I can choose to be bitter and contribute to the racial divide or I can recognize how lucky I am to have the life I do and choose to work for change. That's what I'm trying to do, not always successfully though, brother. I have my bad moments, but I like to think those are fewer and farther between now."

"What about around here?"

"What do you mean?"

"Well, this seems like a pretty conservative white neighborhood."

"Oh, it is. Definitely. Nice neighbors, though. Even a few I'd call friends. A couple of them brought dinners over for the first week I was home from the hospital. But, you know, there're always some on the other end of the spectrum."

"Oh?"

"Sure, especially some of the older folks over at the country club. I get some weird looks sometimes. I even had a cop drive up next to me when I was on a walk over that way a couple of months ago. He rolled down his window and said, 'Can I help you find something, sir?' I remember laughing and shaking my head until it became clear that the officer didn't share my amusement about the stereotypical scene he was creating. Things got serious pretty quickly until I showed him my driver's license with an address a block away."

"Did he apologize?" asked Luke.

"He did, sort of, but for all the wrong reasons. He said something like, 'Oh, Dr. Reynolds, I'm sorry. I'd heard about a professor by that name living around here somewhere but I just didn't think that, you know...' I told him it was okay, but inside I was pissed. I was thinking about my many black brothers and sisters who don't happen to have three letters after their names or don't live in places like this. That encounter probably wouldn't have ended well for them."

"No, I'm sure you're right."

Luke took a long pull on his beer and glanced around the beautifully landscaped yard. He struggled with a difficult thought before deciding to verbalize it.

"But you know what? I'm probably no damn better than that cop. I hate to admit it, but if I'm walking down the street alone and see a black man coming toward me, I get a little nervous, sometimes more than a little nervous. And that's a really shitty thing. I hate that about myself, but there it is."

"So, what are you specifically feeling when that happens?" asked James.

"I don't know. I guess a whole lot of stuff: fear, shame, uncertainty about how to act or what to say, if anything. Discomfort about what this man might think about me."

"Shame?" asked James.

Luke reached up to massage the scar at the corner of his mouth. "Sure; about the way my race has treated this man's race, and still does. And about my own apparent prejudices. What do *you* feel when you find yourself in the situation of the black man in my scenario?"

"It depends on the non-verbal cues I pick up from the white guy headed toward me. Could be anything from fear, to anger, to distrust, to a tentative desire to connect in some way."

"To connect?"

"Like you and I are doing right now, except probably on a much more superficial level. That's the best case. It almost never happens, though. Sometimes just a nod or a single word of greeting can feel like a breakthrough."

"And what if the white person coming your way is a woman? Does that change anything?" asked Luke.

"You bet your ass it does. You wouldn't believe how the old Jim Crow fears still plague most of us. I've even crossed the street or looked down at the sidewalk in a ridiculous subservient kind of way. It makes me anxious, ashamed of myself, or resentful toward the poor woman, or all three."

"Does any of this ever happen to you on campus?"

"Hardly ever; I guess because most people there know who I am. See, that's the key — knowing people, even a little bit. It can make skin color irrelevant, like most people feel about hair color."

"That's a hopeful perspective. But here's another thing I've got to admit: I hadn't really given much thought to any of this until after I met you and then when my stupid brother went off the deep end. I'm ashamed that I was so unaware, James. I suppose I'm still pretty damn unaware."

"Sure, probably. But, man, this is a great start. This is how good things can happen. Another beer?"

"Sure."

What Kind of World

J ennifer followed her sister upstairs to the nursery-in-progress. The walls were still dressed in their original antique white, pending discovery of the baby's sex. A new crib lay along one wall, a colorful toy box from Maggie's childhood adorned another, a changing table was partially assembled next to it, and an inviting oak rocking chair with a soft cushion finished off the décor. A window above the toy box looked out onto the back yard.

"I can't believe my little sister is having a baby," said Jennifer, scanning the room. "Your belly and this room are pretty convincing though."

"I'm convinced," said Maggie. "When you can't find a comfortable position to sleep in and you have to pee all the time, it's impossible to ignore, not that I want to."

"Just another month or so, right?"

"Yes. And I'm ready, Jen. I'm *so* ready to not be pregnant anymore!"

"I'm sure. I can only imagine what it must be like."

"Even though I can feel the baby kick every now and then, it still sometimes seems like I'm just getting fat, hauling around a bunch of extra weight. But I don't mean to sound so negative, Jen, I really don't. When the baby's actually here – outside of me – I know It'll be a whole different thing. There'll be a real little person in our lives, *our* little person, and I know I'll love her so much. I keep thinking it's a girl, but I'll be happy either way."

"How's James feeling about becoming a father?" asked Jennifer.

"I don't think it's really hit him, even now. He talks about it a lot and I know he's going to be a great dad, but with everything else going on, I don't think he's totally connecting. You know what I mean?"

"I think so. But from what I've heard, once the baby arrives and he sees his own child, that'll all change."

Maggie nodded. "He's never said it, but I think James is determined to be the good father he never had."

"I'm sure he is, and I'm sure he will be."

"But I also know there's something else weighing on him," said Maggie, sitting down in the rocker.

"Oh?"

"Yes, and it's on my mind, too. I like to think that the world we live in today has come a long way, but when things happen like the attack on James and the whole thing with Finn, I get really scared about the baby's future. When James and I are out together, we still sometimes get odd looks or people actively ignore us – you know, all that kind of thing. And I've pretty much gotten used to it. I'm proud of us as a couple and I like that we get to be seen out there together. But now, when I think about bringing a baby into this world, a black-and-white baby, it's really getting to me in a much deeper way. What's her life going to be like? Will she be safe? Will we have to teach her how to deal with the police later on? And what about these crazy groups like Finn's that we hear about? Sometimes it makes me so angry, and other times I just want to crawl into a corner and cry. And I know James is going through his version of the same thing."

Jennifer moved around behind the rocker and wrapped her arms around her sister. "I'm so sorry, Mags. That's an awful thing to have to deal with right now, or any time. And it makes me mad too, and sad. For what it's worth in the face of it all, you know that Luke and I love you and James, and that we're always here for you, right?"

"I know, Jen. Thank you. I love you, too. You give me hope."

"I think there're lots of reasons for hope out there," said Jennifer. "Sometimes progress seems slow and sometimes it even seems to back-track a little, like now. But I have to think that we've come along far enough in this country that the long-term direction is set. I mean, look, no matter who's in power in Washington, they'll continue to move ahead on civil rights, equal opportunity and all the rest. And there's just no way that we'll ever have a president who'll condone or ignore the kind of white supremacist hate that rears its ugly head from time to time. Our country's better than that. Your child is going to live in a better world than we do right now."

"I hope you're right, Jen. I truly hope you're right."

The Hotel

L ate Sunday afternoon after another walk, more conversation, and promises to return after the baby's birth, Luke and Jennifer made the short drive out of Fairwood and back down into the heart of Spokane. They pulled up to the old hotel they had thought about visiting for some time. A first for Luke, he handed the car keys to a valet and let the staff take the bags and park the car.

He and Jennifer stepped into a beautifully ornate lobby with heavy dark wood everywhere. Luke glanced around as the desk clerk checked them in. A fire crackled in a large stone fireplace on the other side of the room and subtly scented the air with hardwood smoke. The room's old woodwork was exquisitely hand carved, and Luke couldn't help but imagine how much Finn would have appreciated the craftsmanship. He caught himself wondering how a person who now seemed so bitter could simultaneously appreciate such beauty. It seemed like a contradiction in some fundamental way, but Luke imagined that such mental partitioning was not only possible but common.

"This is gorgeous, Luke," whispered Jennifer as they followed a bellman down the sconce-lit, heavily carpeted, silent hallway to their room.

Once inside, with the tip paid and the door closed, Luke felt himself relax. He reached out his arms to Jennifer and the two stood together in a long, silent embrace. When they separated, Luke returned the smile he saw on his wife's face but sensed something else behind it.

"What is it, Jenny?"

"Oh, I think it's just the last day and a half catching up with me. We didn't get much of a chance to talk last night, did we? Were you as tired as I was?"

"Pretty wiped out, yes. Lots of intensity. I don't know how Maggie and James deal with it all."

"I know," said Jennifer. She reached back to undo her ponytail and shook her head to let her hair flow down. "So… how do you feel about room service tonight? I know you had a nice restaurant dinner in mind, but I don't know… I just feel like snuggling with you in front of our little fireplace over there and not dealing with anyone else tonight. What do you think?"

"I'm right there with you. I think that's a perfect way to finish our weekend."

"Let's promise to always make time like this, just for the two of us, even when life gets complicated and busy," said Jennifer.

"Yes, absolutely. I love you so much, Jenny."

"I love you more."

"I doubt it," laughed Luke as he snatched a pillow off the bed and threw it at his wife.

She tossed it back, missing her mark and sending one of the bedside lamps crashing to the floor.

Jennifer, wide-eyed, covered her mouth with her hands. "Oops," she said.

"No harm, no foul," said Luke, examining the lamp. "The soft carpet saved your pretty little ass. But, you know, this means I win."

Jennifer grabbed a second pillow and this time she didn't miss. Nor did she on the next two attempts.

"Okay, okay; truce?" said Luke, still laughing.

"Truce," agreed Jennifer. "You know, you look kind of warm in that shirt. Don't you think you'd be more comfortable without it?"

"Done," said Luke. "By the way, I really like that sweater of yours, but you look a little on the hot side yourself. In the spirit of our truce, don't you think you should…?"

"Fair is fair," winked Jennifer as she pulled the sweater over her head and shook her hair back into place.

"And?" said Luke.

"You drive a hard bargain, sir. The least you can do is give me a hand here... Oh, that's better... much better."

"I couldn't agree more."

Jennifer kicked the growing pile of clothes to one side. "You know, those pants of yours are looking a tad tight. If I were you, I'd do something about that."

"You're just full of good advice tonight... There."

"And?" Jennifer continued, hands on her hips.

"You're never satisfied, are you?" smiled Luke, tossing his boxers onto the pile.

"Oh, I have a feeling I will be."

Jennifer turned around, glanced back over her shoulder at Luke, then unzipped her jeans and slowly moved them down over the tops of her hips, paused for a moment, then continued, bending over, until she had them at her ankles. She took her time getting her feet free, then straightened up and turned to face Luke.

"And?" he said.

"I don't know; I'm feeling a little shy. I might need some assistance with this last little bit."

"Jenny, help is on the way."

Luke pulled Jennifer close, kissing her neck and savoring the feel of her nipples against his chest. He moved from her neck to her mouth, softly at first, and then with more urgency. As he sensed her breathing escalate, he let his hands slide inside the back of her panties and slowly pulled them down and past her thighs. They dropped to the floor and she stepped out of them. He left her mouth, moved to her breasts, then knelt in front of her and gently separated her legs.

"Let's forget about room service tonight, okay?" said Jennifer.

"Forgotten," said Luke.

Little Dents

"That was a great breakfast," observed Luke in the car the next morning.

Jennifer smiled as she merged onto Interstate 90 out of Spokane. "Not half as great as our non-dinner last night, though."

"Not even a tenth," agreed Luke. "Although... I've gotta say, that omelet came pretty close."

Luke raised a hand to fend off a good-natured swat from his wife.

The clear, cool morning promised a nice drive as the couple headed southwest in comfortable silence for miles in light traffic. Luke glanced over at Jennifer several times to make sure she was awake and alert, and on the third time drew a response about not being such a worrier and that the morning coffee was doing a fine job. He smiled and promised not to be such a pest.

Somewhere around Moses Lake, they took a break and switched seats for the rest of the drive home. Then, miles later, while crossing over the Columbia River bridge, Luke decided to broach a subject that had been on his mind for the last couple of days.

"You up for a little serious conversation?" he asked.

"Uh-oh, this doesn't sound fun."

"Don't worry, it's not about us. Well, it applies to both of us but isn't about *us-us*, if you know what I mean."

"Nope, I have no idea what you mean, so you should probably just say it," said Jennifer.

"Well, it came to mind again yesterday when we first walked into the lobby of the hotel. I was noticing how beautiful the woodwork was, and immediately thought about how Finn would appreciate the fine detail."

"Okay…"

"And then I thought how strange it seems that someone that bitter can probably also appreciate beauty and craftsmanship. And yet, maybe not so strange, because I think people are pretty good at sectioning off pieces of their lives and protecting them from the other pieces. Compartmentalizing, I think psychologists call it."

"Sure, I think we do that all the time," said Jennifer. "I mean, if I couldn't leave Product Review meetings at work and brought home all that tension, I'd be a mess. We'd probably already be divorced."

"Come on, Jenny, don't say stuff like that."

"No, but there's an element of truth there. Somehow I can be Jennifer Mason at work and Jenny at home. It's about protection, right?"

"Yes, I think so. And about trying to stick to the stories we tell ourselves about ourselves. I guess that's protection, too – keeping our self-images intact, even when our various parts contradict each other."

"So where were you going with all this?" asked Jennifer.

"I was thinking, in some ways I'm just as bad as Finn. I mean, my life, our lives, are so far removed from the realities faced by most people of color in this country that we really have no idea what the world is like for them. And, for the most part, we don't even *try* to know. We might hold compassionate political views or even express them in public but, really, we don't know shit. And even worse, we don't do anything about it! We just compartmentalize the little knowledge we *do* have off to one side and go on living in our more comfortable mental spaces."

"Ouch."

"Right. Even the growing number of upwardly mobile black people like James still live under a social cloud and sometimes it's much, much worse than that, like it was for him. But the

190

people who haven't had an opportunity for a good education or a real career, or who've been constantly pushed down by society since birth, wow, I don't know. I really don't know. The problem feels so big. How do you even make a dent?"

"I guess it's like any huge problem – the dents count, as long as there are lots of them and each one fits into some bigger context," said Jennifer. "Look at any large software project, for example. Look at the Windows operating system. If Bill G just said, 'Okay, everyone, go write a few million lines of code that'll make PCs competitive with Apple products,' it'd be hopeless, right?"

"I'm sure it would. It'd be like me telling my students, 'go write the next Great American Novel.'"

"Exactly," said Jennifer. "You've got to break it down into much smaller pieces inside an overall plan. Look at what I'm working on these days – it's like one paragraph in a novel. Nobody who uses Windows will ever see my little contribution or even know it's there. I love it when some obnoxious guy at a party asks what I do at work because then I can tell him that I'm writing the 'garbage-collection algorithm inside the memory management subsystem inside the kernel.' If that doesn't cause his eyes to glaze over and send him wandering back to the bar, nothing will. But even so, my little piece of invisible software is absolutely essential. Windows won't operate without it."

"Makes total sense. But here's another thing," said Luke. "I really want to make a few good dents but I feel like I'm doing it out of guilt. And then I feel guilty about that, too!"

"Why the guilt? Oh, yeah, because of your brother…"

"Right, and more."

"Okay, but I really don't see what's wrong about using that as motivation. Guilt isn't such a bad thing. It's like the guardrails along our life-highways," Jennifer grinned and rolled her eyes.

"Wow, you're a metaphorical maniac this morning!"

"And you're an alliterative animal."

"Listen to us. We're compartmentalizing again."

"Yep."

Brannon Enterprises

"What's up?" said Finn as he sat down for a hastily called meeting with Cal.

"Brannon Enterprises just bit. They left a message on the machine."

"Really? That was quick."

"Yeah, I was kinda surprised myself."

"So what's the plan?" asked Finn.

"They want you to call back right away. Said they have a few questions."

"Okay, I'll get right on it. Alright if I use the phone now?"

"No problem, I've gotta run a few errands anyway. See you later."

Finn picked up the phone and made the call.

"Mr. Brannon, this is Finn Mason of Northwest Premier Properties returning your call."

"Yes, thanks for getting back to me. We got your brochure about the acreage in Spokane and we'd like to have a look at it, both my business partner and me. But first, we've got a few questions."

"Sure. Let me see if I can help with those."

"Okay, first, I'm a little confused. So you're both a real estate broker and a loan officer?"

"Well, not a loan officer, per se, no. I'm a mortgage broker who works with clients to find the best financing for their specific needs. I work with many lenders in doing that."

"And you're also a real estate broker?"

"Yes, that's correct."

"I see. Okay, so kind of a one-stop shop?"

"I guess that's one way to put it, yes. We're a full-service organization."

"Great. That's helpful. How many people do you have in your organization?"

"Seven," Finn lied. "Eight including me."

"And you're the boss?"

"I'm the CEO, yes."

"So, if I could ask, why are you dealing directly with me on this? Not that I'm complaining. But why not a salesperson? I'm just curious."

"The property owner asked me to be involved personally and I'm more than happy to do it," said Finn. "He's a long-term client and besides, I like to stay involved with the day-to-day business when I can."

"Okay, well, I guess that's a plus for me, too. So, another thing: I'm concerned about the up-front fee. Seems a little stiff."

"I understand. It might seem that way, but remember, it's ninety percent refundable when the contract is all said and done." Finn shifted the phone to his other ear and wiped his brow with the back of a sleeve.

"Assuming all goes well," said Brannon.

"Yes, of course. But as I'm sure you know from our brochure, we specialize in helping buyers who require unique financing and we take on some risk in doing that, so we have to account for that risk. Hence the fee arrangement."

"Makes sense, I guess. Just one other thing. It seems your company is running some background checks on us. Our security guy's really sharp and he detected some sniffing around. Brought it up in our staff meeting yesterday."

Finn swallowed hard and hoped that Brannon wouldn't detect the pause. "Yes, we do that with all potential clients. We're very selective."

"Well, you don't have to worry about us."

"I'm sure that's true, Mr. Brannon, but still, you must understand how careful we have to be."

"Hmm."

"Look, we run our business very conservatively. We have to. But if any of that is worrying you, maybe it'd be best for us to part ways now. I'm sure there are other properties out there and other firms you can deal with."

"No, I think we'd still like to move ahead. But I'll discuss all this with my team and get back to you within an hour. Thanks for your time."

Finn put down the phone and stared at it. *What the hell was that? We'd better be extra careful with this guy.* Finn thought about asking Brad to reconsider Brannon Enterprises but rejected the idea almost immediately. *I can't appear weak on this. I'll see what Brannon says when he calls back.*

With Cal away, Finn decided to stay in his cabin and wait for the call. He could get other paperwork done in the meantime.

Forty-five minutes later, the phone rang.

"Northwest Premier Properties, Finn Mason speaking."

"Finn, it's Bill. Bill Brannon. Have you got a minute?"

"Sure, go ahead."

"Look, I'm sorry about the third degree before."

"No apologies necessary. I understand your need to be thorough."

"Thanks. We'd like to go ahead with a showing. How about tomorrow afternoon? Could that work for you?"

"Let me check on tomorrow's schedule with my assistant. Just a sec." Finn put down the phone, waited ten seconds and picked it back up. "Okay, that'll work just fine. How about two o'clock?"

"Two it is. Look forward to meeting you at the property then."

"Great. See you then."

Finn hung up the phone. *Seems like he had a change of heart. Sounded a lot more upbeat. Strange. Oh well, let's do this.*

~

The next morning, well before dawn, Finn stole over to Elsa's cabin and knocked quietly on the door.

"Who is it?" he heard her ask.

"It's me, Finn."

The door opened, and there stood Elsa, smiling, long blond hair disheveled, wearing an unbuttoned work shirt and little else. "I'm sorry, I must look a mess. I was just starting to get ready for the day. Want to come in?"

"Are you kidding? What you call a mess is what most girls can only hope for. I call it stunning. Yesterday with you was... I don't even have words for it."

"I do. I thought it was sweet and warm. I'd almost forgotten what it's supposed to be like. Come on in."

"I wish I could spend the whole day with you, Elsa."

"Me too. But we've only got about an hour before everybody's up, so let's not waste it."

The Showing

A t twelve-thirty, Finn signed out on Cal's log, started up the jeep, and drove out of the compound through Colville and down to Spokane. He arrived at the property at one forty-five, fifteen minutes before the scheduled showing. As he walked across the open field, he was feeling confident about the day but conflicted about the future.

I'll get this deal done and that'll be it. We'll shut it all down after that. Then I can decide what to do. I could stay there and see Elsa whenever I can, but... that's not gonna fly. There's no way we won't get caught, and then what? Or, I can try to get both of us out, but that's nowhere near a slam dunk either – could get us both killed. What if I left on my own? Who am I kidding? I want to be with her one way or another.

Finn wandered over to a high point on the property where the view down to the river was best. He reasoned that this would be the optimum spot to start the conversation with Brannon. Finn would stand with his back to the view so that his client could get the best look at it.

From that vantage point, Finn soon spotted a black Ford Fairlane coming up the road. He guessed that Brannon had seen him as the car moved farther down the road and parked as close as possible to Finn's position. Two men got out of the car and waved. Finn waved back and motioned for them to come up the hill. *Must be Brannon's business partner with him,* Finn thought. *Damn, I wish I'd asked for the guy's name.*

"Hi, you must be Finn. I'm Bill," said the first man as he walked up with an outstretched hand. "And this is my partner, Jeff."

"Good to finally meet you both," said Finn, shaking hands with the two men. "Nice view, huh?"

"Not half bad," said Bill as he scanned the river below. "Not bad at all."

"What kind of development do you have in mind for this property, if I could ask?" said Finn.

"We're looking at a mixed-use kind of thing – retail space below and residential above, with natural open space and walking paths overlooking the river. As far as we can tell, the zoning fits. Is that your reading also?"

"Absolutely. That's exactly the kind of development the county would like to see here," returned Finn. "I don't anticipate any zoning problems at all."

"Great. Let's take a walk over this way. I'd like to see the rest of the land in a little more detail," said Bill with a nod toward the far end of the property.

The men walked together, discussing potential plans, until Bill stopped abruptly at one of the partially overgrown concrete pads.

"So, what was on this land before?" asked Bill.

"Just an old general store and a parking area."

"Nothing else?"

"Not to my knowledge," lied Finn.

"And this concrete? These pipes?"

"Part of the old foundation and plumbing if I'm not mistaken," said Finn, looking down at the rusted pipes.

"We've heard rumors about a gas station or something like that. Maybe some environmental issues?"

"No, I'm sure it's clean," said Finn. "I've checked the county records and, of course, you're welcome to do the same."

"As a matter of fact, we just came from there. Very interesting situation, actually." Bill nodded to his partner.

"Okay, I think we're almost done here for today," continued Bill. "Just one more thing to take care of. Mr. Mason, I'm placing you under arrest for Commercial Real Estate Fraud, Conspiracy to Commit Fraud, Blackmail, and Money

Laundering. I'm Special Agent Mark Hatch and this is my partner, Agent Jeff Abramson. FBI." He flashed a badge.

Abramson pulled out a pair of handcuffs and approached Finn. "You have the right to remain silent. Anything you say can and will be used against you in a court of law…"

A New Reality

F inn sat in a daze in the back seat of the black Ford as the two agents drove toward the center of town.

"Where are you taking me?" he eventually asked.

"Spokane County Jail," replied Hatch. "We use part of that facility as a Federal Detention Center for prisoners awaiting trial."

Prisoners awaiting trial, thought Finn. *Federal Detention Center. This can't be happening to me.*

"What then?"

"You'll get an opportunity to make a phone call. Then there'll be an arraignment within forty-eight hours."

"Arraignment?"

"That's a hearing in Federal Court. A judge will read the charges against you and you'll be asked to enter a plea – guilty or not guilty. The judge will then decide whether to allow bail or not. You might want to have an attorney present."

Finn slumped down in his seat. Guilty, not guilty, bail – these were all words that Finn never expected to hear in connection with himself. *I'll fight this!* was his next thought. But other realizations followed immediately. What the hell am I thinking? They've nailed my ass. *Who ratted on me? I've got to protect Elsa somehow. I don't give a shit about the rest of them.*

When they arrived at the County Jail, Abramson got out of the car, opened Finn's door, and escorted him to the intake area for processing.

"Federal prisoner Finn Mason," Abramson announced to the officer in charge. "Case number 13607."

Case number 13607. That's how they see me. That's how everyone will see me from now on.

"Step over here," directed the officer. "Thumb in the ink. Roll it around. Now press here. Okay, feet on the line, look at the red light."

The next hour was a blur – trading clothes, keys and wallet for an orange jumpsuit, hobbling down the hall in cuffs to the phone, the harsh sounds of the cell block, the clanging of a door.

At the phone, Finn wasn't sure who to call and the clock was ticking. *Luke? No, can't face that right now. Jennifer? Sure, like that's gonna go well. Brad or Cal? Hah! A lawyer? Maybe that guy the old real estate company used. What was his name? Oh, yeah.*

"Phone book?" Finn asked the guard.

"Right there in front of you, Einstein."

Finn shook his head, found the listing and made the call.

"Campbell, Tuttle and Rollins. How may I direct your call?"

"Lyle Rollins please."

"And your name, sir?"

"Finn Mason. I used to be with Meydenbauer Properties."

"I'm sorry Mr. Mason, but Mr. Rollins is in a meeting right now. Can I have a number where he can call you back in the next hour or so?"

"No, that won't work. I'm at the Federal Detention Center in Spokane and this is the only phone call I get today. I need to talk to him now… please."

"Let me see what I can do. Please hold."

Several minutes passed and the guard glanced at his watch.

"Lyle Rollins here."

Finn started breathing again.

"Mr. Rollins, this is Finn Mason. I met you a couple of times when I was at Meydenbauer Properties."

"Oh yes, I remember."

Yeah, like hell you do. "Thanks for taking my call."

"You're welcome. What can I do for you?"

Finn explained the situation as quickly as he could.

"Okay, first of all, have you spoken to anyone there about what you're accused of?"

"No, nobody."

"Good. Keep it that way. Not one word. The FBI might try to interrogate you. Just keep telling them you're exercising your right to have your attorney present. Second, we're going to want to get you released on bail, if the judge offers it. Otherwise, you could be behind bars for at least the next several weeks, maybe months."

"If?"

"Bail's not a sure thing in Federal cases. And it's a lot harder. If they set bail, they'll be looking for a tied-in source of money – someone who's got a personal connection with you. Not just some bail bondsman. Anyone come to mind?"

Finn sighed and gave his new lawyer Luke's name and phone number.

"Okay, I'll contact him today. Finally, you'll probably be arraigned tomorrow or the next day. I'll check the roster and be there to represent you, if you're sure you want to hire me, that is."

"Yes, I'm sure."

"Good. Now, at the arraignment, the most important thing will be your plea. Have you thought about that?"

"There's really no choice. Guilty."

"Okay, well at least that simplifies things. So my main task is going to be striking some form of plea deal. If we do this right, we'll be able to significantly reduce your sentence, maybe even avoid prison time altogether."

"What kind of a deal?"

"That depends. Are there other people involved in this? People you're willing to implicate?"

Finn closed his eyes and swallowed hard. "Yes."

~

After Finn ended the call with his new lawyer, the guard led him down the long cell block past other prisoners in their cells. Most just stared, some nodded, and one shouted something

201

incoherent. The guard stopped in front of the last cell in the row and motioned for Finn to go in. He removed Finn's cuffs.

"You're lucky," said the guard. "You would've had a cellmate but he just got transferred, so you're on your own, at least for tonight. Enjoy the privacy."

"Lucky, sure, great," said Finn.

The guard just glared at his prisoner, then shook his head, turned and left, locking the cell door behind him. Finn watched him walk slowly down the corridor, swinging his key ring around a finger.

Finn stood at the bars of the cell. *How could this happen? An hour ago I thought I was showing a property to a client. Now I'm in a fucking jail cell. Nobody at the compound probably knows where I am, and even if they did, there's no way they'd help. Except maybe Elsa, but I hope she doesn't try. Elsa.*

As Finn thought of Elsa, his mouth quivered, and a single tear escaped one eye before he could do anything about it. *Don't be a pussy, man, come on! What the hell are you doing?!*

He quickly wiped the errant tear away, turned and looked at the rest of his cell for the first time. A double bunk against one wall and a toilet against the other. *How the hell could this happen?*

Finn could hear his father's answer echoing in his head. *You're here because you screwed up again, you moron! Now you're gonna have to suffer the consequences. Won't you ever learn?! Why can't you be more like your little brother?*

Finn tried to shake his father out of his head and sat down on the lower bunk. *The pisser is that I did screw up. I should never have agreed to show that property. We knew Brannon was a risk.*

Finn lay back on the bunk and covered his face with the thin, yellowing pillow he found there, blocking out the harsh light in the cell. *Elsa was right. I should have listened to what she was saying about Patriots' Pride, and about me. I didn't know what the fuck I was doing, even joining up in the first place. I think I screwed up in more ways than one. And now I've probably lost any chance I might've had with Elsa, too. I hope she'll be okay. I hope she gets out.*

Anguished thoughts continued streaming through Finn's mind until they morphed into a dream as he slipped into exhausted sleep. In the dream, Finn and Elsa were on a Ferris wheel at the county fair. He felt the wind in his hair and watched her pull her long blond hair back and hold it over one shoulder to keep it from flying in the breeze. She was smiling. When they reached the top, the wheel lurched to a stop and the suspended seat swayed back and forth before settling down. He held Elsa's hand as they gazed at the scene below.

The hundreds of people on the tarmac looked so small; some black, some white, some in between, all of them milling about, enjoying the day. Then the wheel was suddenly much higher, and Finn could see thousands of pinpoint people across the farmland and towns nearby. And then higher still – roads, tiny cars, plains, mountains. And finally, the entire globe, blue and brown, with large swaths of white clouds, entire storm systems, all set against the infinite blackness of space.

When the wheel started again and let them out at the bottom, Finn was still holding Elsa's hand. They passed by the ride operator and Finn looked up at him, an older black man wearing a Seattle Mariners baseball cap. The man nodded at Finn and smiled. Finn smiled back.

Reading the Scale

When Luke got home from the University just after seven that night, Jennifer was there and looking worried.

"Luke, when I got here a few minutes ago the machine had a message on it. I went ahead and listened to it. You should, too. Like right now."

"What's it about?" asked Luke.

"Finn. It's about Finn. You'd better just listen to it."

Luke's mind raced through several possibilities, none of them good, as he ran to the answering machine and pushed the playback button.

"Mr. Mason, this is Lyle Rollins of Campbell, Tuttle and Rollins in Bellevue. I'm a defense attorney representing your brother, Finn. You're probably not aware of this yet, but he's been charged with several federal crimes and is being held at the detention center in Spokane. It's critically important that I speak with you today, this evening at the latest. Since you might not get this message until tonight, I'll give you both my office and home phone numbers. If it's after six, call me at home."

Luke grabbed a pen and jotted down the two numbers.

"You'd better call him now," suggested Jennifer. I'll throw some dinner together."

"Thank you, Jenny."

Luke dialed the attorney's home number and put the phone on speaker so he could easily take notes. The call was picked up on the first ring.

"Hello?"

"Yes, hello. This is Luke Mason returning your call."

"Luke, thank you for calling back."

"Of course. What's going on?"

"I assume you got my voicemail?"

"Yes, quite a shock. How's Finn doing?"

"About as well as anyone can do in county lockup, I'd say. He's okay – just trying to come to grips with his situation."

"Is he in serious trouble?"

"I'm not going to sugar-coat this or anything else we talk about, Luke. So, the answer is yes, it's quite serious."

"What are the charges?"

"Commercial Real Estate Fraud, Conspiracy to Commit Fraud, Blackmail, and Money Laundering. He was picked up by the FBI this afternoon."

"Unbelievable. I knew he'd gotten into some strange stuff, but nothing like this."

"Strange stuff?"

"I think he'd fallen in with some kind of white nationalist group."

"Hmm, oddly, that might actually help us."

"How do you mean?"

"Well, if he can somehow tie this group to these alleged crimes, the federal prosecutor is going to be much more interested in a plea deal. They're always looking for ways to go after groups like this but it's often hard to find charges that'll stick. These might."

"So, it sounds like you think Finn actually did these things," said Luke.

"All I can tell you is that he wants to plead guilty."

"Oh."

"So Luke, I have one very important thing for you to consider. Would you be willing to come up with some cash to post bail for your brother?"

"I don't know, honestly, I'd have to think about it. And anyway, I doubt if I'd be able to come close to the amount. How much are we talking about?"

"Well, given that Finn is charged with some serious felonies but is a non-violent first-time offender, my best guess is somewhere around fifty grand, but I won't know anything specific until the arraignment. And even then, it's possible the judge won't offer bail anyway."

"I don't have that kind of cash."

"Do you have any property? Sometimes the government will take a lien on real estate but not usually. Cash from a mortgage would be much better if you could pull that together in a hurry."

"I guess that would be a possibility. He and I own some land and a cabin together. But let's say that none of that works out or I just decide not to do it; what happens then?"

"Then Finn stays in jail until sentencing. Could be several months."

"Probably serve him right."

"I'm sorry?"

"There's some bad blood between us, obviously."

"Well, please give it some good hard thought. The county jail is not a nice place. I'll need an answer by tomorrow morning."

"Any chance I could talk directly with Finn before then?"

"Probably. I'll call the county and try to set up a conference call between the three of us. I need to be part of any conversation between now and the hearing. Let's plan on nine o'clock in the morning and I'll let you know if that changes. Can you call my office a few minutes before that?"

"Absolutely. Thank you."

When Luke put down the phone, his hands were shaking. "I guess you followed the gist of that?" he said as Jennifer walked into the room.

"Sounds like we need to talk. I'm so sorry, Luke."

"Me too. Sorry is only the beginning."

Jennifer nodded and leaned her head against Luke's forehead.

"I have no idea how to even start thinking about this," he said.

"Well, maybe starting with the fact that Finn is your brother?"

"Sure, but everything he's done – to you and who knows who else – that just seems heavier when I put it all on the scale. You know what I mean?"

"Yes."

"And if he's really involved with the kind of group we think he might be, then, if we help him out, what does that say about us? Where do we draw the line? When do we take a stand? Or do we just put our blinders on, compartmentalize, and call it a family issue."

"Wait a second. What did the lawyer say when you asked him if he thought Finn actually did the things he's accused of?"

"He said Finn wants to plead guilty."

"Oh... so, what could that say about Finn's state of mind?" said Jennifer. "Could it mean that he's starting to see how wrong he's been? That he's remorseful?"

"Possibly. Or he knows he's screwed and he's just trying to get his sentence reduced. He might not have any regrets at all," said Luke.

"But none of the charges have anything to do with hate crimes, right?"

"Not directly, but they sound like things a hate group might do to raise cash."

"Hmm, they do, don't they," admitted Jennifer.

"I might be able to tell where he's coming from when I talk with him," said Luke. "I've gotta say, though, he's gonna have to show me he's totally turned around before I even think about bailing him out."

"That's not going to be an easy phone call."

"No."

207

The Call

Luke got up at five-thirty the next morning and continued to wrestle with himself. He'd been doing that, unproductively, for most of the night, and sleep had been nearly impossible. Finally, he gave up and went to his desk to write. Ever since he could first remember dealing with personal problems of any kind, writing about them had been his way of processing. In committing his thoughts to paper, forcing himself to put together sentences and paragraphs that made sense, he found he could usually discover a way forward.

He picked up a pen, placed a new pad of paper in front of himself on the desktop, and wrote:

My brother has been, and probably still is, consumed with anger and hate. He has taken positions against minority races that I find appalling. He has badly mistreated at least one woman, now my own wife, and, in general, seems to have become a hardened misogynist. He has apparently joined a group whose philosophy is right in line with all of this. And now he stands accused of several serious crimes. In less than four hours, he will want to know if I will mortgage the cabin we built together so that he can make bail.

I feel infected with his anger, and maybe even hate. I never imagined myself hating my own brother, but here I am. Maybe it's not hate, per se. Maybe it's a level of anger I've never felt before and I just don't know how to interpret it. I don't want to hate Finn. And I don't want to let him drag me down to that level.

What do I want? That's really what I need to understand right now. I think I want to hear him say that he's genuinely sorry, and not just for the crimes he's committed, but especially for his hateful philosophy. But that would mean a radical change for him, and how likely is that? And could I believe anything he might say?

I guess I want us to be real brothers again, but that seems like a fairy tale. I can't see that happening for a very long time, if ever. That would mean forgiveness, and I'm having a hard time imagining ever being capable of that. I hope I'm wrong.

There is no possibility of resolving any of these deeper issues in the next few hours, but I must make a practical decision about a much lesser one. I must decide whether to leave my brother in jail while he awaits sentencing or to give him freedom. Anger biases me toward jail, I admit that. In some dark way, I want Finn to suffer.

But maybe there's another, less vindictive reason for me to deny him bail. If he gets a good plea deal, he might not get a prison sentence at all. And if I bail him out now, he'll only end up spending a couple of nights in jail, total. Maybe several weeks or months would be exactly what he needs to truly understand his situation and see the need for fundamental change. Maybe he needs to sit with his guilt for a while. I could be doing him a favor.

But, then again, there might be others like him in jail. They might just feed his anger and make everything worse.

And here's another consideration. The judge might not offer the option of bail at all. If I postpone my decision until after the hearing, I can avoid confronting Finn now and maybe never have to make a decision at all. I could still start the process of getting a mortgage, just in case. I could privately tell the lawyer what I'm doing so he'll know

I'm working on it, keeping the option open. I don't think he absolutely needs to have an answer today.

Wait a minute. What the hell am I doing?! I'm weaseling out, right in front of my own eyes! I've known what I need to do all along. I've got to make a stand here. Finn needs to feel the impact of what he's done. Even if the judge never offers the option of bail, I want Finn, and others, to see where I am on this.

Luke put the pen down and stared at the paper in front of him. *I know what I have to do.*

Jennifer walked in, wearing a robe and rubbing her eyes. She wrapped her arms around her husband from behind his chair. Luke felt her sleepy warmth. "You okay?" she asked.

"I think so. Could you take a look at this?" He handed Jennifer what he had written. "I'd like your thoughts before I make the call."

"Sure."

Jennifer read through Luke's rambling narrative and then looked up. "Are you absolutely certain?"

"Yes, unless Finn shows genuine remorse – and not just about his crimes. I can't imagine him doing that, though."

"Okay then. I'm totally with you."

A couple of hours later, after breakfast, Luke made the call to the lawyer. It went straight through.

"Lyle Rollins."

"Mr. Rollins, Luke Mason here. Before you say anything, I just need to tell you that I won't be posting bail for my brother, and here's why..."

"Luke, stop."

"No, it's very important to me that Finn understand where I'm coming from. I need to..."

"Stop. Please. it doesn't matter anymore."

"What?"

"I just got off the phone with Spokane County. I am so deeply sorry to have to tell you this, Luke, but your brother is dead."

"No, no, that can't be right… he's just… no…"

"I am so very sorry, Luke. Someone must have gotten to his food last night. They found him in his cell this morning, poisoned."

"No. Oh God, no…"

"Luke, is there someone there with you?"

"My wife. She's… she's in the next room…"

"Good. That's good. Go to her. You need her help a lot more than mine right now. We'll need to talk more, but now is not the time. I'll call you tomorrow. And again, I'm terribly sorry."

Luke put the phone down and wept.

Aftermath

The next morning, Luke rolled over in bed, turning his back to the door as he heard footsteps approaching.

"Can I call in to work for you?" asked Jennifer. "I don't think you could make it in on time even if you got up right now. And besides, you shouldn't even think about trying to work today."

"No, I'll do it. Just give me a minute."

"Luke, I'm more than happy to call."

"I said, I'll do it."

"Okay, okay. Just trying to help."

"Yeah, well, don't."

Luke heard his wife exhale, turn, and walk away.

"Wait, Jen, I'm sorry."

He heard the footsteps stop.

"I'm sorry I snapped at you."

"It's alright."

"No, it's not. You deserve the exact opposite," said Luke, turning toward the door. "You must be struggling too, and yet you're reaching out to help. I'm sorry."

Jennifer walked back into the room. "It's going to be really hard for both of us for a while. We need to stick together," she said.

"Yes, you're right, of course."

Jennifer sat on the side of the bed, touched Luke's scar gently, and kissed him on the forehead.

"Can I make that call for you now, sir?" she said with a little smile.

Luke laughed, but his eyes were wet. "Yes. Thank you, Jenny."

Luke felt his shoulders relax as he listened to his wife on the phone freeing up his day. She just knew how to handle things. She was good at life.

But life, it's so fragile. We try to control it, to protect it, and we cling to the belief that we can. But we deceive ourselves. We say, "life goes on," but one day that becomes a lie for each of us. It only applies to the collective, and even there, given enough time, our species will probably succumb to natural or self-inflicted limits. So what should we do while we're on this ride? What happens to the little bits of meaning that we find along the way? Even if they accumulate over generations, will that matter in the long run?

"What do you think about scrambled eggs and sausage this morning?" Luke heard from the kitchen. He had to smile. From a dark existential dilemma to protein, just like that.

"Sounds good."

After a quiet breakfast, as Luke was cleaning up, he found himself lost in thought again.

"You look pensive. Want to talk about it?" probed Jennifer.

Luke sighed and looked up. "I was just thinking about how I almost threw my brother under the bus. I hope he never knew."

"You mean about the bail thing?"

"Yes."

"He couldn't have known anything about that, Luke. You didn't tell the lawyer until after…"

"I know, but I could've agreed right away when I first talked to Rollins. What if he told Finn I needed time to think about it? That's almost as bad as saying 'no' right up front."

"I doubt if he even had a chance to speak with Finn after that. Don't torment yourself, Luke. You were trying to do the right thing."

"Still, I was being so damn self-righteous. I was ready to stand in judgement of him when I'm almost as culpable myself."

"How could you possibly mean that?"

"In a passive way, I guess. What, exactly, am I doing to counter the hate and division we're being forced to look at? Nothing, absolutely nothing."

"Okay, I get that. I've been thinking a lot about it, too. So far, I don't have anything specific in mind, but I met someone at work who recently joined the company and I think she might have some good perspective on this. I'm having lunch with her tomorrow."

"Oh?"

"I'll let you know if anything comes of it. Anyway, there's something else I think we should talk about. Do you think Finn would have wanted some kind of service?"

"I doubt if he ever even thought about it. I mean, I haven't. Have you?"

"I guess not, no."

"I'm pretty sure he wouldn't have wanted a traditional funeral, though."

"What about a small family gathering, like an informal memorial sort of thing?" suggested Jennifer.

"That might work. Maybe at the cabin."

The phone rang and Luke picked it up.

"Hello?"

"Luke, it's Lyle Rollins. I'm sorry to be calling again so soon, but there are a couple of things that can't wait, unfortunately."

"No, it's okay. Go ahead."

"Since you're the next-of-kin, I'm afraid you're going to have to make some decisions, things you'd probably rather not deal with right now. My firm and I can help with the detailed follow-up, but the decisions themselves must be yours."

"Okay, I understand."

"First, Spokane County needs you to come and positively identify your brother. Only you can do that, I'm sorry to say. Then, you'll need to decide about the disposition of the body — burial, cremation, and so forth. Once you decide, I can assign someone at our firm to handle the details, if you'd like us to.

Otherwise, it'll be up to you. And, finally, you'll need someone to handle the estate."

"Estate?"

"Well, there's really just Finn's half of the cabin property, his vehicle, a modest bank account, and a life insurance policy, but those things go to you and will need to be handled properly. Oh, and there's the matter of filing his final tax return."

Luke swallowed hard at the sound of the word, 'final.' "Can I call you back in about twenty minutes on all this?"

"Absolutely. I'll be here."

Luke sat down with Jennifer and forced himself to go through the details with her. In the end, they decided to handle the disposition themselves but to hire the law firm to deal with the estate and any other related items. Jennifer offered to drive to Spokane with Luke the next day but he insisted on going alone. He called Rollins back as soon as he could pull himself together.

"Rollins here."

"Mr. Rollins, it's Luke Mason. I've made some decisions."

Luke informed his newly hired lawyer and was about to close the conversation when Rollins interjected.

"Luke, I heard from the County Jail this morning about the details behind Finn's death. Do you want to wait until sometime later or would you rather know now."

"I think it'd be better now. I've been stewing over it anyway, so might as well deal with it."

"Okay. A prison guard was arrested last night and charged with Finn's murder."

"A guard? Really?"

"Yes, apparently the guy was being blackmailed and reported Finn's arrest to his blackmailer, whoever that is. Then, when Finn came in, the guard made sure he was assigned to take Finn through processing and to his phone call. Now, I feel terrible about this, but on that phone call I asked Finn to think about how he would plead at his arraignment. He said he had no choice but to plead guilty. Well, the guard must have

215

overheard that and reported back to his handler. Whoever this handler is, he must have been worried enough about Finn's possible testimony to order the guard to take the next step."

"Unbelievable. Is anyone following up on all this?" asked Luke.

"The FBI. It's still very much an active federal case, and I wouldn't be surprised if you hear from them soon."

FBI

The day after Luke returned from his duties in Spokane, he got a call at the university from the FBI. As he expected, they wanted to interview him. Not quite as expected, though, was the timing. They wanted to meet at Luke's office that very afternoon, regretting not being able to fit him into their schedule while he was in their territory. Luke was exhausted from the Spokane trip, having identified his brother's body, decided on cremation, and dealt with seemingly endless paperwork which was dry and tedious on the surface but emotionally charged just beneath. Today, he had hoped to distance himself from anything related to his brother by hiding deep in his work. But now it appeared that his meager attempt at therapy would have to wait.

After teaching his last class of the day, Luke walked back across campus and tried to steel himself for questioning. He knew so little about his brother's life after Finn left the Seattle area and wondered how much value he could really bring to the investigation. When he arrived at his office, two men in dark suits were waiting outside. Luke unlocked the door and invited them into his small workspace consisting of an old wooden desk and chair, two rickety guest chairs, one overloaded bookshelf and piles of papers.

"Thanks for meeting with us today, Mr. Mason."

"No problem. But it's Luke, please."

"Okay Luke, I'm Special Agent Mark Hatch and this is my partner, Agent Jeff Abramson."

"Pleased to meet you both. Here, have a seat. How can I help?"

Luke sat behind his desk and pushed some papers aside.

"First of all, we want to say how sorry we are for your loss."

"Thank you."

"Our job now is to find the people who controlled your brother's killer and get to the bottom of their scheme. We just have a few questions. It shouldn't take up too much of your time."

"Not a problem," said Luke. "I've taught my last class for the day."

"So, you're a professor here?"

"Not technically a professor. An instructor. I teach undergraduate writing courses."

Abramson retrieved a small notebook from his inside jacket pocket and began taking notes.

"And your wife? Does she work?" asked Hatch with a glance at Luke's wedding band.

"Yes, she's a software developer at Microsoft." Luke considered bringing up Jennifer's prior relationship with Finn but dismissed the idea.

"Any other relatives in the area?" Hatch continued.

"Finn was my only direct relative anywhere. My in-laws live in the Spokane area."

"What do they do there?"

"My brother-in-law, James, is a professor of philosophy at Gonzaga University and his wife, Maggie, runs a small environmental consulting firm."

"And the name of that firm?"

"Fairwood Environmental Consulting."

Abramson continued writing and Hatch paused, then continued.

"Were you aware of Fairwood's involvement with the property where Finn was arrested in Spokane?"

"Uh, no. What kind of involvement?"

"They were advising a potential buyer about the property's environmental status."

"Oh, you mean the old truck-stop property? Maggie mentioned something about that. Said it was damn near worthless because of the underground tanks and pollution."

"That would be the one. Finn was trying to sell it using a scheme in which he could extract money from the buyer up front and then terminate the contract using blackmail. We think he'd been successful in doing this several times before one of those buyers decided to risk blackmail and report the fraud."

"My brother did *that?*"

"I'm afraid so. Does the name Northwest Premier Properties mean anything to you?"

"No, it doesn't ring any bells. Finn worked for Meydenbauer Properties."

"How about Patriots' Pride?"

"Nope."

"Are you certain about that?"

"Yes, absolutely. I've never heard of either of those companies."

"Patriots' Pride isn't a company. We think it's a fledgling white nationalist organization that your brother might have been involved with."

"Okay, now that makes some sense, I'm sorry to say."

Hatch looked up with raised eyebrows, prompting Luke to continue.

"When Finn lost his job, he blamed it on the Affirmative Action program. He'd always been politically conservative, but for the longest time I thought his objections to things like Affirmative Action were just based on typical right-wing positions; you know, pro-business, anti-regulation, small government, that sort of thing. Maybe racism was always part of it, I don't know, but I never really saw it in Finn until then."

"When he lost his job?"

"Yes."

"Did he say anything about joining a group like Patriots' Pride?"

"He never mentioned a group by name, but he did talk about some new friends that understood his anger and frustration. I got the sense they were linked with some fringe groups in the Pacific Northwest."

"Did he mention their location?"

"Not specifically, but just before he disappeared, he talked about taking a trip up somewhere in the northeast corner of the state, somewhere near Colville, I think."

Hatch glanced at Abramson, then continued.

"Luke, what do you know about your brother-in-law's mugging earlier this year?"

"Well, I know it was bad. James nearly died as a result of it. But what does that have to do with any of the rest of this?"

"We're not sure yet; probably nothing. Just wondering if there's anything more you might know about the circumstances."

"No, not really. I wish I could be more helpful."

"You have been, Luke, and we appreciate your time."

With that, the interview was over.

Sacrifice?

"How was your day?" asked Jennifer as Luke walked through the door.

"Kind of crazy, actually. Spent the end of it with the feds."

"The FBI came to see you today?"

"Yeah. They weren't there long but it wasn't something I expected to have to deal with today. Still, I'm glad it's done."

"Did you learn anything new?"

"Not really. They asked a lot of questions but I think they knew the answers to most of them before they even asked."

"Checking on your credibility maybe?" asked Jennifer as she handed Luke a glass of wine and sat down with him.

"Probably. They mentioned James, his mugging."

"Really? Is there some kind of connection?" asked Jennifer.

"I don't know, and I don't think they do either. Still, it seems way too coincidental. Maggie was working on something with the same property that Patriots' Pride – that's the name of Finn's group, I found out today – was trying to sell."

"You don't think Finn would've done anything like that, do you?"

"Damn, I'd hate to think so but, I don't know anymore. It's like I never really knew my brother."

"Right; same here."

So, what about *your* day? Isn't this the day you were gonna have lunch with your new friend at work?" asked Luke.

"Linda, yes, she's great. She works in marketing and has tons of good ideas."

"About?"

221

"Mostly education. Remember our talk about making small dents in big problems?"

"Sure."

"Well, I've been doing some thinking about how we could maybe make some of our own, and Linda's been super encouraging about that."

"So, tell me."

"I was thinking, okay, you and I both have skills we could share with others – skills that could help lift people out of poverty or motivate them to go on to higher education. I'm thinking young women and minorities in particular – people who've been pushed to the side and denied a good shot at high-tech careers. What if we were to start a nonprofit organization that provided free or near-free training in computer programming and writing for these folks? I mean, can you think of two more valuable skills in the workplace today?"

"No, those would be right up there, I agree. But how could we ever find the time to do something like that?"

"We'd have to start small, really small. Maybe just a couple of students a week, maybe weekends or evenings. More like tutoring for now."

"What about equipment? How would we get computers? And software?"

"That's one way Linda thinks she can help. She's already got great connections at the company – all the way to the top – and she thinks Microsoft would donate older machines as we upgrade them, which we do all the time. This fits right in with the company's vision of personal computers in every home and on every desk. The more we educate people, the more potential there is for that vision to become reality. But we'd still need funding for things like rent, electricity, desks – that kind of stuff. I don't think we can rely on the company for any of that."

"Yeah, there is that little problem. We can't afford to put much into this, not if we ever hope to buy a house in the next few years."

"Well, what about the cabin?" said Jennifer.

"We can't live up there."

"No, no. I didn't mean that. I know you love the place, Luke. I do too. It's a very special place for our family. But, at the same time, the property tax is now all our responsibility – not just half of it. And on top of that, there's maintenance, insurance and all the rest. We could be free of all that."

"Right, but no, I don't think I could ever sell it if that's what you're suggesting."

"I understand, I really do," said Jennifer, touching Luke's arm. "I'm just trying to help us think about all the possibilities."

"Sure, but not that. It means too much to me. Finn and I built that place. You and I basically met there. It's our Thanksgiving place. There's just got to be another way. I need to go grade some papers."

Luke's tongue probed the scar at the corner of his mouth as he walked away. *How could she even bring that up right now? Doesn't she understand what I'm going through?*

Luke read two student papers before he realized he wasn't giving them the attention they deserved. He'd given them both a "C" but couldn't remember why. He put them back in the pile, shook his head and decided to revisit them when he got around to the rest.

Wait a minute. She's just being reasonable. She knew I was thinking about mortgaging the cabin to bail out Finn, so maybe she was just... No, that's different. That's not an outright sale; we'd still have the place. But, okay, what about a mortgage? Maybe that would be a good way to pull together enough cash to start a nonprofit. We could figure out a way to make the payments. Cut back on other stuff. Maybe find a cheaper place to live.

"Jen?" he called from behind his pile of papers.

Small Infractions

"He had real promise," said Brad between forkfuls of breakfast. "Pisses me off it had to go this way."

"We didn't have a choice," answered Cal. "We would've been screwed to the wall."

"Right; no doubt. That fucking Brannon. What the hell happened? I thought you had some bad shit on him."

"I did. But, remember, he wasn't one of our top ten."

"Don't throw that back at me, Cal. If you had any doubts you could've pushed back."

"I tried, remember? So did Finn."

"Yeah, well, not hard enough," said Brad. "Anyway, let's move on; we've got other shit to deal with. Any other messages from your go-between in Boise?"

"About the guard, you mean?"

"Yes. I'm worried about bleed-through."

"No, it's been quiet. There's no way the guard will connect us to this."

"You sure?"

"Sure as I am about anything."

"You're not building my confidence here, you know that."

"Not my job, boss."

"Okay, okay, you're right. I appreciate everything you do. I really do."

"Thanks."

The two men ate in silence for the next several minutes, there alone in the Capitol. Outside, the sun was starting to break through the morning clouds. Finally, Brad spoke again.

"Okay, next steps. You know how to dissolve an LLC, right?"

"I'll figure it out. I'll dig through Finn's notes and get the money transferred to a new account for starters."

"That part's done. I took care of it yesterday in town."

"The money?"

"Yeah. But let's get that LLC off the map right away, okay? And the phone number too."

"I'll work on it today."

"Good. By the way, have you seen Elsa around recently?" asked Brad.

"No. Not since yesterday morning, I guess. Why?"

"No reason. It's just that she's usually here by now for cleanup."

"She'll show up."

"Uh huh."

Cal nodded, got up and headed for the restroom, leaving Brad alone with his thoughts.

She should be here by now. Where the hell is she? These dishes aren't gonna do themselves.

Brad decided he couldn't let that kind of irresponsibility stand. *Let even small infractions go unpunished and you'll eventually lose control.* He got up from the table, leaving the breakfast dishes there, and headed out the door. He would pay a little visit to Elsa and set her straight. But on his way to her cabin, he passed by the gravel parking area on the far side of the Capitol and was immediately struck by its emptiness. His truck was gone. And so was Finn's trailer.

Elsa's Epiphany

A few days earlier, while scrubbing the floor in the kitchen, Elsa overheard bits of a quiet conversation between Brad and Cal as they entered the Capitol. Clearly, they had no idea she was there, down on the floor out of view behind the cooking island. She froze as she learned that Finn had been arrested in Spokane and would plead guilty to fraud. Cal was trying to convince Brad that they should act quickly and decisively, but Elsa could only hear fragments of the conversation and it wasn't clear what he intended. Still, it sounded ominous.

Fortunately for Elsa, it was between mealtimes and the two men had evidently come into the building not for food but for a quick private discussion. She stayed motionless there on the floor and waited. Minutes later Brad and Cal left, apparently having reached a decision, and Elsa was able to breathe freely again. But her heart was still racing.

After assuring herself that the men were gone and weren't likely to return immediately, Elsa resumed working on the floor, but her mind was elsewhere. *What will happen to Finn? What can I do? Probably nothing, as usual. But I can't stay here. This is Hell. They've created a piece of Hell on Earth and I've been a part of it. I've got to do something, If not for Finn then against these bastards.*

As Elsa finished the floor and walked back to her cabin, she was already formulating a plan.

By the weekend, she was ready. She woke to her alarm at three in the morning, went to the bathroom and got dressed. Her one bag was already packed, and a quick look around the cabin assured her that nothing was left behind – nothing that mattered, anyway. Two hundred fifteen dollars in cash, pilfered from grocery money over the last year, would have to do for a while. Quietly, she opened the door, took one last look up toward the trail that she and Finn had hiked, and walked down to the parking area at the far end of the compound.

Elsa had used Brad's truck many times to run errands and knew that the keys would be in it, hidden under the floor mat. On her way to the driver's side door, she passed by Finn's trailer with his kayak still in it. *No, that's not in the plan,* she reminded herself. *But, when Finn gets out… I know he loved that boat. No, I shouldn't. It's too risky.* She hesitated, feeling an unsettling combination of adrenalin and early morning indecision. *Oh, what the hell. I'm probably screwed anyway.*

Elsa tossed her bag onto the truck's front seat and walked back to the trailer. As quietly as she could, and with as much strength as she could muster, she slowly pushed and pulled the trailer into position at the back of the truck and hooked it up to the hitch. Finally, she stole over to Cal's old car, the only other vehicle on the compound, and took the keys from under its floor mat. She threw them as far as she could, into the woods. *Does he have a second set? Don't think so. Never seen him use any other keys.*

At this point, Elsa knew she had already gone far beyond any possibility of explaining her actions if caught, so the next step of starting the truck's engine didn't add much to her already high anxiety and the dull pain in her stomach. She just hoped the Capitol would block the sound enough from the rest of the compound for her to leave undetected.

The truck started with a low rumble and Elsa drove away without waiting for the engine to warm up. She stopped only to open the gate, then drove through without closing it. Glancing back through the rear-view mirror, she saw the Patriots' Pride sign, faded and barely readable in the moonlight. *Pride in what?*

Several minutes later, Elsa was off the dirt road and in town, then on the highway headed south. Checking the fuel gauge, she found the tank nearly full. *One piece of luck. But I'll need more than that.* With the exception of a few long-haul trucks, the road was empty and Elsa flew past Spokane at around five o'clock as light crept along the edges of a cloudless sky.

I should stop and try to do something for Finn. But what? He's in jail. I'd just complicate things and make matters worse, not to mention putting myself at risk. I'll try and contact him after I'm safe in the next few days. She drove on.

Elsa had an aunt living in Woodinville, a small town across Lake Washington from Seattle, and that was her destination. She arrived unannounced around ten, after stopping for breakfast in Snoqualmie and taking the back roads from there. Aunt Kathryn, never married and now a retired librarian, had been the only family member who had ever taken Elsa seriously. Her parents never had. But Elsa hadn't seen her aunt in years and wondered if she knew anything about her bad choices and where they had taken her.

Kathryn's was a single story, natural cedar-sided house with a welcoming covered entry and a carved wooden door adorned with a large and colorful inlayed peace sign. The home was situated on the banks of Bear Creek and surrounded by acres of forest. Elsa recalled the many times in her late teens when she had escaped from the world to sit with her aunt on the back deck overlooking the creek. Sometimes they would talk. Sometimes they just sat in silence, listening to the soothing sound of the water, something Elsa craved when things got bad at home. Kathryn – or Aunt Kay, as Elsa had always called her – just seemed to know when to ask about things and when not to. And now, some ten years later, what did Elsa want her aunt to ask?

Elsa parked the truck, walked up to the door of the house and knocked. A lady in her sixties, slim, with pulled-back graying hair, a long tie-dyed skirt, a peasant blouse and an enquiring smile, opened it.

"Can I help you?" the lady asked.

"Aunt Kay?"

"Elsa? Oh my gosh – come in, sweet girl! What a surprise! I didn't even recognize you. You're all grown up!"

Grown up? Maybe. Sweet? I don't think so, thought Elsa as she accepted a hug from her aunt. "Thank you! It's so good to see you again. I'm sorry to just drop in like this."

"Oh, Elsa, you know you're always welcome here. Come on in. What brings you here? No, wait, can I get you some herbal tea? Then we can sit and talk."

"That would be wonderful. Thank you so much."

As her aunt busied herself in the kitchen, Elsa glanced around the house. Not much had changed. The big throw rug in the center of the living room hardwood floor. The hanging curtain of beads marking the entrance to the hallway. The large stone fireplace. The old overstuffed couch and chairs. One of Kay's own paintings of a forested Lopez Island shoreline hanging above the fireplace. Several full bookshelves and a large collection of vinyl records with the first Grateful Dead album cover showing on the end. A photo of Elsa when she was ten or eleven. And the large window looking out toward the creek with a padded window seat in front of it, one of Elsa's favorite places to sit and read so long ago.

"Did you see many salmon last Fall?" asked Elsa loudly toward the kitchen as she looked out on the creek. Her aunt was part of a volunteer effort to count the fish as they fought their way up the many streams to spawn on the east side of Lake Washington.

"Fewer than last year, I'm afraid. But, anyway, I just love seeing them. They're inspiring. So persistent. Kind of like you, dear one," said Kathryn as she came back into the living room and set a tray down on the coffee table in front of the couch.

"I really don't know about that," said Elsa, smiling and shaking her head. "Oh, you made your almond muffins!"

"Yes, I haven't done these in quite a while. For some reason, this morning just felt like a good time to bake. Oh, and those are a few 'special' ones there on the left, if you know what I mean. Help yourself!"

"Well, lucky for me. I will!"

Kathryn had never offered weed to Elsa when she was young, but neither had she ever attempted to hide its presence. So, partaking now seemed completely natural and, as Elsa convinced herself, it might just help her tell her story and ask for what she needed. She chose one of the muffins on the left and took a bite.

"Yum, thank you Aunt Kay. Just what I needed."

"Good. That's good. Now, tell me. What've you been doing with your life?"

Catching Up

As Kathryn's 'special' almond muffin slowly began to work its magic, Elsa opened up about her years of isolation. It was relatively easy to describe her struggles getting through college, since Kathryn already knew most of that anyway, including the discouragement doled out on a nearly daily basis by Kathryn's brother, Elsa's father. He had always done his best to convince Elsa that she would never be able to use a college degree, even if she could manage to get one, and that she should just go get a 'normal girl's job.' Elsa's mother hadn't stood up to her husband, and that had been almost as hurtful as the direct attacks on Elsa's self-esteem. But she had persisted, partly to spite her parents, partly because of Kathryn's support, and partly because, by the time her junior year rolled around, she had begun to realize that the study of psychology truly interested her.

It had interested her enough to make her listen to the department chair when he encouraged her to pursue a graduate degree. She'd been flattered by this attention, and the prospect of delving more deeply into a field that had helped her make some sense of her own life was compelling enough to get her started. And it was almost enough to get her through.

But, as she now admitted to her aunt, she let two things get in her way and drive her into isolation. The required advanced mathematical study of statistics had been rough and had allowed the background noise of her father's voice to reassert itself. See? *You'll never be able to do this! You're just getting deeper in debt, and for what?* And then there was Jim.

231

Jim had come into the picture at a bar a few blocks off campus in the University District. Elsa was there trying to decide what to do with her life over a gin and tonic one evening when Jim walked in after work at a nearby construction site. He was tan, blond, nicely muscled, and with a classically rugged, handsome face that both captivated and mystified Elsa. What was in that smile he tossed her way? She saw a certain wistfulness in it, and she took it as an invitation to explore. It seemed to promise much more than the usual come-on.

As Elsa understood now, and described to Kathryn, she had fallen in love so quickly and so intensely that she failed to recognize the potential of the simmering anger that both powered and consumed this man. She craved the intimacy that came from prying Jim open, from helping him – as she saw it – confront his Vietnam demons and the battles he faced after coming home. She longed to be on his side, to empathize and support. But the fact that her support was never really reciprocated didn't occur to Elsa until much later. Her infatuation and her naïve belief that her own very limited psychological training could help her "fix" this otherwise perfect man, led her further down the path of self-deception.

It wasn't until after she and Jim were married a year later that Elsa began to admit to little bits of that self-deception. But just little bits, and those were easily suppressed or rationalized. Then, when Jim had excitedly introduced the idea of going to live with a group of "like-minded people" in northeastern Washington, Elsa had seen the light in his eyes and jumped at another chance to support him, to help him get better. The idea of like-mindedness had just seemed like extra words in a sentence about adventure and renewed intimacy.

"Aunt Kay, I'm so ashamed of my own ignorance. I never paid any attention to politics, or social issues for that matter. You'd think that someone who'd been studying the inner workings of the human mind wouldn't be so blind."

"We all have our blind spots, dear," said Kathryn.

"Hmm." Elsa took the last bite of muffin with a sip of tea and then continued. "I remember you telling me about the time you were in the March on Washington in the early sixties, how you heard Martin Luther King Jr. speak, and how you protested against the war. I was so young and stupid. I just thought of all that as a history lesson – one I wasn't very interested in learning. And, believe it or not, it wasn't until I'd been at Patriots' Pride for a few months that it began to dawn on me that I'd become part of something reprehensible, something you had personally fought against. I think Jim and the others tried to hide most of it from me, but I could easily have seen it if I hadn't had my head so far down in the sand. But then, when Jim died, I started to experience the hate, the lies, and the humiliation directly. That opened my stupid eyes to the broader picture. It wasn't just about me."

Kathryn's questioning look reminded Elsa that she had neglected to fill in some important details of the Patriots' Pride experience. She described Jim's covered-up suicide and her subsequent but slow enlightenment about the organization's real purposes. Then she rolled up her sleeves and showed her aunt the rope burns on her wrists.

"Oh, my poor dear girl," said Kathryn, reaching out to hold Elsa's hands in hers. "Who did this to you?"

Haltingly, Elsa told her aunt about her captivity and the abuse at Brad's hands. Kathryn listened intently, slowly moving her head from side to side, tears building in her eyes. Seeing this, Elsa changed the subject to Finn, his kindness toward her, his arrest in Spokane, her hopes for him and her worries about his safety.

"What did you say Finn's last name was?" asked Kathryn, to Elsa's surprise.

"I didn't say. Mason, I think."

"Oh dear."

"Why?"

Kathryn just sat there, eyes closed, slowly shaking her head. Then, after a long sigh, she opened her eyes and looked up at her niece.

"Elsa, sometimes there's just too much shit in the world to bear at one time."

"Aunt Kay!" Elsa smiled through a developing cannabis haze.

"No, I'm sorry dear. Just too much shit."

Elsa's smile disappeared as she stared at Kathryn, waiting for an explanation. Had she disappointed the only family member she had ever trusted? Was it that she'd stayed away so long, keeping all this from her aunt? Were her decisions and experiences just too awful to contemplate?

"Aunt Kay? I... I'm so sorry."

"No, it's nothing like that. I guess you haven't read the paper this morning."

"No, I almost never do. Too depressing."

"Yes, well, this is worse. For some reason, an article on the back page of the Seattle Times caught my eye this morning. A young man named Finn Mason died in Spokane County Jail last night."

Home

"Oh." Elsa got up and walked to the window. Outside, the stream flowed by, leaves rustled in the late morning breeze and a shaft of sunlight revealed the amber, brown and pale stones beneath the water. Elsa knew if she stepped out onto the deck, she would hear and see life everywhere. To her, all of it seemed at once beautiful and indifferent – beautiful in its entirety, in the balance of plants, animals, water and sun, but indifferent to the fate of any single organism. Within the scope of Elsa's view, she guessed that thousands, maybe millions, of tiny creatures were just beginning their journeys while just as many were ending theirs. And yet, the entire tableau was stable, peaceful, as though none of the comings and goings mattered in the slightest.

"How did it happen? Did the article say?" she asked.

"Poisoning. A guard's been charged with murder."

"Oh."

"Did you know him well, Elsa?"

"Just starting to."

"Would you rather not talk about it right now?"

"Could I have a little more tea?"

"Of course, dear. I'll be right back."

Elsa walked back to the couch and sat with her head in her hands. *I guess I was right when I drove by Spokane this morning. There was nothing I could've done.*

Kathryn came back into the room with a fresh cup of tea. "How can I help, sweet girl?"

"You're helping right now, just being you. I've missed you so much. I'm sorry I've stayed away for so long."

"I've missed you, too, Elsa. But I knew you'd be back someday, and here you are."

"Here I am, selfish as ever." *And not a sweet girl.* "I haven't even asked about you. I'm so sorry. Please, tell me how you are and what you've been doing."

"Are you sure you don't want to talk about Finn?"

"Yes, I'm sure. Not right now."

"Okay, well, I'm doing fine; just the normal getting-older aches and pains I guess, but I'm loving life after retirement."

"Do you miss working at the library?"

"Oh yes, sometimes. I miss the children mostly. But I still volunteer once a week for story time. I get my kid fix that way, I guess."

"I bet they absolutely love you," said Elsa.

"Well, I don't know, but they always seem happy to be there."

"Of course they do. So, tell me, what else are you up to?"

"Oh, a little of this, a little of that. Some local political work for progressive candidates. Working on the never-ending marijuana legalization efforts – no surprise there I guess! Gardening, always. And I'm writing a memoir."

"Really? That's wonderful. How far along are you?"

"It's hard to say, actually. I think a little over halfway. Even if no one ever reads it, it's been good for me."

"I would love to read it. Would you let me?"

"Of course, if you really want to. Maybe after I get just a little further along with it."

"Okay, I'll keep asking. Oh, could I use your bathroom. It's been kind of a long trip."

"Oh gosh, of course dear. What am I thinking? Just make yourself at home."

When Elsa returned, Kathryn was again busy in the kitchen, this time putting together sandwiches for lunch.

"You're always thinking of others, aren't you," said Elsa.

"I got the munchies. Thought you might, too," Kathryn smiled.

When the two women sat back down to eat, Kathryn asked, "Is there anything else you'd like to tell me about Finn? I get the feeling there is, but I don't want to pry, so…"

"No, you're right; there's more. I just can't believe he's gone."

Kathryn nodded.

"He was a smart guy, but very confused. Conflicted, I guess you'd say."

"In what way? Why?"

"He was a conservative gone bad. That's kind of the way I think about it."

"I thought they were already that way," laughed Kathryn. "No, I'm sorry, I don't mean that. Just a terrible attempt at a joke."

"That's okay, I get it. No, what I mean is I think Finn always had a sort of independent, every-man-for-himself, keep-the-government-out-of-my-business kind of outlook on life. And he depended a lot on his career for his sense of self-worth. He didn't get much, if any, from his parents. So, when he lost his job to a new guy who just happened to be an African American, I think he felt like he lost a lot more than the job. Just my stupid armchair psychological diagnosis, probably nothing more."

"No, that's your father talking. It sounds right to me. What do you think he lost?"

"He took it all very personally, I think because it felt like someone was taking away a big part of his identity. His political views were part of what remained, and they gave him a natural path forward. I think he clung to them, but they weren't enough. He was afraid and wanted to feel strong again. So he followed those views to their limits. But ironically, he knew he couldn't get there on his own. He needed someone or something to blame – people of any color other than his. People who, in Finn's view, were taking America away from its rightful owners, taking it away from him. He just about lost his soul, Aunt Kay."

"Just about?"

"Yes, like me, but for different reasons. I was clueless and self-centered, still am. He was angry and afraid, but I think he knew what he was getting into. Both our souls were dying. It's no excuse, though. What we did, what we were a part of, was unforgiveable, hateful, destructive."

"But you said, 'just about.' Do you think he would have turned around?"

"Maybe. There were some things he said when we last talked that made me think so. At least I wanted to think so. And I wanted to think that he and I might somehow get out together."

"Did you love him?"

"I don't know. It was too soon. I'd barely started to know him. Maybe."

"But you miss him."

"Yes."

Kathryn nodded and picked up her sandwich. She and Elsa ate in silence for the next few minutes. Then Kathryn changed the subject.

"So dear, what will you do now?"

"I guess I'll look for a place to stay and try to figure out how to make some things right. Maybe go back to school."

"Well, part of that is easy."

"Oh?"

"Yes, of course! You can stay here. I'd love it if you would."

"Are you sure about that? I don't want to invade your paradise."

Kathryn placed a hand over her heart and smiled. "I'm absolutely sure. And there's no invasion. You've always been a part of this place, in here."

"Thank you. Thank you *so* much. I love you and I don't deserve you."

"I love you too. And stop letting your father's voice tell you what you do or don't deserve."

In Deeper

The next morning, Elsa looked up the number for the FBI office in Seattle while Kathryn prepared breakfast. Elsa had wrestled with her thoughts all night and finally settled on a rough plan, one she outlined for her aunt over coffee.

Later, when they sat down to eat, she continued. "There's just one thing I'm really worried about. It's giving me second thoughts."

"Oh? What's that?"

"The guys at Patriots' Pride are hard core. They're so sure they're right about everything that nothing and nobody else matters. I've heard about some things they've done and now I'm almost certain they were behind Finn's death too. They're dangerous, Aunt Kay. I'm worried about you, about doing anything that could possibly expose you to them."

"Thank you, dear, but don't let that distract you. I've taken a few risks in my time and I'm never opposed to doing it for the right reasons. This is a right reason. And besides, you need more protection than I do. When you talk to the FBI, you need to be clear about that, right up front."

"I will. And I want to meet them somewhere other than here. Somewhere neutral. Maybe down in Kirkland. The thing is, though, I want to hand over Brad's truck, since I, you know, sort of stole it. So I'll need to get a ride home. Could I possibly call you after the meeting is over?"

"Of course. Tell you what; let me give you my new mobile number. I'll run some errands nearby and come pick you up when you call."

"You've got a cell phone? Wow, I'm impressed."

"Hmm, well your old aunt isn't completely out of it," Kathryn smiled. "But just so you know, you can try to hide from Patriots' Pride, and that's a good thing, but keeping secrets from the FBI is a lot harder, believe me. You're better off not even trying."

"Ooh, sounds like there's a good story in there somewhere."

"Maybe it'll be in my book. We'll see."

Elsa wasn't sure what to make of her aunt's comment and just laughed. "Okay, I'm gonna make the call now." She went to the phone in the kitchen and dialed the number.

"Federal Bureau of Investigation, Seattle office. How may I direct your call?"

"Hello, I have some information about a case in Spokane that I'd like to provide."

"One moment. Let me transfer you to an agent."

Moments later... "Special Agent Harris. How can I help you?"

"Yes, hello. My name is Elsa Jorgenson and I have some information related to the Finn Mason murder case in Spokane."

"Okay, we appreciate that, Ms. Jorgenson. What would you like to tell me?"

"I want to do this in person, if you don't mind. A public place in Kirkland would be best."

"Well, Ms. Jorgenson, our resources are stretched pretty thin. If we sent out an agent to follow up on every tip we get, we'd never get anything done. I'm sure you can understand."

"Mr. Harris, I was a member – more like a captive – of a far-right group in Eastern Washington. Finn Mason was also there. I think I know why he was killed and now I fear for my own life. I want to speak with you or someone at the FBI, face-to-face."

"So you knew Mr. Mason personally?"

"Yes. Do you want my information or not?"

"We do. Where would you like to meet?"

Elsa gave Harris the address of a restaurant near the marina in Kirkland and suggested they meet at two o'clock. They settled on one-thirty and the conversation was over.

~

That afternoon, Elsa unhitched Finn's trailer from Brad's truck and, with help from Kathryn, moved it and its cargo into an unused part of her oversized garage.

"You've got a truck, too?" asked Elsa in surprise, looking around.

"That and my trusty old VW Bug," replied Kathryn, nodding toward the far end of the garage. With all the gardening and landscaping work around here, I decided I needed a truck a few years ago. But I use the VW for everyday stuff. You remember it, I'm sure."

"Definitely. You picked me up from school in it. Seems like so long ago."

"Well, it was."

Elsa drove down to the Lake Washington waterfront in Kirkland and parked near the restaurant. She was ten minutes early, as planned, and selected a window table. Moments later, a tall, slender man with short hair, wearing a dark suit walked into the restaurant and scanned the dining room.

So predictable, thought Elsa with a smile. She was about to get up and introduce herself when the man walked over to another table and sat down laughing with a group of two others. *Okay, I guess that'll teach me something about stereotyping.*

At one thirty-five, Elsa glanced down at her watch and missed a young woman coming through the entrance. When she looked up again, the restaurant hostess was directing the woman back toward Elsa's table. She appeared to be about Elsa's age, was dressed in a dark blue pantsuit and wore her light brown hair in a bun.

"Elsa Jorgenson?" the woman asked, approaching the table.

"Yes, hello."

"Hi, Elsa. I'm agent Sue Dorn. Sorry I'm a bit late. Thanks for meeting with me today." Agent Dorn held out her badge for Elsa to examine.

"Thank you, too. I appreciate you taking the time."

A waitress appeared and took their orders, temporarily halting the conversation. When she left, Agent Dorn continued.

"I know you probably expected Special Agent Harris. He was called away on an emergency and asked me to step in. As it turns out, I've been keeping track of the work in Spokane anyway, so this is good."

"Sounds like it. But I have to admit, I wasn't expecting a woman. Terrible, huh?"

"No, don't worry about it. I'm used to it. I'm still kind of a rarity at the Bureau."

"Well, anyway, I'm glad. Makes me feel a little more at ease."

"Good. So, Harris tells me you knew Finn Mason?"

Elsa told Agent Dorn everything she knew about Patriots' Pride, the names of the members, their white nationalist philosophy, the real estate scam, the probable reason for Finn's murder, and Elsa's own virtual imprisonment. As she was wrapping up, Agent Dorn jumped in with another question.

"Elsa, did Brad or anyone else at the compound ever mention any other group they were associated with?"

"Brad always thought of himself as the ultimate leader. I think he wanted to build a kind of white homeland around himself up in that area. But I only remember hearing him talk about one other person as a true leader of the movement. He must have really revered the guy."

"And who was that?"

"I think his name was Richard Butler. He's in Idaho somewhere."

"The leader of a group that calls itself Aryan Nations," said Agent Dorn.

"Yes, I've heard that name. That's the guy."

"Okay, that's helpful. Thanks. Oh, by the way, I noticed your ring. Are you married?"

Elsa paused, having forgotten about the ring and its implications. *Oh no. This could be really bad. But I'd better just lay it all out there. It'll all come out sometime, somehow. Better now than later.*

"Elsa?"

"Sorry, this is painful. And complicated."

"Okay, just take your time."

"Yes, I was married, to a man named Jim. But he's dead now."

"I'm sorry. How long ago did he die?"

"Almost two years now. He and I were at Patriots' Pride together and he took his own life, at least I'm convinced of that. Brad says it was murder, by someone outside the group. I never believed him. Jim suffered from deep depression like a lot of other Vietnam vets."

"Again, I'm so sorry. But how did the court rule on it?"

Elsa closed her eyes and sighed. "Okay, this is the complicated part."

"Alright..."

"His death was never reported."

"Never reported?"

"Right. He's buried in the forest on the hill behind the compound. Brad didn't want to draw any attention to Patriots' Pride."

"Well, it's got attention now."

Hope

"Jenny? Look, I'm sorry I'm being such a jerk," said Luke as he came back into the living room. "Let's talk more about your idea."

"About selling the cabin?"

"Well, sort of. What if we took out a mortgage on it? We could use that money to get your nonprofit started."

"Luke, it can't just be *my* nonprofit if this is going to work for us. It's got to be *ours*. If we do this and you're not really into it, it could end up being a huge problem for our marriage, and nothing's worth that."

"Right, I totally agree."

"And also, it would be a pretty expensive way to go. Did you know that mortgage rates are almost ten percent right now?"

"Uh, no."

"Well, they are. And if we pulled out, say, seventy-five thousand, and if it was a thirty-year loan, then we'd be looking at about six or seven hundred dollars a month. That's more than our rent."

"Ouch. So you've already thought about this, obviously."

"A little. I've got a spreadsheet on my computer at work."

"Of course you do," smiled Luke. "Look Jenny, I'm totally with you on this, a hundred percent. I really want to offset some of Finn's damage and I think you're onto a great way to do that. I guess we just need to keep thinking about how to finance it... Wait, hold on a second..."

"What?"

"Maybe Finn can help."

"Uh...?"

"I just remembered something our lawyer said. Remember he mentioned a life insurance policy Finn had? He was going to get back to me this week about wrapping things up and I bet that's part of it."

"I wonder how much it's worth?"

"Probably not a lot, but hey, if it means we could trim the loan down to a more manageable size, then who knows? It would be so cool if Finn could be the one to make this all happen. I don't know if he'd laugh or cry."

"I love this idea, Luke! What do you think about calling the lawyer right now?"

"I think yes, I think we should do that."

Just then the phone rang. Luke and Jennifer looked at each other. "No," said Luke. "It can't be."

It wasn't.

"Hello?" said Jennifer, putting the phone on speaker so Luke could join in.

"Jen, it's James. Great news here. Raza has arrived!"

"Raza?"

"Our new son! And Maggie was amazing!"

~

On Saturday, Jennifer was up at five in the morning and Luke had a cup of coffee made and placed in the car for her trip to Spokane. She had packed the day before, and Luke doubted she'd slept much during the night. He hadn't seen her quite this excited since their own wedding day, and still, this was different. It was like the new seven-pound eight-ounce addition to the family had switched on something in Jennifer that Luke had never seen before. Invisible now was the methodical software developer, and on full display was an ecstatic, even giddy, sister and aunt.

"Keep your mind on the road, okay Jenny?" he said as he waved goodbye. "I love you!"

"I love you, too! Call you when I get there!"

Luke walked back into the house, shaking his head and laughing. He too was thrilled for James and Maggie and he'd loved their several recent phone calls. But Jennifer's response was qualitatively different. He marveled at it.

Even a call on Thursday from the lawyer about the insurance policy had been largely covered up by the news of Raza's arrival. It wasn't as though Luke and Jennifer weren't happy about their fifty-thousand-dollar insurance windfall – they definitely were. It was just that the news of their expanding family felt so much more significant. To Luke, it felt like the perfect antidote to his brother's hate and divisiveness. Raza came from love, from the union of black and white, and the child gave Luke hope.

Intention and Action

While Jennifer was reveling in aunthood and trying to give her sister the gift of rest, Luke was struggling to plan a memorial service for his brother and finding the task to be even more difficult than expected. His third cup of coffee was half gone and still no words were on paper, no plans were gelling.

For what seemed like the hundredth time, he glanced at the simple urn of ashes sitting on the edge of his desk. *How do we celebrate a life so marred by hate and bitterness? Just emphasize the good parts? No, that's a dishonest attempt to ease our own pain and guilt. Somehow, we have to come to grips with the whole of his life, flawed as it was, flawed as we are.*

It was. We are. That's the key.

Finn was gone, and all that visibly remained was this urn of inertness, this collection of material purged of all vitality, all consciousness. *But* we *remain. We are still here, and Finn has left us with a gift, even if he hadn't intended to. He left us with the will to change ourselves and whatever small part of the world we can reach. He has jolted us into action, given our lives new meaning and purpose. Now it's up to us to follow through. In that indirect way, we can honor him.*

With this thought in mind, Luke's hand moved easily across the page. Within a few hours, he had written the first draft of a eulogy and had come up with a basic approach to the entire memorial. It would be an informal family event and would be held at the cabin. Luke would speak first and would then invite anyone else to offer their thoughts. They would scatter Finn's ashes in the lake. But they would postpone it all for a few months so Maggie and James could safely bring Raza with them.

247

When Luke pushed back his chair that afternoon, he felt relieved. But he also reminded himself not to confuse intention with action. And so, he placed a call to his lawyer.

"Lyle Rollins here."

"Lyle, this is Luke Mason."

"Hi, Luke, what can I do for you today?"

"Well, first of all, I want to thank you for everything you've already done. Jen and I appreciate it so much."

"You're more than welcome. Glad to help."

"And now I'm looking for a little more help on something else."

"Okay, sure."

"Two things, actually. The last time we talked about Finn's insurance policy, I think I mentioned that Jen and I want to use that money to start a nonprofit?"

"Right."

"Would you be willing to help us get it set up?"

"Absolutely. Be happy to. There's somebody in the firm who'd be perfect for that. I'll ask him to call you."

"Good, thank you. And second, we're going to need a little more cash than the insurance provided, so we'd like to take out a small loan on our cabin. Can you recommend a good mortgage broker?"

"Yes, as a matter of fact, there's a woman we've used at Meydenbauer Properties, and my wife and I have also worked with her personally. Janice Mendelson – I'd recommend her highly. Just a sec, let me get her contact info."

Luke wrote down the information and called Ms. Mendelson immediately after he finished the conversation with his lawyer.

"Mendelson Financial Services."

"Oh, hello, may I speak with Janice Mendelson please?"

"Speaking. What can I do for you?"

"My name's Luke Mason and I got your name from Lyle Rollins, my attorney."

"Oh yes, sure. How can I help?"

Luke explained the situation briefly, touching on his brother's death, the insurance policy, his and Jen's desire to create a nonprofit organization, and their need for some additional funding. He concluded by describing the cabin property and asking if Ms. Mendelson would be interested in finding an appropriate loan for them.

"Yes, I'd love to work with you on this. If I could just ask a few questions, we could actually make a start today if you like."

"Yes, definitely. Fire away."

"First of all, how much equity do you think you have in the property?"

"Well, it would be a guess, but we do own it outright. There aren't any other loans. Based on what I've seen around that area of the North Cascades, I'd say the cabin on its forty acres is probably worth close to two hundred thousand."

"Okay, and how big of a mortgage were you hoping to get?"

"Around twenty-five thousand. Actually, we'll want to end up with that much after all costs."

"That shouldn't be a problem. Do you and your wife both work?"

"Yes, she's at Microsoft and I'm at UW."

"Excellent."

After a few more questions, Jan promised to get back to Luke with some lender options and to set up an appraisal of the property. Luke thanked her and hung up the phone, feeling good about the day.

The Real Deal

A t Patriots' Pride, Cal and the rest of the crew were packing up a rented moving truck. Soon after Elsa's departure, Cal had picked up some alarming chatter out of Spokane, and Brad had made a painful decision: they would abandon the compound, at least temporarily, and move the operation to Hayden Lake, Idaho. A much larger group there had offered protection.

Cal watched while Ted and Jonathan hefted his safe into the truck and closed the heavy pull-down door. After removing his car's rear license plate, he connected the car to a tow-bar and hitched that to the back of the truck.

"Damnit!" he spat as the hitch pinned his thumb against the metal mount. He pulled out the bloody mess and stared at it. "Shit! Hey Brad, is there a first aid kit in this rig?!"

"Haven't seen one," said Brad from the driver's seat. "Come on, we've gotta get going. Just wrap it up in your shirt."

"Hurts like a son of a bitch."

"Okay, but you know what? I don't really give a shit right now. We've gotta go. Now."

Cal grumbled but climbed into the passenger seat. Jonathan, Ted, and Steven were already waiting in the cramped crew-cab in back.

"Wave goodbye, ladies," said Brad as the remaining members of Patriots' Pride passed under their faded sign above the gate.

No one waved, no one spoke, and no one looked back.

~

About an hour down the highway, Cal spotted a blue flashing light in the passenger side mirror. "Crap!" he said, turning toward his boss.

"You still complaining?" said Brad.

"Check your mirror."

"Shit."

Brad slowed and was ready to pull over when Cal motioned for him to continue.

"See that dirt road down there to the right? Take that and stop down there instead."

"Why?"

"Just trust me."

Brad turned onto the side road and stopped about fifty yards down in a wider area.

"Okay guys," said Brad, looking back at the rest of his crew. "Remember the story. Cal and I are moving to Walla Walla and you guys are helping. Stick to that and we'll be fine."

Cal felt for his weapon under his jacket and clicked off the safety. Through the mirror, he could see the State Patrol car pull up and stop behind them. The officer was on the radio, taking his time. Finally, he got out and approached Brad's side of the truck.

"Morning, gentlemen. License and registration please," said the officer. "And next time you're pulled over, stay on the main road."

"Just didn't want to block traffic, sir. Wasn't much of a shoulder. So, what's the problem?" asked Brad, digging for his wallet.

"Did you know the car you're towing doesn't show brake lights when you slow down? Noticed that on the curve a couple of miles back."

"Damn. We must've forgotten to hook it up. Sorry officer."

"Hmm, looks to me like there isn't even any wiring for that. How many folks have we got back there?" said the officer, peering through the window into the crew cab."

Brad didn't answer.

Cal glanced back through the side mirror. *No partner in the cruiser. Good.*

"License and registration?" repeated the officer.

Brad handed over one of his several licenses and the truck's registration.

"So, Mr., uh, Campbell, where you fellas headed today?" asked the officer as he scanned the license.

"Walla Walla."

"Uh huh. Pretty big truck. What're you hauling?"

"We're moving – me and Pete here," Brad nodded toward Cal. "So, you know, furniture, kitchen stuff, clothes. The other guys are helping out."

"So, Pete. Looks like quite a lot of blood there. How'd that happen?"

"I, uh, crushed my thumb hooking up the tow bar back there," said Cal.

"Doesn't have anything to do with that gun you're carrying?" said the officer, looking at the bulge under Cal's jacket.

"No sir."

"You got a concealed-carry permit for that?" continued the officer.

"Sure," said Cal. "It's probably stored away somewhere in the back; oh, wait, I've got it right here." He reached under his jacket.

The officer grabbed his radio with one hand and went for his gun with the other. But Cal was faster. If it hadn't been for Cal's injured thumb, it might have only taken one shot past Brad, who instinctively leaned back into his seat. But it took two. The officer was down.

With the shots still ringing in his ears, Cal couldn't hear what Brad was saying but it was clear he wasn't happy with the situation.

Cal decided to ignore his boss and do what had to be done. He put on a pair of gloves, tossed another pair at Brad, got out

252

of the truck and dragged the officer's body back to the cruiser. "A little help here!" he yelled back toward the truck.

Brad ran back, red-faced and cursing, but helped Cal get the body into the back seat. Cal got in and drove the car another quarter mile down the dirt road and off into a wooded area where he left it. *This'll buy us a little time,* he thought as he ran back up the road.

When Cal got back to the truck, Brad was livid. "What the hell was that!? Now we're screwed!"

"Maybe, but not right now," said Cal. "Would've been right now for sure."

"What a choice."

"Well, sometimes that's all you get."

Brad drove his followers back onto the highway and continued the trip in silence for several minutes as the gravity of their situation sank in. Finally, he spoke.

"We've got to get off 395 as soon as we can."

"I know a back way out of Loon Lake," said Cal. "It'll cost us a few hours but nobody goes that way unless they're local."

"Anything to stay out of sight. Let's do it."

Twenty minutes later, the truck was off the highway and on a winding rural route through forest and farmland heading east.

"Look guys," said Brad. "When we get there, we're gonna be under their control for a while. That's just the way it's gotta be. They're pretty structured, disciplined, as they should be. Good men. But eventually we'll be on our own again, so don't worry."

"What's their name?" asked Jonathan from the back seat.

"Aryan Nations. Run by a guy named Richard Butler. He's the real deal," replied Brad. "Like us."

Pride's End

S pecial Agent Mark Hatch glanced at his watch and took another sip of coffee. He and his partner, Agent Jeff Abramson, had been at one of the two roadblocks just outside Hayden Lake for hours, waiting in their car while State Troopers did the tedious work of stopping and searching vehicles. They were looking for the suspects in the murder of another State Trooper. The unfortunate victim had radioed in a routine traffic stop earlier in the day and had described the vehicles involved but hadn't responded to follow-up calls. A search had quickly located the car and the officer's body.

The FBI agents were there because they had heard about the abandonment of the Patriots' Pride compound early in the day and had information from their Seattle counterparts about a likely destination for the group. Mark Hatch had strongly suspected a connection between the officer's murder and the compound's abandonment, and this gave him an immediate opportunity to go after the group. He had been planning a raid on the compound for the next day anyway, but this moved things ahead more quickly and, he hoped, would involve less risk. Still, someone had killed a State Trooper and that signaled desperation. And desperation signaled danger.

Hatch's radio crackled with a call from the other roadblock just above Hayden Lake on southbound 95. They had stopped a moving truck with a car in tow which matched the description called in by the fallen officer earlier in the day. It took the agents less than two minutes to get there.

The scene, which must have been chaotic just moments earlier, was now stable. One man, short and stocky with a prominent black beard lay dead in the street with a gun still in his hand. Another man – bald, fit, and with a large lion tattoo on his neck – was in handcuffs along with three others.

Six Months Later

It was September, and the scattered deciduous trees among the evergreens of the North Cascades were just beginning to reveal hints of yellow and red as Luke and Jennifer drove up the road to the cabin. As always, they stopped at the gate for their arrival ritual.

"I love you, Luke Mason."

"I love you, Jenny Mason."

They parked the truck, made their way down to the dock and basked in the lake-view sunshine before opening up the cabin. The Spokane contingent would arrive in about an hour and they wanted everything to be ready, especially the babyproofing. Jen covered all the electrical outlets near floor level while Luke brought in a supply of firewood and fitted a screen around the hearth. He placed a photo of Finn on the mantle next to a single candle and thought about the eulogy he would soon give his brother. He would look at this photograph, then at the upturned faces of his family, and would try to make sense of a bewildering life cut short. But the eulogy he had written suddenly seemed much too formal and embarrassingly pompous. He felt an irrational panic set in, as if he were about to deliver a deeply flawed talk in front of hundreds of people in a sprawling cathedral.

Thankfully though, that spell was broken when Jennifer asked if he would please start the generator. He smiled and walked outside to complete the task. But on the way to the generator shed, Luke passed by the single remaining kayak under the edge of the cabin and the sight brought unexpected tears to his eyes – tears that wouldn't stop no matter how hard he willed them dry. He slumped down on a log at the edge of the forest and, for the first time, fully yielded to his grief.

In those moments, looking back with blurry eyes toward the cabin and the lone kayak, Luke let go. He let go of his confusion, his anger, his failure to help, his deep sadness, his brother. Two things remained: an urn of ashes, and hope. One, tangible but inert. The other, intangible but shining with potential. This is what he would talk about today. This would be the simple story.

With tears finally stopping, Luke got up from the log, walked over to the generator, and started it.

~

Later, as he finished repairing a baseboard in the cabin, Luke heard the crunch of gravel outside and looked up to see the Bronco with its doors opening.

"Jenny, they're here!" he called toward the kitchen.

Luke opened the cabin door to see his brother-in-law lifting Raza from a car seat. Maggie was pulling a big bag of baby paraphernalia from the back seat. Jennifer joined him and they walked out to greet their family together.

"Raza," said James. "This is your Uncle Luke!"

The baby looked up at his uncle with wide dark brown eyes, and burped.

"Well, Raza," said Luke, smiling broadly. "Welcome to the family. I think you'll fit right in!"

"You've grown up so much since I saw you six months ago!" Jennifer said to her nephew in a high voice that Luke hadn't heard from his wife before. "Can I carry him in for you, James?" she asked. I want to show Luke how to

"Sure. He's replaced floppy with squirmy, so he's both easier and harder to hold. Here you go."

Luke watched with awe as Jennifer seemed to know exactly how to lift the baby from James's arms and hold him to herself.

Remembering Maggie with her load of stuff, Luke turned to help her. "Here, Mom, let me give you a hand. You have one handsome little guy there!"

Maggie put her things down and hugged her brother-in-law. "Thanks, Luke. I couldn't wait for you to meet him."

The family of five walked together into the cabin and settled in. Jennifer sat in a chair near the fireplace holding Raza, playing peek-a-boo and chatting away happily. Luke helped with the bags and stole glances at his new nephew and enthralled wife.

Jennifer must have noticed this and called out to Maggie, "Is it okay if Luke holds him for a minute or two?"

"Yes, of course."

"I don't know, Jen," said Luke. "I've never done this before. I don't want to break the little guy."

"Don't worry, I'll show you how. Here, pick him up under his arms, bring him to your chest and support his bottom. Like this. There, you've got it. Now, just keep one arm under him and support his neck and head with the other. See, you're a natural!"

"Hi, Raza," said Luke.

Raza wriggled around, as if to look for his mother or Jennifer, and began to cry.

"I'm sorry," said Luke, as Maggie came back into the room.

"No, nothing to be sorry about," she said. "He just doesn't know you yet. That'll all change by the end of the weekend, I'm sure."

Maggie left her baby in Luke's arms while she talked softly and reassured her little one. The crying stopped and was replaced with a smile that Luke felt was directed at him. He relaxed and smiled back.

~

Later that afternoon, when Raza awoke from a nap, everyone gathered in the living room as Luke stood by the fireplace with a sheet of paper in hand. The family sat in a circle with Raza exploring the floor in the middle which Maggie had filled with stuffed animals. Luke watched as his nephew paused over the faded old Thanksgiving bloodstain in the floor, apparently interested in the contrast it made with the surrounding wood.

Luke cleared his throat, lit the candle on the mantle next to Finn's picture, and began.

"First, thank you guys. Thanks for making the trip up here today to remember my brother." He held up the paper in his hand. "I, uh, wrote something for the occasion but when I read it again this morning, it just seemed wrong – way too formal for one thing; and much too long. I mean, it's just us, right? If Finn could've read it, he probably would've called BS after the first two sentences anyway. So, instead, let me just talk for a minute. Then Jen and I have something we'd like to ask you."

Luke brought the paper with his prepared remarks up to the candle and touched it to the flame. He tossed it into the fireplace as it burned, then turned back to his family.

"I loved my brother. And I almost hated him. I came pretty close, and that scared me. I'd be willing to bet that all of us, except of course Raza, went through something like that, each for his or her own reasons. Finn gave us plenty of those.

When Finn was alive, I hung onto a vague hope that maybe he'd wake up one day and come back to us; that he'd have some sort of epiphany and try to repair the damage he'd done. And that crazy hope, I think, was what kept me from crossing all the way over the line to hate. But now that he's gone, what have we got to replace that?"

Luke reached down and pulled Finn's urn from a box at his feet.

"Well, we have this: Finn's physical remains. It's just inert ash, not even any recognizable DNA, I'm told. Not a lot of hope there."

"But *we're* still here," he continued, placing the urn next to the flickering candle on the mantle. "Maybe we can use the darkness we saw in Finn as well as the light I once saw in him as a kid and a young man, to push us forward. There's real hope in that, if we act on it."

Luke looked down at his nephew playing with a stuffed bear on the floor at the center of the family. "And for me, little Raza is the best symbol of that hope we could possibly have. In fact,

Jen and I would like to ask for your permission to name something after him."

Maggie and James looked at each other with raised eyebrows, and then back at Luke as he continued.

"Jen and I have been working on an idea that we think could bring meaning to Finn's death, even to honor him in a backwards sort of way. Finn left us with a life insurance payout. We want to use that, in combination with cash from a small mortgage on this cabin, to set up a nonprofit educational organization for people of color and women who find themselves at a disadvantage competing for jobs or trying to get into college. We'd like to call it the Raza Academy."

James and Maggie exchanged a few quick words and looked up, smiling.

"We'd love that," said James. "And I'd like to think if Finn could look down on us now, with a wiser after-death perspective, that he'd have a good laugh at the irony of it all and raise a glass to the Raza Academy."

Life Changes

"Thanks for dinner, again," said Elsa, pushing back from the table with some effort. "I'll get the dishes."

"Oh no you don't, mom-to-be," said Kathryn. "You look tired. Just come sit and keep me company in the kitchen. You haven't said much about your day. How are things at the U?"

"Oh, they're fine. But it feels like this last push is gonna be the hardest; and definitely the longest since I'll need to delay a couple classes for six months or so." Elsa patted her expanding belly and smiled.

"Of course. But you know, whenever you're ready to go back, I'm here, like I've told you before."

"Aunt Kay, you're my angel. But are you sure you're ready to take care of a little one?"

"More than ready. I'm excited about it."

"I don't know what I would have done without you."

"You would've found a way."

"Hmm, wouldn't've been a great one, though. I might've had to track down Finn's relatives and beg for help. That's the last thing I'd ever want to do."

"Don't sell yourself short, dear. Look how far you've already come. Have you thought any more about what you'll do with your degree?"

"I think I'm pretty settled on becoming a psychotherapist. I'll need to do some clinical work as part of the degree and then I want to work with people suffering from depression. And with people struggling to make major life changes."

"It won't be just academic for you, will it? You'll be able to bring some serious real-life experience to your work. Your patients will be the lucky ones."

"We'll see," said Elsa. "Right now I feel like the lucky one."

Intersection

"Luke, I'm scared," said Jennifer on the ride home from a New Year's Eve party at the University where much of the discussion had centered on the new nonprofit. She and Luke had described their rented building in the Rainier Valley, talked excitedly about the computer donations from Microsoft, and tossed around ideas for a writing curriculum.

"Scared of what? Everyone was so encouraging tonight."

"I know, I know. It's just that, I mean, look at us! We're just a couple of white folks with a lot of guilt who think we have some kind of grand plan to parachute in and help black folks."

"Is that really what you think this is?" asked Luke. "You think it's all about guilt?"

"No, not entirely. But don't you think some of it is?"

"Sure, but it's a lot more than that," said Luke. "When did you start feeling this way? I thought you were really into this whole thing – especially the way you were talking tonight."

"I went down to the building yesterday."

"You didn't tell me about that."

"I know, and I'm sorry. I wanted to, but I started having these doubts and I thought if I kept quiet about it, maybe they'd just go away. And then tonight, everybody was having such a great time and, you know, I just didn't want to spoil it."

"Okay, so tell me. What happened yesterday?"

"You know how the building has that big store-front window? Well, I went in and sat down on the concrete floor in front of it and watched people walk by outside while I drew up a plan for arranging desks and computers. And pretty soon, I wasn't planning anymore, just watching."

"What did you see?"

"I saw a whole lot of life I know nothing about. I saw people who were obviously homeless shuffling by – mostly black but a few whites and Hispanics. I saw groups of young black teenagers coming home from school with no books or backpacks. One kid waved at me and smiled. Another little guy – couldn't have been older than twelve or thirteen – took a cigarette out of his mouth, spat on the window and flipped me off. I saw older guys and girls cruising slowly by in cars. One of them came to a stop just outside the window, and a guy, maybe sixteen or seventeen, made a gun shape with his hand and pointed it right at me. After that, I moved to the back of the building and waited until things slowed down outside. Scared the living hell out of me. There's so much anger and frustration there, Luke."

"I'm so sorry, Jenny. Please don't go back there alone, okay?"

"Okay."

"Those people couldn't have had any idea about why you were there. Probably thought you were some rich lady planning to open a boutique or something. Maybe if they knew…"

"Maybe," said Jennifer. "But, at the same time, I have no idea what's behind their actions either, what their lives are like every day. We're so naïve, Luke. Are we even doing the right thing?"

"I… I think so. I don't know."

"I don't know either."

The two drove on in silence for the next few minutes. Finally, Luke spoke up.

"Why don't we call James tomorrow and get some advice?"

"Really? Because he's black?"

"No, because he's wise. Okay, yes, partly because he's black. I just think he'll have another useful perspective on this."

"You're right; it's a good idea."

264

~

The next day after a late breakfast, Luke and Jennifer got on the phone with James. Together, they filled him in on Jennifer's recent experience, being open about their doubts and fears and asking for advice. But when they finished, James was silent.

"James, you still there?" asked Jennifer.

"Yes, just thinking. Give me a moment."

Luke and Jennifer looked at each other and waited. Finally, James spoke.

"Okay, first, don't give up. I think the basic idea is sound, but you're probably going to have to approach it differently. What might feel like a friendly offer of help to you will probably look like an invasion to them. It's a clash of cultures. You can't think of yourselves as rescuers. You can't just bring a piece of white culture into a black neighborhood and expect to be accepted, no matter how noble your motives. There's just too much history, too much legitimate distrust."

"So, where does that leave us?" asked Luke. "Sounds impossible."

"It's not impossible; just really, really hard," said James. "I think you're going to have to forget about moving any computers in for a while, and about teaching any writing classes."

"But... that's the whole point," said Luke.

"Is it?" said James. "Because if it is, you'll fail."

"Great," said Jennifer. "Terrific. So what *is* the point?"

"Well, that has to be your call, but I'll give you my opinion if you want it."

"I'm sorry, James. Yes, of course we want it," said Jennifer. "Just a little frustrated here."

"I understand," said James. He paused before continuing. "I think you've got a great opportunity to help form an intersection between the two cultures, a real connection with depth and authenticity. I think the point should be relationship."

"You mean we should just scrap the idea of the academy and do something different?" asked Jennifer.

"No. Education is vitally important. No, what I'm saying is that you have an even bigger opportunity here, and the educational component can become a natural part of that. In my view, neither culture should ever be fully assimilated into the other. The goal of education is not to convert black to white or vis versa. It's a way for each culture to discover the attributes of the other. It's a way to find and broaden the intersection between the two, not to replace one with the other. Again, this whole thing should be about relationship. It's about living in that intersection."

"Yes, that feels right. Exciting even," said Jennifer. "But abstract."

"Okay, so let's take it down a level or two," said James. "What if you were to invite the community into your new place and just tell your story? Honestly tell it. Lay it all out there –fear, guilt and Finn included. And then ask the people to tell theirs. Have a conversation. Don't assume too much about where you'll go from there. Listen and use what you hear. Resist the urge to make too many plans up front. Does any of this make sense?"

"To me it does," said Jennifer. "Luke?"

"Actually, yes. I love the idea of storytelling. Maybe after the first few get-togethers, anyone who wants could *write* their personal story. We could provide paper and pens for people like me but maybe also computers for others who feel more comfortable writing that way or want to learn. We could post the stories on the walls for all to read, or not, depending on how people feel about that. At this point, we wouldn't teach or edit, unless someone specifically asks for it."

"And," Jennifer jumped in, "maybe later we could make some computers and printers available for people to use for schoolwork, too. Maybe we don't even think about offering computer programming classes at this point. We just wait to see if anyone's curious after using the machines for other things."

"Now you're talking," said James. "But don't get discouraged if this doesn't work at first. It's not going to be easy and you'll probably have to change course a few times. But it could be very, very good in the long run."

"Hey, I just had another thought," said Luke. "Let's change the name of this whole thing. It sounds too formal, too one-sided. What if we call it "Raza House?""

"I love it!" said Jennifer and James together.

Jamal

As the last of spring gave way to summer, Luke was using his construction skills to mount a sign on the front of the building in the Rainier Valley south of Seattle. Jennifer had done the calligraphy – large green lettering against a black background – and Luke now fastened it into place above the window with the help of Jamal, a new friend and part-time employee from the neighborhood. Raza House, nearly seven months in gestation, was finally born.

Luke climbed down from his ladder and stood next to Jamal on the street, looking back at the sign. "Looks good, Lucius," said Jamal. "Looks friendly."

"I'm glad. That's exactly what I told Jen," said Luke. "I hope everyone sees it that way."

"Guess we'll find out," said Jamal. "When's the big day?"

"Next Sunday. You can be here, right?"

"Long as you're not just usin' me as black bait. You know, gettin' people comfortable about walkin' in and then pouncin' on 'em."

"Shit Jamal! Really?" said Luke. And then, with a sly smile, "Hey, you think that'd work?"

Jamal just shook his head and Luke couldn't tell if he was actually offended or just thought Luke's attempt at humor was lame.

"Come on, man," said Luke. "Give me a break. You're like one of the founders of this place: you, me, and Jen."

"I'm just givin' you a load a shit. 'Course I'll be here. Hey, will the real Raza-man be around that day?"

"That's the plan."

"Good. See you then, Lucius."

~

Luke had first met Jamal on a Saturday several weeks before, when he made a trip to Rainier Beach Hardware for a new set of drill bits and some sandpaper. He had asked the young, tall, black man in a blue assistant manager's vest to point him in the right direction, and that young man had said, "Sure, follow me. I'll show you."

When they got to the right aisle, Jamal had asked Luke how he planned to use the drills and then suggested ones with carbide tips. Impressed, Luke had asked the young man's name, given him his own, and thanked him.

"Luke. Like in the Bible?" asked Jamal.

"Yeah, I guess so. The name's actually Lucius, but I hate it."

"That *does* suck. No offense man, it just does. Sounds like the devil or some shit like that."

"I think that's Lucifer," said Luke.

The two had a good laugh, and Luke left the store smiling.

Then, as Luke had painfully learned over the years, no project, no matter how well planned, can ever be completed with a single trip to the hardware store, so he found himself in Jamal's store several more times in the next few days. And each time, if he didn't find Jamal right away, he'd ask for him. One day, Luke asked him if he knew of anyone he could hire to help hang drywall and do a few other odd jobs.

"Sure, me," came the response.

"But you've got this job. Seems like you're here at the store all the time."

"Not nights and Sundays."

"Okay, great. How about Sunday afternoon then, say around one?"

"Sure. You got enough drywall tape and mud, Lucius?" said Jamal with a smile.

"Uh, probably not."

"Aisle seven. And you never said where, on Sunday."

"Right, sorry." Luke gave Jamal the address.

269

"Hey, that's just up from where I live!" said Jamal.

"Perfect. See you Sunday."

~

When Luke arrived at the building on Sunday, Jamal was already there, sitting on the sidewalk up against the building. He had on a pair of headphones, his eyes were closed, and a Walkman lay by his side. Luke didn't recognize him at first, having never seen him dressed in anything but his store uniform. Today Jamal was wearing a Seattle Sonics jersey, ball cap, black pants and white, unlaced Adidas shoes. Luke walked up and tapped him on the shoulder.

Jamal's eyes flew open and he jerked back. "Shit Lucius! Don't ever do that!"

"I'm sorry, I didn't mean to scare you."

"Not cool man. Not cool."

"Okay, okay. But what was I supposed to do? Just stand there until you happened to notice? Could've been all afternoon."

"I don't know, man. Just don't do *that*."

"Okay, well, come on in." Luke unlocked the door and the two walked into the building.

"So... what *is* this place?" asked Jamal.

"It's gonna be called Raza House."

"What the fuck is a Raza?"

"Raza is my one-year-old nephew. And look, the F-word's part of my vocabulary too, but I'd appreciate it if you don't use it in the same sentence with Raza."

"Okay, sure. Sorry. Hey, Raza sounds like a black name."

"I think it's actually from the Urdu language, but his parents liked the name because it means 'hope.' His dad's black and his mom's three quarters white, one quarter Cherokee."

"Wow. Sounds like you'd need hope for that. How's it working out?"

"Great. Really great."

"So... I still don't know what's the story on this place."

"I'll tell you the whole thing while we get this drywall up."

270

As they worked, Luke and Jamal gradually shared the highlights and lowlights of their lives. Luke learned that Jamal had graduated from Rainier Beach High School three years earlier and had been working ever since. He'd done well in school, but not quite well enough to get a scholarship to UW where he'd hoped to study engineering. A failed quest for a student loan had left him dejected, and when a school counsellor suggested community college, Jamal had walked out of her office and into the hardware store where he applied for a job stocking shelves. He'd done well there, too. The pay wasn't bad and he'd been promoted quickly. The downside, as Jamal explained it, was that he was starting to feel too comfortable with it all, and thoughts of finding a way to get to college were rapidly fading.

Luke had tried to be encouraging and mentioned his connections at UW, including a couple of casual acquaintances in the Mechanical Engineering and Computer Science departments. And, of course, he also answered Jamal's original question about Raza House, starting with the painful story of Finn and ending with Jen's and his evolving plans.

"The idea is to create a place where we can all tell our stories, kind of like you and I just did. I'm convinced if we can learn to do that, and do it honestly, then we can make a start toward listening. And if we can learn to really listen, then we'll have inched toward a better world. And inches of action can combine into feet of results, and feet into miles."

"Sounds good when you say it," said Jamal.

"Saying's one thing. Doing's another. You want to help me make this happen?"

"I'm in, Lucius."

The Big Day

J ennifer had done some shopping at a Goodwill store down the street, and the front area of Raza House now looked a lot more like a large living room than the storefront it had once been. There were ten comfortable chairs in various styles and sizes strewn about, two overstuffed couches, some end tables, floor lamps and a couple of large coffee tables. A set of metal folding chairs was stacked in the back room in case a large group showed up. The floor was dark walnut salvaged from an old hotel scheduled for demolition. Over this lay an enormous area rug with dark red and blue paisley patterns. The room smelled comfortably old.

Luke and Jamal had painted one wall with what they thought would be a tasteful shade of indigo, and the others with a light gray. Jennifer wasn't sure about the scheme but decided to live with it for a while. An old but very large coffee percolator donated by a local church sat on a long folding table against the back wall, along with paper cups, powdered creamer and sugar. A selection of fresh-baked cookies and juice lay at the end of the table.

Luke, Jennifer and Jamal had been there since early morning and had run out of things to do by eleven. Jamal had been uncharacteristically quiet, and Luke asked him about that.

"Nervous, I guess. What if nobody shows up? Or what if people do show up but think this is lame? Just more white folks with their white plans, knowin' what's best. And here I am, right in the middle of it."

"Yes, I get that," said Jennifer. "I'm nervous too."

Luke nodded in agreement. "Me too. I guess we just have to be who we are and hope for the best."

The somber mood was broken when James and Maggie arrived with little Raza an hour before opening time. Luke saw them first, out on the street, Maggie holding Raza and excitedly pointing up at the green and black sign with his name on it. Luke ran to the door and opened it for them.

"Welcome to Raza House you guys, and especially you!" said Luke as he took Raza from Maggie's arms and carried him in.

"Jamal, this is James, Maggie and Raza. Guys, this is Jamal. He's our partner in making all this happen," said Luke.

"The place looks great!" said James. "Hey, Jamal. So good to finally meet you. Heard a lot of good stuff about you."

"Yeah, me too. I mean, about you all. Hey little man!" said Jamal, redirecting his attention to Raza. "You the guy gonna really make this work, right?"

Raza looked at Jamal and smiled. The ice was broken and everyone chatted easily, catching up, telling Raza stories and killing time.

Days earlier, Jennifer had created a flyer which she and Jamal had distributed around the neighborhood – on telephone poles, bulletin boards in stores, anywhere they could semi-legally put it. It was an invitation to come hear the story of Raza House and it counted on curiosity generated by the recent construction activity at the House and its new sign.

Still, at the scheduled opening time, no one was waiting outside. Luke opened the door and looked up and down the street. Nobody in sight. He came in, threw up his hands and looked questioningly at Jamal.

"Don't worry, man. Nobody'll come right at opening. Wouldn't be cool. Just give 'em a little time," said Jamal.

And, sure enough, about twenty minutes later a few people began to filter in. A pastor and his wife from a church down the street, a friend of Jamal's from high school who was now working at a car wash, an older man who looked like he might

273

be homeless, a woman who owned a local bookstore, and two teenage girls who'd seen one of the flyers and said they were curious. It seemed to Luke that they were more curious about Jamal and his friend than they were about anything else.

Jennifer and James made sure everyone who wanted refreshments got some, and little Raza, crawling around on the rug and pulling himself up along the edge of a low table, instantly became the center of attention.

About a half hour later, as conversations began to lag and three or four others arrived, Jennifer stood up and cleared her throat.

"Thanks for being here everyone, and welcome to Raza House. I'm sure you're wondering what this place is all about. Maybe you're even a little suspicious about it. I don't blame you a bit if you are. I even have my own doubts about it. But I also have a lot of hope. The best way to describe this experiment in hope is that it's a place where we can all share our stories. It's really as simple as that. I'm sure that sounds a little vague but I hope by the end of today it'll become a lot clearer.

I see you've all met little Raza. He's my nephew and the inspiration behind this place. But if you're anything like me, you've probably forgotten the rest of our names by now, so I'll just mention them again real quick. Over there are James and Maggie, Raza's parents."

Jennifer paused as she noticed the two teenage girls frowning, whispering together in the back of the room and glancing over toward Maggie. She wondered what they might be thinking about the white woman who married this obviously successful black man. She tucked the thought away for later consideration and continued.

"Right here is Jamal who's our neighborhood partner in getting this all going. This is my husband, Luke, and I'm Jennifer. There's another name you'll hear around Raza House and I'll let Luke tell you about him because he's a big part of our story. Luke?"

"Thanks, Jen. Yes, that other name is Finn. He was my brother and, in an ass-backwards sort of way, he's responsible for the startup of Raza House. Finn never met little Raza. He was murdered just before Raza was born, and his life insurance policy got us going. But the thing is, my brother would never have dreamed of doing anything remotely like this with his money. That's because he was a white supremacist."

The room couldn't have been more silent if it had suddenly been thrown into the hard vacuum of space. Luke looked around at the people and nodded his head. "And that's where my story begins."

Luke's Story

L uke began with his early childhood, growing up with an angry and violent father, a passive mother, and a protective older brother. As he listened to his own story spill out, he knew that the relative stability he enjoyed as a child was probably not anything like Finn's experience of that same time. Finn had been the buffer between Luke and their father, and had created a safe and relatively sane little bubble for Luke to live in. But in doing that, Finn had to absorb much of the chaos and the rage before it could reach his little brother.

Luke admitted that he had only very recently begun to understand the depth of his brother's sacrifice and regretted that he had never thanked Finn for any of it. And perhaps, Luke worried, that lack of recognition was partly to blame, that *he* was partly to blame, for the path that Finn ultimately took.

Luke could only speculate now that his brother was gone, but it seemed to him that Finn, in his young adult life, had begun to see the natural misfortunes of the world as another form of attacker, taking the place of his father. And since Luke no longer needed protection, the energy Finn had previously directed that way now needed another outlet. He also needed to find a new target for all the anger and resentment. Luke had received some of the spillover, but Finn clearly hadn't wanted Luke to be his main target. He needed someone or something else to play that role. He found it in the non-white races – the "others" which he'd become convinced were out to displace him, to take away his self-esteem, to beat him at his own game on an increasingly tilted playing field. And to see himself as unjustly punished, he had to believe that these "others" were somehow inferior to him and unworthy of any success they might achieve. He connected with a group who felt the same way and began to look for acceptance and validation there.

Luke paused and looked around the room.

"So, I've lived partly under a kind of delusion. I grew up in what seemed to me like a pretty normal, stress-free environment. I ate three good meals a day, had friends, enjoyed sports, got a good education, and found it easy to get summer jobs and later a real career. But all this was partly because I had an older brother who decided it was his job to protect me, to isolate me from the harsher realities of the world. Finn never went to college and he always told me it just wasn't for him. Later I discovered there was only enough money for one of us to go."

Luke was quick to point out that he was in no way absolving his brother, only trying to understand why things happened the way they did. Finn's actions at Patriots' Pride, to the limited extent that Luke knew about them and was able to describe them to the people gathered that day, were not things to be tolerated as just another political viewpoint. They were simply wrong.

Luke looked over toward James.

"My brother-in-law over there, the philosophy professor, helped me understand this the other day. He helped me see that we can't always expect to change people like Finn. But we can still make progress. We can stop trying to change that one person and go bigger, but not in the abstract. Work with other people, he said, and always personally, one-on-one whenever possible. I guess Raza House is that other way for me.

Here's the reason I bring all this up. As a kid, I wasn't only protected by my brother. I also had another form of protection – and still do – that's almost invisible to people in my world but supports us in deep and powerful ways every day, and that is White Privilege. I never had to worry that I might get hassled by a cop or accused of something I didn't do, or that I wouldn't get a job I really wanted, or that someone might think of me as

277

dangerous and cross the street to avoid me, or that I might even get killed just because I had a certain skin color. Sure, I knew a little about racism. I read the papers and saw the news on television, but it all felt like something in a different world, something I had no control over and no responsibility for. Just like living in Finn's bubble, I was able to get on with life without having to bother with any of that. Other than feeling a little guilty from time to time, I was fine, and as I got older, I dealt with the guilt by giving a little money to charity every now and then.

I guess it took the shock of my brother spouting racist and misogynist bullshit and running off to a white nationalist compound to wake me up, at least to the extent I am awake. I feel like I've got one eye partly open now and I'm working on the other. And that's one of my hopes for Raza House – that it can be an eye-opener for white folks like me. But not so we can somehow feel better or less guilty. It's more likely to be the opposite, at least for a while. No, the goal is to grow new connections by honestly sharing our stories in the hope that those connections will lead us to work together on practical solutions; solutions that bring more opportunity for education and careers; solutions that bring hope. Raza House isn't some kind of charity. It's meant to be a place where we can all do the hard work of genuine connection-building. It's meant to be a place of change for all of us, starting from the gut and working outward. That's why our stories are so important. We *are* our stories. When we tell them, we reveal ourselves. When we listen, really listen, we connect. And when we connect, we have a chance to work together to build a better world."

Luke sat down and looked around the room. He saw a few nodding heads, a smile or two, but skepticism on other faces. One man stared out the window. That was okay. It was a start.

278

A New Story

Each Sunday throughout the summer, the team at Raza House told their individual stories and invited people from the community to tell theirs. And each day, the number of people coming from the community grew until, by the fourth Sunday, the count seemed to level off at around thirty. At first, only a handful of people were brave enough to speak, but over time, as the group became comfortable with itself, more joined in. Others wrote their stories on a page or two and pinned them to the indigo wall. Some writers stayed anonymous and no one was ever pressured to speak or write. Some never did. But almost everyone listened. That was the one ground rule: when someone spoke, you tried hard to listen; you put as much energy into your listening as you did into your speaking.

The stories ranged from inspiring accounts of personal success against long odds, to candid admissions of failure and despair, all the way to experiences which led to a deep distrust of white people and white institutions. In a nearly inaudible voice, one woman haltingly told of her rape by a white man she had worked for years ago, bringing out more than a few tears of compassion and rage in the group.

And then there were the outliers who just liked to hear themselves talk. One man boasted of a long, mystical conversation with Jimi Hendrix in Seattle a day before his death and was met with raised eyebrows. Another – not the pastor – preached the Gospel for a good twenty minutes. Luke encouraged everyone to find something of value in every story, even when it was buried under ego or fear. And it didn't always work. Sometimes people would interrupt, argue, or try to hijack someone else's story. It was messy. It was life. It was good.

By week four, Jennifer had brought in a printer and three computers which she set up in the back room and encouraged people to use for writing their stories or doing homework. Jamal had some experience as a computer user at the hardware store and volunteered to supervise "Raza's Lab," as it came to be known. He opened up the lab three nights a week and refused to be paid extra for it. All he wanted in return, he told Jennifer, was to learn how to write software. Jennifer, of course, was thrilled with this and agreed to stay late on Sundays teaching him the basic concepts of computer science and the C++ programming language. Luke stayed too, first just using the time to catch up on maintenance work around the building and later helping people with their writing as they began to ask for it.

But one Sunday in late November, when Luke and Jennifer arrived at Raza House for the weekly group meeting, Jamal met them at the door with a long face. "I fucked up," he said.

"How? What do you mean?" asked Luke.

"Take a look around." He stepped back from the doorway.

"Oh," said Jennifer.

Except for the large area rug, the front room was almost bare. The couches were both gone, as were most of the chairs, tables and lamps. The big indigo story wall had been spray painted with the words, "Whitey Go Home!"

"What about…?" asked Jennifer, looking back toward Raza's Lab.

"Gone. All of it."

"The floppies?" asked Jennifer, hoping that the little discs with people's stories and homework on them hadn't been taken.

"That's the one good thing," said Jamal. "I kept them in that little safe in the back of the closet. It's still there with everything in it."

"Whew!" said Luke. "All the other stuff is replaceable. The stories aren't. So, what the hell happened?"

"Like I said, I fucked up, bad. I feel like shit."

"Okay, we appreciate that but… how did this happen?" said Jennifer.

Jamal stared at the floor. "There's this girl I've been hangin' with, okay?"

Jennifer squinted at Jamal.

"No, no. It was all my fault, not hers. She was here with me last night and I was kind of, you know, showing off our computers and she was coming on to me like I was really important or something. I let it go to my head. She wanted to get out of here with me and go someplace so I ducked out the back with her and forgot to check the front door. I guess it wasn't locked."

"Any idea who got in?" asked Luke.

"No idea, but it must have been somebody who knew about all the shit we had in here, or somebody who knew somebody who did. Probably some cat who's gonna snort it all up his nose."

"Maybe, but what about that? That's what really hurts," said Luke, staring at the vandalized wall.

"There's some extra paint in the back room," said Jamal. "I'll get it done before anyone shows up today."

"No, wait," said Jennifer. "Of course it's painful but it belongs right where it is. It's another story – maybe the most important one so far. If we ignore this, we might as well close up shop."

Luke and Jamal stared at Jennifer and nodded.

Now What?

"At least we still have coffee," said Luke as he measured the ground beans and loaded up the giant percolator. "Wonder why they didn't take this along with everything else."

"Thing looks like an oil refinery been through a fire. Probably figured they couldn't sell it," said Jamal.

"Coffee kinda tastes like that, too," smiled Luke. As he looked up from his measuring, he noticed people gathering outside the building in a light rain. "You mind getting the door, Jamal? It's kind of early but it's getting wet out there."

"Got it."

Five or six people walked in silently and gazed around the room. More followed, and soon there were over forty. Word of the break-in had apparently gotten around. Some sat on the rug and others just stood or leaned against the walls. But it seemed to Luke as though most people were either looking down or away from the story wall, avoiding it. He heard some muted discussion but couldn't make out the words from where he stood in the back of the room.

"Coffee's ready!" he announced. Then, "Oh crap, no cups. Sorry everyone. I didn't notice."

A woman who Luke knew as the owner of the bookstore down the street got up. "No problem," she said. "I've got some at the shop. Be right back."

"Thanks, Celine," said Luke. "Appreciate that."

Luke walked over to the group and sat down on the edge of the rug. He felt the eyes of everyone on him. "The room seems a lot bigger without all that damn furniture cluttering it up, don't you think?" he joked.

A little quiet laughter came from the group, then silence again.

"While we're waiting for Celine to get back with those cups, seems to me maybe we should all just gather our thoughts for a while. We'll have a lot to talk about in a minute and I'm sure we all want her to be part of that."

There were lots of nods around the room.

When Celine returned with a big stack of paper cups, a line had already formed at "the refinery." Coffees in hand, the group finally settled back onto the rug and against the walls. Luke pointed to the spray-painted story wall and opened the discussion.

"So, we've got a new story. Well, maybe not so new because I know this is far from the first time these words, or ones like them, have been written. As we thought about cleaning up and rebuilding, Jamal and I immediately figured we'd just paint over the wall right away, even before you all arrived here today. But Jen disagreed. She pointed out that the words on that wall are in exactly the right place for now. They're a story, or maybe more like the first line of many stories. And those stories are exactly the ones we should be listening to and understanding, particularly the few of us here in the room who happen to have white skin. So, with that in mind, let's talk."

Daniel, the black minister from the local church, spoke first.

"Whoever did this probably has no idea what goes on here. That's no excuse; I'm not saying that. Just that it's a good example of ignorance."

"Maybe not, though," said Jackson, the homeless man with his trash bag full of clothes in the back of the room. "I respect what you're sayin', Pastor. It's jus' that we don't really know, do we? Maybe this guy knows exactly what goes on here. Maybe he's even been here with us. Maybe he jus' thinks we shouldn't ever be together – blacks and whites. That you white folks," he continued, nodding toward Luke and Jen, "are jus' tryin' to keep tabs on us – you know what I'm sayin'? Learn about what we're thinkin', what we're up to, so you can keep us down."

"Could be," said Luke. "I mean it could be what this person was thinking."

"Thing is, we don't know what this guy's own story is, right?" said Jamal. "We could sit here and make shit up all day."

"Hey, I'm not makin' shit up, man!" said Jackson. "I hear stuff like this all the time on the street. There's a lot of folks out there think this Raza place is bullshit, that it's jus' whites comin' in to push us out or convert us or whatever."

"Sorry, Jackson. Didn't mean that. I guess I was just thinkin' that it'd be great to really know what was in this guy's head – to hear his real story. He's gotta have his reasons, right?"

"Maybe he's here right now!" said someone. "You here, man? Not gonna jump on your ass. Just wanna hear you."

Silence.

"Too much to hope for, I guess," said Daniel. "Maybe we could get the word out. Maybe he'd come around and talk if he knew we weren't out to get him. Did you call the police?" he asked, looking toward Luke.

"No, not yet. Maybe we shouldn't. Maybe that'd be better. What do you all think?"

"Depends on if you want to get your stuff back," said Celine. "There's a chance you could."

"Stuff's just stuff," said Luke. "Jen?"

"Agree. This place is a whole lot more than the things we had here, at least that's the hope. Naturally we don't want to lose things, and we'll make everything more secure, but this place is about us, all of us here, not about furniture and computers."

Several people nodded and more than one "Amen!" sprang from the group.

"But you guys haven't really said much about how *you* feel about what happened," said Janelle, one of the two teenage girls who'd been in most of the meetings. "You're always asking us to talk. How about you?" She looked toward Luke and Jen.

284

"Janelle, you're right. Thanks," said Jen. "I uh, I guess it feels personal to me. I know it wasn't – this person can't know me – but that's how it feels. Makes me feel angry and small at the same time. Attacked, vulnerable, I guess."

"Same," said Luke. "Can't really add much to that, except maybe that it makes me feel misunderstood."

"Uh huh," said an older woman leaning against the back wall. "Now you both talkin' my language. Maybe other folks here, too."

"Yeah," said a young man sitting on the carpet. "Like when that white cop stopped me for no reason last week. Never did tell me why."

"Or when I was in the Safeway yesterday and the manager asked me to show him what was in my purse 'cause it was too big and he thought I was puttin' stuff in it. I wasn't. He didn't even apologize. Just walked away," said a young woman standing in the back.

Others jumped in and the stories came pouring out: an arrest and release never explained; a car vandalized with a swastika; a threatening phone call. They just kept coming, and at the end of the meeting people were still talking as they left.

Luke smiled at Jen and Jamal as he closed the door. "That was good, I think. Now what?"

Date Night

L uke looked up from his table in the back of the room, smiled and waved. Jennifer had just walked through the door of their favorite restaurant at the base of Queen Anne Hill and Luke was looking forward to spending a relaxing dinner with his wife, catching up on the day's events. Life had been busy and chaotic, filled to overflowing with demanding jobs and increasing commitments at Raza House. Jennifer had recently been promoted to Development Manager and It had been hard to find time just for the two of them until she suggested putting a regular date night on their calendars and protecting that time just as they would any important meeting. Luke had objected at first, complaining that the idea felt too structured, too lacking in spontaneity. But he had eventually warmed to it after realizing that the status quo wasn't what he wanted either.

"Hey, you good lookin' guy! Mind if I join you?" she asked.

Luke stood, trying to ignore the pain in his lower back which had started bothering him recently. "Tempting, but I'm saving this spot for my wife. Wait. You know what? Until she gets here, have a seat. I'll tell you all about her. She's amazing. And sexy."

They laughed, kissed, and sat down to wine that Luke had already ordered.

"So, tell me about your day," said Luke, adjusting his posture to counter the back pain.

"It was one of those days you look back on and say, 'did I actually get anything done?' Seemed like never-ending meetings. We had our regular Development Meeting, a Code Review, a meeting with my boss about performance reviews, and then a bunch of drop-ins in my office. But one of those was Linda and that was good."

"Oh? What happened with that?"

"Well, we caught a good break. The Windows User Interface team just replaced all their development machines and Raza House can claim as many of the old ones as we want. They're faster than our stolen ones; better monitors, too."

"Great. How many do you think we should get?" asked Luke.

"I'm thinking maybe four or five. We've got the space and more people have asked when we're going to have machines again. I'll stop in at the Goodwill store and see if I can find some replacement furniture too."

"What about a printer?"

"Doesn't look like we're going to get one from Microsoft this time. They're keeping the ones they have for now. We'll probably have to buy one."

"Hmm. Have you seen our bank balance lately?" asked Luke.

"I know. I'm getting a little concerned."

"Me too. But, at the same time I feel like we need to expand. Those two things don't go together very well, do they."

"What do you mean, expand?" asked Jennifer.

"Well, I'm really liking what's going on with all the dialog at the House and I definitely think we should keep encouraging that. I'd love to fill up that whole wall with people's stories. But more and more people are asking for help with their writing and more of them want to use a computer, too. The thing is, I don't think either one of us has any more time to give right now. Jamal probably doesn't either. I mean, look at us, scheduling time for a date? I'm not complaining – just saying I think we're really up against it."

Jennifer reached across the table for Luke's hand. "I know. I'm feeling kinda overwhelmed too."

"So what I was thinking was let's recruit some volunteers. Some from the U and some from Microsoft, maybe just two or three for now."

Jennifer frowned. "Sounds like more work for us, at least in the short run."

"Maybe. We'd have to screen them super well. They'd have to be totally in tune with what we're doing, and passionate about it – can't be people who only want another volunteer position on their résumés."

"That's for sure. And then once they're on board we'd have to manage the group – scheduling, training, coaching, monitoring progress, dealing with attrition. You know, all that stuff. Let's give it a little more thought, okay?"

"Sure. It's just an idea," said Luke.

"And a good one," smiled Jennifer. "I just don't want us to burn out trying to prevent a burn-out."

"Right. So, what about the money situation?"

"We've got to figure out a way to make Raza House pay for itself. We can't just keep dumping money into rent and utilities each month," said Jennifer. "Before long we're gonna have to take out another loan."

"Ask for donations when people use the computers?"

"Maybe, but even that could discourage people. It might even give the impression we're trying to start a business and make money off the community."

"A fund-raiser?" tried Luke.

"That's a thought. Maybe a big one once a year? I could see us doing that."

And so the conversation continued, through dinner and into desert when Luke changed the subject.

"You know, I keep wondering what Finn would think about Raza House. You still wonder?" he asked.

"All the time. Sometimes I wish we could have a kind of magic window into his last days. But then I also think, no, we probably wouldn't see what we hope for. We're probably better off not knowing; just being thankful in a weird way. If he hadn't done what he did, Raza House wouldn't exist."

"Yeah, you're right. I just wish we could have both. You know what I mean? Both the House and knowing where Finn's head was. It's hard not knowing, even if it's all bad."

When the check came, Jennifer paid it and looked across the table at Luke. "Meet you at home? And if we're not too tired, maybe...?"

"Race you."

Several Years Later

I t was 1998 and had been eight years since the World Wide Web first emerged as an obscure academic tool built upon the Internet. The first Iraq war had been fought seemingly successfully, Bill Clinton was in the White House, the Cold War had been over for a while, and a general feeling of positive anticipation infused everything. Venture capital was pouring into Silicon Valley and limits of all kinds were seen as anachronisms. The only thing on the horizon that seemed even mildly ominous was Y2K. The impending turn of the millennium was causing trouble for some of the older software providers but was only a minor annoyance for the newer ones like Microsoft.

As was her habit, Jennifer arrived at her corner office on the second floor of Building 15 with a double tall mocha before six in the morning. This gave her time to catch up on the hundred-plus emails which had flown into her inbox since the night before and allowed a few moments for thought and planning. Early morning was a quiet time at Microsoft, as most of its young employees arrived by nine or ten and worked late into the evening, sometimes staying overnight. Long hours, personal sacrifice and unflinching commitment to goals were badges of honor, as was the coveted "Blue Badge" itself, which identified permanent employees and allowed access to the many buildings now spreading across the sprawling Redmond campus.

Jennifer sometimes wondered how she had managed to survive the pace, the brutal review process, the stress of deadlines, the intense Bill G meetings, presentations at ever-growing industry conferences and the many other elements of life at the center of the software universe. But she knew the answer: it was Luke.

Luke had plugged away at his university teaching job, provided the love and stability she needed at home, and kept Raza House going with a dedicated team of volunteers and fund-raising events. Jennifer knew that the people who had graduated from college and returned as Raza House volunteers while pursuing their own careers, Jamal being the first among them, were clear evidence of Luke's persistence and passion. She had contributed financially and with a continuous flow of donated equipment from Microsoft but sometimes wished her career had not been so all-consuming.

Windows 95 and the Office products had launched Microsoft into a new phase of rapid growth despite the company's failure to recognize and exploit the internet early enough. Jennifer had seen the opportunity and pushed for deeper network integration but had achieved only modest success in getting the necessary funding. Still, her efforts had been enough to earn her several promotions, leading to her current position as General Manager of Server Products. That was one step away, albeit a large and uncertain one, from a Vice President slot at the company.

She didn't see this kind of advancement as a strong personal goal and disliked the internal politics which sometimes demanded more physical and emotional energy than she wanted to apply. She also distrusted the euphoria she was starting to see around the company's stock price. The Blue Badges were starting to pay a lot of attention to their stock options and some hallways were beginning to sprout monitors showing live updates to the MSFT ticker symbol. Of course, Jennifer wasn't immune to the optimism and occasionally glanced at her own options, but generally regarded the phenomenon as a distraction.

Unfortunately though, this heady mix of euphoria, stress and rapid change was taking a toll on personal lives, even as most people tried to ignore or repress it. Jennifer saw this in her product teams, particularly around performance review times, and lobbied hard, along with several people from HR and the executive ranks, for confidential psychotherapy sessions for employees. She had taken on this effort as a personal objective, and today she would assist HR in interviewing the last round of psychologists as a representative of the technical management team. The plan was to hire three therapists as contractors and run a year-long pilot program.

Jennifer worked her way through four interviews before lunch, finding one applicant qualified for the job and the other three marginal. All four were men. She walked over to one of the many cafeterias available on campus, built herself a large salad, and reviewed the next résumé as she ate. This one showed promise. The applicant had an MSW degree from UW and was currently a PhD candidate there. This person had been pursuing the degree while also working as a therapist in private practice for the last several years specializing in the treatment of depression and stress-related disorders. Jennifer glanced at the name at the top of the résumé before slipping it back into her purse: Elsa Jorgenson. She walked back to the HR building thinking, good; we need another qualified female in the mix. *I hope this one interviews well.*

The Interview

Elsa arrived twenty minutes before her scheduled interview and was enjoying a wall full of photographs depicting the early days of the company. One fascinating set showed aerial views of the Redmond campus as it was being developed. Another, at the very beginning of the display, was a picture of Bill Gates and Paul Allen standing on either side of an Altair 8800 microcomputer, the target for their first software product developed for a small company in Albuquerque. *They were so young!* thought Elsa. Bill, smiling, looked to Elsa like a skinny kid she remembered from high school who was always finding clever ways to avoid gym class. And Paul, so serious with that long hair and beard, seemed more like someone her aunt might have known from a commune in the sixties.

"Ms. Jorgenson?" came a voice from the other side of the waiting room. "Hi, I'm Jennifer Mason. Come on in; let's get started."

Elsa's ears perked up at the mention of Jennifer's last name. *No, couldn't be related. It's a common name.*

"So, Elsa, welcome to Microsoft. Is this your first visit to the campus?" asked Jennifer.

"Yes, it is. But I feel like I've been here before because I've heard so many descriptions of it."

"Oh? From newspaper articles or...?"

"Mostly from my patients. I've worked with several people from Microsoft over the last few years."

293

"Oh, that's excellent. I know you can't talk about specific cases, but how's your experience been with our people, in general?"

"In general? Well, I've enjoyed it and I'd say it's worked out well for almost all of them. Some just needed help with basic coping skills. A few people felt they couldn't talk honestly to anyone at the company for fear they'd appear weak. Others had stress-related relationship issues, both at work and at home. It pretty much ran the gamut, as you'd expect."

"Was there any common thing about their work experience that seemed to stand out in terms of stress?"

"You mean as a cause of stress?" asked Elsa.

"Yes."

"Well, there were several. But the one thing that came up over and over again was the performance review process. And I wasn't just hearing this from people on the receiving end of reviews. I also had several managers who were having terrible difficulties giving reviews to their employees."

"Can you say more about that?"

"Sure. It was actually very interesting. Almost everyone who'd had prior experience with performance reviews at other companies felt that Microsoft's approach was far superior to the soft "everybody's above average" kind of thing they'd seen elsewhere. You know, like when every kid gets a trophy just for showing up at games. They liked the rigorous attempt to use measurable goals and to run a very objective process. But, at the same time, when it came down to using mandated curves which forced managers to always identify the lowest X percent who would get no bonuses and no new stock options, even in small teams with all good performers, that's where things got tough. It's a classic case of agreeing with the strategy but struggling with the tactics. All this causes a great deal of anxiety and makes managers feel disingenuous when they have to find and amplify even the smallest faults and weaknesses in order to justify the required low ratings."

"I won't argue with that," said Jennifer. "Even though I think the process does helps people continually reach higher. But, back to you, what do you generally do to help people with this struggle?"

"Well, there's no single approach. Everyone has slightly different issues, based mostly on their own personal histories. And they need different paths back to health because of that. But overall, I try to follow three general steps. The first is active listening; this is so important not only because I need to understand what events in the patient's past might be contributing, but also because people simply need an outlet for their feelings; there's usually no one at work to talk to. Exposing even a hint of weakness can be dangerous in a highly competitive environment like this. And second, I try to find specific evidence to help people re-build their sense of self-worth. This is usually not too hard because only highly capable people ever make it into jobs at Microsoft in the first place. And finally, we work together on specific strategies for dealing more constructively with the system at the company. I never take sides, even while providing an empathetic presence. It's not my place to try to change Microsoft, as much as I might like to sometimes."

"Thanks. So, tell me about your academic work. Do you have a thesis topic yet?"

"Yes."

Elsa described her work on the measurable physiological effects of cognitive dissonance, and then the conversation turned to her career goals and her specific reasons for seeking a contract with Microsoft. Since this was the last interview of the day, Jennifer spent over an hour with Elsa and, by the end of the session she knew she would provide a "Strong Hire" recommendation to HR in an email that afternoon.

1999: Full Circle

S till suffering from the lower back pain brought on by his ruminations over the fate of the cabin, Luke abandoned the idea of getting his flyrod from the truck and slowly turned, walked up from the dock, and picked his way carefully through the thorny blackberry vines which had invaded the path. The place had clearly gone downhill over the last several years. How much money would it take to bring it back into shape? Would the investment be worth it, particularly in Jen's eyes? Should he just give in and put the place on the market? They could use some of the funds to help keep Raza House afloat. Maybe finally buy a place of their own in Seattle; pay off the cabin loan; seriously consider having a baby before it became too late. None of these questions were new. Luke had turned them over in his mind a hundred times before, often agonizing over them alone, occasionally daring to explore their prickly surfaces with Jen, but never allowing himself to get to the point of resolution.

Why is that? Why am I so reluctant to commit? At some level he had always known the answer but second-guessed himself every time it rose high enough in consciousness, like a trout rising to a poorly-tied fly and then turning, whipping its tail, and escaping back into the depths at the sight of the truth.

Now Luke stepped up to the partially open cabin door again, just as he had left it minutes before to let the darkness seep out while he checked the dock. And indeed, the morning sun was starting to throw a narrow shaft of light into the room. Luke pulled the door all the way open, the hinges creaking, the light expanding, the darkness receding.

And there, on the living room floor, was the truth – a familiar sight but one now illuminated more fully. Luke knelt down on the floor slowly, fighting against his back pain, and traced the dark outline of his old bloodstain with a finger as the long-ago fight with Finn replayed in his mind. He had instinctively stepped between his brother and Jen to protect her from his wrath. Or was it his first awkward attempt to tell her he loved her? Or to steal her away from Finn? Or to try to save his brother from himself? Luke had never replaced the three stained floorboards despite Jen's several requests over the years, and he could easily have done so. There were ten or fifteen spare boards stored under the cabin near the one remaining kayak.

The pain in Luke's back began to subside as he made his decision. He would replace those three boards today as the first step toward selling the cabin. It was time.

Finn and I built this cabin together, working side by side. We fished this lake together. We loved this land. We tried to figure out our young lives here. But our differences? We kept those buried until that day, on Thanksgiving no less. I can never be thankful for our fight, our separation, or Finn's tragic decisions. Definitely not for his death. But I am thankful for the path this put me on. What an odd thing to think, but there it is. Without all this darkness there would never have been the bright lights of Jenny, Raza House and the little bits of hope and change we've been able to bring to the world together. Life's been good. It's time to accept that and make it even better. It's time to let go of the past.

And so it was that Luke got up off the floor, fetched his tools from the truck, and began to pry up the three bloodstained floorboards. They came away easily and he carried them down by the lake where he sawed them into smaller pieces and placed them into a makeshift firepit near the spot where he and Finn had camped while building the cabin so many years ago. He walked back up the trail, crawled under the cabin past his kayak, and retrieved three new boards. Then he spent the rest of the afternoon cutting them to size, sanding them thoroughly, applying two coats of sealer and fastening the boards into place in the floor. The next day before leaving, he would carefully brush on the finish coats just like his brother had taught him.

Luke stood back and looked at his work. *I've tried my best to build this to last and make it worth lasting, Finn. Now let's go finish up our business.*

As the afternoon was blending into evening, Luke washed up, selected a bottle of Argentinian Malbec and took two wine glasses with him down to the firepit. There he stuffed some old papers under the cut-up bloodstained floorboards and struck a match. With the wood beginning to flame and crackle, Luke poured two glasses of wine and held them both up in front of the fire, one in each hand.

To you, my brother! If there is a God, let Her have mercy on your stained soul. And on mine.

Friends

W hile Luke was busy at the cabin over the weekend, Jennifer had decided to catch up on work at the office. Five days a week at twelve or thirteen hours a day just weren't enough to do the job, let alone do it well. At least the ancillary task of establishing the on-campus psychotherapy service had been behind her for nearly a year. Even though she still monitored status emails from Elsa Jorgenson and occasionally responded with encouragement or advice, Jennifer's own time-consuming efforts in the planning, funding, organizing and staffing stages were well in the past.

But an email from Elsa this morning had an unfamiliar subject line. Normally it read, "Monthly status: EMWP," using an acronym for the program name, Employee Mental Wellness Program, and was sent to the entire upper management team at the company. But today, it simply read "Meet for coffee?" and was sent only to Jennifer.

Having recently thought a lot about her sadly limited set of friends, almost all of which were colleagues whom she never saw beyond the confines of the campus, Jennifer was intrigued by this invitation from someone who was not an integral part of the company. She read the email for the second time, trying to decide what to do about it.

Jennifer,
I'm about to make some changes in my personal life which will affect my involvement at Microsoft and I'm wondering if you could take a few minutes away from the office to chat with me about that. I've always enjoyed working with you, even though

our time together has been scarce. Would you possibly have time to meet me for coffee today or tomorrow?

Thanks,
Elsa

Jennifer smiled. You could always tell when an email was written by someone not steeped in Microsoft culture or tech culture in general. Too many words. Not badly written; just something more like Luke would produce. But this sounded important and also offered the potential for a new friendship. Jennifer replied:

love to. when? where?

Five minutes later, as Jennifer was responding to other emails, a new one popped up from Elsa.

How about Starbucks on NE 24th? 10:00 today?

Now she's getting the hang of it, thought Jennifer.

great. see you there.

Jennifer glanced at the time on her computer monitor. This would give her a little under two hours to plow through the remaining emails and set an agenda for Monday's staff meeting with her Product Unit Managers. She created an appointment in Outlook for her meeting with Elsa and got back to work with renewed focus.

At a quarter to ten, up popped the Outlook reminder about Elsa. Jennifer dismissed it, quickly saved her agenda, and ran out the door.

She arrived at Starbucks only a minute late and spotted Elsa waving to her from a table in the back of the room. She waved back and ordered a double tall mocha. When the hissing from the espresso machine stopped and she picked up her drink, Jennifer made her way back to the table and sat down.

"Thanks for taking the time to talk with me," said Elsa, smiling.

"Not a problem," said Jennifer, returning the smile. "I was over at the office catching up on things anyway. So tell me, what's going on? How can I help?"

"Well, a couple of things, one specifically related to Microsoft and the other not so much."

"Okay, sure; fire away."

"I'm getting close to finishing my dissertation and I feel like I really need to give it a lot of attention right now. With my private practice and Microsoft taking pretty much all the rest of my time, something's got to give. Also, my aunt's been watching my nine-year-old daughter when I'm not around and I'd like to give her some relief from that."

"I didn't know you had a daughter; that's wonderful! What's her name?"

"Samantha. We call her Sam. And you? Do you have kids?" asked Elsa.

"No, we keep putting that on the back burner. With me at this job, my husband at UW, and us both trying to run a non-profit, that burner is starting to feel kind of permanent, I'm sad to say. But what about your husband? I'm guessing he must be pretty busy too?"

"That kind of gets to my second topic, but I guess we should finish the other one first."

"Of course. So, your contract must be coming up for renewal pretty soon now."

"Yes, next month. I've loved my time here and feel like I've been able to make a difference. I hope you agree."

"Absolutely. From where I sit it looks like you've become the natural leader of the team. We all appreciate your good work and how you've kept us in the loop all along. We'll be sad to see you go. Particularly me, personally."

"Thank you, Jennifer."

"Of course. So when will your last day be?"

"August thirty-first would be good, if that can work for you all."

"I'm sure it will. I guess you'll need to give your formal notice to HR."

"Yes, will do. I'll also provide a couple of recommendations for a replacement."

Jennifer watched as Elsa ran a finger around the rim of her coffee cup and seemed ready to speak more than once but hesitated each time.

Finally, Jennifer tried to break the tension. "So… there was something else you wanted to talk about?"

Elsa looked up and Jennifer thought she saw a mix of anxiety and hope in her new friend's eyes.

"Yes, there is. I might be way off the mark, but there's something personal I've been wanting to ask you for a long time. And now that I'll be leaving, I thought it might finally be okay to do that."

"Sure, go ahead," said Jennifer.

"Okay; does the name 'Finn' mean anything to you?"

Finn

"Finn Mason?" asked Jennifer, stunned. Then seeing Elsa nod, she continued. "Uh, yes, actually. I dated him briefly a long time ago. And, this probably sounds pretty weird, but I'm married to his brother now. Luke."

"Oh my God. I've wondered for so long but never let myself pursue it, because, you know, conflict of interest and all that. No, I'm sorry, that's not exactly true. That's just an excuse. It's really because I was ashamed and afraid."

"I'm sorry, so... how do you know about Finn?" Jennifer asked.

Elsa closed her eyes and paused. She bit her lip, sighed, and looked up.

"There's something about my past that's not on my résumé, Jennifer, something I'm terribly ashamed of. I was a member, well really more like a captive, of a white nationalist group called Patriots' Pride near Colville. I met Finn there. I was with him a couple of days before he died."

"Oh, Elsa, how awful for you. Luke and I know a little about Patriots' Pride from the FBI – how Finn was a part of it, but we know next to nothing beyond that. I'm so sorry you got caught up in it. I hope Finn didn't harm you in any way."

"No, no, he was good to me. It was the others, one in particular, not Finn. Finn actually tried to protect me."

"I'm sorry, but it's hard for me to imagine Finn being good to any woman."

"He was, Jennifer. He really was. I want you to know that. But he was deeply conflicted. I think he was just starting to come to grips with his situation. Given time, I don't know, things might've changed. For the better, I mean."

"I... I don't know what to say."

"I know. I'm so sorry to spring this on you. It's an awful lot to deal with."

"It is, yes. But I need to know, do you think Finn ever understood the damage that groups like that do? Did *you* understand that?"

"Jennifer, I was so naïve when I followed my new husband to Patriots' Pride. I should've known I was about to become part of a hate group, but I didn't, not at the beginning anyway. I have no excuse other than blind infatuation and that's no excuse at all, only a bad reason. I was complicit in something evil."

"And Finn?"

"I think Finn pretty much knew what he was getting into. I'm sorry to say that but I think it's true. He was the mastermind behind an illegal scheme to fund the group. My best guess is that he felt victimized when he joined, and then the affirmation he found there helped him deal with that. But, in the end I think he was starting to question his decisions, and maybe even his motives. He confided in me."

"So, you two were close?"

"In some ways, yes. We were definitely getting there. He opened up to me about his doubts and I think we were both struggling with similar things."

"Can you remember anything specific he said?" Jennifer asked. "Anything that led you to believe he might be ready to look at things differently?"

"Yes, one time in particular. He and I were on a hike near the compound. I had just told him something I'd overheard about the group's plan to grow from within – to have kids there, maybe even a school. He seemed revolted by this. He said he couldn't imagine children growing up around people like... and then he couldn't finish his thought. I asked him if he meant people like himself and me, and that seemed to stop him in his tracks. He was so confused but I thought maybe that moment was the beginning of something good for him."

"And was it?"

"I don't know. It might have been. He was vulnerable – so in need of a friend or a lover. I was touched by that and couldn't help myself. I guess I needed the same things, so I talked him into going back to my cabin."

"Ah. Okay... but... what about your husband? Where was he during all this? I'm sorry if I'm..."

"No, it's okay; I haven't told you everything. Jim took his own life long before I met Finn."

"Oh, gosh, I'm so sorry Elsa. I never would have imagined any of this just seeing you on the street somewhere."

"We all have our stories, I guess. And I still haven't finished telling you one of the most important parts of mine."

Jennifer looked up and then, thinking about the timing, made the connection. "Is it...? Is it about Samantha? Sam?"

"Yes."

"Is she Finn's?"

"Yes."

"Oh my."

"Are you okay, Jennifer?"

"Yes, just trying to process all this. Why are you telling me now? Why didn't you try to track Luke and me down a long time ago? We could've helped."

"I don't know. I've tried to analyze myself so many times. I think it was a big mix of things. I was ashamed, for one. It was still a time when being a single mom put you way out on the edges of society. And then I was afraid I'd lose Sam – that I'd somehow be forced to give her up because I didn't have the means of supporting her like I imagined the other side of her family might. I know, crazy, but I was so paranoid about that. And then my dear aunt offered to step in and help, and at that point I think I just wanted to put everything behind me, to start over. I'm so sorry. You and Luke deserved to know. How do you think he'll take the news?"

"I think he'll be thrilled to know he has a niece. And when he hears that Finn might have been ready to re-think some things, well, that'll be a big deal."

"Good. When do you think you'll tell him?"

"You know, I was just thinking – would you be willing to tell him yourself? The whole story? Everything you know about Finn, how he treated you, how he might've been having doubts?"

"I could do that, yes."

"Would you really?"

"Of course. It's the least I can do after all this time. I'd be honored."

"Wonderful. It'll be hard to keep from telling him myself in the meantime, but I think this would be so much better. I'll set it all up as soon as I possibly can. Oh, there's another thing I want to ask you. I wonder if you know anything about it."

"Sure, I'll tell you anything I know."

"My brother in law, James…"

"His attack?"

"Yes."

"That was Patriots' Pride too. Our security officer, Cal, he was the one. He went down to Fairwood to shut down your sister's relationship with a client – one of the target clients in Finn's scheme. I guess James showed up and, oh God, I'm so sorry about what happened. I wasn't supposed to know anything about that but I overhead the guys talking about it one day."

"Was Finn involved?"

"No, absolutely not. He didn't know anything about it until I told him. It just about made him sick. I remember he said something about James being a peaceful man. I think it brought a lot of things home for him. It made everything suddenly personal. That was the day before he was arrested."

"This Cal you mentioned, was he one of the men who ended up in prison over this whole thing?"

"No, he wasn't. But if you heard about the incident on the news, you might remember that one of the guys was killed during the arrest. That was Cal."

"Oh. Was he... Did he also..."

"Finn's death?"

"Yes. Was that him, too?"

"In the end it would've been Brad's decision but I'll bet anything it was Cal's plan. He had contacts everywhere, even at the jail."

"Will you tell Luke about this too, when you talk with him? I want him to hear all this directly from you."

"Of course. I'll tell him everything. You'll be there too, right?"

"Yes, I'll be there."

"Good. I'll pull all my thoughts together in the meantime so I don't forget anything."

"Thank you. Oh, before I go back to the office, do you have any pictures with you?"

"Pictures?"

"Yes, of Sam."

Elsa smiled and reached for her purse.

Options

J ennifer decided to skip lunch after her meeting with Elsa
and put in another few hours at work before going home
for the day. Her thoughts were still spinning from Elsa's
revelations as she parked below her building, and she hoped that
some focused work might help clear her head. It would be so
hard to keep all this from Luke until the right time. So unnatural.
But still, this was the best way.

She used her blue badge to access the elevator and rode to
the second floor. She walked past the large window of the test
lab used by one of her product groups and saw seven or eight
people there, hard at work on a Saturday afternoon. She waved
to them and moved on.

Jennifer glanced at Friday's closing price on one of the
MSFT stock ticker displays outside an office as she made her
way down the hallway. The price was a little over half what she
remembered it being just a few days earlier. *Oh, that's right, another
two-for-one split. Heard a lot of chatter about that last week. This is crazy.*

Even though Jennifer was proud of the company for doing
so well, and for her team's part in that, she had been very
disciplined in ignoring the whole stock option thing and
encouraged her employees to do the same. She had even
avoided discussing it at home. Here at work, keeping the focus
on product quality, features and schedules was paramount, and
employees daydreaming about buying cars, houses and boats
didn't help.

But today the conversation with Elsa had brought family
financial needs back into sharp focus. She and Luke had talked
about wanting to contribute to the college fund her sister and

James had started for Raza, and now they had Sam to think about too. And, of course, that was all on top of the need to keep Raza House afloat.

Fundraisers had kept the House going year to year, but the events took a tremendous amount of time and energy away from more important things and they weren't allowing any real expansion. All this, and knowing Luke was up at the cabin, probably agonizing over its fate at that very moment, made Jennifer realize that she needed to have another look at their personal finances. She decided to temporarily violate her own guidelines and scheduled thirty minutes at the end of the day to throw together a spreadsheet evaluating her options.

She glanced at the time and got back to work reviewing status reports and thinking about specific feedback she would provide to each of her four product units. When she had thoroughly digested all reports and considered both the literal content and the between-the-lines implications of each, she fired off an email to each Product Unit Manager with specific questions, concerns, and directions. In one case, she asked for a one-on-one meeting for Monday morning to discuss an ongoing conflict between a development team and a test team within the same product group. She was careful never to cloud necessary critique with unwarranted praise. When praise was deserved, she was always pleased to give it, but *only* when deserved, and only in a separate context. Mixed messages, she felt, only resulted in confusion and mistrust.

When the last email left her outbox, Jennifer checked the time and switched gears. She opened a spreadsheet and began populating it with information about her various stock option grants and strike prices over the last decade. She had never factored in the last three stock splits and did so now – half the price but twice as many shares each time. She had been aware that the price had recovered quickly after each split but hadn't allowed herself to explore the personal implications until now.

When the last of the data was in and the basic formulas were in place, Jennifer created a bottom line to sum everything up.

What she saw so astounded her that she went back twice, carefully checking for errors and bad assumptions. There were none. She closed the spreadsheet, emailed it to her personal account, pushed back her chair, and left for home. Luke would be there late the next morning and they needed to talk.

Choices

Uncharacteristically, Jennifer found it hard to sleep that night. She kept waking up, her mind grappling with new opportunities and the decisions she and Luke would need to make in the coming days. Luke had called from the cabin earlier in the evening, and Jennifer had wanted to tell him everything immediately but decided that sitting down face-to-face would be much better. A big part of it would have to wait for Elsa anyway. So, she had demurred. Luke had sounded good, more settled, and had said something about wanting to talk with her about the cabin when he got home. Jennifer hadn't tried to pry anything out of him because she knew that would have naturally forced a discussion of her own topics. As a result, the conversation had stayed on a superficial level and felt awkward. That bothered Jennifer, plaguing her sleep and infecting her dreams.

The last time she woke up, the clock said 5:13. She abandoned all hope of further sleep, put on a pair of jeans and a T-shirt and walked into the kitchen, bleary-eyed and thinking about coffee.

With a pot made and a cup poured, Jennifer settled down at her desk, opened her email and downloaded the stock option spreadsheet. She stared at the bottom line again, still finding it hard to believe. She sipped at her coffee, shook her head, and thought about the many possibilities that lay ahead.

~

Just before noon, as Jennifer was keeping herself busy reviewing a set of features and schedule tradeoffs for a future release of

Windows NT Server, she heard Luke open the front door and announce, "Jenny, I'm home!"

"In here!" she responded. "Want half my grilled cheese? Just made it and I'm not all that hungry."

"I'm okay. Had a couple of protein bars on the trip down."

Jennifer stood to kiss Luke. He was smiling broadly and looked good, seeming more relaxed than he'd been in a while.

"Are you interruptible? Looks like you're deep into it there," said Luke, glancing at the screen.

"Just give me five minutes and I'm all yours for the rest of the day."

"You got it. I'll grab a few things from the truck and be right back."

Jennifer finished up her notes and sent off two quick emails, then went to see if Luke needed anything. She found him toting a heavy toolbox to the garage. "Can I help with something?" she asked.

"Thanks, but we're good. That's the last of it. Just some stuff we haven't used at the cabin for years. Thought it was time to bring it back," said Luke as he shoved the toolbox into a spot under the work bench.

"Hmm, what got you thinking about that?"

"I think I finally got my head straightened out about the cabin, Jen. I think we should go ahead and put it on the market as-is. There're a lot of things we could do to fix it up, and maybe we should tackle one or two just so it'll pass inspection, but most things are just going to cost money we don't have right now and probably wouldn't add much to the value of the place anyway."

"Let's take a walk and talk more about that, what do you say? A quick one around the neighborhood?"

"Sure. Just let me wash up and I'll be right back out."

Jennifer gazed down on the scene below. Up on Queen Anne Hill, the sun was out but patches of fog persisted down below, covering the lower half of the Space Needle and parts of the many large office towers which had recently begun to dominate the downtown area. Most of Elliott Bay was blanketed in fog but Bainbridge Island was still visible in the distance across the sound. A ferry was emerging from Eagle Harbor, bound for Seattle.

"Let's go," said Luke as he rejoined Jennifer outside. "Beautiful day for a walk up here."

Jennifer offered her hand and the two started off together, enjoying the warmth of the sun and the view below.

"I love you, Luke, and I love that you're feeling more settled. You seem happier."

"I think I'm feeling relieved. Letting go doesn't seem nearly as hard now as I always imagined it would."

"Seems like a really healthy place to be," said Jennifer, squeezing Luke's hand. "Look, I know my timing is a little weird here, but what if you were able to keep both that feeling of relief and the cabin itself?"

"I don't know. What're you talking about?"

"Luke, yesterday I decided it was time to have another look at those stock options I've got at work. You know, the ones I used to joke about being worthless wallpaper someday?"

"Yes?"

"Well, James was onto something years ago when he said he had a good feeling about those options. I've known for a while they'd be worth something, maybe enough to get us a couple of new cars someday, but I didn't understand just how much. I didn't want to get distracted by the whole idea, and I wasn't fully vested then anyway, so I never did all the math, until now."

"Okay…"

"Let me put it this way: if we exercise our options now and sell the shares, our tax bill alone would be several times more than I ever imagined our entire lifetime *income* would be."

"Our tax bill? That doesn't sound like great news. What are you saying?"

"Yes, just the tax bill. The rest of it would pay that bill and then fix us up for life."

"You can't be serious."

"I know. It's hard to believe, but yes, very serious."

"Are you saying we can keep the cabin?" asked Luke, incredulous.

Jennifer laughed and took both of Luke's hands in hers. "Yes, we can keep the cabin. That's a drop in the bucket."

"And what about Raza House? Can we do more there?"

"We could set up a foundation that'll keep it going basically forever. We could even expand it."

"Jenny, this is unbelievable. Is there enough to help out with Raza's college fund too?"

"More than enough. Way more than enough for all of this. And we can start thinking differently about how we spend our own time, too, if we want to."

"You mean our jobs?"

"Among other things, yes. We can choose to keep them if we want."

"If we *want*?! What did we do to deserve all this?"

"Nothing really. That's the thing. Why us? Why not some of the folks at the House?"

"I know. But Jenny, you've been working your butt off for years."

"Sure, but do you think our friends at the House haven't worked just as hard, or harder? I can think of at least a half dozen people there who have two or three jobs and are still struggling."

"Of course. You're right. We need to think more about what we can do. Actually, no, now we *get* to do that!"

The Arc

J amal had been one of the fortunate ones at the House. He had graduated from UW in 1993 and then again in 1995 with a Master's degree in computer science. His experience at Raza House had left him with much more than a head start in the world of software development and an acceptance at the university. It had also left him fascinated with the idea of community. With Luke and Jennifer, he had been an integral part of building their diverse, open, loosely structured group in Rainier Beach, and he saw the nascent World Wide Web as a way to extend this idea beyond its geographical boundaries. At that time, the Web was used mostly as a one-way service on the internet for publishing information, at first academic, and then inevitably, commercial. But Jamal was one of a handful of people who first saw it as a new platform for community, for discussion, for bringing people together who might otherwise never encounter each other.

As part of his Master's thesis, Jamal built websites for both Raza House and the little hardware store where he continued to work, and hosted them on a server provided by Jennifer at Microsoft in exchange for technical feedback on the use of the company's Internet Information Server. The Raza House site even had a private area where people could log in and post their stories. Almost no one saw these websites for the first couple of years because very few people used the Internet for anything much beyond email at that time. But a small startup out of a garage in Bellevue *did* take notice, and in the Spring of 1996, they made Jamal an offer to come help them improve their own fledgling book-selling website called Amazon.com.

Jennifer had tried to interest Jamal in a role at Microsoft but he wanted to take some time after graduating to think about his next move, or that's what he told her at the time. What Jamal really wanted was some independence. He had loved working closely with Jennifer, but it was time to move on. It was time to see what he could do on his own.

And so he took the job with the little dot-com. But only after he made that commitment did he sit down with Jennifer and tell her what was really on his mind. The new job was a risky choice compared to Microsoft, but it was a chance to test himself, to see what he could do on his own, to be Jamal. Not that he wasn't grateful; he made sure Jennifer knew that. And when he told her he'd miss working with her at Microsoft, he had barely hidden the catch in his voice.

After graduation, he never returned to the hardware store, except as a customer, but Jamal continued to be a regular presence at Raza House; and by 1999 he was leading some of the weekly meetings and providing computer tutoring and coding classes three days a week after work. Both Jennifer and Luke had encouraged a few people from the tech and academic worlds, most of them white, to come to the weekly meetings to share their stories and listen to others. More people came from the local community, too. Sometimes the meetings got a little confused and heated as new folks from very diverse backgrounds met for the first time and clashed with each other. But the old hands, especially Jamal, eventually helped the new ones understand and appreciate the values of active listening, honesty and kindness which had become hallmarks of the Raza House culture.

Jamal noticed that the House seemed to run in a cycle: chaos followed by healing and re-integration, followed again by disorder, then more healing, and so on. It wasn't always easy or pleasant, but it was real, and it seemed to be heading in the right direction over the long haul. He thought about the words of Theodore Parker, the 19th century abolitionist, that were made famous by Martin Luther King Jr. when he paraphrased them as, "The arc of the moral universe is long, but bends toward justice." Jamal had posted those words on both the story wall and the website.

As he walked out of Raza's Lab through the front room on his way to lock up one evening, Jamal was thinking about the healing part of that cycle. At the House, it felt like things were moving forward again, bending the right way.

But looking out through the front window after securing the deadbolt from the inside, something was bothering him. He was feeling good about his own life, yes. But what about some of the folks out there on the street? What about Jackson, looking older by the day, trudging by with his entire net worth stuffed into a garbage bag? Or even Celine, seeming to do better than most, but, as Jamal knew, barely keeping the bookstore afloat. What about the thinly disguised hopelessness he saw under the hoods of the boys hanging out on the corner after school? Or Janelle, pregnant for the second time at twenty-two. Or the drugs starting to flood the streets, promising escape from misery but delivering only captivity. Was anyone out there feeling the arc bending toward justice, or was it just him?

Even though Amazon had yet to turn a profit, it was well funded, and key technical staff like Jamal were being paid very generously with bonuses, 401Ks, and promises of stock options to come. Other than student loan payments, Jamal's expenses hadn't changed much, and his savings account was getting so large that the bank was constantly sending him offers of investment accounts and lines of credit. It was ironic, he thought, that only those who didn't need more money could get it, and easily. Things were getting so much better for a few like him, but so much worse for many others.

Jamal sat down on one of the couches in the front room and stared at the indigo story wall. He dug his phone out of a pocket and selected Luke's number. The call went to voicemail and Jamal left a message.

"Lucius, my man! We need to talk. Could you, me and Jen get together soon? Thanks. Call me."

Bending the Arc

L uke was just finishing up at the office when he noticed the voicemail on his phone from Jamal. He listened to it and returned the call right away, curious about the urgency in Jamal's voice.

"Hey, Jamal, it's Luke."

"Hey, Lucius. Thanks for the ring-back. So, could you and Jen get together with me in the next day or two? Maybe for dinner or something? I need to run some shit by you."

"Well, sounds tempting – running shit by us over dinner. Who could resist that?"

"Come on man, you know what I mean! How 'bout you meet me down at that little Italian place on 47th not far from the House? Maybe tomorrow night at seven?"

"Sure, that should work; just let me check with Jen and I'll get back to you. Are you gonna give me a clue about what you want to talk about?"

"Nope."

"Okay then. I'll call you back a little later."

"Okay, thanks. Bye."

Luke looked at his phone, smiled, and shook his head. Six years at the university and a key role at Amazon hadn't changed Jamal much at all, and for that Luke was thankful. He called Jen, told her he was about to leave work and asked about the mystery dinner the next night. She checked her schedule and quickly agreed to the time.

~

The next evening, Luke and Jennifer arrived at the restaurant a few minutes before seven to find Jamal already seated at a quiet table in the back. He smiled and waved them over. An open bottle of Chianti Classico Reserva and three wine glasses sat on the table.

"Nice. You buying?" joked Luke.

"As a matter of fact, yeah, I am," said Jamal with a smile. "Since I'm on my way to becoming a rich ol' bastard like you guys – no offense – I thought it was about time."

"Okay, well, thank you, I think," said Luke.

After everyone ordered their meals, Jennifer asked, "So what's on your mind, you rich old bastard?"

"It's kind of about that, actually. It just hit me the other day. I was sitting there at the House, just staring at the story wall, reading some of the new stuff, when I started thinking about the people in the neighborhood. You know, friends, folks that come to the House, folks that don't – black folks mostly. And it hit me. I've almost always had enough money to get by – pay the rent on time, eat, buy something to wear every now and then. And now I've got more money coming in than I know what to do with. Most of them? They don't have shit. Never have and probably never will. Thing is, the difference is getting worse and worse. I keep getting raises and bonuses and they keep getting shit.

Now here's the thing. It isn't just about being able to buy stuff. You guys know this. It's about choice. It's about hope. It's about feeling like you could do something different if you wanted to, or not. It's about not feeling stuck. I mean, who knows? Maybe ol' Jackson always wanted to open a fuckin' shoe store. Maybe Celine wishes she could pay writers to come to her shop and give talks. Maybe she wants to do something completely different. I don't know and you don't know. And that's because these folks can't even afford to dream out loud. Can't let themselves have that kind of hope. And in the meantime, we just get richer. You know what I'm sayin' here?"

"I think I know exactly what you're saying," nodded Luke. "Things are getting more and more out of balance, and faster."

"And here's something else," said Jennifer. "I don't mean to minimize what's happening to the black community – not for a second. But there're also some white folks who get stuck on the bad end of this division, and yes, they've got a big advantage because of the color of their skin, so many of them can get unstuck. But there're some, like Finn, who seem to have this idea that when one group wins, the other has to lose. I think he believed that way down in his gut. I think he felt like he was made to lose because others were given an unfair chance to win. I think he felt like he had to reverse that – make the others lose. So I guess what I'm saying is that this growing economic disparity is also partly responsible for the rise of the despicable white supremacy movement we're seeing."

"Makes sense," said Jamal. "I mean, sure, I like winning, but not by pushing other folks down. I don't think it has to be what us tech-heads call a zero-sum game. Not if there's enough room for all of us to grow."

"So, I'm guessing you've got some ideas? Some things we could maybe do?" asked Luke.

"Yeah, one idea. I don't think that just flat-out giving people money is always the best way, okay? And that's not because I think they're gonna use it wrong or lose it or something. It's mostly because I think it hurts people's pride and they don't really feel like they're in control. You know what I mean?"

"I think so, yes," said Jennifer.

Luke nodded. "So what're you thinking then?"

"I'm thinking small loans. Very low interest, if any. I heard about something like this going on in Africa. People can apply for these loans if they want to start a small business or maybe even just get themselves out of high-interest debt that's killing them. I know our loans would have to be bigger than the ones I've heard about because, hey, things are a lot more expensive here. What if us three could put some cash into a kind of pool that we could make loans out of? I'm thinking small loans from anything like a couple hundred to maybe a few thousand bucks each. A loan like that could make a huge difference for some folks. And since they'd have to pay it back over time, it wouldn't be a handout and it wouldn't feel like one."

"I think that's a great idea," said Luke.

"Me too, Jamal, but I'm wondering, have you thought about how we'd deal with situations where someone couldn't or wouldn't pay us back?" asked Jennifer.

"A little. I haven't got a good answer for that one yet, except that we'd have to be at least a little hard-ass about it. We couldn't just let it go because then the whole system would probably fall apart. And then there's that pride thing again, too. Maybe extend the time, work out other payment plans. I'm not sure. That's the kind of thing we'd all have to agree on before we got into this. There's probably a bunch of other shit like that we'd have to work out ahead of time."

"For sure," said Jennifer, looking at Luke, then back at Jamal. "But I really like this idea, Jamal. This is good. Let's work on it. And hey, I've got another idea to toss into the mix. I haven't even told you about this, Luke. It just came up today at work. You guys want to hear about it?"

"Sure," said Luke, "But Jamal, was there anything more you wanted to say about the loan idea?"

"Oh, sorry!" said Jennifer. "That was rude – got too excited! Please tell us more."

"No, that's pretty much it. Go ahead, Jen."

"Okay, well, I think I've told you both a little about the free employee counselling program that I helped put together at Microsoft? It's been pretty effective helping people deal with their problems. So I was thinking – there're a lot of people at Raza House with stress in their lives for a whole bunch of reasons – what about us offering free counselling there too? Jamal, do you think people would be open to that?"

"I don't know. Not most of the guys. Seeing a shrink is sort of a weak-ass white thing to do. Maybe some of the women might try it. I'm not sayin' it'd be a bad thing to do; it's just not a slam dunk."

321

"Hmm," said Jennifer. "Sounds like we'd really need to think more about this before doing anything. It's just that my psychologist friend Elsa brought it up yesterday. She has some colleagues who want to do some volunteer work and thought of us."

Thinking of Elsa made Jennifer wish, for what seemed like the hundredth time, that she could tell Luke about his niece and all the other news without waiting a moment longer. But, once again, she suppressed the urge, reminding herself that the current plan was best. It wouldn't be much longer.

"You know what?" said Luke. "I think it's time we spend a couple of days away from the city and hash through a bunch of ideas like these – really work on the details and set some new directions for Raza House. What do you think about the three of us, your friend Elsa, and maybe even James and Maggie and Raza, all spending a weekend up at the cabin? We could do all this planning and have some fun too. What do you both think?"

"I'm in. Definitely," said Jamal.

Jennifer nodded. "Let's do it. You know that quote you put up on the wall, Jamal? Maybe it's time we help that arc bend a little faster."

At the Dock

Having just delivered his last lecture of the day, Luke was back in the office reading papers and putting together a plan for the coming week, the final one of the semester. But no matter how hard he tried to focus, his thoughts continued to stray toward the weekend ahead. So finally, after several fruitless attempts, he gave up, stuffed the remaining work into his backpack and set it aside. He would get up early and deal with it all on Monday morning.

Propping his feet up on the desk, Luke leaned back with a smile on his face and let his hopes for the weekend stream through his mind one more time. He and James would take Raza fishing off the south shore of the island. His nephew, now almost ten years old, had developed quite a good cast and had earned himself a spot with the older guys. Maybe Jamal would like to join them. He wasn't really into fishing, but he loved spending time with Raza.

Brainstorming and decision-making would take most of the time. But unlike the planning at work, this was exciting stuff. He and Jen had decided to renovate the cabin, adding more bedrooms, upgrading the kitchen and expanding the living space. The idea was to create a kind of retreat – a place where small groups from Raza House could come for special events or workshops. They would talk about all this and decide on specifics. They would also flesh out Jamal's idea of providing micro-loans for those in the community with great ideas or pressing needs, and then determine the amount of money they would each contribute to the initial pool. And James had recently mentioned the idea of starting a scholarship for minority students at Gonzaga and wanted to discuss fund-raising for that. Things were moving fast and Luke felt the weekend would probably be one of those times they would all look back on someday and celebrate.

Finally, Luke thought about Jen's friend, Elsa, the psychologist. He looked forward to meeting her and exploring the possibility of starting a counselling service at the House. Apparently, she would already be at the cabin when they arrived. She had asked Jen if she could come up a day early for a little R&R. Luke had agreed, emailing driving directions and a checklist for opening up the cabin.

~

Early the next morning, Jamal picked up Luke and Jen in his new Jeep Cherokee and drove up to Rockport. On the way, they talked through some of the issues and opportunities surrounding the micro-loan program, laying some of the groundwork they would need for a fuller discussion at the cabin. Jennifer suggested the ideas of a Mission Statement and Business Plan, and they all agreed to have the statement in place and maybe the skeleton of a plan by the end of the weekend.

"You know," Jamal said. "As part of this loan thing, I've been thinking about Celine's bookstore a lot lately and feeling kind of bad."

"Oh?" asked Jen.

"Well, I think Amazon's amazing and is gonna be a giant convenience for a lot of people, but I also think it might be kind of a killer for small bookstores like hers. It'll be so damn easy to order books online and have them delivered right to your door. And someday, we'll probably even sell electronic books. People will be able to start reading their books seconds after buying them, all from home. Don't tell anybody I told you that."

Luke and Jennifer shrugged and nodded.

"So, I've been thinking," continued Jamal. "What could Celine do that Amazon can't or won't? What could she do to protect her shop? Well, she could make it into more of a hangout place. A cool place to read, have a cup of coffee, something to eat. Maybe have a private room for discussions, maybe a classroom or two. She'd still sell books but she could also bring in authors to give talks, stuff like that, maybe charge a small fee. Then I was thinking, hey, some of this sounds kind of like what we do at Raza House. Maybe there's a way to put the two together that would be good for Celine and good for the community. I don't know, just thinking out loud."

"Wow, maybe there's something to that," said Jennifer. We should toss it around this weekend."

The conversation continued, on and off, all the way up to Rockport where Jamal put his new vehicle into four-wheel drive and started up the road into the woods. When they got to the cattle gate across the road, Jamal stopped to let Luke out. Jennifer turned to Jamal.

"Excuse us for a second. Something we always do…" She stepped out and joined Luke at the gate.

"I love you, Luke Mason."

"I love you, too, Jenny Mason!"

Luke glanced back to see Jamal looking up, rolling his eyes and shaking his head. Jennifer swatted at him as she climbed back into the Jeep. "You're just jealous!"

They continued up the road and parked alongside a pickup truck at the cabin.

"Must be your friend's truck," said Luke.

"Borrowed it from her aunt, I think," said Jennifer. "Down to the dock first, as usual?"

"Absolutely," said Luke. "We'll be right back, Jamal. The last part of our little ritual." And smiling, "Don't give us any crap."

Luke took Jennifer's hand as they walked down toward the dock together. As they were about to round the last bend in the tall blackberry thicket surrounding the trail, Luke felt her squeeze his hand. He turned to look into her eyes and saw that they were wet.

"Jenny, you're crying. What's wrong?"

"Just happy," she smiled through her tears as they stepped beyond the thicket and onto the dock. "Look."

There, floating side-by-side in the still water, were two kayaks. And standing on the dock was a woman with a young girl at her side, smiling brightly.

"Hi," said the little girl, holding out her hand. "I'm Sam."

~

About the Author

Don Thompson is a retired software professional with a degree in Applied Physics and Information Science from the University of California, San Diego. He is currently writing fiction, running a small business helping senior citizens with technology challenges, and assisting in the development of a permaculture-inspired farm. Writing has been Don's passion for the last twenty years, and *Bending the Arc* is his fifth novel. He and his wife live with their golden retriever on the Olympic Peninsula in Washington State.

Don can be reached at don@bendingarc.com.

A Personal Note from the Author

My biggest challenge (and fear) in writing this book stems from the obvious problem that I am a white man writing, at least in part, about the black experience in the United States. I've grown up in a society of white privilege and therefore cannot truly understand the depths of anger, despair, suspicion and pain experienced in various forms by nearly all people of color in this country. Nor can I fully appreciate both the pride and the internal tension which must arise when the same people succeed or rise to positions of power and wealth. And of course, there is no single black or brown experience, just as there is no single white, female or male experience.

Fortunately, some excellent books and journalism, insights from the Southern Poverty Law Center, and from friends with direct experience have helped chip away at a portion of my ignorance. From that starting point, I've tried to tell a realistic but hopeful story of discovery and transformation, but primarily from a perspective I *do* have some experience with—that of a white middle-class family working their way through a variety of challenges at the end of the twentieth century.

But it is now two decades into the twenty-first century. Is the kind of hope expressed in this story still justified today? I'm tempted to despair when I see implicit permission being granted at the highest levels of government to treat hate speech as a First Amendment right, white nationalism as just another political option, human kindness as liberal political correctness, misogynism as normal male behavior, and withdrawal, isolation, and fear as foreign policy norms. Perhaps these are new regressions—in practical effect they certainly are. But they are also windows, now blatantly thrown open, into longstanding realities we've historically preferred to hide.

Maybe it's a good thing that these windows are so open right now. My hope is that the long lens of history will ultimately reveal today's ugly rhetoric and policies as eye-openers helping to shock us back on track. My belief is that the moral arc of the universe will continue to bend toward justice, but it will need a lot more help from all of us in doing so.

One way you have already helped is by buying this book. That's because all author royalties from the sale of *Bending the Arc* go to an amazing organization in Maryland called The Kindness Corps. To find out more about them, please visit their Facebook page at www.facebook.com/thekindnesscorps/.

You can also find more information about the book and the Kindness Corps at www.bendingarc.com. For author information, please see www.DonThompsonAuthor.com.

Did you enjoy my book?

If so, I would be very grateful if you could write a review and publish it at your point of purchase. Your review, even a brief one, will help other readers to decide whether or not they'll enjoy my work. And remember, anyone who buys this book is helping to bend the arc in a very practical way. Thank you!

Do you want to be notified of new releases?

If so, please sign up to the AIA Publishing email list. You'll find the sign-up button on the right-hand side under the photo at www.aiapublishing.com. Of course, your information will never be shared, and the publisher won't inundate you with emails, just let you know of new releases.

Acknowledgements

First, I want to thank my wife, Donna, for her many readings of the manuscript and her honest and helpful contributions to its improvement. Her love and encouragement during the entire writing, editing, and publication process has meant the world to me.

To my "kids," Ben, Gracie, Matt and Katie: thank you for your reading time, your insightful suggestions and your encouragement.

There were two other beta readers who provided feedback, not only from a literary standpoint, but also, and most importantly, from a cultural/racial one. Leathia West and Carol Morrison, thank you both for your very valuable contributions of time and insight.

Susan Friend and I had wonderful discussions about characters, race, theme, and plot early in the process. I'm grateful to her for those times and for introducing me to Leathia.

Finally, I want to thank Tahlia Newland of AIA Publishing for her professional manuscript appraisal and editorial advice. I'm grateful for her many specific suggestions, for her teaching, and for her encouragement.